Chris F̶ ⎯⎯⎯⎯ ⎯⎯⎯ ⎯s all aroun
the wor ⎯⎯ntly living in London. This is his
second novel. His first, *Twelve Step Fandango*, has been
shortlisted for the prestigious Edgar Allan Poe Award for
Best Paperback Original.

Also by Chris Haslam

TWELVE STEP FANDANGO

Alligator
Strip

CHRIS HASLAM

ABACUS

ABACUS

First published in Great Britain in June 2005 by Abacus

Copyright © 2005 Chris Haslam

A CIP catalogue record for this book
is available from the British Library.

ISBN 0 349 11839 6

For permission to quote lyrics from 'Poison':
Words and Music by Alice Cooper
© Ezra Music Sony/ATV Music Publishing Limited
All Rights Reserved

Typeset in Bembo by M Rules
Printed and bound in Great Britain
by Clays Ltd, St Ives plc

Abacus
An imprint of
Time Warner Book Group UK
Brettenham House
Lancaster Place
London WC2E 7EN

www.twbg.co.uk

To Frederick, who knows
'gators ain't all bad

Alligator Strip

Part I

1

The Maître d' was furious. He was also pretty breathless, but we had both run a long way. I had chosen the two-hundred-dirham Menu Royal from the *carte du jour* at the somewhat overrated Hôtel de Foucauld, but any advantage of speed gained from skipping the dessert had been offset by the effects of doubling up on the couscous. I tried to eat well at least once a week – it was part of my new regime of self-improvement – but decent restaurants were thin on the ground in North Africa, and I had already fled from the best of them.

The late setting sun shone pink upon the walls of Marrakech, and already the feeble lights of dangerously wired bulbs twinkled beneath the pall of greasy smoke rising from the lethal food stands in the Place of the Dead. Long, ragged Berbers and short, sharp-eyed Arabs gaped as I dashed through four lanes of traffic, their gazes turning lazily to my yelling pursuer. The meal I had just stolen had been very rich in the ingredients that the body needs time and a good liqueur to digest, but heartburn was the least of my present worries. I was uncertain of the legality of my Moroccan residency and uninterested in any clarification that the local police might provide. I was also fairly unhappy about the prospect of the kicking that I was bound to receive if this furious Maître d' caught me.

I leapt the low wall into the Place Foucauld and ran through its urine-tainted trees, ignoring the ludicrously optimistic offers to polish my boots *à la Parisienne* from the geriatric shoe-shiners. I emerged gasping from the little park on to the street, side-stepping a horse-drawn *caleche* and pausing for the briefest moment to throw a look of withering disdain to a family of five on a moped who had missed me by the will of Allah alone. From here, it was a five-hundred-metre dash across the Jemaa el Fna to the stinking, hustling anonymity of the souks. Once I had slipped like a drop of rain into that ocean of thieves and liars, I would be invisible. No one in Marrakech had ever pursued me this far before, and I found it disturbing that this dark and oily man in his badly tailored dinner suit should have taken my dishonesty so seriously. Most Thursdays, the restaurateur would make a show of chasing me for half a block, then let his curses alone pursue me, thus saving both his face and his legs. This middle-aged fool, however, had hunted me over twice my effective range and he was closing fast. By now I had gathered a mossy following of excited kids and earnest-eyed suppli-cants who jogged alongside and offered me everything but sanctuary.

'Why you move so fast, English?' cried a ragged bandit with a home-made badge that described him as an 'Official Gide'. 'Come with me now and I show you the secrets of Marrakech!'

'Piss off,' I wheezed.

I was halfway across the square, less than a hundred metres from the Café de France, and now I realised I would never make it. My flight had caught the attention of the evening crowds, and they pressed in from every side. My elegant linen suit, while a little on the large side, wrongly identified me as a rich Western tourist in need of urgent relief, and if there was anybody in Morocco who could help me, it was everybody and nobody in this smoky square. Brown hands reached out to grab me as I stumbled through the throng, responding to some promise of reward yelled by my pursuer, and I was still fifty metres from safety when I slipped on a pomegranate and fell heavily into the dust.

The crowd quickly hemmed me in, and I rolled into a foetal curl. I expected the Arabs to fall on me like hyenas on a downed warthog, but when I looked up they were staring down like clueless witnesses to a freak accident. Unfortunately, though, there was one heaving, red-faced new arrival who knew exactly what to do. The crowd parted as he pushed his way through, loosening his bow tie with the tight-lipped vigour of a man about to gain satisfaction. He shrugged his white tuxedo from his broad shoulders and tossed it to a gap-toothed boy, then stood above me, undoing his cuffs.

'So, was there something which was not to sir's liking on the menu tonight?' he hissed in exotically accented French, passing his sweat-stained shirt to a bemused Berber.

'There seems to have been some sort of misunderstanding,' I stammered. 'Would you believe it? I'd just ordered my coffee when I remembered I'd left my wallet back at the hotel, so I was just jogging back here to fetch it.' I always timed my exit to occur just after I'd ordered my coffee. It was a sacrifice, but it allayed any mounting fears on the part of the establishment that I was planning to do a runner, and, if I was ever caught, it served equally as proof that there had been some terrible emergency. The maître d' replied with a spitball in the dust.

The Berbers were chanting something that might have been '*Fight, fight, fight*', and the maître d' obliged by launching a series of kicks at my midriff, his dusty toecaps thudding into my ribs and encouraging the crowd to join in. Kids and old men followed his lead, cursing me for a scoundrel as they laid in to my scrawny *infidel* body. I tried to roll with the blows, coldly aware that the stoning that was surely imminent was not going to be the type I was used to enjoying of an evening. Unshod toes cracked as they collided with my bones, and I realised why this square was named the Place of the Dead. Laughter made crueller for its innocence was punctuated with exhortations to greater violence, but, as I resigned myself to my just deserts, a loud voice punched through the mob and pulled me back.

He was pushing his way from the edge to the middle, his Southern accent advocating reason while his build commanded respect. I opened one eye and chanced a glance at the man who appeared to be my saviour. He was wearing bright white sneakers that shrugged off the desert's dust, beige slacks from the Gap, and a polo shirt. Something heavy and golden flashed from his wrist every time he waved a conciliatory hand, but I could see neither his face nor the halo that surely lit it. 'Gentlemen, gentlemen,' he cried. 'Please! There's been a terrible misunderstanding. Tell them, kid.'

His interpreter babbled out a translation of the American view of events, and as the crowd listened, the big guy took a step closer to my kicked body.

'Get up, stand behind me, and keep looking down. Got it?'

I struggled to my feet.

'There you go,' announced the American. He grabbed the arm of his guide, a nervous-looking youth with a dark, anorexic face, and held up a jewelled hand to still his tongue. 'Ask the guy how much he wants.'

The kid turned to the maître d', then back to the American. 'Him say he speak English good. Him tell me fuck myself.'

'Oh yeah?' mused the American. 'So how much will do it, big guy?'

The Moroccan remained indignant. It wasn't about money, he blustered. It was a point of honour, an issue of standards, a matter of law. Still, a hundred US would do it. Twenty-five, sighed the American. Eighty, minimum, insisted the maître d'. He settled for thirty.

'Turn around and follow the kid to the taxi stand,' murmured my hero as he handed over the greenbacks. 'Keep looking at the floor – don't make eye contact with the ragheads. I'll be right behind you.'

'*Vous êtes foutu,*' hissed the maître d' as I passed him. He pointed at the police station. '*Mon cousin est au commisariat. Vous êtes fini a Marrakech.*'

I shuffled away, head down, glad that I was still near enough to the scene of my beating to hear his wails of distress as he realised that his jacket and his dress shirt had been nicked.

'You're a lucky guy,' declared the American as we stepped into a taxi.

'I'm a grateful guy,' I replied. 'Very grateful. You probably saved my life back there. Jesus! I was just strolling through the square, thinking how beautiful the place was, when they set upon me like a pack of bloody wolves.' I turned and offered him my shaking hand. His grip was limp and wet, his eyes sparkling in the reflected light of the Koutoubia Mosque.

'My name's Martin Brock,' I announced, feeling that he deserved at least that much truth.

The smile that cracked his thin lips and narrowed his close-set brown eyes was one of amusement. 'Gene Renoir,' he offered, 'and don't be giving me no more of your Limey bullshit, y'hear?'

The cab stopped outside the Hôtel la Mamounia, an art deco palace with a leather-lined bar to which I'd never succeeded in gaining entry. Smiling at the fez-wearing security guard, I followed Gene inside, knocking the dust from my jacket. The clientele were a mixture of aspirational natives, European interior decorators and rich tourists, wasting the last minutes of a desert sunset with overpriced cocktails and anodyne jazz piano. We took a low table and appraised each other's potential.

'You didn't get hurt so bad,' he reassured me. 'I hope it was worth it.'

'You hope *what* was worth it?' I replied, giving the barman a nod.

'Dinner,' he replied, hiding his smile with a lick of his lips. I opened my mouth but he stopped it with an outstretched hand. 'I saw it all, Troop. I was there.'

The barman hovered like a disapproving hummingbird.

'Beer, imported,' I ordered, like it made a difference. 'What can I get you, Gene?'

'I'll have a Coca-Cola,' he replied. 'Lots of ice.'

The barman nodded.

I shook my head. 'No ice.'

The American had saved my arse, and now I had saved his. That squared us, but he didn't notice.

'I saw you as soon as you came in,' he smiled. You kind of stood out, and as soon as I saw you, I figured you for a grifter. Ordering the coffee and dessert is a nice touch – it lulls them – but you spoiled the scam by running into the men's room, and by the time you'd worked out which way was outtahere that fat bastard near enough had you.' He laughed out loud, shaking his head. 'He damn near had you.'

I nodded slowly and met his eyes. He had me at a disadvantage, but I was in no position to begrudge him the high ground. He had saved me from a severe beating, and deserved my gratitude. I repeated my thanks and he shrugged.

'Hey, I slipped out while they were clearing up that dessert trolley you knocked over, so I figure we're just about even. Wanna see a show?'

It was an unusual request, and one I felt bound to refuse. I necked my beer, dropped a hundred on to the dark table, thanked my saviour once more and limped into the Arabian night.

Life was too short to waste making friends.

Life in Marrakech can be hard for a hustler, and the only way to stay ahead of penury is to be constantly alert for a new angle of escape. It's a common and unfair misconception that the conman is bent only upon the pursuit of easy wealth: more often than not, he is merely in flight from poverty and thus should be seen not as a raptor, but as a ragged rook. As an *infidel* in a city populated by genetically modified shysters, I was equally cursed and blessed. On the upside, I was a fellow European in an eccentric and not inelegant white linen suit with an adequate knowledge of local history and geography. I was a friendly face in a foreign place upon whom the nervous tourist could rely to provide an acceptable level of service for a reasonable price. Furthermore, I could always lay my hands on the whole chocolate box of Moroccan delights, from lowest-grade commercial gear, through the sticky kif, right up to the famous double-zero, the soft-centred, handmade, champagne truffles of the hashish harvest. Conversely, it was admittedly easy to mistake me for a low-down opportunist in a grubby jacket with a bluffer's knowledge of local culture and a desperate expression. I therefore lost as many clients as I won, and the result was an uncertain, hand-to-lungs existence made tolerable only by the soap-sized block of resin I carried around in a painted tin box like a fetish. At the starlit end of every long, hot day spent dragging increasingly sweaty and apprehensive tourists through the souks and across the Berber-infested squares, I would retreat to the shack I rented upon the roof of the abattoir and smoke two or three long, fat joints of the finest organic hashish, filtered through silk of a double-zero mesh, and I would hallucinate that the life I was leading was one of fulfilment and satisfaction. Three floors below me, nocturnal flies got high on the spilled pools of sheep's blood that encrusted the gutters while I fell asleep gazing into the heavens, worrying about my health and trying to see hope in the stars. Every morning the sun hit my face like a jabbed pool cue, coming around the side of the Atlas Range and over the cracked pink parapet of my roof. I rolled out of my hammock only when I began to sweat, brushing the creases from my trousers and shrugging my jacket on to my back. I suffered pains in my chest, aches in my teeth, shivers down my spine and permanent diarrhoea. It was kind of like having a family.

Three times a week a sympathetic barber with one eye and no teeth would pare the beard from my face and calm my belly with hot mint tea while I studied the ruins before me and contemplated the means by which I would arrest their decline. As my face was shaved, an autistic boy – possibly the unfortunate barber's son – would gently scrape the grime from beneath my fingernails and soak my nicotine-stained fingers in steaming, scented water. Hot towels, bound like swaddling clothes around my naked face, sucked the grease from the pores, and thus groomed I would head to the Place Foucauld to meet the first Chicken Bus of the day.

Tourists – call them backpackers or travellers if it sounds cooler – have invariably heard all about Marrakech long before they step into its dirty embrace. Keith came down here in the sixties – or was it the seventies? – and got wrecked with Marianne – or was it Patty? Clapton came, too, and didn't Jimi spend some of his pitifully short life all along the watchtowers of the city walls? There was something cool drifting through that hot desert air, and I knew what it was. The Moroccan Tourist Board will try to sell you the living city, with its musicians and its snake-charmers. The guidebooks will push the delights of the souks and the Koutoubia Mosque. The travel sections of the Sunday broadsheets will enthuse about the sweetest boutique hotels, the Gardens of the Menara and the best places to buy hand-tooled leather magazine racks. I'll sell you ten grams of the reason why you really came to Morocco, and I'll bet you your money back that you'll remember me the longest.

After a couple of days' sick leave I put the post-traumatic stress of my kicking behind me and ventured warily into Saharan society to scavenge the rent. It was a poor day for photography: dust blurred buildings blended into a colourless sky against which the Atlas stood unfocused like a rolling bank of distant cloud. Out to the east, behind the mountains, the Sherghi was biding its time. A vicious, angry bastard, this feverish wind sucked the dirtiest grit from the desert floor and spat it at the city, turning sweat to mud and spit to slime and sending good Muslims running for the *hammam*. It would be here in a day or two, and right now the light seemed to fall upon the city as through a lens of applied imperfection. I bought a shot glass of oversugared mint tea from the dour owner of my favourite café and listened to the indignant-sounding chatter of my robed companions at the bus terminal. Soon, the first of the day's flagged minibuses would enter the city, pregnant with tourists and thirsty for gas, and we would fall on it like jackals on a lost and wounded wildebeest. Those who succeeded in sinking their cracked teeth into the blinking passengers would depart sated, leaving the rest of us to await the next arrival. There were always more hustlers than buses, and it was inevitable that some would go hungry, but their misfortunes didn't concern me. This sordid business was the same as any other, and it followed that one needed an edge to succeed. Mine were inherent: a white skin, an English accent and a charming smile. Added to that, I possessed a basic understanding of tourist psychology.

I followed the snapped gaze of four hundred eyes as a mirrored minibus dragging a ragged flag roared through the street like the vanguard of a desert army. Painted up like the Yellow Submarine, it bore the legend 'Marrakech Express' along both sides, although its promise of wild rides on the boho highway was tempered somewhat by the subtexted passenger benefits: 'Air Conditioned', 'Videos' and 'Frequent Rest Stops'. I knew this bus, and I knew that its driver – a tall, tanned South African named Hector – already had his passengers stitched up.

They stumbled from the van like zombies, a pale cortège of board shorts, sandles and thousand-litre rucksacks, ready to follow Hector right back to his house. He led them through a plague of tour guides, accommodation experts, whispering dope dealers and beggars like the Pied Piper.

I let them go: the second bus had already arrived. This one oozed promise like its brakes bled fluid: a dusty, yellow ex-American schoolbus named, in bold, hippy script, the 'Magic Bus'. I shifted in my seat, watching like an impassive Peter O'Toole as the dreadlocked ingénues stumbled, blinking, from the doorway. A tattooed youth wearing the back-packer's uniform of cargo shorts and trainers scrambled on to the roof, elbowing aside the Arabs as he threw his compan-ions' luggage down to them. A group of girls, their unity rent by a night on the road with the backpacking boys, joined in the fun or stood moodily to one side as their camp dictated. Three of the girls wanted to go with the boys, but their surly companions insisted that they make their own arrangements. Swatting away persistent hustlers with a guidebook as though they were tiresome insects, the girl in charge led her friends into cover, as I had known she would. There were three cafés within sight of the bus terminal, yet tourists always chose the one I sat in. I knew why, but I never told anyone. I smiled as they entered, a simple acknowledgement, a friendly greeting, nothing more, noth-ing less. There were fourteen tables on the terrace, and only three of these had room for rucksacks. I was sitting at the middle of the three, and the girls installed themselves to my right.

Within three minutes, they were mine – accommodation only – and I led them away before the cursing waiter could pounce. I left them at a no-star *riad* down an alley in Kennaria that deserved five if stars were awarded for position, ambience, beauty, friendliness and value for money. I always told my clients that they could stay there only if they prom-ised to tell no one else, and they always laughed. Marrakech is a town where old jokes work for a living: ask any carpet salesman.

Pocketing my commission, I hurried back through the awakening souk to meet the next bus: I had two double rooms available in a French-owned place with a lemon tree and a fountain, and I needed affluent young couples to fill them. The right people would last me all week, earning me commission all over town and paying me directly for my local knowledge. This was my business, and as long as it allowed me to retreat to my rooftop solitude at the end of the day with enough to drink and enough to smoke, it would suffice until circumstances changed.

Three days later, they did.

I had snared a foursome from Winchester, young and pleasant company, and had just led them on a lucrative full-day excursion to a hash farm high in the hills to the east of the city. By the end of the trip, they had known more about the cultivation, harvesting, preparation, packaging and export of commercial-grade Moroccan hash than anyone else in Hampshire, but they had since smoked so much that they couldn't even remember where Hampshire was. Now the two blokes wanted to go drinking. The two girls wanted to buy a carpet. Much as I wanted to side with the gentlemen, I felt honour bound as their objectively minded guide to mention that I had a friend in the *Criee Berbere* who would cut them the deal of a lifetime on a carpet. Both ladies and gentlemen were sceptical, but I led them into the pungent murk to prove myself a man of truth.

The American, who knew otherwise, must have been following me. I saw him approaching as my charges admired a twelve-by-eight Messulan weave, and sent him a nod of recognition that said, 'Don't embarrass me in front of the customers,' but the smirking Renoir ignored it. Oblivious to the wonders being held up for his approval by grinning stall-holders, he pushed his way deep into my personal space and started talking … Loudly.

'Hey, Troop, how's your spleen?' he started. 'Run from any good restaurants recently?'

The smile he received in reply said, 'Very funny. Now

fuck off,' in most languages, but Gene, trampling over my part of the desert like a US Marines expeditionary force, didn't get the message, and before I could think of a verbal response he was introducing himself to my clients.

'This is one lucky sonofabitch,' he told them. 'Hadn't been for yours truly, his ass would have been dragged to fuckin' Mauritania by now.'

'I make you very good price for this carpet,' interjected Mohammed, the stallholder from whom I collected 8 per cent on every sale.

'From a restaurant: one of those classy uptown joints,' Gene was explaining. 'Motherfucker chased him right into the square! Ran him to ground and started kicking the shit out of him. Ain't that right, buddy?'

My clients were no longer admiring the near perfection of the eight by twelve. They were deaf to Mohammed's once-in-a-lifetime, zero-margin offers. A new light had fallen upon Marrakech, and, thanks to a drunken American, I was standing in it. I shrugged. I had presented myself to these people as a Cambridge linguist making a study of the language employed by sophisticated dope smokers – slightly eccentric, granted, but trustworthy and well connected. Scarpering from restaurants and having the shit kicked out of me in the Jemaa el Fna seemed somewhat inappropriate to that representation.

The American had sequestered the two women, and, with a hand on the shoulder of each, was swaying close in conspiracy. 'So I start checking on this guy, and I find he's one of the biggest goddamn hustlers in town! Would you believe it? The locals call him a hyena because he preys on the weak and the vulnerable. Where I come from, we'd call him a grifter – that is, a swindler or cheater, generally one who steals small amounts of money on an irregular basis. You guys, from the UK, you'd call him a conman: charming, persuasive and slippery as a goddamn cobra.'

A cobra, I could have told him, is as dry as a bone, but it wouldn't have made any difference. The damage to my reputation was reflected in the eyes of my clients, and already I could detect those tiny changes in body language indicating that one has been sussed as a lying bastard. My Grand Tour of the Gardens of Marrakech with Connoisseur Dope Sampling, planned for tomorrow, was in serious jeopardy, but I couldn't understand why this Septic was pissing on my fireworks.

He pushed the women back to their men and looked directly at me, wobbling slightly. 'Guys,' he grinned, 'I'm only kidding you. This is a great guy. Stick with him and you'll have a ball.' He smiled, not like a drunkard but like a schoolteacher, then leaned forward and as deftly as a Colombian pickpocket slipped a card into my linen suit. His breath smelled of nothing stronger than mint tea. 'Just watch your goddamned wallets,' he advised, suddenly distracted as a banner-dragging Cessna flashed across a narrow strip of sky. 'I'm heading off to watch some snake charming.'

My prospects evaporated shortly afterwards. A looming cloud of doubt had overshadowed my client's appetite for floor coverings, and they cried off happy hour at the hotel on the grounds that both women had simultaneously developed nauseous migraines. Unsure if they would be adequately recovered to enjoy tomorrow's Gardens of Marrakech with Connoisseur Dope Sampling Tour, they cancelled and left me with nothing to do on a Moroccan Sunday but go visiting.

2

'It would have been cool if I had got them developed,' observed Gene airily. The three rolls of exposed film that sat on the low, marble table between us purported to contain one hundred and eight pictures of me hustling tourists in Marrakech. Apparently, I had been stalked.

'Why?' I asked.

'Because you've got talent,' he replied. 'You're not that good, because you have no discipline, but you're a talented boy. Trust me.'

Twenty minutes earlier I had arrived uptown on foot and in a sweat, like the indignant hero of a social drama. Failing to notice the sophisticated entryphone system, I had hammered on the studded sixteenth-century door until a robed servant had invited me in. Until the moment I crossed the threshold, my driving emotion had been one of slightly overplayed fury, but as I passed through a miniature citrus orchard and crossed a tiny bridge over a stream that ran the length of the courtyard from the fountain on a mosaic bed I felt my rage replaced by a sense of apprehensive wonder.

I could smell the money.

Given command, I would have ordered everyone in the house to skin up and spend the day watching the fountain and raiding the fridge. Gene, however, was quite clearly the master of his temporary home. He greeted me from a first-floor salon, looking like a dangerously gay uncle in his silken housecoat and shiny slippers. 'Cold one?' he asked, and it would have been rude to refuse. I sat down and placed my stash tin in plain view on the table. Gene invited me to put the tin away.

'I'm a liberal kind of guy,' he announced, 'but you got to understand that I am one hundred and ten per cent opposed to drugs. I saw too many good guys go under in Vietnam to that stuff, and I won't have it in my presence. Sorry to be a bummer and all that.' He placed a sweating can of Bud on the table, cracked himself a can of Coke and took a long slurp, his eyes leaving mine only when he blinked. 'Bottoms up!'

I didn't like the way I was being played. I'd dragged my miserable arse two klicks uphill in the heat of the Saharan day to register my disapproval of this buffoon's drunken disruption of my career, and somehow I'd ended up accepting his hospitality and acceding to his ridiculous views on the consumption of cannabis. I'd always been under the impression that it had been the NVA and the VC who had got GIs KIA in South-East Asia, not THC, but maybe I'd been wrong. I shrugged and went with the flow, sipping Bud, smoking Marlboro, accepting US cultural imperialism and feeling pretty cool about it. The longer I sat beneath the aircon the more inclined I was to forgive and forget Gene's bizarre behaviour back in the souk, but my reputation was at stake, so I made an effort.

'You were out of order last night,' I told him.

He stuck out a lip and shrugged. 'Look at it as an exercise in damage control.'

'No, seriously, man,' I protested, 'you blew me a week's wages there. They were all up for my Gardens of Marrakech and Connoisseur Dope Sampling Tour, but after you came by both the birds got headaches and everyone got nervous and I got nothing. Like I say, you were out of order.'

A shaft of sunlight struck a thread of gold on Gene's housecoat, ricocheted north and spun a halo around his monk's scalp.

'Diddums,' he said, crossing the shiny room and bending before a piece of furniture older than the USA. 'Does that square you away, Troop?'

Two hundred and fifty US dollars fluttered into my lap: two hundreds and a fifty. I bit my lip like a Mississippi gambler. 'What's that?'

Gene hid his admiration well. 'Based on my observations' – he swung a languid hand towards the film rolls – 'it's a week's wages.'

'Get the fuck out of here!' I snorted. 'I make twice that, and more, if I'm lucky.'

That got him. He sighed and turned back to the dresser. I held his eyes in an unblinking stare as another four hundreds fell like banana republics before me. 'That do it?' he muttered, and I nodded, but suddenly and deeply I felt, like a Colombian kid in a CIA T-shirt, that I should have demanded a whole lot more. Nevertheless, it was a result, and I only wished I was allowed to smoke in there. I grabbed a Marlboro instead.

Gene slapped something wooden with a crack that made me sit up and listen.

'OK, let's stop fucking with each other. Here's the deal: I want you to forget your pissy little grifting and come and work for me instead. You're too damned good at what you do to end up dead in some raghead jail, and I can guarantee you'll make more in three months with me than you'd make in a goddamned lifetime anyplace else. I mean it Troop. You have a high earnings potential.'

I adopted an expression of casual nonchalance that might possibly have looked like one of flattered vanity. 'What's the catch?'

Gene exhaled, long and hard like a builder with bad news. 'The catch is that you'd have to leave Morocco, enrol on a

19

frequent-flyer programme, wear expensive tailoring and wash a little more regularly.'

Later I would discover that at least one of these was true.

'What will I be doing?'

I had an uneasy feeling that I was being invited to embark upon on of those dark homoerotic odysseys untouched by popular culture, a sordid adventure as a rich man's toyboy, a whore's holiday where the abuse would be repaired by Doctors Smirnoff and Armani. Gene was pitching for me to do his bitching, and I'd probably have to get a skinhead and grow one of those dumb little goatee beards.

'You'll be my office boy,' he replied. 'You will answer telephones, write letters, send faxes, maintain records and accompany me on business trips. I expect you to learn quickly and be professional at all times. You will be my right-hand man and my personal assistant.'

I wasn't so sure about the last two duties.

'And what is it that you do?'

He stared at me for a long moment, then smiled. 'You ask a lot of questions. I like that. I'm a businessman. I have an enterprise – a solid gold venture – and it's moving into phase two. To proceed, I need help, and you'll do just fine.' He made a steeple of his forefingers and tilted it towards me. 'You're wondering "Why me? Why not some hotshot Harvard MBA?"' He spoke like an Evangelist, and he was good, even if I had no idea what a Harvard MBA was.

'I'll tell you why, Troop. On top of your natural talent you're poor, and that makes you hungry. You're smart, and that makes you ambitious. You're English, and that, through no fault of your own, adds my organisation an essential touch of class, and finally, you're wanted by the Moroccan Police, and that makes you keen for a career change.'

I'd almost forgotten about the maître d's cop cousin. If I was busted, the least I could expect was deportation to the country from which I arrived, and I was in no hurry to return to Spain.

I shrugged and tried to look cool.

'So what do I do now?'

Gene lit a Marlboro and jabbed it towards me. 'First thing you do is to lose the dope. I'll give you until five-forty tonight to get rid of it. Then it's gone for ever. That is the foundation of our agreement. Is that acceptable?'

Gene dissing my stash only made me want it more. 'Why five-forty?'

He sucked the last three swallows from his Coke, crushed it in his hairy hand and belched. ''Cos five-forty is when I check in at the airport, and it's gonna be with or without you. Your call, Troop.'

It was best not to think too hard when opportunities for free air travel arose. 'Where we going?' I asked.

'Cape Coral, Florida,' replied Gene, striding towards me and sweeping me from the room. His urgent momentum seemed to push me down the stairs and back across the lush, narrow courtyard. 'Give it some thought,' he suggested from his little footbridge as his butler ushered me on to the street.

'You don't need to come to Marrakech to recruit an office boy,' I remarked. 'Why don't we take some time on the flight to discuss the exact terms and nature of my employment. That way we won't get off on the wrong foot.'

Gene shook his head. 'That, I'm afraid, will be impossible,' he sighed. 'You see, I'm holding a first-class ticket, and you, Troop, are holding a lady's purse. The six-fifty you've got in your pocket will cover a coach seat, so if you're still interested in coming to work for me the next opportunity for a staff meeting will be Stateside. My offices are at eighteen-seventy

Sunrise Drive, Cape Coral, Florida. That's the quality side of Fort Myers. Report to reception when you get there. Have a nice flight.'

I beat him to the airport by fifteen minutes.

3

US Immigration singled me out for their special attention as I arrived in Miami. I had reason to believe that they were acting on intelligence rather than intuition, as the half-ounce of hashish I had eaten twenty hours previously still had me firmly crushed in its hairy monkey fist and my behaviour on the Air France flight had probably betrayed my intoxication. My luggage worried them, too.

'The rest was lost in Paris,' I lied as the son of a Cuban refugee rifled through my handbag. 'I made a complaint.'

They wanted to ask me about the handbag, but there had to be some regulation against it. A vague, red-eyed Englishman in a stained white suit carrying a beaded purse came straight out of the problem pages of the training manual, and no one had ever read that far.

'Where you staying in the United States, sir?'

Something – Gene would have called it innate talent – made me lie. 'The Bluegrass Motel, Memphis, Tennessee,' I replied, the exact address I had written on my immigration form, and then my attention wandered. There was a clever question on the form designed to trap fugitive Nazis. 'How many people ever actually admit to being members of Hitler's National Socialist Party?' I enquired.

Neither the Cuban nor his redneck supervisor looked up.

'None,' said the redneck. 'How long you planning on staying?'

I told him two weeks and he gave me back my passport. I passed through Miami airport like an excited rat, my nose twitching beneath my twelve o'clock whiskers for the first whiff of the New World. The cops were an easy score: plumper and more innocent than they looked on TV. The smoked-glass doors opened and I stood at the low-tide line of the American shore, blinking in the midday heat like a refugee who couldn't tell north from south. The cost of my dream ticket and the entertainment I had purchased to while away the journey had left me with thirty-five dollars and some change. A connecting flight to Fort Myers cost over one-fifty. I was surrounded by business travellers in rumpled suits who could have told me where I'd gone wrong in the booking process, how I'd missed the most efficient itinerary, and why I'd failed to get an upgrade, but I didn't really care. Air travel was either expensive or cheap, but it was always stressful and uncomfortable. You turned up ludicrously early and spent every minute thereafter being herded and bullied like unwanted Gypsies by self-important people in menacing uniforms. I could have told US Immigration where all the Nazis had gone.

America wasn't built to be overflown, and Route 66 was never a flightpath. If I hadn't wasted so much money on overpriced in-flight experiences I might have been able to afford a cheap rental car with which to ease myself into the American Experience. As usual, however, my self-indulgent nature and pitiful short-sightedness had left me with no onward travel options but the thumb or the bus. I watched my trembling hands for a moment and made up my mind: I would ride the Dog to Fort Myers, but not until I had scored. The long-dormant dragon that nested in my brain had been awoken by the aroma as soon as I had left the aircon of Miami International. The dry, chemical fragrance rose from every banknote and every cistern in the country, and the reptile licked his cracked lips with an ulcerated tongue as he sucked the spores into his starved nostrils. After seven lean years in the African desert the worm had turned around and found himself standing in the USA looking at the Real Thing. This corporation manufactured and distributed the world's favourite product, the substance that the planet craved. It made you want to teach the world to sing or stare in chattering wonder at the Northern Lights. Its consumption underlined your confidence in yourself and the planet upon which you stood, your belief in quality and consistency, and your everlasting optimism for a brighter future. It was a strong brand, and someone had named a soft drink after it. I bought a cold can of Classic from an oversized vending machine and shuffled towards the taxi rank, wondering if I could afford Vice City's smallest deal.

'You get Coca-Cola in England?' asked the cabby as we headed east on the Dolphin Expressway.

'Sometimes,' I replied, wondering if it was true that all taxi-drivers knew where to score.

'You should come to my church,' he suggested. 'We got a twelve-ounce bottle in every niche.'

There was a picture of my driver in a frame on the bulkhead that separated us. It looked like the cover of a forties blues album. Below it, on the paintwork, someone had written, 'fuck you!' in perfect four-point script. The Devil was always in the detail.

Depending upon how you looked at it, the Greyhound bus station on 6th Street was the beginning or the end of the American Dream. Lower-caste salesmen sat beside trailer-park teenage mothers and fed quarters into the flickering pay per views while homesick, shaven-headed recruits in stiff uniforms read comic books alongside alcoholic geriatrics on row upon row of fixed plastic chairs.

One way to Fort Myers cost twenty-nine. The taxi ride had cost me fifteen, so as I counted and recounted my sweaty notes, I realised that it was looking more like the beginning of the end for me. I was an immigrant on a tourist visa, down to his last twenty bucks in a bus station on the wrong side of the tracks with nothing to look forward to but a grifter's promise. I was tempted to save the last of my money, just in case, but what good was twenty dollars? Twenty dollars was a liability, a sum that fell between usefulness and insignificance. Managed wisely, it could be stretched out for days, buying a little sustenance here and a little necessity there, and then, like an ice-cube dropped on the prairie, it would be gone. It made far more sense to squeeze the maximum enjoyment from the last twenty in the shortest possible time, and the Before You Go Lounge was the place to do it.

The barmaid was a wrung-out blonde who had been employed for her empathetic attitude: like everyone else in the bar, she was wishing she was someplace else. She slid a cold draught on to the bartop without taking her eyes from the TV. I followed her gaze and tried to make conversation.

'So it's going to rain?' I guessed, as the local news station broadcast a severe-weather warning. The barmaid nodded and changed the subject.

'English, huh?'

I replied with a nod and a shrug.

'Cute accent,' she announced, as though little else about me appealed to her.

It is important to slake one's thirst before embarking on a drinking session, so I necked my beer and ordered another, studying the bottles behind the bar as I considered my next move. Tradition demanded that I spend my remaining bucks on sour mash and brew, but ambition suggested that I ran the length of the tequila shelf. Ultimately, however, it was a question of economics.

'What's your cheapest shot?' I enquired, realising as I asked that there were numerous answers to this question.

The barmaid scratched her belly ring. 'Generic, I guess,' she answered. 'What time's your bus?'

'What bus?' I replied, watching her pour two fingers of caramelised alcohol into a shot glass.

She screwed the lid back on to the clear glass bottle. 'Most people drinking in here have a bus to catch.'

'Can't afford a ticket,' I shrugged, looking up to gauge her sympathy.

'Tough,' she shrugged back. 'Can you afford your tab?'

I listened to a little music, watched a little TV, and tried to plan for the future. Five beers and six shots later, as a thick tropical dusk fell like a soiled curtain, I did as I was told and spread my cash on the bartop. There was a shortfall of four dollars and the barmaid was unimpressed.

'I might have some Moroccan cash,' I offered, but her expression remained unchanged. I rummaged in my hand-bag and pulled out something I'd nicked a couple of nights and a lifetime previously.

'Here,' I slurred magnaminously, 'take this in lieu of the difference. It's a bottle opener from the Hotel Mamounia in Marrakech.' I placed the opener on the bartop and we appraised it.

'Hey!' cried the guy on the next stool. 'That's a fuckin' antique!'

Somehow I had failed to notice him before, but I watched him now as he leaned across and snatched my artefact from the bar. This was a man who boozed for a living, a cheap suit selling coast-to-coast crap as an excuse to drink in every bar in every state except one of sobriety.

I felt an enormous respect for him in spite of his soup-stained cuffs.

'Give you five bucks for it,' he offered. To me, his offer was an exit visa from the bar. To him, it was proof to his wife that he had an international career.

'Ten,' I shot back.

'Get fucked,' he growled. 'Five.'

'Fair enough,' I shrugged, taking his cash. I dropped the sweaty five on to the pile and took a single. The barmaid snatched it back.

'Over here,' she explained, with a wolverine smile, 'we tip.'

A cold Atlantic downpour drenched the dirty street as I lurked in the shadows of the bus terminal, watching slick, wet Greyhounds come and go. The last bus to Fort Myers left at ten-thirty, and I intended to be on it. Tickets to ride were checked at the door of each bus by tip-hungry drivers keen to help passengers enjoy their trip. It seemed likely that this was the only control, and it followed that, once seated, I would be safe, as long as I didn't draw any attention by taking a paying passenger's reserved place. The chances of this happening diminished as the bus filled up, so ideally I would sneak aboard at the last minute. I cringed as a squall snapped the rain like a wet towel, stinging my face and reminding me how dearly I wanted to be safe and warm on that bus when it left. Orange street lights and the nauseating neon flicker of fast-food joints, discount call centres and all-night liquor stores shone back from the running gutters, reminding me of where I'd be if I missed this connection. All I needed was a diversion.

'Jew need some help?'

The voice leaked insincerity like the bus shelter dripped

rainfall. It came from the shadows beneath a hooded top, its owner short, thin and full of troubling ambition. The high sodium lights that illuminated the bus station flashed across a pencil moustache and goatee. I pulled my hands from my pockets.

'I'm all right, mate,' I replied.

He nodded towards a bus, his hands hidden, hopping from foot to foot like he needed to pee.

'Jew waiting for a friend?'

I sighed. The poor have been hassled by bandits at transport terminals since before Paul decided to hitch to Damascus. The method was the same the whole world over, and I doubted its application was limited to humanity. Hyenas hung out where wildebeest assembled, and packs of long-tongued wolves waited for lost reindeer. I dearly wished I was carrying a large, black handgun that I could jab into his face and so close this testing conversation. Then again, this was Miami, and he probably had an even bigger gun stuffed in the waistband of his baggies.

'I don't have any friends,' I replied, 'and I don't have any money. None. Not a fucking dime. I got nothing to give except this here lady's handbag, and that's cursed.'

He looked up at me and I saw his face. It looked slightly puzzled. 'Jew need a place to stay?'

I shook my head. 'I got a place. Fort Myers. You ever heard of it?'

He shook his. 'Nope. Jew gotta cigarette?'

I leaned against the ugly graffiti of the shelter wall and offered him a Marlboro. He sucked smoke and blew it out hard.

'Jew got a ticket?'

I stared at the floor. 'Nope.'

'So how you gonna get to this Fort Myers?'

I shrugged. 'How the fuck should I know?'

We watched a cop car flash by, sirens whooping and lights flashing, then the little guy jabbed me with his elbow.

'Follow me,' he growled. 'I show you how to ride for free.'

We crossed the forecourt to where the big white coach of Greyhound Lines Incorporated Service 1174 stood in the floodlit rain. The driver was still in his seat, pretending to be working on important paperwork and killing time until he had to meet his charges.

'Soon as he steps down from that bus, those people in there gonna come through the door. Some of them got big bags.' He nodded towards the terminal building, his hands still in his pockets. 'I ask them they need a hand, or they got any spare change, and when the driver's busy calling security or telling me to get the fuck out or whatever, jew come around the back and step on to the bus. Go down the back and hide in the restroom. Stay there until the bus leaves. Jew getting this?'

I nodded. 'Sure I am. Thanks, man.' I extended my hand. 'I'm Martin.'

He left his in his pocket. 'Whatever. I'm Salvador. Gimme another cigarette and I tell you something else.'

I passed him another Marlboro and he stashed it away.

'Take my advice: get a car. You meet all kinds of bad people on the bus, man.'

Salvador's plan was by no means flawless, but it got me out of Miami. I laid low through Hollywood, and feigned sleep in Fort Lauderdale. Then the big white bus headed west on I-75, speeding down a rainswept highway across flashlit flatlands. Every mile I travelled was a bonus, and I was beginning to relax and enjoy the ride when it all went wrong. We pulled over at a crossroads close to the middle of nowhere to let two passengers step down. A car was waiting for them, and the driver made sure they were safely away before leaving his seat and striding slowly down the aisle. I swapped glances with the guy on the next seat, an old man with a bad cough and white shoes that matched his flat cap, and shrugged. When I looked up the driver had stopped beside me, as I had suspected he might.

'May I see your ticket, sir?'

'Hmm?' I glanced up, showing only polite surprise. 'Er, yes, of course you can.'

I went through the predictable charade of searching my pockets, patting my ribs and rummaging through my bag. 'Must be here somewhere . . .'

He let me sweat for a couple of minutes, then put his hand on my shoulder. 'My paperwork says at this point I got forty-one passengers on this here bus. You make forty-two.' He grinned like a rat-catcher. 'You're busted, pal.'

They clapped as the bus pulled away, leaving me standing in rain that fell so hard it hurt. I was sure I'd been in worse situations. The road lay like a length of shiny tape across a soft, black landscape. Sheets of lightning flashed like distant artillery, backlighting the dripping, drooping trees and throwing even darker shadows on to the sodden ground beneath. Millions of warm raindrops fell on millions of greedy leaves, drowning the growling of whatever was abroad in the gloom beyond the road. Glad for once that I wasn't stoned, I put all thoughts of night-crawlers from my mind and raised a thumb over the road. There is a belief that it is easier to hitch a ride in poor weather than in fair, but this is not strictly true. Precipitation works in the hitch-hiker's favour for only the first five to ten minutes of the storm. During this period one has pity on one's side and the driver has only nagging conscience. Once the water has soaked through to the skin and the spray from passing traffic has pebbledashed your legs with road dirt, conscience has been dropped at the verge and the driver is riding with practicality. Who wants some dripping hippy messing up the velour and steaming up the windscreen?

The rain, I noticed, moved in waves of varied intensity, as though successive storms had collided somewhere over my head. It fell like an explosion of hot hypodermics, stinging my back and shoulders like a tattoo, then washed my wounds with a gentle spray before falling cold and heavy. It ran down my legs and pooled in my boots, and as I shuffled my feet I sucked mud in through my cracked soles. Conflicting winds gusted through the treetops like competing settlers in a land grab, sighing in disgust as they rushed around my sodden body. Jagged bolts as wide as highways staggered skywards, lighting the night in blue-tinged monochrome, tearing the darkness to shreds and setting off explosions like the carpet bombing of Cambodia. Suddenly wildly exhilarated by the spectacle I began dancing in circles, whooping and cheering with every strike, understanding exactly why the next car to pass didn't stop. What kind of madman would pick up a long-haired maniac in a disco suit who was dancing to the thunder on a storm-lashed swamp road at midnight?

But I didn't have long to wait.

Yellow beams pierced the deluge, and I fixed my biggest, friendliest smile to my face and stepped into the road, the headlights lighting me up like a dirt-splattered scarecrow. I kept on smiling and the huge pick-up truck kept on coming before swinging off the blacktop and into the lay-by in a spray of pale mud. I jogged across to greet the driver.

'Need a ride?' he drawled, like he was on his way home from the beach. An ugly hound dog awoke on the bench seat and barked.

'Shut the fuck up, Clinton!' bawled the driver, his thick gold necklace reflecting lightning.

'Sure I need a ride,' I nodded, eyeing the big black dog with disdain. He curled his lip in return, flashing two rows of shark's teeth.

'Pleased to meet you,' said the driver, offering his hand and shaking mine in a perfunctory manner. 'My name's Brad. This here's Clinton. Who the hell are you?'

'Martin,' I replied. 'Nice to meet you, Brad. Likewise, Clinton.' The malevolent dog jostled for space between Brad and me while Elvis wondered about that mystery train comin' down the track.

'Cool sound,' I commented.

'*El Rey*,' Brad replied. 'That accent – where you from?'

'UK,' I said. 'England.'

Brad nodded. 'Cool.'

Clinton yawned, farted and growled at the same time, glancing at me in an unspoken challenge to do better.

I lit a cigarette, noticing as I did that there was another light in the cab, something wild and flickering independent of the Ford's electrical system. I looked into Brad's face and saw the same light in his blue eyes. It was reflected in the vulgar gold chain draped around his neck and looked suspiciously like the glow from a distant but all-consuming blaze of insanity. He caught me looking, so I bluffed it.

'What's that HK stand for on your hat?' I asked.

Brad smiled, pleased to be asked. 'That HK stands for Heckler & Koch, boy, the finest corporation on God's earth.'

'Cool,' I nodded. 'They make tractors or something, don't they?'

Brad stepped on the brakes. 'You sayin' I'm a hick or something?' he growled.

I held up my hands. 'No!' I insisted. 'Not unless you want

33

me to. I just thought that you people wore hats with tractor names on them, or baseball teams.'

He appraised me like a hanging judge and decided that no offence was meant. We rolled.

'HK make firearms,' explained Brad. 'They make the finest firearms on the planet and I'm not dissin' the flag by sayin' so neither, not when our Special Ops boys have got the SOCOM. You know what the SOCOM is, Martin?'

I shrugged.

'SOCOM's the Special Operations Command tactical firearm solution, boy, a big motherfucker of a firearm endorsed by the DOD.'

'Wow,' I gasped, like I knew what the hell he was talking about.

'You know something else, boy?' asked Brad, warming to his theme.

'It's Martin,' I reminded him.

He looked at me in mock-horror, as though he'd committed a gross offence and cared. 'Well, pardon me, Marty. I was just fixing to tell you that HK is owned by a Brit company, British Aerospace, so that makes you a welcome guest in my vehicle, Marty.' He grinned and dipped below the dashboard, ignoring the road. 'Let's have a little drink to the boys at British Aerospace!'

He bobbed up and swung the wheel as we clipped the verge, passing me a bottle in a brown bag.

'To the boys at BAE, HK and SOCOM,' I proposed, before taking a long, medicinal suck on the liquor. I took another pull and passed the bottle to Brad.

'Life is a mystery,' he sang. 'Goddamn wise words from an otherwise talentless piece of kike ass, wouldn't you say?'

I was still trying to filter the facts from his last statement when Brad had another idea.

'You guys drive on the left, right?' he said.

'Right,' I confirmed.

'Thought so,' grinned Brad, whirling the wheel. 'This make you feel more comfortable?'

The truck crossed the glowing median and rolled through the storm in a reckless English style.

'Easy, man,' I warned. 'This is kind of insane.'

Brad shook his head and switched off the headlights. '*This* is kinda insane, wouldn't you say?'

I scrabbled on the bench seat for a safety-belt, pushing my hand under the indignant dog's backside in my search. As he growled a heavy thud knocked him into the footwell.

'Shit!' cried Brad, and then the pick-up pitched nose-down in the darkness and plunged into a shallow ditch.

I rose and headbutted the cabin roof, falling back into my seat stunned and fearful. There was a moment of apprehensive silence, ended by Brad's delighted laughter.

'Y'all okay?' he called, wiping the blood from a split eyebrow. 'Musta been some kinda corner back there. Fuckin' highway goes straight as an arrow for miles and miles and then some dumbass puts a corner on it.'

I was squeezing a bleeding nose, reasonably satisfied with the outcome of the inevitable crash. I told Brad that I was fine and climbed out to push the pick-up back on to the road. He spent fifteen minutes trying to coax his big, ugly dog back into the cab and was subdued as we resumed our journey. Eventually he spoke.

'You're pretty goddamn reckless riding on the wrong side of the highway at night in the rain with no lights in a stolen pick-up. 'Specially with this here untrained dog in the cab. I wouldn't want to go far with you, you crazy motherfucker!'

Elvis was singing 'That's Alright'.

I looked at Brad. He was far from all right.

Some time later we stopped for gas on the outskirts of an unlit town. Brad grabbed a broom and swept the swamp weed from the front of his ride as I huddled in the neon. Clinton sniffed the pumps for diesel and splashed each one with a hillbilly autograph.

'C'mon, let's git,' yelled Brad. 'Want some sulphate?'

Of course I wanted some sulphate. I took his wrap and poured powder on to my tongue like sherbet. I'd forgotten how bad it tasted.

'Gimme that booze,' I gurned. 'Quick!' Suddenly alert, I tried to concentrate on the road ahead. 'Where we going?'

Elvis had left his job down at the carwash and his momma a goodbye note. Brad had been singing along, but now he frowned.

'I'm going to kill my girlfriend,' he announced. 'You're going to Cape Coral.'

I waited until Elvis had roamed a hobo jungle and a thousand miles of track. Wrong king, wrong song. Should have been Hendrix.

'Hey, Brad, where you goin' with that gun in your hand?' I asked, taking another long pull on his brown-bagged liquor.

'Good call,' he nodded. 'Gonna shoot my old lady. She been messin' around.'

'Then what?' I replied. 'You gonna head down Mexico way?'

Brad took a thoughtful swig and wiped his mouth with the back of his hand. 'Dunno,' he admitted. 'Hadn't really thought that far ahead.'

I tried to change the subject. 'How come your dog smells so bad?'

Brad grinned like a proud parent. 'Crazy bastard ate a skunk last week. He's been farting like that for days. Ain't that something?'

Elvis's forty greatest hits rolled from end to end and back again as Brad outlined his past, present and future with the lucidity and clarity that one gets from only the truly wired. Brad was twenty-nine, and the last time he had got any satisfaction he'd been twenty-four. The past half-decade had been spent in the Crossroads Correctional Center in Cameron, Missouri: five years for the contravention of State Law 404 and the possession of twenty-eight kilos of poor-quality Mexican weed. He stared through the windscreen wipers and they sighed for him.

'You been in prison, Marty?'

I shook my head. 'Not yet.'

Brad shook his head, smiling at something undeclared. 'You know what I missed most while I was in that shiny, new correctional facility?'

'Women?' I tried.

'I mean apart from women.'

'Drugs?'

Brad sniffed impatiently. 'I mean apart from screwing, drugs, brew, liquor, TV and bowling.'

'I give up.'

'Firearms,' he revealed. 'I missed my goddamn firearms almost as much as I missed my old hound dog.'

'Oh,' I said. '*This* hound dog?'

He shook his head and slapped Clinton's. 'Uh-uh. This here's my *new* hound dog.'

'Why's he called Clinton?'

''Cos he's friendly, dumb and fucks anything. Tried it on with a pig couple of weeks back, didn't you, boy? Just like his goddamned namesake.' He took another swig from the brown bag and gasped. 'I know you got all them IRA terrorists living in the woods over there in England, Marty, but this here's a dangerous country, too. Look at what happened tonight: I'm driving along, minding my own business, and you're there in the rain waving me down like you just broke out of some cuckoo's nest.' He gave me a long, serious look. 'Anything could have happened, man.'

We stared out into the darkness for a moment, each considering the implications of our meeting under such dark clouds.

Brad brought us back to the present. 'That's why I cherish my firearms. I got a Ruger Thirty-ought-six and a Benelli Twelve, and a Thirty-eight Special stashed back there with the digging tools and the ropes,' he confessed, nodding towards the covered rear of his truck. 'It's better to be prepared.'

'Prepared for what?' I asked, aghast.

'Anything that might come along in an average twenty-four,' he explained.

'Yeah, but they're no good to you back there,' I pointed out. 'Supposing I pulled a knife on you in h—'

Brad touched the brakes and swerved, and when I had recovered my balance he was pointing a pistol at my head. 'You were saying?' he asked melodramatically.

Clinton started barking.

I swallowed. 'That the one you're going to shoot your fiancée with?' I winced as he scratched his ear with the muzzle.

'Don't know yet. Would be nice, though. Shut the fuck up, Clinton!' He dropped the magazine on to the seat between his legs and, with one finger on the steering wheel, worked the slide to drop the chambered round. 'Check it out,' he suggested, handing me the pistol. I curled my fingers around the plastic grip and turned the weapon over. It felt solid, well engineered and dependable, a matt-black extension of my hand and my will. It felt absolutely right.

'That', announced Brad, 'is a Heckler & Koch USP forty cal., the finest handgun in the world. You can keep your faggy Desert Eagles and your P-Ninety-nines and your Sigs – they don't come close. That, Marty, is a precision tool and I urge you to acquire one a.s.a.p.'

I dragged back the slide, savouring the perfect tension in the spring, felt it lock, then let it snap forward. Pointing out into the rain, I pulled the trigger, hearing only the disappointed click of the hammer on an empty chamber.

'What happens if we get stopped with all these firearms?'

Brad had it all worked out. 'We escape,' he replied, 'or we die there and then. Arrest is not an option tonight.'

The storm was still following me, a whirling frenzy of backlit cloudbursts, and there was nothing beyond the road but rain-lashed shades of black. I smiled a tight little smile, like a man on the wrong train.

'This pick-up really stolen?' I enquired breezily.

'Fresh out of Florissant,' nodded Brad, 'and a good thing for you, too. You reckon if I was the legitimate owner of this vehicle I'd have messed up the leather with your drippin' butt? Hell, no: you'd have been out there drowning in the rain like McArthur fucking Park.' He scanned me from head to toe and shook his head. 'Who the hell else would have picked you up? You're a lucky guy, Marty!'

Amphetamine sulphate and hollow fear tormented my colon as we emerged from the swamps and passed from cattle country to the first orange lights of the sprawling communities of Florida's west coast. State Troopers' cruisers lay submerged in the shadows by the side of the freeway like waiting 'gators, and there was little prey to choose from on tonight's storm-swept carriageways. Brad, I had learned, had tracked his fiancée from St Louis to Fort Myers, and he was going to kill her because she was a cheating bitch.

'And she ain't my fiancée no more, neither,' he pointed out. 'If she was, she'd still be wearing this.' He fumbled at the grubby neck of his T-shirt and dragged out a cheap ring on a flashy chain.

The slick highway was lined with neon, and Brad had taken his eyes from the road. 'Let's get some coffee and work up a plan,' he suggested, swinging into the parking lot of an all-night diner called Terry's. 'Guard the car, Clinton.'

Exhaustion had risen like unexpected flood water behind the flimsy chemical dams that were keeping us both awake and it was with aching limbs and slow reactions that we stumbled blinking into the restaurant's brightness. A worn-out waitress with a tattooed tear brought us coffee, water and a slice of cherry pie while we stared out at the rain like strangers on a train.

I sipped coffee that was as hot and weak as me, and broke the silence. 'I don't think you should be doing what you're thinking of doing,' I declared.

Brad gave me one of those languid jailhouse stares. 'And what the fuck would you know?'

What did I know? I'd been in the United States for less than twenty-four hours and I had drunk all my money, been thrown from the Greyhound into alligator-infested swamps and rescued by a homicidal St Louis ex-con with a bad dog, a truckload of guns and a mission to kill his fiancée. It was raining so hard that I thought the world was trying to tell me something. And I had no cigarettes. I took one of Brad's and stood up.

'I don't know anything at all, mate,' I replied, and left.

Brad waited long enough for the rain to reach my skin, then soaked me some more by skidding into the gutter. He threw open the passenger door and leaned past his baying hound. 'Get in,' he said. 'C'mon, don't make me apologise. Shut the fuck up, Clinton.'

We drove another fifteen insignificant American miles before he spoke again. 'It's not like you think, man,' he sighed. 'It ain't like she just upped and left me while I was inside. She *put* me inside, man.'

I held up my hands, noticing that they were trembling. 'Listen, Brad. I'm just a hitcher. You shouldn't be telling me all this. It's not wise.'

He snorted, as though unimpressed by my modesty. 'Hey, it's good to talk, Marty. I been locked up with a bunch of criminal losers the last five years and you're the first smart guy I've met since I got out.'

I lit one of his cigarettes, shivering as I inhaled. 'So what did she do?'

'She was clever,' he admitted, shaking his head in reluctant admiration of her genius. 'She took me for a fool. I do two things good: I get dings out of bodywork, and I sell weed. You been to Mexico?'

I shook my head. 'Not yet.'

'Yeah, well, Mexico is a source of good weed. Always has been. Nothing spectacular, just your regular generic reefer. Very good friend of mine called Rufus tells me he's been invited in on a shipment: five hundred kilos, five ways, only he ain't got the ante. I ain't got it neither, but a guy I know from St Louis is willing to front me the capital.'

He shot me a narrow-eyed glance. A tiny light, not very bright, was flashing somewhere in the back of his head, warning him to check his speed-fuelled tongue. Spilling your guts to complete strangers was traditionally considered unwise in some parts of society, but Brad, all fired up on the bitter taste of amphetamine, was having too much fun to stop. This was as close as he'd ever get to a chat show, and I was a captive audience. He licked his lips and let rip.

'The scam is foolproof – we got a converted van with secret compartments and all – and the plan goes like clockwork, man. I never even met the other four guys. Me and my buddy Rufus worked out the after-sales policy and decided no cash, no flash. We wait until we've sold the whole consignment, and then we wait some more. Then, and only then, we start spending. Most fools go out buying fancy clothes and custom pick-up trucks right off, and that's what gets them caught. Me and Rufus: we were foolproof. You been to St Louis?'

'Not yet,' I replied.

'It's a big party town, man, and me and Rufus had customers lined up all over. Five kilos here, ten kilos there, and in the first week we've unloaded sixty per cent of the consignment. I pay back my man and the rest of the cash is bagged up in ten-k bundles and stashed out on my step-daddy's place in Crawford County.' Brad blew a long plume of smoke into the windscreen. 'Me and my buddy did a lot of pacing and a lot of scratching, but we learned how to be cool. Come Labor Day we got twenty-eight kilos left, and I'm sitting outside Denny's with it stashed in the pick-up truck waiting for my buddy to show. It's ten in the morning and the parking lot is crawling with joggers, strollers, faggots arguing on cellphones, and me. Turned out everyone else was packing for the city, and suddenly they're all over me. Rufus saw it all from across the street – told me they even had a sniper on the roof and a helicopter. Charged me with, and I quote, "the class A felony of trafficking in the second degree, and the class B felony of possession of a controlled substance with the intent to distribute". State wanted to keep me for fifteen. Judge gave me five. To be continued.'

We were driving through working-class suburbia – cheap wooden houses on unkempt plots, each and every one flying the flag.

'Maybe I missed a bit,' I said, 'but where does your ex-bird fit in to all this? It sounds to me like your good buddy Rufus sold you out and did a runner with the cash.'

Brad sighed. 'I'm cutting here, Marty, but you ain't bleeding. My buddy visited me in jail. Warned me that Sherry-Lee was coming in wearing a Federally sponsored wire. Next thing he's clashed heads with a forty-five slug and lost everything. Sherry-Lee and the sixty-four thousand dollars are still at large. How does that sound to you?'

I nodded like a moron. I was too tired to argue any more.

I awoke and the panic of displacement pulled my seat from under me. When I landed, I was still lost. Clinton had pushed me hard against the passenger door with his huge hind paws. The pick-up carried a pack in his simple canine view, and I was at the bottom, with the bitches and the pups.

'Where are we?' I asked fearfully.

Brad was smoking and staring into the pre-dawn dark. 'We're there,' he replied.

I stretched, wincing as I dragged my neck muscles back to where they belonged. My tongue felt brown and unhealthy and my scalp itched. 'Where's there?'

After a moment's reflection Brad turned to me. 'Here,' he said.

We were parked on a dirt road, our tyres washed by an unmapped river of brown rainwater. One side of this flooded track followed the curve of a swampy wasteland of sawgrass and windblown garbage, and the other abutted a chainlink fence backed by a freakish, dripping conifer hedge. An unlit signboard identified it as the boundary of the Bridgeview

Trailer Park, RVs welcome, weekly and monthly rates available.

Brad pointed at the open gate. 'That's where she is,' he nodded. 'She ain't done bad for herself with all that cash, has she?'

The clock on his dashboard said 4.15, time for me to be going.

'Is this Cape Coral?' I asked.

Brad shook his head. 'Nope. Cape Coral is twenty minutes that away. This here looks like the cheap side of Fort Myers Beach. I'll drop you off after I'm done here.'

'No,' I insisted. 'You've been kind enough already. I'll make my own way from here and let you get on with your business.'

Brad grabbed the wheel with both hands. 'Man, it's no problem at all. Shit, it's on my way back north. We'll grab breakfast or something.'

I dropped my head and rubbed my eyes. 'Look, Brad. You and Sherry-Lee have got a lot of talking to do . . .'

'No, we ain't.'

'Well, whatever. It's been great riding with you and talking and everything, and thanks for the whiz and all the fags, but I'm only here on a tourist visa and I can't be getting involved in murder.'

Brad removed his hat and scratched his greasy blond head. He stared ahead, looking for words. None came, so I filled in the gap.

'I'm sorry, man, but I hardly know you.' I opened the door and stepped into the rain. 'Good luck, Brad.' I ignored the dog.

Brad nodded. He looked hurt. 'Whatever, man,' he muttered.

I walked back towards the highway, wishing I'd scrounged

a cigarette before falling out with him. Something huge and dark loomed up to my left, its definition increasing with the dawn's early light until I could see the blurred grey span of a bridge arcing into the murky distance.

Bridgeview Trailer Park.

Somewhere in there, sleeping or weeping in one of those prefab boxes of broken lives, lay Sherry-Lee, unaware that death was psyching himself up in a stolen pick-up truck on the swamp side of town. Any time soon Brad would coast up to her trailer, crack the door with his lock-knife and take care of business. There would be wailing and begging and pleading and then there would be shooting. I wondered if I would still be in earshot when Brad's chosen firearm discharged. I wondered how I would feel, whether the sound of those shots on the early morning air would carry through the flimsy walls I had built around myself since I'd last heard pistols at dawn. Brad wasn't heading north any more than I was turning over a new leaf, and the last of the shots I would hear would be the one he put through his own head. One made one's choices and one had to die with them: who was I to intervene?

I'd stopped, I noticed, and was standing, half-turning on the wet, yellow track. I'd been thinking about multiple gunshots, a series of muffled pops, then a pause, then one more, and yet the aural image was inconsistent with what I knew of Brad's character. He loved his firearms, and respected his ammunition, so the most I would hear would be two shots: his 'n' hers. And maybe another, for the mutt.

Unless Sherry-Lee had guests. Or a dog of her own. Or kids.

It had been four years since Brad had seen her, and kids were always a possibility where women were concerned.

Given time to think, I'm usually on the hostile side of

ambivalence towards children. Innocence and trust are short-comings that should be eliminated from a kid's character before the pain and disappointment hit. Kids are small humans with too much time on their hands and a shortage of respon-sibilities, and I have no sympathy for them. It wasn't their fault — I just didn't like them. But something neural, some-thing autonomic, wouldn't let me walk away, and I found myself running back towards the Bridgeview Trailer Park.

The dog heard me coming and heralded my return at unnecessary volume.

'What the fuck are you doing back here?' hissed Brad as I skidded, breathless, to a halt. 'Shut the fuck up, Clinton!'

He checked that I was alone and carried on preparing the USP, which had more than doubled in length.

'What's that?' I asked, pointing at the weapon.

'Tactical silencer,' he replied. 'You forget something?'

'Yeah, but I remembered it before it was too late,' I mut-tered. 'Brad, we got to talk.'

He gave the silencer a final twist and placed it beside him. 'So go ahead and talk,' he said dismissively, bending to pull a narrow box of Winchester 40-cal. pistol rounds from beneath the seat.

'I don't think you should go in there,' I began. 'Suppose she's not alone.'

Brad shrugged. 'I got bullets for everyone. Even you, if you want.'

I shook my head. 'That's not what I meant. You're not thinking tactically. Where's your recon? What's your plan? You're going in there like some kind of gangster, and if you come up against a sawn-off you're fucked.'

I saw the momentum drop from his determined prepara-tion of his weapon as my words thudded into his brain. I was talking Brad's language, and with admirable fluency, I

thought. I let another volley fly. 'You got to know your
route in, your targets, their locations and their tactical dis-
position, so you need recon. You cannot perform this task,
'cos if she knows you're coming, she'll be looking out for
you. I, however, am just a dumb tourist off the plane from
wherever, checking up on weekly rates at the trailer park.
You get what I'm saying?'

Brad was reeling. This was the closest he'd ever come to a
real special operation, and it seemed that the hippy he'd
saved from the storm was a tactical genius. 'Sounds cool,' he
admitted. 'Makes sense, I guess.'

'What number?'

'Thirty-four C.'

'I'll be back in fifteen minutes,' I promised, checking my
wrist. 'Quit loitering – drive around the block or something – and I'll see you later.'

Clinton glared at me like I was glass, his ears half cocked:
he saw right through me. 'It might be advisable to kill the
dog,' I added, backing into the darkness. 'He makes way
too much noise.'

I strode through the gates before Brad had time to recover
and realised that I had no idea what I was doing. I didn't
even have a watch. Rows of immobile homes in disparate
states of repair sat on tired plots of similar upkeep. Every
home owned a car – some had two or three – and most had
a barbecue of one sort or another in the front yard. Paddling
pools and tricycles and bright plastic toys were scattered
across the park, and on every corner of every plot something
wild had scattered the garbage. In some a dim light burned
behind a screened window, while others were lit by the electric blue of a TV screen. One row of a dozen or so homes
was entirely vacant, as though a virus had wiped out the
street, and their plots had grown thick with straggling weeds.

I spotted 34 C on the next street. A rusting blue Mazda was parked outside and I registered with relief that there were no toys scattered on the unused front yard. The trailer seeped the uncomfortable air of something worn out of necessity rather than desire, like a windcheater or a bullet-proof vest. How bulletproof, I wondered? The rain had faded to a light drizzle, a grey sea mist that crept in on the dawn to mingle with the vapours from the swamp.

Sherry-Lee was home – I could see the flickering light of her TV through the trailer window – but I didn't know what to do next. I slipped into the shadows behind the mobile home to consider my next move: knocking on the door at 4.30 a.m. in a stained white suit and sporting an English accent seemed ill-advised. Wishing I had something to smoke, I crept up to the window and peered inside. Sherry-Lee was keeping company with a bottle of Jack and a black-and-white movie. Her hair was long and dark, her shoulders narrow, and that's all I could see. I moved around the trailer and mounted the steps to the front door, letting my body take the initiative. Railing against the folly like the bound master of a ship in mutiny, I watched my hand knock hard and loud on the trailer door.

The TV volume decreased immediately, but no one came to the door.

I knocked again, urgently.

'That you, Solomon? You locked out again, Solomon?' The voice was soft and sweet and full of concern.

'That you, Sherry-Lee?' I replied. There was a long pause during which I envisaged six rounds of thirty-eight being quietly woken. The glow of the TV died and the sound of quiet movements came from within. I stepped away from the door frame. 'Sherry-Lee? My name's Martin – Marty if you like. I'm British. I don't know who the hell you are or what's going on, but I'm here because of Brad and I got a message from him. I know it's late and all that but we gotta talk, like right now. You don't even have to open the door. You okay with that?'

Injuns were out there and Sherry-Lee needed time to corral the wagons. She tried to buy time. 'I got a Twenty-four pointed right at you, boy,' she cried, after a long pause.

'What's a Twenty-four?' I called back.

Another pause. 'A Glock Twenty-four, Compact Nine. You know, a handgun.'

I stepped a little further away from the door. 'Oh, right,' I replied. 'We don't have guns in England.'

Sherry-Lee was clearly freaked, but her voice dripped like honey. 'You really from England?'

'Absolutely,' I confirmed. 'I'm from Cornwall, near London.'

I heard her feet shuffle across the floor. When she spoke, she was nearer. 'Where's Brad?'

I leaned towards the door and spoke quietly. 'He's out front, in a stolen pick-up, with a shitload of firearms. He's pretty mad, and I think you should split right now because –'

A cheap lock turned and the screen door was pushed outwards. Sherry-Lee stood in the frame in a T-shirt and long legs. Her hair tumbled from her shoulders like the rain ran from mine and her eyes turned the words to pebbles in my mouth.

'– because I'm trying to avoid a tragedy.' Christ, the way Brad told it she sounded so big and so clever and yet here she was, small and vulnerable and beautiful. My guts had turned to slush, my heart had melted and my knees were weak. I closed my eyes and kept them shut. 'Look,' I sighed. 'I'm trying to do the right thing. I hope I've done it. I'm out of

here. Thank you for your time and I'm sorry to have disturbed you. Goodnight.'

'Goodnight, Martin,' she replied. 'You tell Brad he ain't
got no reason to be mad about nothing. And don't fear the
reaper – ain't that what they say?'

'Only the lunatics,' I mumbled, turning on my sodden
heels and slipping back into the dark.

I know she watched me go.

Brad was waiting where I'd left him.

'Shut the fuck up, Clinton, you goddamned loudmouth,'
he hissed as I approached.

'Your lucky night, pal,' I told him, shaking my head and
waiting for him to ask me why.

'Why?'

''Cos if you'd done the Angel of Death thing you'd have
scored an own goal, as we say in England. Tonight is party
night at thirty-eight C, mate, and there must be forty people
in that place. They got a barbie burning on the outside, kids
playing, motorcycles lined up down the street, people dancing and singing . . .'

'I can't hear nothing,' protested Brad.

'Wind's in the wrong direction,' I explained.

'And it's raining,' observed Brad. 'How come they got the
barbecue going?'

I shook my head. 'Hardcore biker motherfuckers, man.
Probably cooking with gasoline.' I pointed at the lightening
sky, then I pointed at Brad. 'Rain, rain go away, come back
another day. Let's get out of here.'

Brad bought breakfast at Denny's, and after I'd finished my
$3.99 grand slam I ate his short stack with sausage patty. A
blonde waitress poured weak coffee without waiting to be
asked as Brad stared with mild shock at a morning I was sure

he hadn't planned on seeing. Having deceived him, I felt the urge to reassure him, but I sealed my lips with maple syrup.

'How you set for cash?' he asked distractedly.

I showed him my palms and kept chewing. He slapped a fifty-dollar note on to the table. 'That's for the recon, man. Now we're straight, right?'

I nodded, and he rose.

'Gotta go,' he sighed. 'I'll see you around.'

I swallowed hard and fast. 'Where you going?'

He shrugged. 'Dunno. Like I said, I ain't thought that far ahead. Guess I'll head back to St Lou and see my parole officer.'

'What about your bird?'

He looked at me for a moment as if he had no idea what I was talking about, then he shrugged again. 'Sherry-Lee? I'll deal with her later. In the meantime . . .' He gave the matter a few moments' careful consideration. 'Fuck her,' he decided.

I shivered at the memory of her silhouette. It would have been churlish to refuse.

4

A wet blanket of grey clouds was dragged over the Florida coast by a warm south-westerly as I walked down Del Prado Boulevard in search of Gene's Cape Coral address. The efforts I had made to improve my damp and unshaven appearance in the washroom at Denny's didn't show, and the polo-shirted pedestrians of this shiny, new town were brutal in their disdain. This unfinished development, raised from the swamps, was the second-safest city in the USA, proclaimed an honest-looking poster sponsored by the Cape Coral Realtors' Association, and it didn't want the likes of me ruining its chances of reaching the number-one spot.

I had to agree: I was a disgrace, but I had potential. Gene had seen that back in Marrakech; Brad had used it only this morning; and Sherry-Lee, above all others, had benefited from it. I let my mind show off its latest composite images of Sherry-Lee for a moment and noticed to my delight that they now came with sound. 'Stop by for a beer,' she whispered, 'I haven't had the chance to thank you properly for what you did last night.'

I caught my reflection and cringed. I was wearing a soiled linen suit two sizes too big, a Guns N' Roses T-shirt and a pair of pointed brown cowboy boots with soles that flapped like lizard jaws. My fingers were stained yellow and my lips scabbed from an amphetamine-sponsored chewathon. I hadn't showered in a month and my teeth were a whitish shade of brown. I stank, I sucked, and I failed to shape up.

Sherry-Lee deserved better; America deserved better. Gene
certainly expected better.

From a distance he looked cool in a smug, bourgeois fashion,
dressed like he owned a boat: chinos, polo shirt and deck
shoes.

'Stay the fuck out of my way,' he hissed when he saw me.
Two fat guys in flight jackets with George Michael facial hair
were chewing like brain-damaged sheep on the veranda
while Gene and a small Hispanic man argued in the kitchen.

'You the help?' asked Tweedle Dee as I retreated to Gene's
brown lawn to light up a Marlboro.

'S'pose I am,' I replied, with more grace than either of
them deserved.

'Guess you're fired, then,' grinned Tweedle Dum, goading
me with a stare like a short, sharp stick.

I took a couple of long drags, my eyes never leaving his,
then I blew smoke. 'When was the last time you let Jesus into
your heart?' I asked him, but he was summoned by his boss
before he could remember. I watched the three climb into
their Jeep and screech out of sight before giving Gene another
chance to welcome me to his sumptuous suburban home.

'Can you just disappear for a couple of months?' he asked
when he remembered I was still on his premises. 'Now is not
a good time for me.'

'Where am I going to go?' I asked. 'I spent all my money
getting here.'

Gene managed to shake his head and scratch it at the
same time. 'Jesus, I don't know. Go to the fuckin' beach or
something.'

'What about the job?' I demanded with as much indig-
nation as I thought appropriate, considering my appearance.

Gene sighed impatiently. 'Troop, right now there is no

fuckin' job. There isn't even a home, nor an office neither. I've just taken a direct hit and I got thirty minutes to evac.' He looked at me for the second time and raised his curiously symmetrical eyebrows. 'Bye-ee. Go on. Git.'

I stood my ground, fumbling for another cigarette. 'No way,' I insisted. 'No way are you chucking me on to the streets after I flew from fucking Africa to be here.'

Gene pointed out through his kitchen window and down the leafy street. 'Those repo bastards are chucking *me* on to the streets in thirty minutes. What do you want me to do? I got no address, I got no business. I got no business, I got no need for staff. See where I'm heading?'

I couldn't see where he was heading. All I could see was Sherry-Lee standing in the doorway of her trailer with her long legs, short T-shirt and long hair.

'I got a place we can stay,' I announced, my mind casting ahead to catch my mouth's drift. 'No neighbours, no questions, and weekly or monthly rates. I think it's quite near the beach.'

Gene rubbed his face. 'I need an aromatherapy,' he sighed.

The greaseball manager at the Bridgeview Trailer Park had ketchup on his unshaven chin and something nasty in his eyes. He could have found a gay subtext in a Bugs Bunny cartoon and it took him a single glance to categorise Gene and me. 'Insurance assessors, you say,' he smirked as Gene filled in the forms. 'That what they call it now, is it?'

'Certainly is, sir,' smiled Gene, handing over an Alabama state ID and driving licence.

The manager studied both for evidence of sodomy, then returned them. 'That all seems fine, Mr Renoir,' he nodded, pronouncing Gene's assumed name as 'Renoyer'. 'Just one week?'

'Yes sir,' replied Gene. 'Just one week. And it's *Ren-wah*, by the way, like the philosopher.'

The manager was reluctant to learn anything from a faggot. 'Why, ain't that a surprise, I wonder,' he shrugged, dangling a key between a finger and a thumb. 'Thirty-seven D. It's down by the fence at the back end. Don't go breaking through that fence, neither, for your own sakes. There's 'gators in there and patches of quicksand that'll suck you down quicker than a garbage disposal. You have been warned. Now y'all keep your *ass*essing to yourselves, now, y' hear?'

Thirty-seven D delighted me as much as it disgusted Gene, and he had donned rubber gloves and an apron as part of a chemically dependent attempt to bring our new home up to his somewhat acute standards of hygiene. I hoped the manager could see him camping it up with the Shake 'N' Vac. My joy at having somewhere to live was tainted only by the absence of Sherry-Lee's Mazda from the next row of trailers. If she had any sense, she'd be driving for the state line right now, hauling her life and her savings out of harm's way and wondering about the knight in tarnished armour who had saved her life.

As I dropped the last of his cartons on the sagging bed in the better of the trailer's two bedrooms, Gene called me to my first ever corporate briefing. A single coin the colour and diameter of a Ritz cracker lay on the table in our new home's kitchen-diner in a clear plastic wallet. Gene pointed with a yellow rubber finger. 'Take a look,' he said.

I picked it up. It seemed too heavy for its size. 'What is it?'

'Krugerrand,' explained Gene. 'From Kruger, Paul, and rand, after Witwatersrand, where the gold was mined. '

'Why are you showing it to me?'

'Because you need to know. It's a certified bullion coin, as good as cash anywhere in the world. The latent value of these beautiful objects fund the operation here in Florida, an operation which, thanks to your assistance in its relocation, now requires an assistant. That brings me to you. I want you to take three of these into town and sell them for the best price you can get. Consider it an aptitude test. If you get arrested, or if you disappear, I'll tell the cops you stole them from me. If, on the other hand, you come back with a decent amount of cash, I'll consider your engagement as my PA. Got it?'

Seemed simple, I thought, as I drove Gene's Toyota the few miles of steaming freeway into Fort Myers. My mission was to sell three coins for as much as I could without showing any ID, accepting any cheques or attracting any unwanted attention. Mindful of this latter concern I swung into the lot of a thrift store and spent a few minutes replacing my wardrobe.

'Lookin' good,' nodded the septuagenarian store girl with pencilled eyebrows and sun-cured hide.

Inclined to agree, I handed over ten of Brad's bucks and returned to the Toyota wearing flared Wranglers, a white T-shirt and an Oahu print shirt. I ripped the relevant pages from the International House of Pancakes Yellow Pages and set off in search of disreputable coin dealers, wondering why every thought in my head began and ended with Sherry-Lee. Sitting back and watching myself drive, I conjectured on the causes of this infatuation. What love I had in my self-absorbed carcass was easily stirred, but just as easily misplaced. I fell in love all the time, especially with waitresses, which was odd, considering my indifference to food. I also had a much more reasonable attraction to barmaids, although my affections were rarely reciprocated. These, however, were merely passing fancies, sweet, self-inflicted wounds that stung and ached then faded away like shopping-mall piercings.

Compared to these flesh wounds, Sherry-Lee hurt like Moroccan dentistry, and I couldn't work out why. Maybe it was the stress, I thought, as an eager man in a bow tie explained the difference between proof and circulated krugerrands. Perhaps it was the nostalgic threat of sudden death attendant at our first meeting that had drawn me to her, I mused, as a fat guy in an Elvis T-shirt escorted me nervously from his coin shop. Most likely my sickness was caused by Sherry-Lee's unattainability, I concluded, as an unscrupulous pawnbroker paid me two hundred and fifty dollars a piece for coins that were worth three-sixty each.

Sherry-Lee was gone, lost in the urban wilderness of the United States, and I would never see her again.

Gene hid his pleasure at my return as I struggled through the screen door. He was lying on his back on the floor of the trailer, feeding computer cables behind the chipboard furniture. 'What the fuck is that?' he asked.

'Beer,' I replied, dropping the first brown bag on to the Formica table. 'I also got us some tequila, some over-proof rum and a bottle of Jack.'

Gene shook his head in dismay. 'You get any food?'

'You bet I did,' I confirmed. 'I got potato chips, a selection of weird American chocolate, four lemons and half a dozen limes. I also got us a bag of ice. Fancy a Bud?'

Gene stood up, brushing the arse of his ironed jeans. 'How much you get for the krugs?'

'Six-fifty,' I grinned, cracking a cold one by way of celebration. Gene watched as I took a long suck on the can, studying me as a farmer might observe a badly behaved mutt.

He was trying to put three into six-fifty and failing, but maybe he expected me to cream the top. What self-respecting apprentice conman wouldn't? He rubbed his nose as though struggling to reach a decision, then sighed.

'Okay, here's the ground rules,' he announced.

I carried on swallowing, and reached for another can. 'Go ahead,' I belched.

'Okay. We start work at seven a.m. We got coffee all day. One midday rest break of thirty minutes and we finish when we finish. Then, and only then, you may drink. I don't care how much you drink so long as your operational effectiveness is unaffected at seven the next morning. Fair?'

His tone precluded dissent, and, in spite of my concerns over the length of the working day, I nodded.

He nodded back. 'Another thing: we're near the beach, but we're not on vacation. You do your partying on this trailer park, in this trailer, and nowhere else. That's the way it is. Happy?'

I shrugged. 'Not really. I don't even know what my job is.'

'Your job', explained Gene, 'is to do what I say, when I say, and if you can manage that we'll shake hands in a few weeks and part as extremely rich men. Happy now?'

'How rich?' I asked.

Gene stared through the freshly washed windows at a passing plane and snatched a figure from the air. 'Say half a million. Now tell me you're happy.'

Happy? I was flabbergasted.

Gene reckoned I'd been ripped off by the pawnshop but conceded that six-fifty wasn't a bad result for a rookie. He counted me fifty, tipped my beer down the sink and invited me to join him at the table.

'Tear out a single page and take notes,' he directed, tossing me a yellow pad and a felt-tip.

The sun slid steaming into the Gulf of Mexico, its exit unseen by Gene and me as a white moon rose in the east and the aircon buzzed like the king of the bugs. Gene paced the narrow precinct of the trailer like a deposed dictator, determined and optimistic. He seemed to have thought of everything and forgotten nothing, and as he filled in the white spaces on his map of the future I felt a rising admiration for this sober and determined man. Less than twelve hours before he'd been thrown out of his house, and if I had been in his bright white sneakers, I would have jogged to the nearest bar to wallow in cheap liquor and self-pity until fortune dealt me a break. Gene, however, had hit the ground running, and here we sat, in a DeLuxe air-conditioned trailer home, planning a short-term future with a fat dividend. It was a shame he hated drugs.

'What we got so far?'

I started, shocked by his intrusion into my thoughts.

'Don't press so hard on the paper,' he advised. 'That's why you're using a felt-tip: no impressions on the tabletop. So what we got so far?'

I scanned the list. 'We've got to get me a driving licence and some business cards. We've got to tell Fedex about our change of address and add your London pictures to the web page. You've got to activate the Credit Suisse account and I apparently need to get a haircut, or a trim, preferably.'

'Cut,' growled Gene. 'What else?'

'We need a strongbox or floor safe for this place, and I need an executive convertible with aircon, CD changer and whitewall tyres.'

Gene sprayed detergent onto the hotplate. 'Very funny. Keep your nose clean and do as I say, and in a few weeks' time you'll be able to buy yourself a Cadillac,' he promised. As it happened, he was telling the truth.

Later that night, I sat on the steps, slapping mosquitoes and sipping Jack. The shaved moon had reached its zenith and in its dusty light I stared at Sherry-Lee's trailer. The previous night she had been available; now she was untraceable. There was something viciously ironic about that. If I had never met her potential killer, I would never have met his potential victim, and the fact that I had spoken to her preordained that we should never meet again.

'God bless her,' I belched, suddenly and comfortably aware that there were many more women in Fort Myers Beach upon whom to spread my charms, regardless of Gene's code of professional conduct.

I spent the next twelve days learning my trade. Gene would wake me with the merciless superiority of a teetotal Christian at a nighttime hour that he called 'o-six-hundred'. We would breakfast together: Gene, dressed in a sweat-stained, dove-grey jogging suit, would shovel dirt-brown bran and skimmed milk into a face flushed by a three-mile run. I slumped silently opposite, scraping the crust from my eyes, seeking succour in a Marlboro and stimulation from Gene's weak coffee as he scanned the latest *Coin Collector* magazine or last month's *Recreational Flier*. My daily mission was to absorb enough about the coin trade to pass Gene's oral examination when he returned from the field. If I passed, I could drink myself blind, but if I failed, he hit me with a two-night suspension.

And there was always backgammon.

'So we're coin dealers?' I hazarded one clammy midweek night as we faced each other across the kitchen table.

Gene rolled a five and a three and used them to establish a forward position deep behind my lines. 'Kind of,' he nodded.

I rolled a one and a two.

Gene sniggered. 'Big mistake,' he said as I slid my men further towards his minefields.

'You always take the tactical view,' I countered. 'Me? I think strategically.'

Gene made a safe move out of home. 'That so?' he smirked. 'That what you were doing in Marrakech? Thinking strategically?'

I sat back and lit up another Marlboro. He was beating me on all fronts. I rerouted the subject before it knocked me down. 'What kind of coin dealers are we?'

Gene looked up through his eyebrows. 'Extremely dishonest ones,' he declared. 'Your move.'

Coin dealer is a vulgar term, and any numismatist worth his forty pieces of silver will tell you that it takes a lifetime to learn the trade. In twelve days, if you work hard, concentrate and avoid memory-impairing chemicals like alcohol, you might learn enough to bluff, as long as you keep your mouth shut and say absolutely nothing.

'Just keep your mouth shut and try to nod when I nod,' hissed Gene through the side of his shiny face as we approached the Northwest Georgia Convention Center in Dalton. 'And leave the fucking handbag in the car.'

We'd driven for fourteen hours, slept four hours in a truck stop, washed and changed in the bathroom of a Texaco, breakfasted at Denny's, then pulled in to the parking lot on Dug Gap Road.

Dalton, Georgia, had found its fame as the place where Johnny Reb crushed a superior Yankee force by rolling boulders down on to the Bluecoats, but these days, like a decorated veteran with an unambitious agent, it liked to be known as the Carpet Capital of the World.

I checked my reflection as I crossed the air-conditioned

threshold of the Northwest Georgia Convention Center. My suit had been tailored for a man of average size sometime in the sixties; Gene had picked it out for me in a St Petersburg thrift shop. It had set him back twenty bucks, but, as he had so waspishly observed, style never came cheap. My hair, for so many years an abandoned, overgrown roof garden, had been pruned, trimmed and cut back by Gene's favourite hairdresser. This time I paid, and the haircut cost five bucks more than the suit. I also bought a pair of shades, so I wouldn't have to look myself in the eye. In the fingerprint-smeared glass doors I saw reflected a slick-suited, sharp-shooting, fast-talking hustler. The girl at the reception desk saw a fat salesman's scrubbed assistant. She smiled and kept on chewing. I smiled back and followed Gene into the hall.

The hangar-like space had been transformed into a souk of narrow alleyways between velveteen partitions and polished glass display units. These precincts were strolled by cautious-looking couples of retirement age who believed in the reliability of gold and trusted in none but God. They walked the line like they'd had a bad idea, sticking to the middle of the aisles and avoiding eye contact with casual-shirted coin dealers who tried in turn to look like they didn't need the business. Gene checked his Rolex, then scanned the hall for a clock.

'You go thataway,' he said quietly. 'Move briskly, like you're late for an appointment, but make sure they see you passing. You see someone in your way, you say, "Excuse me," loud and clear so they can hear your accent. Try to sound like you got some class, and meet me in those rest-rooms in thirty minutes. Do not engage anybody in conversation. Understood?'

I nodded and he was gone. I met him half an hour later in the men's room. 'What was all that about?'

He checked no one else was around, and brushed the dandruff from his tweed shoulders. 'Meet me at Herdmann Heirlooms, Stand E Forty-one, in, say, ten minutes. I'm gonna tell you a coin is mint state. Look at it hard, then tell me it's not.' He checked himself in the mirror, then turned to me. 'This is not an exercise, boy: that's the enemy out there.' The urinals flushed like a round of applause as he left the room.

Herdmann was a fat guy in a Hawaiian shirt who looked like he should have been getting stoned somewhere. His stand consisted of a series of glass display cases and a lucky-dip bin full of foil bags of coins.

'Hey, Marty,' yelled Gene as I approached. 'Check it out, baby!'

'Frightfully sorry,' I began, my words falling like Caithness Crystal. 'Martin Brock-Crossfield!' I shoved my hand at Herdmann.

He recoiled and bounced back, grabbing my hand in a surprisingly dry grip and squeezing it softly. 'Herbie J. Herdmann Junior,' he announced in an accent that Boss Hogg would have taken for a Confederate.

'Delighted,' I smiled, turning to Gene. 'Have you bagged one, old boy?'

He pointed into Herdmann's display case. '1892 five-dollar Liberty Gold. Mint state sixty-four. Five K. Check it out.'

'Marvellous,' I brayed. 'May I see?'

Herdmann was clearly freaked. 'This is a very rare piece,' he whispered, his eyes widening as he watched me pull on a pair of white cotton gloves.

I slid the yellow coin from its polythene envelope and squinted at it from arm's length. ''Fraid not, old boy. I see bag marks, at least two nicks and numerous abrasions. I'd declare this coin closer to sixty than sixty-four, and worth considerably less than five thousand dollars.' I dropped it on to a velvet pad and locked a lethal look on to Gene. 'My client's collections are among the finest in Europe. I can consider nothing less than proof or mint state sixty-five.' I let Herbie see the slightest shake of my head, then swung my gaze to him. 'I'm so sorry, Mr Herdmann, but may I take your card?' I stuffed a hand into my inside pocket, holding the jacket open long enough for Herbie to clock the exotic label. I smiled, handing him a card that said, 'Whitehall Numismatics'. 'Have you been to London recently?'

Herbie shook his head.

'You should,' I suggested. 'Let me know if you're ever going and I'll have a word with my people.'

'You're a fucking natural,' grinned Gene as we dropped back into Florida. 'I knew when I saw you. I'm a goddamned genius when it comes to judging character!'

Somehow he had managed to skim the merit from his compliment for himself, but he was no judge of character if I was anything to go by.

I changed the subject. 'Why haven't we bought anything?'

Gene smiled like he was riding a Huey back to Danang with a necklace of ears. 'Didn't need to. We went to Dalton to make impressions, not purchases.' He leaned over the steering wheel to point at a small white aeroplane. 'See that? That is not the way to execute a gliding approach.'

It was late on Sunday night when we rolled back into Bridgeview. Dimly lit trailers flickered fifty-seven shades of blue as we coasted to our corporate HQ, swerving to avoid a clearly disturbed middle-aged black man who loped nervously through our headlights. Gene's racial consciousness had seen no need to develop since 1959 and his description of our neighbour was as offensive as he could manage at this late hour. I watched the big, broken man scurry back to his trailer, his progress impeded by a curious need to stop every three paces and check over his shoulder. He looked like a man pursued by demons and I knew how that felt.

Gene checked out as soon as we had checked back in, so I grabbed a pack of smokes and the emergency bottle of Jack and took them both out on to the steps. The night was dark, overcast and close, the humidity rising like swamp fever and smothering the laughter from the late night TVs. Aircon units hummed and cicadas sang, and I wondered what the black guy was running from.

An electric flicker from behind the drapes, like distant lightning behind storm clouds, dragged my bleary eyes to Sherry-Lee's trailer, and I gazed dumbly, like a man who needed slapping, wondering if she was watching anything good. It took me another fifteen seconds to recognise the car parked outside as hers, and five more for the penny to drop.

I choked on my whiskey and rose to my feet, scratching another cigarette from an obstructive pack and lighting it with shaking fingers. Sherry-Lee was back, and my sweating, trembling body was giving away my feelings. I checked my breath with a sticky palm: it seemed to smell of whiskey and cigarettes, the scent of a man. I polished up the bottle of Jack with the tail of my shirt, then tucked it into my second-hand pants, straightened my tie and grabbed my handbag. Next time I checked I was more than halfway to her trailer and still moving, like a kamikaze on autopilot. Part of me wanted to sit back and enjoy the glory. The rest wanted to bale out, but they didn't give parachutes to the likes of me. I crept up the metal steps and knocked on the door, then jumped back into the shadows.

'Sherry-Lee?' I called. 'It's me, Martin, remember?'

The TV died and I heard her move across the thin floor. I remembered her Glock and moved further away from the door.

'Martin? Martin the realtor?'

I took a hard drag on my cigarette. 'No. Martin the saviour. I'm sort of connected to Brad.'

That did it. I was in.

The time that had passed since I had seen her last had added carats to her beauty. She wore an ankle-length pink housecoat in some sort of inflammable material that matched her fluffy slippers and would have suited a woman twice her age, yet she managed to model it with an ironic chic that made me wonder if I was getting old.

'What the hell you doing back here?' she growled, her big eyes more curious than angry beneath her dark fringe.

'Nice to see you too,' I replied. 'Shall we have a drink?'

She padded off like an overwrapped candy bar, the pistol in her pocket banging against her thigh like she was glad to see me. She punched the radio with a white-painted nail and mournful hillbilly bluegrass, straight down from the mountain, poured into the trailer.

'What you doing back here?' I asked.

She rose on tiptoes to retrieve two pretty glasses from a shelf above the curtain rail. 'This is my home,' she replied defiantly. 'It's where I live.' She made *live* sound like *leeyuv*. She turned and approached me, the shot glasses in her hands. I closed my eyes just long enough to thank the Lord for His mysteries. I poured us two deep ones. 'Have you seen Brad?'

She sighed. 'I was going to ask you the same thing.'

We picked up our glasses and raised them to our lips at the same time. We were less than an arm's length apart. Before we drank, our eyes met like head-on trucks. For one of us, it was a deeply meaningful moment. I choked on my bourbon like a freshman. 'No,' I wheezed. 'I haven't.'

Sherry-Lee swallowed and licked her lips. 'He'll be back,' she shrugged. 'He's looking for closure.'

'That what you call it?' I grunted.

She looked at me for a moment longer than was necessary, then glided away. 'Sit down,' she suggested, pointing at a torn blue vinyl couch.

I sat down and sent her a smile that she neither acknowledged nor returned. She gave me a head-to-toe scan with nervous eyes, seeming to note every detail yet looking for something more that could not be seen.

'You make me twitchy,' she declared. 'You scare me. What's with the purse?'

I shrugged. 'It's something I carry around. Can't get rid of it. It's all that's left of a doomed relationship. At least my baggage is visible.'

'That's funny,' she smiled, as though it wasn't. 'Why are you here?'

'I live here,' I replied. 'Next street over. I can see your bedroom from mine . . .'

She raised an eyebrow.

'. . . probably,' I stammered, feeling the heat beneath my stained collar. 'I've never actually checked. Not that I *would* check.'

She smiled again. My heart rate increased. 'Why Bridge View, for Pete's sake?' she asked.

Because I wanted to be near you, Sherry-Lee. Because I wanted to be there when Brad skidded up to your trailer. Because I wanted to catch the bullets for you. Because I wanted to see you naked.

'Because it's cheap,' I replied.

She gave me a short look of intense curiosity, then sat

down opposite me on a kitchen chair. She was no longer scared of me, but then again, I didn't have a Glock in my pocket. There wasn't much in her trailer to remind her of home. A casual glance would have made the place as a weekly rental, no questions asked, but there was one expression of the resident's taste.

'Those glasses are nice,' I commented.

She pointed at the row of coloured shot glasses lining the shelf above the window. 'From my collection,' she smiled, stretching deliciously to reach one. 'See this one here: it's got a picture of a cowboy painted on its side saying "Phoenix Arizona 1949".'

She poured us two more shots. Misery and regret from the radio filled the trailer like a nerve agent. 'You like Tanya Tucker?' asked Sherry-Lee. 'I *love* Tanya Tucker. Seems like no matter what you're going through, Tanya's been through worse, don't you reckon?'

I nodded. 'Sounds like it.'

We worked on the bottle, and while we were waiting for it to empty we explained ourselves. Sherry-Lee had taken off after my last visit, seeking refuge with a congregation over in Okeechobee County. They had prayed together, and after a whole lot of soul searching she had acceded to the will of the Lord and driven back to Bridgeview. 'I put my life in the hands of the Lord,' she smiled, scaring me a little. 'What about you, Martin?'

'That's beside the point,' I argued. 'I'm not being stalked by a heavily armed lunatic.'

She tipped her head to one side, her eyes twinkling in the lamplight. 'You most certainly will be, honey, if my ex finds out you've been here.'

I shook my head. 'Sherry-Lee, I think you're gorgeous, you're lovely, don't get me wrong. But I also think you're fucking crazy sitting here waiting for Brad to deliver unto you his wrathful vengeance.'

She stabbed a white nail at me. 'You don't know shit, buddy!' Her anger drained like a flash flood and the sun came out again.

I blinked, and suddenly she was standing over me, her soft hands on my shoulders, her brown arms receding into the folds of her housecoat. Her dark hair tickled my cheek as her perfume short-circuited my brain and my body went heroin-numb. I felt her hot breath, then the wet blessing of her lips on my cheek, then she was gone; still shining over me, but as unreachable as the moon. 'I know why you came, Martin,' she whispered. 'You're a sweet guy.'

I wafted back to Gene's trailer on an intoxicated, incredulous cloud of delight. The Ramones wrote a song specifically for this moment, but I couldn't remember it. I looked up through the low cloud to a heaven full of bright, twinkling stars, each and every one a sparkling witness to my self-delusion.

She'd said I was a sweet guy. She'd kissed me on the cheek, then she'd wished me goodnight. It was neither porn nor love, and there had been neither promise nor incentive in her gesture. I was a little brother to her, one who would become a good and trusted friend, a nice guy to whom she would one day confess her passion for another, and I didn't care. I dismissed the swooping, grinning bats with a drunken sweep of the hand she had grabbed as I'd slipped on the trailer steps and scoffed at the mocking stars. The only deluded person in this relationship was the beautiful Sherry-Lee.

It was hard to sleep that night, but easy to dream.

Gene and I spent the next day sending letters to dealers we'd met in Dalton. Our company notepaper was a heavy ivory vellum, with a letterhead announcing 'Whitehall Numismatics'. It listed addresses in London, Hong Kong and, incongruously, Fort Myers, FL, and was backed up by a company brochure. This discreet document was printed on matt ivory A5 to match the notepaper, with a glossy, navy-blue cover and the company name embossed in gold. I hadn't realised that I was working for such a prestigious organisation and I was impressed.

'What happens if someone calls us in London?'

'Try it and see,' grunted Gene.

What little atmosphere there was in the trailer had settled somewhere between us, and our working environment was overcast with an impending storm. Whatever it was, it was my fault. It was written into my contract.

'Did you call yet?' he growled.

I sighed and dialled the number for our central London office. The call was answered after three rings by a woman who explained that both Mr Renoir and Mr Brock-Crossfield were out of the country on business. She offered to pass a message on to us, but I declined. I wouldn't have known what to say. I dropped the receiver.

'See?' said Gene. 'One hundred and sixty bucks a week. Office Management Services in Kowloon. No questions asked.'

'What if they want to visit us?'

Gene looked up from his paperwork, peering over his glasses like a perturbed pedagogue. 'On the highly unlikely off-chance that one of these crackers should dare to cross the Pond, they'll climb three flights of stairs to find an empty office with a note on the door saying we've relocated to larger premises with the same telephone number you just called. I made an appointment with the realtor and stuck it up while he was showing me round. No more questions.'

I had one more. 'You pissed off with me, Gene?'

He didn't look up. 'Yes.'

He was still pissed off with me two days later as we drove to the Interstate Coin Fair in Mississippi. After eight and a half hours at a steady sixty-five we pulled in to a sprawling, low-rise, prefabricated development somewhere between Tallahassee and Pensacola that called itself the 'Frie dship Mot l' in buzzing neon. A cautious roach scuttled into cover as I entered our room, its walls speckled brown with the mosquito-digested blood of everyone who had ever stayed. I dropped on to the bed and lit a cigarette. 'Gene . . .' I began.

'You know why,' he replied. 'You're compromising security by hanging out with that slut.'

I had intended asking him why he was mad at me. Now I was mad at him. 'She's not a slut,' I cried. 'How dare you call my . . .'

'Your what?' he interrupted. 'Girlfriend? Fiancée? Virgin intended?'

He had a point. I lay back and blew smoke. 'My friend,' I sighed. 'I was going to say "my friend".'

Gene took a long, critical look at himself in the flaking mirror, plucking at strands of his thinning hair and rubbing expensive face cream into his fat jowls. 'You ain't got no friends, Martin,' he observed. 'You just got me, you and that goddamned fag handbag.'

We left at six the next morning and drove another four hours across America to reach the Days Inn on I-49 South in Hattiesburg, a once-compact lumber town built around a railroad junction in the yellow pine woods of southern Mississippi.

'What's the mission?' I asked as we watched the coin

collectors of Forrest County congregate at the convention centre entrance.

Gene looked at me through his mirrored, prescription shades. 'Hey,' he drawled, 'I'm impressed. You're beginning to talk the talk!'

'Yeah, whatever,' I retorted. 'What's the mission?'

Gene leaned on the steering wheel and watched the faithful. 'Follow and support. Definition: a tactical mission task in which a committed force follows and supports a lead force conducting an offensive operation. You're my Brit partner. You know the European coin trade inside out but you're out here to source certain rare pieces for your Old World clientele. You're particularly pissed that you were outbid on that 1875 mint state sixty gold five-dollar piece last month that went for a hundred and sixty-five thou. You've got a lot of catching up to do, and if I show you something and mention Lady Monroe, you ask me to negotiate on your behalf. Today we got to buy a lot of shit.'

'Lady Monroe,' I repeated.

Gene nodded.

'Like Marilyn?'

'Yes,' he sighed. 'Like Marilyn.'

He turned to leave the car, then turned back. 'What now?' he hissed.

'Nothing,' I said.

We bought a lot of gold in Hattiesburg: extremely fine 1866 gold eagles, flawed Mexican pesos and about uncirculated sovereigns, different nationalities, different ages, but all the same race, nurtured by the touch of Midas and suffused with the DNA of Mammon. Gene wrote big Miami cheques with a flashy fountain pen while I made delighted one-sided calls on a dead cellphone to my excited and entirely fictitious

British clients. Every troy ounce of gold I touched left a little of itself to sink through my thin subcutaneous flesh and settle in my bones, until I could taste it on the back of my teeth and feel its weight on my spine. Gold fever, I realised in Hattiesburg, MS, is a physical condition perfectly suited to complement a cocaine addiction, and I could easily have embraced the life of a coke-head coin dealer. The salesmen shook our hands and invited us to strip joints, bars and nightclubs, and Gene politely refused each and every offer.

I challenged him on his social policy as we walked away from Finklemann Fine Gold. 'We should get out and circulate with these people,' I suggested. 'They seem to like us and we're supposed to be making friends, aren't we?'

Gene shook his head. 'That's your big failing, Troop: you can't see the difference between making a friend and making an impression.' He stopped and grabbed my arm. 'I buy old gold coins. I screw them on the price, but only 'til it hurts, then I write them a cheque and leave the bullion behind. You know why?'

'Saves us getting robbed in the parking lot,' I sighed.

Gene nodded as though I'd missed the point. 'Sure it does. It also gives these hicks time to bank the cheque and see it clear before sending the coin to us. Know what that does?'

'Makes sense?' I tried.

Gene shook his head and poked the sharp edge of my lapel. 'It makes an impression. Now keep the fuck up and listen out for Lady Monroe.'

It was too hot to be indoors, but Gene just didn't seem to be the outdoor type. We traipsed up and down carpeted aisles, the static raising the hair on the back of my neck as Gene appraised and dismissed one antique coin after another. When we sat at a dirty table to sip thin coffee from cardboard cups he rubbed his forehead as though the metal was bringing him down.

'Where's all the goddamned romance gone?' he mused, not expecting a reply. 'Shouldn't gold bullion be stored in velvet-lined chests of English oak and guarded by eunuchs or something?' He looked up at the polystyrene ceiling and sighed. 'This place cheapens it all. Gold wasn't made to be sold in a goddamned Days Inn.'

He shook his head as an elderly couple clad in golf-club casuals wobbled past. 'Fuckin' pitiful,' he decided, finishing his coffee and sweetening his breath with a pocket-sized aerosol. 'Let's go.'

He found the coin we'd been looking for at a stand with a sign that read, 'Ned's Solid Gold Investments'. He feigned excitement. 'I believe we're in luck,' he cried, hooking his thumbs into his waistband. Ned stubbed out his cigarette and pulled the top half of his body to attention. He looked like Kenny Rogers the day after Ruby had taken her love to town, but he smiled as he rolled his chair towards us, clearly impressed by the two sharp-suited professionals stepping into his corner of the Hattiesburg Days Inn Teepee Suite. We appeared to be making an impression; as was Ned, in his own way. He wore a fishing hat with flies attached, a short-sleeved shirt with horses on the front, khaki shorts, white socks and, in deference to the executive nature of his position, a pair of black brogues. A tiny yellow pin with a diagonal black stripe drew Gene's attention to the hat.

'Air Cav, huh?'

Ned nodded down at Gene. 'You too?'

Gene shook his head and stretched out his hand. '*Semper Fi*, pal.'

Ned pumped Gene's manicured hand. 'Goddamned Marine Corps! What about your buddy?'

I started to say something and Gene cut me off. 'He's a Brit. Ex-Household Cavalry.'

Ned's eyes widened in what might have been disbelief. 'A fellow cavalryman, eh? What do you say, Brit?'

'*Habeas corpus*,' I winked, confidentially.

'I worked out with you guys in 1970; some freezing place in Germany.'

'Not me,' I replied. 'I was still in short trousers then. My father, maybe? He's, er, recently retired from the Staff.'

I dropped the baton and Gene caught it. 'So what happened to you, Ned?'

The big man shrugged. 'AK round, lower spine, Long Ben, 'seventy-three. Didn't kill me.'

Gene had locked on to something old and yellow in Ned's glass case. 'Let me see that 1872 half eagle there, will you?'

Ned waved a big, Gook-killing hand. 'Help yourself, Gyrine.'

Gene picked up the coin with deft gloved fingers and looked at me. 'I think we've found Her Ladyship's desire.'

I looked at the coin and raised my eyebrows. 'She'll be delighted. I'll call her right away if you can sort out a price.'

Ned grabbed me as I turned. 'Do you know what you're looking at, son?'

I paused, staring at his grip upon my sleeve until he let it drop, then rolled my gaze across the coin. 'It's an 1872 five-dollar half eagle. It was designed by Gobrecht and first minted in 1866. That particular specimen comes from the Carson City Mint in Nevada: ninety per cent gold, ten per cent copper, just over eight grams. From the wear around the wingtips and neck of the eagle, I'd judge it as EF forty – extremely fine, as they say. Other than that, I'm clueless. That's why my colleague is going to handle the purchase.'

★

It was still light outside as we crossed the near-empty parking lot. The wet evening air was thick with insects and heavy with misheard promise. I wanted to unbutton my shirt and throw my tie into the slipstream of a passing truck, score an ounce of weed and a gram of coke and hang around in bars until I got lucky or drunk. Gene wanted to catch up on some paperwork. There was no chance that he would agree to us going our separate ways, but I had nothing to lose by inviting him to walk with me.

'Fancy grabbing a cold one before we hit the road?' I asked, nodding towards the tavern at the far end of the lot.

Gene was watching a light aeroplane climbing out of a nearby field, shaking his head and muttering. 'Too much flap, not enough throttle. Fucking moron.'

'Come on,' I urged, 'it's Miller time.'

He watched the plane bank into the haze, then pointed at the passenger seat. 'Get in. You're still at work.'

I stuck a Marlboro to my lower lip and chain-smoked in seething silence as Gene drove us fifty-five miles south-east to the JetWay Motel on the outskirts of Saucier, MS. Heavy bugs swarmed around the floodlights as Gene checked us in. When he returned to the car he seemed to notice my ire for the first time. 'What's the goddamned matter with you?' He coasted past the reception hut and into a compound of lodges circled like wagons on the edge of town.

'Gypsies, tramps and thieves,' I replied. 'That's what the people of the town they call us.'

'What the fuck are you talking about?'

I sighed. It was too hot to talk, but not to fight. 'I'm getting pissed off with driving around dressed like a man in black with no cash and no fucking idea of what I'm doing or where it's going to end. I'm getting pissed off with always staying in motels with no minibar and rubbish TV. I'm getting pissed off with working seven fucking days a week and never getting any time off. Most of all I'm pissed off about not being allowed to go out. That and having no money, or did I mention that already?'

Gene shook his head sadly, scratched his nose, picked up his vinyl attaché case and left me sitting in the car. It was not the reaction I had expected. I took a deep breath of Dixie dusk and followed him into our motel room, scarcely noticing the depressingly worn and torn fittings on the set of a hundred great songs. A nervous roach scuttled into a crack beneath the flecked melamine kitchenette and a dozen hungry mosquitoes danced along the neon strip. Gene cranked up the aircon, hung his suit on a wooden hanger he'd nicked from the Georges V in Paris, loosened his tie and slipped his shoes on to sprung cedar trees. Still looking like he'd trodden in something, he opened his case and removed a fresh surgical mask from an economy pack of fifty and placed it carefully over his tight-lipped mouth and flared nostrils. Satisfied with the fit, he pulled on a pair of orange rubber gloves, dug an industrial-sized can of Raid from the case and set off, clad in mask and baggy skivvies, on a tour of the perimeter, dispensing insecticide with the smug determination that comes only with massively superior firepower. No wonder the roach had looked nervous. His search and destroy mission complete, Gene dropped the mask and looked at me, his white cotton shorts hanging lower than a homeboy's.

'Okay,' he conceded. 'Payday.'

He sat on the bed and pulled five hundred-dollar bills from his billfold, fanning them out on the nylon counterpane. 'Five hundred, right?'

I nodded, and lunged for the cash, but he blocked me, taking one hundred back in a manicured pinch.

'That's for rent – fair?'

I shrugged. I could get by on four hundred.

'Food and other essential consumables, both indoors and on the road: we'll round that down to a hundred. Agreed?'

Another note dived back into his billfold. My hackles began rising, and Gene felt the static.

He looked up like a long-suffering father. 'Nobody likes paying their debts, Martin, but what do you expect me to do? You want me to feed you, clothe you and house you, and then pay you? Where do you think the money comes from?'

'Trees?' I mumbled.

'Yeah, right. Listen to me: you're an employee, and you get a salary, right? However, you're also a lodger, and you need to pay your bills. It's what everybody else in this country does, okay? Is that understood?'

I shuffled my feet in a non-committal gesture of defeat. Gene took that as an affirmative.

'Great,' he sighed. 'Now, look: you've still got three hundred left for beer and liquor consumption.'

'Fair enough,' I muttered.

He dragged another two hundred from the pile.

'Oi!' I cried. 'What's that for?'

He pushed the cash back into the silver clip. 'Beer and liquor consumption,' he replied.

I grabbed my handbag and took what was left of my salary fifteen miles in the wrong direction before three rockers in a heavy-metal pick-up truck showed me the way out of their wickedly dry county. Two neon-lit liquor stores leaned hard on the county line, and a gang of kids in baggy jeans and keychains flagged me down as I pulled up at the first. They wanted liquor and brew and had nothing but cash and weed to trade. I took both and followed a two-lane highway at a steady thirty-five, my smile widening beneath the bright night sky as I sucked on a mouth-watering joint and sang along with track after track of solid rock. When all else was spattered with the dirt of commercialism, it was uplifting to know that the lowdown purity of rock could still be found on the warm night air. They played 'Black Dog' as I rolled through farmland, 'Guerrilla Radio' as I waited for the lights to change at a deserted crossroads, 'Rocky Mountain Way' as I wondered what Sherry-Lee was listening to back at the trailer park, and 'Since You've Been Gone' as I wondered what Sherry-Lee was doing back at the trailer park. I leaned low over the steering wheel to relight the joint, grinning like a man who'd hit radio paydirt, and then the KKIK 106.5 announcer explained the facts of life.

'KKIK 106.5 Just For Kicks is lifestyle radio,' he beamed. 'KKIK will bring your business a listening audience of today's young adults establishing buying habits, well-educated professionals with significantly discretionary income. KKIK listeners are in the acquisition mode of life and are buying homes, cars and making other major purchases. The time is now to capture new customers. KKIK's interactive format can mobilise its audience like no other radio station in southern Louisiana. Here's Heart!'

I blew smoke and punched the dial. I just didn't match the listener profile. Over on KRCR Pastor Reverend Tony Caruso was giving a lecture on herpetology, and he sounded angry. 'Now, like a strong man in a hurricane, I look around me in the chaos and what do I see, people? What do I see? I'll tell you what I see: I see you folks running scared, like mice fleeing a tornado, and what are you running from? We all know what you're running from, brothers and sisters, because every time we look through the Devil's window we see him looking right back at us and we hear our so-called leaders and advisers telling us to take up our children and lock our doors, stay low lest the Great Dragon breathes fire on our quaking carcasses. What are we scared of, brethren? Biological strikes? So-called dirty bombs? Weapons of mass destruction? Plagues and pestilence? Fire and famine? Is my brother's faith so weak that he fears Death, people?'

Someone near the preacher yelled, 'Yeah man!'

The Pastor Reverend lowered his voice and leaned in to the mike. 'Why fear Death, people? Why deny the Lord's omnipotence? Why take the hard road when it's so darned easy to acknowledge the greatness and glory of God?'

'Hallelujah!' came a distant cry.

'All we got to do is open our eyes, sniff that sweet air, taste that cool water, hear that happy birdsong and reach out and touch someone.'

The road had dragged me to a river, and I pulled off before the bridge, parking in a picnic area overlooking the water. The kids at the liquor store had fronted me a generous wad of sage-coloured weed in return for the use of my seniority in the acquisition of beer and vodka, and it was doing nobody any good sealed in a snappy bag.

'Don't think about the Dragon,' advised the Pastor Reverend. 'The Dragon is a device of the Devil, and this beautiful life is but a message from our sponsor about the life everlasting. I don't want to talk to you no more about dragons, brothers and sisters. I want to talk to you about snakes. That's right, snakes. Serpents. Crawling things. Vipers. Now you've all been looking out so hard for the big reptiles that you didn't see the scaly serpents sliding into your lives, did y'all? That's the way Satan planned it, people, but it's not too late to thwart his evil. Forget the Dragon. Let the Dragon come and we'll rise as one and slay that ragged Dragon, but only if we've not been struck down by snakes from within. Listen for their hissing. Listen for their rattle. Seek out the serpents and banish them. St Patrick did it, and so can we. Look out for their shiny suits, their silver tongues, their golden promises. They're smooth, they look slimy but they're dry, and you're their prey, people.'

I tugged a cold can of Bud from the damp brown bag on the passenger seat and left the Pastor Reverend's chapel to walk down to the water's edge. Something significant slipped into the water with a smooth splash as I stepped in the mud, and as fireflies danced above the swaying reeds I wondered for one sober moment what the hell I was doing. Far above me unseen debris whirled through space in directions determined by the gravity of opposing spheres, and down here, on the Pastor Reverend Tony Caruso's bright planet, I drifted like space dust from one cosmic encounter to the next, and one day I would burn up in an unnoticed split-second streak of faint light. I had no long term plans: the furthest ahead I ever thought was the next drink, the next spliff, or, God willing, the next line. I had nailed myself to a small wheel, and I was rolling downhill. Rock 'n' Roll radio couldn't help me, and the Christians had made me for a snake. I drained my can, flicked my roach, started the car and slithered back to where I belonged.

Gene was waiting up for me, but he didn't want to argue. He wanted to play backgammon, and how could I have refused?

'I think we should make an effort to get to know each other better,' he declared, rolling a six and a one with his first throw. 'Let's say that every time one of us rolls a double, the other has to answer a question.'

A cockroach as long as my little finger lay in spasm at the corner of my eye. I ignored its death throes and cracked a beer. 'What kind of question?' I rolled a one and a two.

'A personal question,' explained Gene, rolling a double three. 'Here's an easy one: where are you from and what did your pa do?'

'That's two questions,' I protested.

'I rolled a double,' pointed out Gene unconvincingly.

'I come from a place called St Moody in a place called Cornwall in a place called England and my dad was a tractor driver.'

I spun the bones and landed a double one. 'My question: when does this end?'

Gene sipped his Diet Coke and sparked up a Marlboro Lite. 'Labor Day. First Monday in September.'

He raised his eyebrows as I did the best I could with my roll.

'I'm gonna fuck you right up,' he promised, rolling a five and a four that put two of my men inside.

They stayed there for two more moves, and even the double six I rolled wouldn't help. 'Why don't you have a drink?' I asked.

Gene replied with a long look that wondered if I was trying to trick him, then shrugged. 'Yeah,' he smiled. 'Why not? My go.'

I broke the seal on a bottle of Wild Turkey and poured us two deep ones. My next roll put me over the wire, but I was still a long way from home. Gene worked on building barriers that left my men floundering like the 29th on Omaha Beach, and the doubles I rolled gained me little intelligence. Gene was an army brat from everywhere. His dad had been killed in Korea and his mom had been a schoolteacher. He joined the Marine Corps in '66 just to piss off his dad's shellshocked ghost and served two tours on the Laotian border as a platoon leader in some tough-sounding parachute recon outfit. He took his third tour as a company commander and was honourably discharged as a ranking major in 1974. He had a drawer full of medals somewhere and a changed mind full of unwanted memories. He didn't like to talk about Vietnam.

Then my luck changed. Lying to Gene had always been easy, but under the artificial constraints of the game it felt wrong, so I chewed on the Turkey and answered the questions. I owned up to my fatherhood and abandonment of a kid who was three weeks past his eighth birthday. I expressed the appropriate amount of flippant remorse, like a coward acknowledging a tumour, arguing that the boy was better off fatherless than having a dirty old man like me. It was ironic, I agreed with Gene, that one so unsuited to childcare should have chosen to become a teacher, and unsurprising that it had all gone so badly awry.

Gene hated kids. 'Fuckin' rugrats,' he growled. 'Just the sight of them, downwind, far enough away that I don't have to hear their whining, is enough to kick my black dog. It's the easiest fuckin' thing in the world to get a kid.'

I wondered if he was referring to procreation, kidnap or sniping, but his attention had returned to the game. He took a double gammon with no more doubles rolled, setting up his pieces for the next game even as he bore them off. I rolled the next double and poured out two inches of celebration. I was running out of ideas.

'You a Republican or a Democrat?' I asked.

Gene grinned. 'I'm a grown-up. Politics is a means by which the community is bound and I've chewed through the knots. I'm like the snake in the fruit cellar, among y'all, beneath y'all, around y'all, and while those fools try to shine a light on society I'm gliding through the shadows they've made, making a profit from chaos.' A four and a three snapped the tip from his smugness. He lit a cigarette and sucked hard, his hand covering his mouth as he slid a white man deep into my manor. 'I don't give a fuck about the next attack, the next recession or the next fucking war. I don't give a shit about welfare, healthcare or clean air. I don't care about GM, Ford, Boeing or Microsoft, and I don't believe a word of what I hear on ABC, CNN or Fox. To each according to their need from each according to their fucking gullibility, as Lenin once said.' He rubbed his shiny forehead as though he'd been slapped, then drained his Wild Turkey. 'You think your vote makes one fuckin' lick of difference to your life?'

'Don't know,' I shrugged. 'Never voted.'

'Why not?'

I wanted to tell him that I'd never voted because I believed that any individual seeking public approval was clearly self-interested and so lacked the altruism necessary for public service, but that wasn't true. 'Dunno,' I replied. 'Just never got round to it.'

Gene shook his head. 'You're like one of those autistic kids: dumb and smart at the same time. The reason you never voted was because subconsciously you knew it was wrong to belong. Makes sense when you hear it out loud, don't it?' He picked up his glass and sucked on the dregs. 'None of it's gonna mean a thing when Jesus comes back, that's for sure.' He raised his eyebrows in delight at my expression and laughed, high and short. 'Don't worry, Troop: Jesus ain't coming back. His body was cut up by the Romans and buried all over the Empire. Last thing Pilate needed was a martyr. I'll tell you what I know someday. In the meantime, all you got is me, and I'll lead you out of the wilderness.'

I poured us two more, spilling drops on the board. 'Cheers!'

Gene raised his glass and held it out to me, a big smile on

his sweating face and an unnatural glint in his eyes. I met his gaze until it unnerved me, and when I looked back he was still smiling. I lifted my glass to break his eyeline.

'Here's to us,' he suggested, like a solemn fiancé.

'To us,' I confirmed, with deep reservations.

The barking of a gas-crazed dog woke me soon after day-break. I swung my aching legs to the floor, swaying queasily and noting with disappointment that I was still wearing my shoes. On the upside, I was also still wearing my trousers, and it was only my throat that was sore. I limped to the bath-room, my bladder stretched like a hog-choked anaconda, and rattled the door.

Locked.

'Gene,' I cried. 'I need to piss.'

'Leave me alone,' he croaked.

I heard a cough, a rush of liquid and a groan. I cursed him and opened the front door. A hot and unhealthy day tried to block my access to the lot, but I squeezed past and relieved myself in the weeds at the end of the block. In the shim-mering mid-distance a mad dog yelled canine obscenities at passing traffic. I bought an ice-cold Coke from an eight-foot vending machine, drained it in three gulps, belched and bought two more. Gene took his time over his ablutions, running steam from a clanking shower stall and flushing the WC every time it filled. I sat sipping soda and surveying the remains of last night. Cigarette packets crushed into balls lay like fallout on the ash-speckled carpet. Every hard surface above floor level had been squatted by empty beer cans, the demobbed ranks of an army of dissolution. Generals Bourbon and Vodka stood drained and open-mouthed on the battlefield, both unrepentant. A prickle of fear prodded a droplet of sweat from every pore as I realised that I had little useful recollection of anything that had happened after the Wild Turkey had been tamed.

Gene limped miserably from the bathroom and fell on to the bed. His face was the colour of sour apples; his eyes the colour of cherries. 'Get my gel-mask from the icebox.'

He soaked up booze badly for a US Marine, I thought, as I passed him his eye-mask.

'Can't drive today,' he croaked, raising himself to sip on a Coke. 'Pass me my attaché case and get your ass shaved, showered, shat and dressed in number twos.'

Ablutions, like number twos, meant different things to Gene and I. He carried a fake Louis Vuitton toiletries case the size of a breezeblock. It contained three types of shampoo, two conditioners, a bottle of Grecian 2000 and a shower cap from the Waldorf Astoria. He had smoker's tooth-cream, whitening toothpaste, Ultraglide dental floss, two plaque scrapers, one electric and four manual toothbrushes, three of which were still in their packaging. His moisturisers, cleansers, rescue creams and skin tonics came from London, New York and Paris, and two of his deodorants came from Tokyo. The overall impression was one of excessive vanity, I thought, unwrapping one of his toothbrushes and selecting a shower gel.

Especially for a US Marine.

'Yesterday Whitehall Numismatics spent nineteen thousand, seven hundred and fifty-five dollars on public relations,' announced Gene as I emerged, scrubbed and fragrant, from the bathroom, wearing beige jeans, a black shirt from Western Outfitters and a pair of black python-skin boots I had picked up in Goldberg's Dixie Thrift for fifteen bucks. It was an outfit that teetered between Rodeo Rider and Hairdresser, but it was better than Gene's recommended Gap slacks and polo shirt. 'We've damn near emptied the war chest, so let's go sell what we're holding.' He lifted one side of his eye-mask and squinted at me like a camp buccaneer. 'You been using my moisturiser?'

I didn't bother asking Gene where he had scored my new driving licence. It bore my photo, my name and the stamped approval of the State of New York. I studied it while I was waiting for my HungaBusta in a diner on the outskirts of Perkiston, Mississippi. Gene sat opposite me in the far corner booth, sipping thin coffee from a bottomless cup and studying the local Yellow Pages.

'Put it away,' he hissed, without looking up.

I shrugged, slipped it into my wallet and started a pyramid of Lovin' Cup non-dairy creamer. It toppled as I was placing the capstone. Gene closed his eyes and concentrated on his breathing.

'You always this chipper after you've been drinking?'

I shook my head. 'That wasn't drinking, Gene. Drinking is when you wake up burned, or married, or tattooed. Last night was just refreshments.'

Gene didn't need to know why I was so cheerful, I decided, patting the snappy bag of weed in my hip pocket. In two days I had gained legitimacy *and* drugs: things were coming together nicely.

A forty-year-old redhead in a miniskirt and bobby socks with an alluring air of clairvoyant resignation arrived at my shoulder.

'One HungaBusta, gone large, with extra hash browns and one order of wheat toast?'

Gene sighed. 'The toast is for me, ma'am.'

I let him have it.

As we sowed, so we reaped, and the most tedious part of any coin-show operation was the road to redemption. Back at

Bridgeview Gene had consulted the Internet, his coin magazines and his American Numismatic Association handbook to plot the location of thirty dealers in close proximity to the highway home.

We followed Route 49 south till it hit the Gulf of Mexico and turned east at a harbour crowded with expensive yachts.

'This is Gulfport,' announced Gene, as we cruised past a fleet of third-class liners. 'Big vacation town. Can you think of a better place to do a little anonymous trading?'

The souk at Marrakech came to mind, but Gene had been there too, and he was the expert. We drove slowly along the seafront in the warm mid-morning sunshine, the ozone tang of the sparkling sea ebbing and flowing through the fug of exhaust fumes, donut stands and seafood grills. The boardwalk was a trail to contentment, and the proof was in every bulging bag from every bustling outlet store. Spend and be saved, buy and be forgiven, consume and ye shall not be consumed. I wondered if the Pastor Reverend Tony Caruso was out here this morning, moving purposefully through the flocks of overweight, myopic tourists, a wolf in sheep's clothing with a Banana Republic carrier-bag and Oxbow boardshorts. Hadn't he heard the First Commandment?

'The what?' asked Gene.

'Eh?'

'You were mumbling like some goddamn hermit.'

I was shocked. 'Do I still do that?'

'Clearly,' sighed Gene, shaking his head as two bikinis rolled past on blades.

I turned to watch them go. 'That was nice,' I grinned.

'Whores on wheels,' grunted Gene.

Legalised gambling, a tastier bait than sun, sea, sand and factory outlets combined, had come to this catholic coastline and transformed the twelve-mile stretch of Route 90 between Gulfport and Biloxi into a coastal Las Vegas with less choice and two kinds of Sea Breeze. The liners I'd seen were floating casinos, and the only place they'd take you was straight into debt. The sharks who ran the coast had learned their trade in Gomorrah, and to one as easily impressed as me they were doing a fine job. Low-priced hotels occupied elegant edifices designed to make the guest feel like a high roller and temptation was never more than a whim away. In a society where money could buy a state of grace, gambling was like dicing with the Devil. Win or lose, it was a test of one's faith, and when your cash and your credit had been tested to the limit, the pawnbrokers would take your earthly goods and give you a second chance.

'Not the pawnbrokers,' said Gene. 'Not here. They only got one sort of rate: desperate. You get nothing out of those sons of bitches but Saturday Night Specials and a poor return.'

We turned away from the coast and headed a few blocks north. Gulf Coast Collectibles looked like an upmarket jewellery shop. Stickers on the door offered a 10 per cent discount with the Gulf Coast Casino card, and it seemed likely that many of the tear-stained trinkets in the seafront pawnshops had once rested on beds of velvet in this marble-floored emporium.

'Good morning! How are you doing today?' cried Gene before the bespectacled proprietor could ask him the same question. He placed three coins on the glass counter.

'Half eagles. One 1867, two 1870s. What will you give me?'

The proprietor pushed his glasses on to his forehead, screwed in a loop and dragged a large, pedestal-mounted magnifying glass on a flexible stem across the counter. 'What do you know about the 'sixty-seven?' he asked in a quiet, wavering contralto.

Gene's tone deepened in reply. 'San Francisco Mint, I'd say AU fifty.'

'About uncirculated, eh?' grinned the proprietor, a golden glister in his unscrewed eye. 'Let's have a look.'

He removed the coin from its transparent case with gloved fingers and laid it on a black velvet mat. 'See Lady Liberty?' he asked, indicating the obverse.

'Real pretty, ain't she?' said Gene.

The proprietor let out a little sigh. 'She is pretty, yes, and if she was uncirculated she would show the merest traces of wear on the tip of her coronet and the fringe above her eye.'

'Well, she do, don't she?' Gene was playing the hick.

'Yes she does,' agreed the proprietor. 'Sadly, there's a little too *much* wear − look, the "L" in "Liberty" has been quite badly rubbed.'

Gene looked through the magnifying glass and shrugged. 'So what you saying?'

The proprietor flipped the coin and examined the reverse. 'See the Birdy? See his wingtips? Look at the wear on the gold. Look at where the feathers have been worn away around his neck. Did you buy this as an AU?'

Gene shook his head. 'My daddy bought it at the Tuscopsie Coin Fair in 'sixty-nine.'

The proprietor unscrewed the loop from his eye and replaced his spectacles. 'Well, you're welcome to take this coin elsewhere for appraisal, but I'd say that either your daddy was conned or he didn't look after the coin right, because this here is a near-perfect example of an EF forty.'

Gene looked hurt. 'Extremely fine? Is that all? What's it worth?'

The proprietor checked his computer. 'Today's price is

twenty-seven fifty. At AU it would have been worth sixty-eight sixty. Want me to take a look at the others?'

'What a bummer,' I declared as we followed the coast east to our next stop. 'We got well ripped at that fair.'

'Did we hell!' Gene scoffed, lighting a cigarette with his grin. 'You go into a coin shop and tell the man you got a B-class coin he's goddamn honour bound to persuade you it's a C-class. You got to tell him it's an A-class straight off, and then you'll get what the coin is worth. We did okay – came out evens.' He leaned low over the wheel to study a passing aircraft.

'Beechcraft Baron Fifty-eight,' he announced, as though I cared. 'Fool's got the mixture too rich. Now keep a lookout for Cemetery Road.'

I spent the rest of a sunny Saturday within sniffing distance of the Southern peaches on the sunny beaches of the Gulf Coast, locked inside a selection of air-conditioned boxes made from armour-plated glass. I learned that the value of a collector coin is based, like that of any antique, upon its rarity and its condition. America took her money from the country that found her, the coinage of Conquistadors and the currency of piracy. Pieces of eight were Spanish-milled dollars, struck in the more stable colonies of Mexico, Bolivia, Chile, Guatemala and Peru. The Spanish dollar was valued at eight *reales*, and was legal tender as late as 1857. The *real*, as one-eighth of a dollar, equated to 12½ cents, or one bit. I wouldn't have cared two bits for this knowledge, but it was all that was going on, so I listened. Coins were struck in different mints, in varying quantities. This was important to the collector. A half eagle, a gold coin with a nominal value of five dollars, struck in Philadelphia in 1861, is one of nearly seven hundred thousand identical coins minted in the same place at the same time. In mint state condition it's worth about twelve hundred dollars.

An 1861 half eagle struck in Denver, on the other hand, is one of only fifteen hundred and is worth over thirty grand. As a dealer or a collector, it helped to be anal.

We saw six scrupulous numismatists and traded our bullion for six honest cheques. Gene sold the last batch of low-value coins to a licensed pawnbroker for one thousand dollars cash, no questions asked. He slid me two hundred and told me to drive him home. He lay down on the back seat, his hands behind his head and a Marlboro in the corner of his mouth, loving it when a plan came together like a cut-price Hannibal Jones. Despite the glare of the setting sun in my rearview, I remained in the dark. We were visiting coin fairs and making impressions. We were having some expensive pieces mailed to us, and we were taking others away. We were selling all the pieces to other dealers, generally breaking about even. We were calling up dealers in our contacts book and buying over the phone, receiving little packages from Fedex and the US Postal Service three times a week. We were, to all intents and purposes, proper coin dealers, although we had no ANA accreditation. For an American company, this certification was essential, but, as Gene was tired of explaining, we weren't an American company. We were Whitehall Numismatics, registered in London, and that explained everything. We bought from and sold to the trade alone, and yet we weren't making any appreciable profit, but I had enough faith in Gene to know that something good was coming. Cunning, dishonest, lowdown and deceitful, but good all the same.

I patted the baggy in my pocket, just to make sure it was still there, and smiled. I was beginning to like Gene. I turned on the radio and stepped on the gas, heading south to Sherry-Lee with Kid Rock.

'Turn that shit off, you schmuck!' Gene growled.

We rolled back to Bridgeview through the swamp fog at

a little after four in the morning. Sherry-Lee's car was outside her trailer, but the lights were out.

Gene patted my back as he climbed the steps into our
mobile home, making me jump. 'Take tomorrow off,' he
mumbled. 'Stay out of trouble.'

A sixth sense awoke me just after eight the next morning.
I lifted the shade and looked outside. Sherry-Lee, wearing
cut-down denims and a man's white shirt knotted around
her midriff, was standing beside her car and chatting with
one of our overweight neighbours, a single mother of four
prone to fits of midnight wailing. Sherry-Lee looked like
she was going somewhere, so I dragged on jeans and a T-
shirt and flew barefoot into the sunshine.

'How are you this morning?' cried the neighbour as I
soared over the dust.

Sherry-Lee turned and smiled, melting my wings. 'Hey,
Martin!'

'Say, you ain't seen my eldest, Solomon, around recently,
have you?' asked the neighbour.

I thought for a moment. Solomon was one of the dumbest
kids I'd ever encountered. A grubby, barefooted eleven-year-
old with a shaved head and a puzzled expression, I'd first met
him when he asked me to tow him behind the car on his
skateboard. When I'd pointed out that his board had only
three wheels he shrugged and said that he'd stand on one side.

I shook my head. 'When did you last see him?'

The mother rolled her eyes skywards. 'Thursday, probably,
about seven. He was headin' swampwards, goin' possum
huntin'.'

A quick and easy meal solution for even the slowest alligator.

'Sorry,' I shrugged.

The mother shrugged back. 'Oh well. Guess he'll turn up somewhere. Just so long as Turn Back Jack ain't scared him off.'

'Who's Turn Back Jack?'

'Crazy black man, lives in that trailer there.' She pointed a flab-heavy arm towards the bridge.

'He ain't crazy,' argued Sherry-Lee. 'He's just scared. He got cursed by a voodoo priest when he was in prison and now he's got zombies looking all over to kill him.' She shrugged like it happened every day.

The fat woman shrugged back. She still thought Turn Back Jack was crazy. 'Whatever, but you ain't gonna get nothing accomplished in life if you keep on looking over your shoulder like that. Y'all have a nice day, y'hear.'

Sherry-Lee watched her go. 'What would she know?' she asked herself.

I smiled at her. She looked like Daisy Duke. 'Where you headed?'

'Church.'

'Wow!' I raised my eyebrows and let my eyes roll down her legs. 'Dressed like that?'

'No, stupid,' she replied in mock rebuke. 'I'll change into a dress when I get there.' She made dress sound like *drayuss*. My breath was shortening.

'Can I come?'

She frowned. Only slightly, but I saw it before she could recover. 'To my church?'

'Sure to your church. Why not?'

She chewed at the knuckle of her thumb. ''Cos you might not like it, and it sure is a long drive. Take us a couple of hours to get there.'

A couple of hours alone, in a car, with Sherry-Lee. I could suffer it if there was a good sermon at the end.

'So?' I cried. 'I like all churches, just so long as they're Christian, and I must confess it's been a little while since I last praised the Lord in company . . .'

As Gene would have observed, her body language was hesitant. She needed a little more persuasion.

'What does it say in Mark sixteen, verse nine?' I wasn't even sure if there was a sixteenth chapter, or even a ninth verse, in the Gospel According to St Mark. It was a shot in the dark, and it hit Sherry-Lee CBM – centre of body mass – as Brad would have said. Her dark eyes widened and her pretty mouth hung open for a moment. 'Do you want to change or anything before we go?' she whispered.

We hit the road ten minutes later, my suit, shoes and a clean shirt laid beside her dress on the back seat. I couldn't help but notice the symbolism, and I'd enhanced its effect by leaving behind my handbag. Sherry-Lee was still stunned, answering my questions with distracted monosyllables. At last, as we headed east on Route 80 beside the Caloosahatchee River, she spoke a complete sentence.

'You are what you are whether you know it or not. Ain't that the truth?'

'I guess,' I replied, switching on the radio. 'Cool station.'

'The Devil's music – that's what Pastor Zachary calls it.'

'Absolutely right,' I concurred, switching it off.

Sherry-Lee punched the button and cranked up the volume. 'Come off it,' she scoffed. 'That is so not genuine. Got any weed?'

I rolled us an effective little number, wound down the window and pretty soon it felt like we were driving a convertible. Sherry-Lee's hair rolled in the breeze like a field of ripe tobacco and her brown skin gleamed in the sunlight like glazed terracotta as, laid back in my seat and behind her line of sight, I examined every inch of her on show.

'Voodoo Chile' was on the radio and I sang along with Jimi. Sherry-Lee looked back at me and grinned. She was wearing Vuarnets and could see what was going through my mind. I felt slightly cheap ogling her from so near without stating my intentions, but it was a feeling I was used to and I could live with it as long as the sun was shining, Hendrix was on the radio and we were doing this romantic road-trip thing. At La Belle we swung north on Route 29 and picked up US-27 at Palmdale. We were in Bad Company, and Sherry-Lee took over the vocals.

A signpost offering Venus flew past and I pulled myself upright. 'Next left,' I cried. It seemed a shame to waste so synchronicitous an opportunity.

We parked in the shade of a spreading chestnut tree and I bought us a couple of Dr Peppers from a shingle-built roadhouse.

Sherry-Lee chewed thoughtfully on her sunglasses, watching me as I rolled us another joint. 'You are what you are whether you know it or not,' she said again, quietly.

'I know,' I replied, looking up and into her eyes.

She shook her head slowly. 'I don't think you do.'

She waited until I'd licked and sealed the joint, and then she kissed me, under the boughs of the spreading chestnut tree, just outside Venus, on State Road 731, in Okeechobee County, Florida. I closed my eyes as my heart swelled and exploded into a hundred little hearts, each one sprouting little wings and circling our embrace. The radio played 'Angie' and Sherry-Lee entwined her arms around my neck, pressing herself into me as I ran my hands through her hair and down her back, tracing the curve of her spine with my fingers and holding on tight so I didn't float away.

Then I spilled my Dr Pepper.

Sherry-Lee broke off the kiss, licking her lips and opening

her eyes. 'We got to go,' she whispered. 'We'll be late for church.'

I climbed numbly back into the Mazda, the little wings vanishing as my heart became whole again. One hundred had flown out, and ninety-nine back in: a little piece of my heart was lost just outside Venus, FL.

You haven't been called honey until a Southern woman calls you honey, and now that our friendship had been sealed with a kiss, Sherry-Lee was pouring it on like she'd been saving it up.

'Well, who'd have thought it?' she cried, making it sound like a line from a Dolly Parton song. 'I never went with an Englishman before.'

'Me neither,' I replied and she laughed.

'Honey, I just love that English sense of humour.'

I placed my hand on her lean right thigh and her eyes flashed.

'Mostly I operate a no-touch policy, honey, but in your case I'm happy to make an exception.' She gave me a low-lidded sideways look. 'You've got nice, soft hands. Guess I'm used to rougher types.'

I could see the effete Englishman cliché warming up in the back of her mind and took immediate steps to prevent his appearance. 'It's my brain that's got the calluses, baby,' I growled, but it didn't sound quite as good out loud.

The sawgrass swampland of the South had given way to broad, green pasturelands, dotted with stoned-looking cows beneath an enormous sky. Cumulo-nimbi as big as Antarctic icebergs drifted across the blue, carrying the Gulf to the Atlantic and avoiding the sun. I passed Sherry-Lee the joint and leaned back in my seat, looking for the future in the clouds. I was at the front end of a love-affair, the top of the slide, when all was sweet hope and delicious anticipation.

From here, I had learned, it was pretty much all downhill, so I lay back, ready to enjoy the ride.

'Martin, honey, I think you're gonna be freaked today.' Sherry-Lee had pulled over on a dark, serpentine county road that wound through the woods. She bit her lip in a way that I thought cute and misread my smile for ridicule. 'No, seriously,' she protested. 'This ain't no ordinary church.'

'So?' I replied, looking for clues in her dark brown eyes.

She held my gaze, then shrugged. 'Whatever.'

We started up again and traded the county road for a local road. Following it away from the gentle pasturelands and bulrush-fringed ponds, we climbed through a silent forest of oak dripping with Spanish moss as though the branches had caught the clouds. A left turn took us on to a rough track, from which long drives to sinister, unseen properties branched off at quarter-mile intervals. I could imagine what lay beyond the crude signs deterring trespass: dented old fridges, the rusting carcasses of classic cars and chained-up hog hounds; beer cans, unlicensed firearms and big arms tattooed with Old Glory. I was beginning to feel like an effete Englishman after all.

Pulling over in the middle of nowhere, Sherry-Lee reached into the back and grabbed her dress. 'Get your Sunday best on,' she commanded, and slipped into the woods.

I peered through the trees, hoping that a blessed shaft of sunlight would pick her out, but in moments she was back, her lithe body graced by a simple floral frock.

'You ain't ready,' she hissed, tilting the rearview and snatching back her hair. 'Hurry up! We get seen here there'll be hell to pay.'

I donned my suit in double time, hopping on one leg and maintaining an all-round watch for hillbillies. 'Where's my shoes?' I called, my voice an urgent whisper.

'How the hell do I know?' retorted Sherry-Lee, deadpan. 'Hell, honey, we only just met.'

'Must have forgotten them,' I muttered, lacing up my All-Stars. 'Check it out: black jacket, white shirt, black pants and, er, blue baseball boots.'

Sherry-Lee gave me the once over. 'You'll fit in just fine,' she declared.

It was no ordinary church. Situated in a wide clearing at the intersection of three tracks, it was a long, low building of stained white breezeblocks. There was neither spire nor steeple, just a shallow-pitched roof that was half moss-covered shingle and half rusty tin. A dozen or so cars and pick-ups of varied age and condition were parked randomly in the weeds around the building.

'Shit! We're late!' hissed Sherry-Lee, and then I heard the singing. We were still a good furlong from the church and the voices strengthened on a warm south-westerly.

'Go tell it on the mountain, go tell it on the shore,' I sang.

Sherry-Lee looked at me in delight. 'You know it!' she exclaimed.

I nodded, still smiling in spite of my sinking heart. I knew it, and I knew 'Kum Ba-Yah', too.

Sherry-Lee abandoned the car and dragged me by the hand through a haze of butterflies and bees and up the metal steps to a wooden door. The wooden cross and plaque announcing, 'The Church of Jesus Christ with Signs Following' had been tauntingly defaced by marker-pen-wielding teenage heavy-metal Satanists and the door was peppered with shotgun pellets. Suddenly it felt safer to be inside.

A narrow man in a tall black suit with a head like a rook's stood facing the congregation and he smiled as we came through the door.

'Sherry-Lee,' he beamed, showing more gaps than teeth. 'Brother, welcome!'

Twenty scrubbed and shaven faces turned to greet us with looks of intense, country-bred curiosity, paying no never mind to no fancy cityboy manners. I smiled back as Sherry-Lee dragged me to a pew.

'That's Pastor Zachary,' she whispered, bowing her head. 'You're gonna be freaked.'

'Let us lift up our hearts!' implored Pastor Zachary, and the meek replied, 'Amen.'

'Let us lift up our hearts!' he insisted, and the faithful called, 'Amen.'

'Let us lift up our hearts!' he roared, and the chosen yelled, 'Amen.'

'Is there any more outside, Sherry-Lee?' called Pastor Zachary.

Once more the congregation swivelled, the long-haired women seeming as disapproving of Sherry-Lee as the short-haired men were of me.

Sherry-Lee shook her head demurely. 'No, sir, we're the last.'

'But many that are first shall be last; and the last first, my child,' smiled the Pastor. It was a feeble joke, and he got a weak laugh. He stood now with his hands by his sides, opening and closing his fists as he ran his eyes across the congregation like a nervous anchorman awaiting instructions from a hidden earpiece. The guitar man took the opportunity to wind up his D-string, plucking harmonics in a shaft of sunlight, and then the congregation, responding perhaps to the preacher's twitching, started calling encouragement.

'Tell it, Pastor!'

'Praise Him, Reverend!'

'We're ready for you, Pastor Zachary,' cried Sherry-Lee, urging me to show some enthusiasm with a ranged glance.

'Get on with it!' I called.

The Reverend closed his eyes as the ripples became a swell of exhortation to glory in the name of God, and as the tension rose to the flimsy wooden rafters I chanced a look behind me, half expecting the Blues Brothers to come cartwheeling through the door. Suddenly the frequency locked and the Pastor spun around, raising his hands before the plain wooden cross on the back wall of the church.

'Blessed is he that cometh in the name of the Lord! Blessed be the kingdom of our father David, that cometh in the name of the Lord! Hosanna!'

'Hosanna!' cried the congregation.

'Hosanna in the highest!' affirmed the Pastor, spinning round to face the people. 'And Jesus said unto them, Have faith in God, for verily I say unto you that whosoever shall say unto this mountain, Be thou removed, and be thou cast into the sea and shall not doubt his heart, but shall believe those things which he saith shall come to pass; he shall have whatsoever he saith!'

I was beginning to lose track of the message. I was on my own. The Reverend paced back and forth, quoting the Scriptures and proving the faith of those gathered before him. I glanced at Sherry-Lee, sitting straight-backed beside me, her bare face radiant and her glittering eyes locked on to the Pastor. Some unseen sign prompted the Pastor to hand the floor to a middle-aged man wearing Gene's number twos and the certainty of a believer: 'Tell it, Brother Vaughn.'

'And he said unto them, I beheld Satan as lightning fall from heaven,' stammered Brother Vaughn, nodding as though he were passing on some recent news. 'Behold, I give unto you power to tread on serpents and scorpions, and over all the power of the enemy; and nothing shall by any means hurt you, praise Him!'

I flexed my toes as Brother Vaughn sat down and two more congregants rose to bear witness. My feet were tingling, as though the bones were vibrating in tune with the guitar man's D. It was becoming curiously hard to breathe, and I felt the sting of sweat across my upper lip as a sister in a cotton dress with waist-length wiry hair and the quiet voice of a woman who knew that everything would be all right in the end addressed the faithful. By now, people were coming and going like a Broadway audition and the fever was rising.

Suddenly Sherry-Lee was up there, her hands twisted in front of her and the sunlight shining through her dress. 'Now when Jesus was risen early on the first day of the week he appeared first to Mary Magdalene, out of whom he cast seven devils.' She was looking right at me.

'St Mark, chapter sixteen, verse nine.'

My shot in the dark had ricocheted from Sherry-Lee's heart and caught me in the temple. I fought for control of my jaw, pulled my face from shock to sincerity and sent her a little nod of encouragement.

'For whosoever shall call upon the name of the Lord shall be saved,' she cried fervently. 'But how, then, shall they call on Him in whom they have not believed?' She was still looking at me, and the sun had shifted in the heavens to send a beam that lit her up like a latter-day saint. All eyes were on her – especially upon the slender silhouettes of her long legs through that thin dress – and a numbness like hemlock had reached my unbelieving gut. 'How then shall they believe in Him of whom they have not heard? And how shall they hear without a preacher?'

'Hallelujah!' and 'Amen!' cried the congregation as

Sherry-Lee slid back to the pew. She squeezed my hand as the guitar man and two tambourines led us into 'To God be the Glory'. I looked in vain for a hymnal. It was like looking for a lyric sheet at a Metallica gig, so I opened and closed my mouth when and where it seemed appropriate. It didn't fool Pastor Zachary. He fixed me with a wide eye and strode down the aisle towards me, tapping on a triangle in a slow, measured tattoo. I shrank as he approached, expecting to be undone.

'Seeing as you don't know the words, Brother, why don't you just bang on this?' he whispered before wheeling like a raven and adding his voice to the multitude. I grinned like a fool and gave the triangle a hammering, and as we started another round of the hymn, the Pastor busied himself with a simple wooden box that he dragged front and centre. The sad-looking sister with the wiry hair had taken so much of the spirit that she was heading way out of tune as we joined the chorus, and by the time we reached the second verse she was wailing. The singing died away, but the sister didn't notice. Her head tilted up and to the left, her body twisted and rigid like she'd been cut down from the rope, she keened in the Sunday-morning silence with tears rolling down her ruddy cheeks, the words guttural and alien. Sherry-Lee seized my wrist, and I felt her trembling.

'Tongues,' she whispered. 'She's been anointed.'

The Reverend was bent over the box, and when he turned I thought for a moment that he was holding a stole above his head.

'And these signs shall follow them that believe,' he declared as the stole transformed itself into a four-foot rattlesnake, its shiny scales the colour of straw and shadow.

'Jesus Christ!' I yelled.

'Praise Him!' agreed the worshippers.

'In my name shall they cast out devils; they shall speak with new tongues; they shall take up serpents; and if they drink any deadly thing it shall not hurt them; they shall lay hands on the sick and they shall recover.'

'Amen!' they cried, and a young man in jeans and a white shirt buttoned to the throat dipped into the box and raised another writhing serpent. He draped its rippling length upon his crown, then framed his face with its diamonds.

I was shaking now, shivering with feet of lead, my trembling causing the striker to vibrate against the inside of the triangle. The tone it emitted was startlingly clear, a pure resonance unattainable by conscious effort, like the sound of a glass harp in perfect pitch with the sad sister's singing. The congregants turned and smiled at me, nodding like they thought that I knew what they knew that I knew. I grinned back, then turned to Sherry-Lee and shrugged.

'It's not me playing this triangle,' I whispered through clenched teeth.

Her big eyes sparkled with tears. 'Bless you, Martin,' she replied with a Madonna's smile. 'The Spirit is upon you.'

Three men and the preacher were now handling serpents at the front of the church, all in a trance and all quoting snakeproof passages from the Gospels. The sad sister was twisting the last words of a lost language from her anointed soul and an unearthly sound was spilling from a length of twice-bent steel. Everyone else was either weeping or crying 'Hallelujah' and I was in bad need of a drink.

'Good to see you today, Brother,' smiled the Reverend as I stood in a state of stunned disbelief in the Sunday sunshine. I blinked hard.

'Praise the Lord, Pastor Zachary.'

The sad sister was sitting on a grassy bank, waiting, like

me, for her earthly senses to return. Sherry-Lee was trying to give her something and she was trying to refuse. Sherry-Lee won, sealing her victory with a kiss. Suddenly the Pastor leaned forward and pressed his lips hard against mine.

'The Churches of Christ salute you,' he declared. 'Brothers and Sisters, let us salute one another with a holy kiss.'

Fourteen men aged between nineteen and seventy kissed me on the lips that morning. I didn't ask why.

'Do not light up that cigarette,' hissed Sherry-Lee as we drove in convoy away from the church. 'Drinking and smoking are taboo.'

'Jesus!' I sighed.

'Don't be blaspheming, neither.'

I pushed the Marlboro back into the packet and hid it under the seat. 'You were right,' I admitted. 'I am freaked.'

Sherry-Lee smiled wide. She was glowing from the inside out. 'Don't you feel amazing, though?'

We were heading for a church luncheon back at Pastor Zachary's farm over Basinger way, an invitation that Sherry-Lee had enthusiastically accepted. My plan had been to get drunk and stoned and pick up where we'd left off in Venus, but Sherry-Lee was still a sweet, white bride of Christ and I had nothing better to do until the honeymoon was over.

Pastor Zachary ran 700 feeder cattle in 32 watered pastures on 442 acres of Okeechobee County.

'Thank the Lord for that,' I replied, as though I knew what he was talking about. The farm had been in the family since the Civil War, and George Hensley himself had paid several visits back in the forties and fifties.

'He don't know who you're talking about, Daddy,' observed a muscular dude with a military crew cut in board-shorts and a singlet.

'You're right, Brother, I don't,' I concurred with a smile.

'I ain't your brother,' he smiled back, with an upbeat kind of animosity.

'Little George was the founder of our church,' explained Pastor Zachary. 'It was him that started the whole thing, God rest his soul.'

'What happened to him?' I enquired.

Pastor Zachary looked back to the ranch-house from where the women were carrying out the lunch. 'Got bit,' he replied.

Lunch began as a pleasant if sober outdoor affair of rice-based dishes and lemonade, then descended into a furious theological discussion. As the afternoon grew old Sherry-Lee played with one of her dungaree-clad cousins while the women thanked the Lord again for His bounty and the men reopened an old and potentially mortal wound to the Church of Jesus Christ with Signs Following. Someone, somewhere – Yankees, Jews or Islamites, it was assumed – had tried to prove that the sixteenth chapter of the Gospel of St Mark actually ended at verse eight. Verses nine to twenty, the foundations upon which my relationship with Sherry-Lee and the whole snake-handling church were built, were alleged to be the work of a medieval forger. It was a conspiracy theory that implicated everybody from the Florida Department of Fish and Wildlife to John Travolta and the Aga Khan. Feeling that I could add little to a debate that had become a ritual, I slipped away to find Sherry-Lee.

I found her sitting by an outhouse with her blue-eyed cousin on her knee, talking to the Pastor's son.

'Have you and Eight already met?' she asked, shielding her eyes against the sun.

Eight was pulling some bicep curls, a shiny silver

dumb-bell shrunken in his fist. 'We met already,' he confirmed. 'Brit, huh?'

'That's right,' I nodded.

He kept on curling. 'That's kind of like a Yankee, ain't it?'

I let it go. 'Why they call you Eight?'

He dropped the dumb-bell and showed me his hands in mock-bemusement. 'Damned if I know.'

The little and ring finger from his right hand were gone, taken, I assumed with a weary discomfort, by a crawling, rattling thing. I turned to Sherry-Lee. 'So, what you doing?' She lifted the kid into the air. 'I'm torturing this here prisoner to get information.'

The little girl screamed in delight, wriggled free and scarpered.

'Release the dogs,' cried Sherry-Lee.

I tucked my shirt into my trousers. 'I'll get her,' I promised. 'I'm an expert at torture.'

Sherry-Lee went thisaway and I went thataway and we caught the kid hiding behind an avocado tree.

'I'll hold her,' said Sherry-Lee, 'and you ask the questions.'

'Nobody escapes the Spanish Inquisition,' I warned, wagging a finger at the giggling child. 'Name?'

'Angie,' she squealed.

'Age?'

'Four and a half.'

'Favourite colour?'

She shrugged in her big cousin's arms. 'I dunno. What's your favourite colour, Sherry-Lee?'

'Blue, like the sky and the sea and your eyes, honey.'

The kid nodded. That was good enough for her. 'Blue. What's your name?'

'Tomás de Torquemada,' I replied, 'and it's traditional for me to ask the questions.' I was about to step my interrogation up a gear when two fat ladies waddled into the barnyard.

'Angie!' There was trouble in that name. The kid struggled free and jumped to her feet.

'Yeah?'

'You know you ain't allowed to play by that barn. What are you thinking of, child?'

Sherry-Lee raised her eyebrows and went to the kid's defence. I heard no words, only voices, but it was clear that Sherry-Lee was being scolded as much as the child. Hot air rose, the child was escorted away and Sherry-Lee wandered back over.

'What was all that about?' I asked. 'Aren't you allowed to torture kids in this country?'

She shrugged. 'You can, but not near the barn. Eight's got some watermelon wine if you want some.'

'Love some,' I replied. 'What is it?'

'Southern delicacy,' grunted Eight, leading us around the outhouse and across a small yard with sheds on three sides.

'Tell him how you make it, Eight, honey,' urged Sherry-Lee.

The endearment rankled, but I let it go.

Eight couldn't have cared less how I felt. 'Get yourself the biggest watermelon you can find,' he advised. 'Cut a plug out of the top, fill her up with vodka, put the plug back in and leave her in the coolbox for as long as you can. That's it.' He dragged a huge blue coolbox from the shade of a shrub.

'Let's go drink some watermelon wine.'

Eight had a problem: the woman he wanted was seeing another man. I sympathised with him, for I too had a problem. I was seeing the woman he wanted. Sherry-Lee seemed oblivious to our mutual plight, being equally sweet to us both. Eight's animosity diminished in inverse proportion to the amount he drank, which was heartening, considering his build. We settled in the long grass at the top of a gentle slope leading through soft-focus, cow-speckled pastures to the wooded banks of the Kissimmee River.

Sherry-Lee lay on her front, chewing a stalk. 'Eight and me, we're almost family, ain't that right, Eight?' She didn't wait for a reply. 'My daddy, Pastor Lewis, he was a preacher too, and after my mom ran off my daddy brought me down here to live on the farm.' She rolled over and looked me in the eye. 'He couldn't be taking me on no evangelising road-trip at the age of six, now, could he?'

Bees buzzed and flies hovered as the striped melon was passed back and forth between us, its sloshing heart becoming lighter with every draught. Eight's, on the other hand, was growing heavier. Eventually he could hold it no longer.

'So this is your new boyfriend?' he slurred, waving a big hand in my direction.

Sherry-Lee giggled. 'No, honey, he's just a friend of mine from where I live.'

'He a customer?'

'No he is not,' she snapped. 'I won't stay if you're going to talk that way. He's just a friend, that's all.'

My heart sank. The tiny part of my mind that remained high and dry knew that she was just keeping the peace, but my emotions were way below the waterline. I stood up, misjudged the slope, and sat down again. Eight rose unsteadily to his feet, drained the melon and hurled it down the slope to explode among the cattle.

'Happy cows,' he sighed. 'I wish I was a cow. Let's go out and get some brew.'

I closed one eye and focused on Sherry-Lee. 'What's he mean by "customer"?'

She jumped up, brushing the hayseed from her dress. 'He don't mean nothing by it. He's drunk, that's all, and so are you.'

Nothing more was said until we'd made it back to the barn.

'Listen, Eight, we're going to head back now,' said Sherry-Lee. 'It's a long drive, and it's Monday tomorrow and all . . .'

Eight raised a dismissive hand. 'Whatever,' he belched.

Glad to be going before the situation deteriorated further, I leaned back against the barn wall, underestimating the distance by nearly two feet.

'Your new boyfriend has fallen over,' grunted Eight.

I climbed to my feet, shaking my head in wonder like the innocent victim of a personal earth tremor.

Sherry-Lee shook hers in dismay. 'You better stay here while I go get the car. Pastor Zachary would be perturbed to see you – either of you – in that state of inebriation. Stay out of sight 'til I bring the car around.'

Eight shrugged and sloped into the barn. I followed, blinking in the warm, dusty gloom. The air was heavy with a dark and oily odour, the smell of something unfamiliar, yet known.

Eight took a pee against the dry wooden wall. 'That's a 1937 Buick Eight under that tarp,' he announced. 'My granddaddy's car.'

'You want to watch out or the rats'll have it,' I replied.

Eight laughed, short and loud. 'Ain't no rats round here except you, boy.'

I had followed his lead and was peeing in the dark when he came up behind me and shoved me forwards. I stumbled and turned to face him. Our physical differences were fractional: I was three-quarters his width and four-fifths his height.

'I seen guys like you come, and I seen guys like you go,' he sneered, prodding me in the chest.

I kept my balance and poked him back. 'And what is this going to achieve? You think that giving me a beating will make her like you better? Don't you get TV out here?'

Brad wouldn't have put up with this crap. Brad would have popped a cap in Eight's arse long ago. Brad wouldn't even have let Sherry-Lee go and fetch the car on her own. Somewhere near my shrivelled liver my adrenals realised the futility of the affair and retired from the fray, leaving me wide-eyed and speechless. Eight was too dim to see what was going on, to realise that none of us had any chance whatsoever with Sherry-Lee while Brad still roamed the earth in a stolen pick-up truck loaded with exotic firearms. Obliquely, I wondered if Eight could further my knowledge of Heckler & Koch's goodwill ambassador, but now was not the time to ask. Eight shoved me again, hard on the left shoulder. The musky odour of sour leaves and excretions was stronger now, as though something sinister slept in the shadows at my back.

'I ain't gonna beat you for my sake,' he declared. 'I'm gonna beat you for her sake. You ain't no good for her – look at you! You got piss down your pants, you're so drunken you can hardly stand up, you ain't even got your own car. You're a goddamned disgrace. What in hell do you think you can do for her?' He took a step closer, but I'd sent down roots. He drew fast, shallow breaths, fanning a testosterone fire as he stood, hands on hips, his face a handspan from mine. 'Tell me, now, 'cos I'm interested to hear.'

Brad would have told him to mind his own cotton-pickin' business, nutted him and left. Brock, on the other hand, exercised the spiritual option.

'I'm going to save her,' I announced, aghast at the sound of my intentions.

Eight had braced himself for a less ambitious goal, and the statement knocked him off balance. He took a deep breath and frowned. 'Save her from what, precisely?'

Through the alcohol-induced night and fog that obscured my lucidity came a narrow shaft of light, a reflection of the clarity I had felt at the service, an echo of the pure tone I had drawn from the triangle. The light was the truth, and the truth was the way, and the way was the light. I should have ignored it and let Eight slap me.

'From you,' I replied. 'From you with your watermelon wine and your weight training and your, your . . .' It was actually quite hard to tie Eight down to anything especially unwholesome. He was a simple farm boy whose dad was a part-time preacher, and then I remembered that he was about to give me a walloping. '. . . your violent nature. From Brad and his no good ways with his firearms and his marijuana. From that trailer park full of those who have left the straight and narrow and foundered by the wayside. From all the bad things in life and beyond.' I paused for breath.

'And beyond?' Eight scowled. 'What the hell you talking about, boy?'

I shrugged. I hadn't given it much thought. 'You know,' I bluffed, 'Satan and stuff.'

Eight's eyes widened in mock-astonishment. 'You gonna save her from Satan? Where her daddy and my daddy failed, you're gonna save her from the Devil?'

It was a metaphysical concept, and one I could never see myself having to prove. I hooked my thumbs into my pockets, stuck out my chest and nodded. 'Yup.'

'Go on, then,' growled Eight, thrusting me backwards with a blow to the breast.

I fell against a wooden box, hearing something heavy move within. Eight snatched up a broom and I raised my hands to ward off the blow. He sidestepped and jabbed the handle against the box.

'Hear that?' he asked. 'That's the Devil in there.'

The reaction from within was half-hearted and disgruntled, the first bleary-eyed warning from a rudely awakened snake. I spun around and leapt backwards. Eight thrust me forwards, one hand on my shoulder and the other on the broom. He bashed the box again and the rattling doubled in volume and intensity.

'Here, take a look,' he whispered, stretching past me to lift the lid. I peered inside, the feeling draining from my legs. Two coiled serpents looked straight back at me, heads like fat men's coffins, their tails rattling like the low-voiced threats of a scrapyard dog.

'Which one's Satan?' I asked.

'Both of them. Either of them. Any of them. They're all the Devil incarnate. You gonna face up to them, or have you seen enough now?'

'I am facing up to them,' I protested. 'I'm looking, ain't I?'

'Looking at the Devil ain't touching the Devil, now, is it?' he pointed out. 'If you're the man who's gonna save our Sherry-Lee from the Devil and herself you got to brush the serpents and the scorpions aside, like Luke said.'

I closed my eyes. 'You're not telling me you got bloody scorpions in here as well, are you?'

'Uh-uh.' He shook his head. 'Just these canebreak rattlers here, a breeding pair of cottonmouths over there and an injured timber type. Now you gonna sit on the pot all day?'

The snakes flicked their skinny tongues across the air, tasting the panic that was pooling in my armpits and running down my back. I could hear my heart trying to beat its way out of its cage while my lily liver wrapped itself around my spine and hid.

'Just reach out and touch faith,' taunted Eight, 'or ain't she worth it?'

He clouted the box hard twice, three times, then stabbed the broom handle inside. The rattling exploded like killer hail on an old tin roof, and as I was wondering whether Sherry-Lee really was worth all this herpetological aggravation I stepped forward and thrust my left hand into the box.

Instantly I felt like I'd been hit by a baseball − a violent, bruising slap that knocked my knuckles hard against the wooden side. I snatched my arm back and smiled at Eight, my mind an evacuated city awaiting two inevitable and devastating attacks.

'Holy shit!' he cried, dropping the broom. 'You just got bit, didn't you?'

I nodded and giggled, feeling slightly hysterical, and turned my hand over to inspect the palm. The rattling diminished.

'Jesus Christ, he got you good,' breathed Eight. 'You are a crazy motherfucker.'

The wound was already swollen, fat and shiny, the blood falling in heavy drips to the dirt floor. My mouth was dry, and the first terrifying flashes of a deep and frightening pain were reaching my brain. I slumped against the old Buick 8. Now I knew why the rats kept clear. Consciousness seemed altered, as though reality had passed through a wet muslin filter. Smooth muscle made itself known as I became aware of the effort required to draw breath. For the time being, breathing was easy, but if gambling hadn't been a sin I'd have put good money on the chances of respiratory failure sometime in the near future. I looked at Eight. 'What happens now?'

He rubbed his chin and shrugged. 'Wait for the angels, I guess.'

I heard a car door slam and looked up. Sherry-Lee stood in the barn doorway.

'They're here,' I said.

Sherry-Lee looked at Eight, then me, then Eight again. 'You two been fighting?'

'He got bit,' mumbled Eight. 'Show her.'

I showed her my bloodstained hand, already as fat as a blown-up rubber glove, grinning like a bull-whipped dog.

'Oh my God!' shrieked Sherry-Lee. 'How did you get bit?'

'Stuck his arm into a box of canebreaks,' explained Eight. 'Crazy bastard did it to prove he was good enough for you. You should be impressed.'

Sherry-Lee gave him a long, hard look, then glared at me. 'That the truth?'

'It's the light and the truth and the way,' I replied.

'We got to call EMS,' decided Sherry-Lee. 'He's delirious.'

Next time I looked there were half a dozen people standing over me and none of them was a paramedic. Black pulses of the purest pain rolled into my brain, obscuring all thought and sensation with the devastation of a wrecking-ball. Between the blows I determined that there was a difference of opinion based upon the strict theological principle as to whether an ambulance should be called. The bite was a test of my faith, the consequence of getting ahead of the Lord.

'I saw him take the anointing today with that triangle,' declared some gummy old-timer.

I closed my eyes as another boulder of snakebite crushed my arm.

'Still bleeding a lot,' observed another. 'Must have got the vein.'

'Your intended is being tried for past sin,' announced Pastor Zachary. 'Only his faith will prove his innocence.'

'You're mistaken,' insisted Sherry-Lee. 'Martin's not one of us, and he ain't my intended, neither. We got to get the EMS here.'

I concentrated on drawing breath. The gathered witnesses to my envenomation had become whispering shadows in the gloom. My stomach lurched and I could taste Charon's penny on my tongue. Sherry-Lee continued to argue the case for my evacuation, but my attention was drawn increasingly to the fight between good and evil raging through my veins and lymphatic system. I only wished I knew which side I was on.

'Get up, you idiot!'

Sherry-Lee was pulling my shirt, and I rose numbly to my feet.

'I'm taking him to the Poison Center,' she declared. 'I don't care about what Daddy would have said, what Little George would have said, nor what you're gonna say, Pastor Zachary. Lord knows it should have been me that got bit, not this fool, and He knows what I'm doing is righteous.'

She led me towards the light, and the shadows parted to let me through.

'Walk slow, now,' she advised. 'We're going to get in the car and get you some help. You got Mediplan?'

I sat myself in the car and watched as Sherry-Lee ripped a strip from the white shirt she had been wearing when all I'd had to look forward to was another kiss.

'Show me your hand.'

It didn't feel like my hand any more. Hot and heavy, it throbbed as though the blood had turned to acid, and as I studied its black, stretched back I saw nothing I could recognise. Sherry-Lee turned it carefully, inspecting both sides before tying her torn bandage around the still-bleeding wound.

'See that?' she asked, pointing at a palm that looked like it had been shot. 'You got four holes there. That's pretty near a perfect bite.'

I was delighted.

She slid back my suit jacket sleeve to expose my arm.

'Okay,' she decided. 'Leave the jacket on.'

She sprang to her feet and crossed the yard, glaring at the men gathered around the barn. Stretching on tiptoe in the shade of a tree, she reached up and plucked an avocado.

'Stick this in your armpit,' she ordered, then sighed. 'The same side as the bite, dummy.'

She started the car and spun out of the barnyard. I winced as another barrage exploded along my left arm.

'You know what you're doing, don't you?'

Sherry-Lee changed up and pressed down. 'Sure do. My daddy got bit nineteen times, and I was there for eighteen of them.' She lit two cigarettes and poked one between my numb lips. 'Get some nicotine into your blood.'

'Who was there for the nineteenth?' I asked, sucking back the healing smoke.

'No one,' she replied, looking straight at me. 'He died.'

There was one good reason why I needed to see a doctor, and several bad reasons why I couldn't. None of them impressed Sherry-Lee.

'I'll write a cheque,' she countered when I explained my financial position.

'I'll tell them you're my fiancée,' she argued when I outlined my alien status.

'Fuck him,' she advised when I wondered what Gene would say. 'He looks unreasonable, anyways.'

I wanted to smile, but my face felt like it had overdosed on novocaine. I wanted to breathe, but my lungs felt like they were a long, long way away, inside a pensioner in a nursing home sixty miles down the highway in West Palm Beach.

'Can't breathe,' I gasped, dragging hard on the Marlboro.

She put her hand on my shoulder. 'Listen: you'll be fine so long as you stay calm. Try not to worry about your breathing . . .'

'I've had this coming,' I admitted. 'I've had this coming a long time.'

'Yeah, baby?' replied Sherry-Lee. 'Keep talking. Tell me all about it.'

Telling wouldn't make it better. I shook my head. It seemed too heavy for my neck to support. 'Can't be bothered. Can we have some music?'

'Sure, honey,' she nodded, punching the radio.

'*Your cruel device, your blood like ice . . .*' sang Alice.

'I love this song,' I said. 'Haven't heard it for ages.'

'I hate it,' muttered Sherry-Lee. 'Reminds me of work.'

'*. . . I want to taste you but your lips are venomous poison,*' continued Alice, and even if I had drawn my last breath I wouldn't have been able to resist singing along. 'You're poison running through my veins,' I sang. 'You're poison – I don't wanna break these chains . . .'

'That's enough of that,' snapped Sherry-Lee, switching stations. 'Now calm down.'

There was country playing as I faded away, my arm now swollen to the shoulder as the haemotoxin washed through my vascules like a chemical spill. A bruise like a thundercloud had cast a shadow from forearm to fingertip, the lightning brewed in its churning core flashing through my bones with a spiteful urgency. The wound had stopped bleeding and a cluster of tiny blisters had popped up on the stained and distended skin around the bite.

'Is it bad?' I asked, hearing my voice as though it were coming from the trunk of the car.

Sherry-Lee turned and smiled, her face and hair haloed by a golden glow. My heart was boarding up the door like a scared little pig, and I couldn't hear her reply for all the hammering. Sweat dripped from my yellow skin and I shivered in the shotgun as the fever rose. The venom was breaking down my blood vessels, burning through capillary walls and letting them bleed into the surrounding tissue. My blood pressure was falling like a Hurricane Coast barometer, and the sudden nosebleed that sprayed over the suit in which I made impressions merely pushed it lower. My head spun like a drunk's as hot waves of nausea threatened to drown me in my own fluids, and even though I could hear Sherry-Lee's shouting, there seemed little point in staying awake. I took half a breath from the empty sky and let myself drop into the depths.

It was a long way down, an uncontrolled and inelegant freefall through dark chaos to a distant end. How far I would fall I neither knew nor cared, for I would never be coming back. Anticipating the end, my mind broke up the furniture and threw it on the embers, casting absurd shadows of half-forgotten faces against the flickering, half-lit wall. I had done things which I should not have done, and left undone those things I should have done and now it was too late to do anything more. I had been handling serpents with neither skill nor respect long before I ever smelled the dark musk of *Crotalus* and felt the whiplash sting of his bite, and the aptness of my end seemed to prove the existence of the God, faith in whom alone could save me. I could hear myself laughing as I tumbled down, laughing and crying, crying and choking, choking and coughing.

There was bluegrass playing as I came around, slumped on my knees on a grassy verge. Swooning with a bungee-jumper's vertigo, I coughed and vomited rice and watermelon wine into the weeds. Sherry-Lee's voice came and went like the sound of the sea from behind a highway wall. 'Lord,' she said, 'I thought you'd gone, honey. Puke it all up now – this is a good sign.'

I nodded, hoping that she wouldn't notice that I'd been sick on my suit. The blackness loomed behind my left shoulder like a warm bed on a cold Monday morning and every spasm, every twist of the screw, pushed me back towards its promised oblivion. Sherry-Lee held me back, helping me into the car and dashing around to the driver's side. I let my head loll forward to rest on my flecked chest, and was again snatched back by her yelling. 'Wake up, you fuck!' she screamed, beating on my shoulder with her tiny fists. She slapped my face until it hurt, then pulled my hair until I yelled. Holding my head up with one hand, she started the car with the other and spun the radio to full volume. 'Chantilly Lace' was playing and as we sped through a blurred landscape I tried to sing along: the Big Bopper in a small Mazda with Sherry-Lee Lewis.

5

Gene stood at the top of our steps like a confused Terminator in a red silk dressing-gown. He folded his arms and stared blankly as he searched his databanks for the appropriate response to my return. He scratched his ear and then his eyebrow as Sherry-Lee helped me from the car, my arm in a sling across my chest and a carrier-bag in my good hand. He took Sherry-Lee's hand in an absent grip as she bounded up the steps to meet him.

'Good morning to you, Mr Renoir,' she cried. 'You look after this fella now, y'hear? I'll just hang his suit here on the screen. I sponged most of the stuff off of it, but I reckon it'll need a good dry clean. Have a good day now!'

Gene nodded and shook his head at the same time, twitching slightly as Sherry-Lee came back to help me up the steps.

'Good luck, honey,' she whispered, brushing my cheek with her lips. 'I'll come by and see you later on, y'hear?'

I nodded, and Gene stepped aside, holding open the trailer door to let me pass. He followed me in, still silent, then showed me his palms in a gesture that asked, 'So?'

'Got bit,' I explained. 'Fucking great rattlesnake – the canebreak variety, apparently.'

Gene twitched some more. I reached into the carrier-bag and pulled out some of the three hundred and ninety dollars' worth of medication Sherry-Lee had bought me.

'Check it out: I got loads of good pills here.'

Gene scratched his head and turned a full circle. 'Jesus Christ!' he barked. He turned again, this time a quarter revolution to stare at his reflection in the kitchen window. 'Jesus Christ! I give the help one, single day off, a fucking Sunday, for Christ's sake, and he comes back on Wednesday with a fucking snakebite!' He spun back to face me. 'How did it happen?'

I shrugged. 'Bent down to pick a flower: got bit.'

'It's "got bitten", for Christ's sake,' hissed Gene, and I couldn't disagree. 'Where?'

'Here,' I replied, half lifting my bandaged hand.

'I can see that!' he yelled, a vein throbbing above his right eye. 'What was your goddamned location?'

'Lake Okeechobee,' I lied, but only slightly. 'Out on a hiking trail.'

Gene watched my face for a moment, then opened the trailer door and brought my bloodstained, mud-soiled, vomit-flecked suit inside. 'What the fuck were you doing on a hiking trail in a fucking business suit?' he howled.

'Hiking,' I replied unhelpfully. 'It was a nice day.'

'It's fucking Florida,' yelled Gene, his cheeks glowing. 'It's always a nice day!'

'What's that got to do with anything?' I asked.

Gene slapped his forehead hard and looked to the floor for advice. His cheeks were redder still when he looked up. 'Have you seen your face?' he asked. There was a knock at the door. Gene pointed at me. 'Go check yourself out in the mirror while I deal with Fedex,' he commanded, 'then tell me what contribution you're going to make to the rest of this operation.'

I inspected myself in Gene's long mirror and shuddered. Before me stood a man who had been set on fire, hit by a truck and drowned in a vat of acid. My entire face was swollen like it had been bee-stung, my lips scabbed and ulcerated and my eyes sunk deep within puffy folds of tender flesh. My arm lay dead and heavy across my chest, the fingers of my left hand fat and black like scorched chipolatas. The thumbnail had already gone, and the rest were curling away to fall like dead leaves from a rotting tree. A Salvadorean doctor with a special interest in pit-viper envenomation had limited the necrosis to a black disc the size of a silver dollar in the palm of my hand, but the gangrene raised concerns about liver failure and renal damage. I understood that to mean that I'd be pissing blood but wouldn't lose any fingers. My job, however, was another thing entirely.

Gene was staring at thirteen pieces of gold spread across the dinette table, trying to see the future.

'You're right,' I concurred. 'I look terrible. I'm sorry.' I sat down on our lumpy sofa and waited for the performance to begin.

Gene's productions were as polished as one might expect from a covert showman and generally examined the themes of treachery, disaster, forgiveness and nobility in a world of suffering and disappointment. The dramatic device was built around the actions of an antagonist who served as both foil and audience, a buffoon whose thoughtlessness and selfishness had brought the world to the brink of oblivion. It happened when I got drunk, when I lost the mail, when I left the chequebook on the roof of the car. And it happened when I got bit. Got *bitten*.

The upshot was my confinement to base. Dr Alfaro had estimated that my body would need twenty-one days to return to normal. I told Gene twenty-eight, and he gave me fourteen, pointing out curiously that this was the field, not the world. Having a team member grounded gave the operation the opportunity to step up the admin, and while Gene was out on the road I was to keep myself occupied. Gene drew up a list of two hundred coins sought by fictitious collectors, and pushed me towards the filing box.

'Prove your worth, Troop.'

'Good morning, Ray! My name is Martin Brock-Crossfield, from Whitehall Numismatics.'

'Whitehall Numis . . . Hold on: you're the Brit company, right?'

'That's right – we met at the Pensacola show. You had that beautiful proof 'seventy-seven Indian head dollar.'

'Yeah, yeah, sure, it's Martin, isn't it? Sure I remember. So what can I do you for?'

'Client was delighted, Ray, and he wants more. I see from your website you're holding a 'seventy-six mint state Indian head. What's the trade on that?'

'Hold on, buddy, let me see . . . Yeah, that's PGCA certified. You want the trade? Call it . . . call it twelve.'

'Ray: call it a grand.'

'Jesus, Mikey, I got kids in college. Call it eleven-fifty.'

'I can't afford kids. Ten-fifty.'

'Eleven, and you're closing me down.'

'Eleven, including shipping and insurance.'

'Christ Almighty! You're lucky I've just given up wheat, Mark. Have I got your address?'

'I'll email you. Will you send it today?'

'United States Postal Service, guaranteed.'

'Cheque's in the post on signed delivery. Cheers, Ray.'

One down, one hundred and ninety-nine to go. Gene left on Thursday morning, still huffing and puffing, heading off to the Leon County Fairgrounds for the Eighth Annual Tallahassee Coin and Jewellery Convention. He mentioned that he'd be stopping off in Daytona Beach to unload, adding that it was the number-one party town on the Treasure

Coast. He asked me not to call him on Saturday night as he'd probably be in some loud and lairy strip-club with some of his old Marine buddies down by the beach, then paused to ask if I'd be able to manage without the car. Unconvinced, I waved him away and picked up the phone.

'Hi there! George? Hi! It's Martin Brock-Crossfield from Whitehall Numismatics . . .'

Gene headed north on I-75 and I spent fifteen thousand dollars before he got to Tampa. Then I shut up shop and concentrated on my social life.

Turn Back Jack was shuffling past as I laid out my lawn chair, stopping and spinning every two or three paces like Caesar Augustus.

'Hey, Jack!' I called. 'How's it going?'

He stopped to reply, glancing over his shoulder first.

'It's John. Don't be calling me Jack. Not out loud.'

I gave him a thumbs up. 'Want to take cover for a while?' I pointed past the trailer. 'Ain't nothing behind there but a big chain-link fence. I like to keep my rear covered.'

Jack nodded. 'Me too. Can't do no harm, can it? You got a glass of water?'

'Sure,' I nodded. 'Sit down.'

He shook his head. 'Prefer to stay on my feet.' Six feet-plus and two twenty-five, Turn Back Jack was the kind of barefoot black man who turned crackers into hound dogs and reminded the illiterate of Caliban. Pursued by earthly troubles all his life, he was now hunted by devils, licensed by an irrevocable curse that would drag him to a gruesome end. I pushed a cold Bud through the door. 'How about a brew?'

Jack paused in his scanning to shake his head. 'No, sir, not for me. I can't be drinking or smoking or carrying on with any kind of sin that gives them an excuse to take me. I got to stay pure and vigilant.'

It was good practice, and I kept watch for him while he sipped his water.

'You get bit by a snake?' he asked, inclining his head towards my sling.

'Canebreak rattler,' I confirmed. 'Hurts like hell.'

'Snakebites is lucky,' he replied. 'Live and let live is what I say when it comes to snakes.'

'You know something, Jack?'

He cringed.

'Sorry, John. You should move out to a place right in the middle of nowhere. No neighbours, no trees, no shadows and no ditches. An island down there in the Keys, maybe, or some place in the Everglades with only one road in. That way you could see anybody coming a mile off, and take appropriate action.'

Turn Back Jack shook his head with a madman's vigour. 'I already thought of that, but I ain't doing it.' He drained his glass and wiped the rim with the hem of his heavy plaid shirt. 'When they come, I want there to be witnesses. What's your name? I want to thank you for the water.'

'Martin,' I told him, holding out my hand.

He nodded.

'Well, thank you for the water, Martin. You got a little bit of snake inside you now. You be sure to use it. I'll bid you good day.'

I watched his back as he went, his progress a grim Southern two-step with a grinning horned partner. Spooked by his passing and in need of medication, I went back inside and watched Mid-Western lesbian transsexuals confess their indiscretions to shocked men with mullets until Sherry-Lee came visiting. She brought me a pizza as big as a tractor-wheel, a plate of dough stacked with pepperoni, cheese and jalapeños that she made me eat while she unloaded the groceries.

'Got you two presents,' she smiled. 'Sauza Hornitos, and this here little baggy of Mexican Red. Thought they might help you while away the hours.'

'I thought *you* were going to help me do that,' I replied, but it was hard to be smooth with cheese dripping off a face like a bruised grapefruit.

Sherry-Lee looked deeper, however: either that or she was drawn to freaks. 'I'd be happy to while away some time with you, honey. Show me that hand.'

I abandoned the pizza after ninety degrees, washed it down with a slug of tequila and struggled to roll a joint while Sherry-Lee tended to my wounds.

'Swelling's going,' she announced, holding my hands side-by-side for comparison. 'You're going to have a big old scar on the palm of your left hand to match this one here on the right. How d'you get that one?'

A long time ago, in a place called La Mendirosa, an Ulsterman had scarred my palm with the muzzle of a hand-gun. I closed my fingers over his mark. 'Can't remember,' I shrugged, 'maybe I'm developing stigmata. Maybe you got your own personal Jesus.'

She leaned forward and kissed me softly on the lips. 'Wanna go to the beach?'

Beauty and the Beast hit Fort Myers Beach with a coolbox full of beer and a bag of weed. I looked rough, but kind of tough, with my envenomed face and slung arm, and Sherry-Lee looked like a dark-haired angel in a yellow bikini. I'd never shared sand with the sweetest peach on the beach before, and the lascivious, lip-licking grins she attracted from the pumped-up beachboys unnerved me.

Sherry-Lee noticed my discomfort and smiled. 'There's no need to be feeding yourself to no sharks, now, y'hear?'

she drawled, passing me a bottle of bronzer. 'Just rubbing that into my back will show the creeps I'm occupied.'

Or preoccupied. Was she yet mine? Lying in the sun at the edge of the Gulf with a cold Bud and a crackling joint was just fine, but I felt the need to summon clouds. 'Sherry-Lee?'

'Yes, honey?'

'Tell me about Brad.'

She groaned. 'Now why d'ya have to go and spoil the day by bringing up Brad?'

I rolled on to my side and studied her oil-slick belly. ''Cos I don't understand.'

'Understand what, for Pete's sake?'

I took a long drag on the Mexican. 'Why he wants to hurt you.'

'Hurt me?' She pulled herself into a sitting position and looked at me over her Vuarnets. 'Why should he want to hurt me? Beg my forgiveness, maybe, but *hurt* me?'

I shrugged, my attention suddenly drawn to a detail on her bikini. 'Maybe all those firearms and stuff gave me the wrong idea.'

Sherry-Lee lay down again. 'Maybe they did. Now shut up and let that sunshine heal your snakebit hide.'

It was snakebitten, but whatever.

I had always believed envenomation to be an acute condition: you were bitten, then you lived or died; simple as that. Sherry-Lee told me my misconception was common as I lay shivering and sweating in the Florida sunshine with a napkin from Cap'n Jack's Crab Shack stuffed up my bleeding nose.

'You'll be sick for a few days yet. You'll get bruised by the slightest thing, you'll get all covered in blisters, you'll twitch all over like you got ants under your skin, you'll get breathless and then you'll panic and then your nose will start bleeding all over and you'll feel kind of depressed. Best cure is to stay high, and that's why I got you the weed.'

'Mexican weed.'

She let my drift pass her by. 'Some people say that a snakebite can give you clairvoyance. My daddy Pastor Lewis believed it be so, and so do some of the Seminole people.'

I sat up and pulled the bloody tissue from my nostril. 'I'm seeing a week of utter discomfort ahead of me.'

'Maybe you'll see more than that. Is this a good joint?'

I took the spliff from her and licked it into shape. 'See more than that? Like what?'

She tossed her hair, the ringlets sparkling. 'I dunno. My daddy used to get some pretty clear ideas of what was going down while he was suffering. He always said he knew my momma was cheating on him, and even after he forgave her and she left him for Cousin Gary, he knew that Gary would-n't be coming home from the desert. He called her up and he told her that Gary was going to die on active service, and that she should come on home or else she'd be lost, and that he still forgave her and all, but she just took it as Daddy being mean.'

'What happened?' I croaked, taking a long tug on the joint.

Sherry-Lee dug her fingers into the sand. 'Daddy was right: Cousin Gary got blown up in Beirut and Momma got lost.' She stared at her toes.

'I'll let you know if I see anything significant,' I promised. 'Like a stolen pick-up full of firearms.'

She caught her breath, holding her reply on her tongue. Maybe she thought I'd let the matter drop. No chance.

'Brad told me what happened. Told me about his business, how it was set up and how it fell down. No wonder he's mad.'

Her eyes slashed my face. 'Mad? No wonder *Brad's* mad? You mean mad as in crazy, right?'

Tricky question, considering the American use of English. 'I mean mad as in pissed off.'

She jumped to her feet, brushing the sand from her legs. 'What in hell has he got to be mad about?' she seethed.

I shook my head in bemusement. I'd thought the issues were acknowledged between these two, but Sherry-Lee seemed to have no idea why Brad might want to put her in the ground. It didn't cross my mind for one second that she might be bluffing. I struggled to my feet and followed her across the beach to the shoreline. Tiny waves rolled in from the Yucatan to break at her feet as she stared longingly towards Mexico.

'Brad and me were planning to settle down there. Get a place on the coast right over there.' She pointed westwards, beyond the yachts and the tuna boats, across the curvature of the horizon.

'Big *hacienda*, east of Ciudad Victoria.'

A tremor in my arm had crept up to rattle my face like a diamondback's tail. 'I bet it's great down there,' I remarked, hoping she hadn't noticed my twitching.

She turned and looked right at me. 'Never been. Brad recruited some local ass down there. Left me in a two-room apartment in St Louis. And you're telling me that he's mad at me?' She turned and walked away, following the tideline, her footprints melting in the white sand. 'You know what's weird about Brad and me?' she called.

I knew plenty, but I kept it to myself. 'What?'

'We're exactly the same age. I mean exactly, give or take a couple of hours. Same birthday, same year. Is that weird?'

'You should have baked him a cake with a file inside.'

She stopped and turned, waiting for me to catch up. I thought she was going to kiss me.

'Hey! You're a funny guy!' she cried, whirling away and

striding forth. 'I met him in a bar I was working in. He kind of stood out. Country boy from out in the Ozarks, come to the city to make a name. He told me he owned an auto-repair shop – turned out he only worked there. Wasn't hard to figure out: the sign above the door said "Luther's Bodyshop". Me and him started dating, then he moved into my apartment, then he started getting big ideas and making promises he couldn't keep.' She looked up at me, smiled and grabbed my hand. 'That's men all over, ain't it, honey?' She didn't wait for a reply. 'Brad loved four things in this world: guns, hound dogs, weed and me. At least that's what he said. Talked me into this dope-dealing scam he'd been suckered into by this creep who ran a gunshop out in Black Jack, St Louis. This guy Rufus Cooper the Third thought he was Burt Reynolds or something. Brad thought he had hit the big time.'

She shook her head slowly, as though in silent denial of some unspoken memory. 'Rufus sold guns to cops and coke to all the other creeps. Brad was always hanging around there, playing with firearms and getting himself impressed with Rufus's bullshit. Brad thought Rufus had it made – he was always going on about it. But Brad was wrong. Rufus was living on borrowed time. One of his cop customers got wind of the coke sideline and muscled in, offering Rufus jailtime or the opportunity to sideslip a shipment.'

Sherry-Lee raised an eyebrow. 'Now I doubt you know anything about drug dealing, honey, but most times a consignment gets busted the losses are absorbed by the investors. This time, though, word got out that the bust was down to Rufus's buddy. Nothing's proved, but the rumours were enough to get Rufus thrown out of the coke business and straight into debt. That got the creep sweating, but then – can you believe it? – he invites Brad to join him on a hunting trip and when they get back it's been decided that him and Brad are going into big-time weed. Brad's boss Luther fronts him his share of the investment and next thing I know Brad's heading off to Mexico in a Dodge van that him and Luther have converted for the purpose.' She paused to lift a shell from the beach, turning it over and passing it to me. 'That sure is a pretty shell,' she declared.

I stuffed it into my sling. 'I'll keep it for you. So what happened in Mexico?'

She stared over the horizon and shrugged. 'Brad and me were supposed to get married down there and live off the proceeds of his dealing, only it never turned out like that. Way Brad tells it, they were in and out like a couple of pros. That ain't exactly what happened. First off, they don't speak Spanish. Second, no one down there trusts them. The guy who liaised with the growers in Chihuahua was the guy who Rufus'd replaced in the deal. He'd died of a heart-attack in a whorehouse in Carson City and the reason Rufus has been invited in is because none of the other investors in this enterprise want to get involved in the actual trafficking, but it ain't working out so well because none of the *narcos* in Mexico want to do business with the new guy.

'So Brad and Rufus waste most of the summer going back and forth between St Louis and Santa Clara. Come Labor Day, Brad just about knows how to order a beer and a tamale and Rufus is still getting sunburned, but they tie the whole deal down and then they're back, like Cheech and Chong without the intellect. As far as I know, there were five partners in the deal, so the shipment goes five ways. Brad had Rufus tied down to a safety clause – kind of country-style, but I got to admit it was pretty smart for him. Brad's terms were that they sold the whole of their share, no matter how long it took, paid Luther his interest, then sat on the rest of the cash for ninety days before moving. If Rufus didn't like it, he could look elsewhere for his ante, and this was just peachy at the beginning of their partnership. Trouble is, it's taken them the best part of ninety days just to get the weed back to St Louis, and now the guys Rufus owes for the lost cocaine are getting itchy.'

She gave me a sideways look. 'Itchy like they want Rufus scratched, but country-boy Brad is still insisting that the cash is bundled up like sheaves of corn and stored in his daddy's barn until the Harvest Festival. They started bickering and the next thing I know Rufus is knocking on my door, telling me Brad's been busted and is fixing to turn state's evidence against him. No way, I said, but then Rufus tells me that Brad ain't quite the guy I thought he was.'

She stopped walking and slumped on to a bench, as though the memories had made her old. 'Then he shows me a picture. Brad and this goddamned fifteen-year-old Mexican. Guadalupe, she was called – stupid damn name – and she's the niece of the guy who they bought the weed from in Santa Clara. Turns out Brad's been planning on going to Mexico without me, and he's willing to turn state's evidence against his partner to get there.' She shook her head. 'Got a cigarette?'

We sat and smoked in the sunshine, the light and the view and the seaside soundtrack an incongruous setting for Sherry-Lee's ashen nostalgia. Or inventions. I wanted to believe her, but it was hard to trust anybody these days.

'That was that,' she sighed. '*Bang!* All over. No wedding. No future south of the border, and not even an explanation from Brad. Sucks, don't it?'

It sucked.

'Didn't you visit him inside?'

'Sure I did, in spite of Rufus telling me not to. I figured

he'd have an explanation – didn't even care if it was believable. Just figured he'd make the effort for me.'

'What did he say?'

She flicked her dog end on to the sand. 'Didn't say shit. Wouldn't see me. Refused to come out. That said it all to me.'

It didn't say it all to me.

'Did you ever find out how Brad got busted?'

She screwed up her nose as though recalling an irritating detail. 'His boss. Rufus heard it from one of his cop friends.' She leaned forward, resting her forearms on her thighs and staring at the tiny dust devils two-stepping along the pathway. When she sighed, she sighed so hard that it came out as a moan, and then she looked at me, holding back her hair with one hand. 'You heard enough now, honey, or do you want the next episode?'

'What do you think?'

She tilted her head in consideration. 'Okay, but I warn you: it contains scenes of a disturbing nature that may cause you to revise your opinion of me.'

I gave her what I hoped was a long, romantic look. 'My opinion of you will never change.'

She laughed sadly and put her hand on my knee. 'Oh yes it will, honey. You ain't seen the whole farm yet.'

'So show me.'

'Well, would you believe that Rufus and me started seeing each other? He came on all sweet and caring, calling by almost every night to see how I was doing, and before you know it, he's asked me out on a date. We went and had seafood and nice wine and he told me he'd been sweet on me ever since he laid eyes on me, but he'd been too honourable to make a move while him and Brad were business partners. Told me it just ate him up how Brad treated me, and how Brad cheated on me in Santa Clara, and all points in between, and now that Brad had gone and shown his true colours he felt it was time to tell me how he felt. I guess I just lapped it up. Rufus says he's got nothing to lose by telling me all this, seeing as he won't be around much longer. If he don't take off before Brad starts naming names, he's going to end up doing ten to fifteen, and he says he won't be hanging around for that. I ask him where he's going, and he says he's leaving the shop to his brother and going down to Mexico. He left it at that.'

'And then he calls you up the next day, after you've been thinking about it all night, and asks you if you want to go with him.'

Sherry-Lee stared at me for a moment. 'How d'you know that?'

I shrugged. 'Snakebite-induced clairvoyance.'

'So what did I say?'

'You said yes, even though you knew it was a dumb thing to do.'

'And then what happened?'

I waited for my face to stop rattling, flexing my numb fingers inside the sling. 'Don't know, for sure,' I admitted, 'but I reckon Rufus needed you, as Brad's girlfriend, to get the cash off his dad's farm.'

'Smart boy,' she declared, shaking her head. 'Smarter than me. Rufus told me he only wanted his share of the cash, but Brad's daddy would never have given it up to Rufus alone. We went out there on the Saturday and I told him that I needed the money to pay Brad's lawyer and we needed bail money to post in the event the judge let him out. Brad's daddy? He's a nice guy but he's kind of dumb, like Brad, and he just handed us the key to the barn. Right there and then Rufus counts out seventy-five thousand dollars and some change, takes out five G for Brad's dad and gives me half of what's left, good to his word.'

'Sounds fair enough,' I conceded. 'You never went to Mexico, though, did you?'

She hugged herself, the goose-pimples raising her skin, despite the warm sunshine. 'Nor did Rufus,' she said quietly. 'Everything was fine. We were heading back to St Louis from Crawford County when Rufus pulls over at this rest area on I-44 and starts cutting lines of coke, saying he feels like celebrating. Next thing he's unzipped his fly and he's asking me to blow him. I say no. "Why not?" he says. "You blew Brad." I tell him that's none of his goddamn business, and then he grabs me by the back of the neck and starts pulling me towards him. I'm yelling and cursing and scream-ing but there's no one else there, just me and him, and then he's punched me in the mouth and I've punched him right back in the balls and I've hit that central-locking button right on the nose and I'm out of there, running down to the highway. The next thing I know there's a gunshot. I just kind of froze. "You know, I missed you on purpose," he yells, "so come back here before I blow your whore's head off your whore's shoulders."'

Her voice was very quiet, and she bit on her knuckle to hide her trembling lip. 'Martin, I ain't never told nobody about this and I don't rightly know why I'm telling you now.'

I showed her my stigmata. ''Cos I'm your own personal Jesus,' I replied. 'Keep talking.'

'I just walked back to his SUV, meek as a lamb,' she said, 'and he raped me. It didn't take long, and he didn't hit me no more.' She looked at me as though it were an important point. 'He only hit me the once, and then he raped me, and then he zipped up and asked me where I wanted to be dropped. Lot of women go through a lot worse.'

'Hey, come on,' I protested. 'That's bad enough. It's a fucking terrible thing that bastard did to you.'

'That's what I thought at the time,' she nodded. 'You know what I did?' She didn't wait for a reply. 'I picked up one of his guns – the Smith & Wesson 625, since you ask, kind of heavy but easy on the wrist for a .45 – and I told him to get out of the car. He laughed, telling me that the safety was still on, so I shot him right there, *BOOM* – she pointed to my inner thigh – 'and then I told him to git. That time he went. He couldn't walk no more than a couple of yards before he went down, bleeding like a hog. Now it's him doing the yelling and the cursing, and then he's telling me to take off, to take his share and go, and I figured that was what I was going to do anyway. I told him to roll over and crawl across to the trees, and he's saying, "Okay Sherry-Lee, okay, take it easy, Sherry-Lee, I'm going," and he's trying to crawl with one hand raised, but he keeps falling on his face and I'm thinking, You dumb, arrogant, stupid, undeserving individual. He was bleeding real bad by now – the stuff was pumping out of him – and before I knew it I shot him twice more in the back of the head.'

She closed her eyes. 'I'll never forget it. I got sprayed like a truck going through a puddle of blood. Right after I've done it, his cellphone starts ringing.' She shrugged. 'I never answered it. I took his life, his money, his firearms and his car. Drove back to St Louis, dumped the 625 in the Missouri and the SUV in the lot outside his shop. Wiped everything down with Wet-Ones. Took a long shower that scalded my back. Then put the money, the Glock and a suitcase into my old Camaro and drove all the way to Okeechobee without stopping. End of series one.'

She twisted the silver rings on her fingers for a moment, like a schoolgirl who'd just confessed to smoking in the girls' room, then she looked at me coyly. 'How do you like them apples?'

6

Sherry-Lee dropped me back at the trailer at five.

'I'll come by after work,' she promised. 'I'll bring some supper.'

'You work in a restaurant?' I asked. I've always been attracted to waitresses.

She waved with studied vagueness in the direction of the bridge. 'Kinda. I'll see you later.'

She stood me up.

I saw the lights go on in her trailer just after two in the morning and I started clearing up the mess in mine. At three I looked across the void between us and saw the flicker of late night TV from behind her nets. Maybe I should have just gone to bed, but I hadn't been anticipating retiring alone, so I grabbed the Hornitos, the weed and a packet of smokes and went visiting.

Sherry-Lee met me at the top of her steps, wrapped in her inflammable housecoat with her arms crossed high on her chest. She needed rest and reflection, she said; she was just tired and she'd see me tomorrow. I nodded, feeling both dumb and disappointed, but I managed a smile. She blew me a kiss in return and told me not to worry.

It hadn't occurred to me to worry, until then.

Calling up the coin shops, working through the list, catching up on the admin and doing what I wasn't being paid to do kept my mind under control the following day. The USPS called three times, dropping security-sealed padded envelopes of old gold, and the regular postman delivered six cheques to the front desk for the bullion I'd sold. Gene had spent three days teaching me how to keep the cash flow on the level, but his methods were always too anal to comprehend and I had resorted to my own system of dead reckoning. As far as I could remember, I had spent just over twenty-five grand and recouped nearly fifteen, with another ten or so in hand. Gene called at five-fifteen for my report and at five-thirty I shut up the shop, switched on the TV, and started worrying.

Drifting through the channels on Gene's RCA, I sat and wondered, a rudderless ship with decks awash in an ocean of voices, pictures and unabsorbed information. I couldn't believe what I'd heard down at the beach, and I couldn't believe she'd told me and then blown me off later that night. Come to think of it, I couldn't believe a rattlesnake had changed my blood chemistry. But it had all happened. A post-traumatic shiver rattled my spine and I shuddered like a man who'd just come in from the cold. Maybe it was nothing to do with me. Maybe she'd just needed to be alone with her memories. Maybe she'd just had a bad night waitressing. Maybe she had thought it unfair to unburden herself on me. Maybe all that talk of Brad had backfired on me, reminding her of what she had lost instead of showing her what she had gained. Maybe the marks on my hands were the proof of nothing more than a pistol-whipping and a snakebite. Maybe I was nobody's personal Jesus after all.

On the obverse of the coin, however, I had a bag of Mexican weed, what was left of a bottle of Sauza, five cans of cold beer and the trailer to myself. My gold purchases were up to date and inbound, and with Gene upstate there was plenty of hot water and room in front of the mirror. It was Friday night and the woman I was falling in love with had promised she would see me tonight. Considering that I'd landed here less than a month ago with twenty-odd bucks and a handbag, America was treating me pretty well. I should have been delighted, or happy, or at the very least content, and yet, like Turn Back Jack, I had a terrible feeling that something bad was about to happen.

Maybe it was just the venom poisoning my mind. I slipped my arm out of the sling and examined my hand. The oedema was still fresh and shiny, my fingers like a bunch of ripe aubergines that should have been kept in the fridge. I couldn't remember whether icepacks were a good idea or not, but I figured that the walk to the vending machine would be therapeutic in itself.

It was sundowner time at Bridgeview, and as I walked along our dusty street with the plastic bucket swinging in my good hand, sprawling men in boardshorts and singlets called lazy greetings. Some rested in lawn chairs, their feet in the dust, while others tended barbecues, leaning back from heat and yelling at kids not to come too near or go too far. The Florida sunset smelled of smoke: Marlboro, Cubanos and Mexican weed; car exhausts and the sweet summer smell of a two-stroke lawnmower. Above all, the Gulf Coast smelled of mesquite and hickory as fish, fowl and prime rib sizzled beneath a pink-striped sky. I sucked it all in, letting the peace and the comfort promised by other people's dinner chase the rattlers into the undergrowth. The snakebite had given me clairvoyance, and now I could see that nothing bad was going to happen.

Brad, however, had other ideas.

A trio of police cars, two marked and one unmarked, were raising dust as they cruised through the park towards the home of the still-missing Solomon Bender. I'd been watching them pass with the prickly nonchalance of the disingenuous when a huge cherry-red Chevy Silverado pick-up creaked to a halt at my side.

'Good God Almighty, Marvin,' cried Brad from the cab. 'What in hell are you doing here?'

I gaped at my reflection in his shades, trying to form a reason.

Brad gave me one, as Clinton yelled his opinion of me to the world. 'Cleaning the johns or what? Shut the fuck up, Clinton, you goddamned idiot!'

I followed his nod to the bucket in my one good hand. 'Kind of,' I grinned. 'Gotta start somewhere in this great land.'

He nodded again, slowly, as though unconvinced. 'So you work here?'

'Yeah,' I replied. 'Here and there.'

'What you do to your arm?'

'Oh, this . . .' There was little conviction in my voice. 'Burned it. On a barbecue.' The dog narrowed his eyes in disgust. I returned his glare, with bells on.

'And they still got you working?'

I shrugged. 'I got no rights in this country, and I need the money.'

Brad shook his head in pitiful bemusement. 'Seen Sherry-Lee?'

It was a question that required a careful and considered reply. Whatever I told Brad now would form the foundation of our relationship, however long it lasted. 'Hell, no,' I blurted, blinking as a vision went up in smoke like a rudely interrupted dream. Frantically I scoured the air for a memory, but I saw only Clinton and Brad, their laughter drifting like rodent ghosts towards the Gulf.

'Wanna get a beer somewheres?'

'Sure,' I nodded. 'Why not?'

'What about the bathrooms?'

'Hell no, let's go to a proper bar, Brad.'

He closed his eyes like it was him talking to the moron. 'I meant your job: cleaning the bathrooms.'

I tossed the bucket into the back of the pick-up and climbed in. 'Fuck 'em.'

Part 2

7

'Surprised you ain't run into my ex-fiancée,' mused Brad as we joined the traffic heading over the bridge for a night on the coast. 'I have it on good authority that she is still at large in these parts.'

'Don't get out much,' I shrugged by way of explanation, digging the dog in the ribs with my bandaged elbow. 'All I do is work and get high. Wanna smoke?'

'Absolutely,' he replied, straight-faced. 'I been buzzing like a heavily armed little bee all the way from east St Louis on some fine crystal meth and I could do with unwinding a little before the evening gets going.' He rubbed the speed-wash from his lips with the back of his hand and spat black into a Starbucks cup.

I began rolling a joint one-handed, ignoring the sensation that every one of my internal organs had shrivelled a little through fear, apprehension and the disappointment familiar to only the truly stupid. Once again I'd accepted a ride from Brad, and I could feel that nothing had changed. He still looked as though he'd mistaken Limp Bizkit for a fashion house, but he wore his trailer trash labels like they were his alone. His necklace seemed bigger than ever.

'Where've you been for so long?'

'Locked down on twice dailies by my fucked-up parole officer. I missed an appointment a few weeks back and he slapped a fifty-day double-reporting order on me. Kinda fucked up my travel plans for a while. Been training Clinton here to hunt hog.'

'That's nice,' I conceded. 'I see you've upgraded the gold chain.'

'This?' He rolled the vulgar rope between greasy fingers. 'Ten point nine mil. switchblade curb. Fourteen K, man, twenty-four inches, one-fifty grams. Classy!' He tossed me a glance like he expected me to be impressed, then shook his head at my apparent ignorance. 'Pearls before swine,' he sighed. 'Like you'll ever need to know about gold.'

I let it pass. 'You packing?'

He conceded a tight little smile. 'Of course. USP and an Eighteen.'

'Glock?'

He pulled off his shades and looked at me, blue eyes glittering in an unkempt face. 'A Glock indeed. I'm impressed with you, Marvin. You learn that at citizenship school?'

'It's Martin,' I reminded him, lighting the joint. 'Marvin's some other guy.'

'Whatever,' he replied, his attention focused on the neon strip at the end of the bridge.

'So where am I likely to find my ex-fiancée on that there Redneck Riviera?' He took the joint and sucked a quarter from its length.

I shook my head. 'Don't ask me. What makes you think she works on this side of the bridge?'

Brad blew smoke at the dog and pointed downtown. 'See them coloured lights? That's where she'll be, and we're gonna have fun tracking her down.'

We pulled in to the State Rec car park, its sandy surface littered with beer cans, dog-ends and gritty prophylactics. Brad reversed into a slot, checked his surroundings, pushed the muttering dog to the floor and placed two black hand-guns on the bench between us.

'What do you reckon: HK or Glock? Just what is the well-dressed redneck packing on the coast this season?'

'Neither,' I replied. My heart rate was knocking like a locked-out kid on All-Hallows and my mouth was drying up. 'No one packs here. It's a fun place, for Christ's sake.'

Brad made a conciliatory gesture with his hands. 'Okay, fair enough. But if they *did* pack, which would it be? Huh?'

I dragged the last from the joint. 'Like I say: neither. I'm not coming with you if you're taking either of them.' I shuddered to think what Gene would say if he chanced upon us now.

Brad gave me a long, hard look that could have gone either way, then smiled. 'Okay. No guns, you crazy fucking Brit. One more question, though.'

'Go on,' I sighed in weak-kneed relief.

'That weed we smoked: is it Mexican?'

'Dunno,' I shrugged. 'Scored it on the beach. Why?'

Brad was looking at me as though he didn't quite trust me. It was an expression I'd seen on a lot of faces. 'Just wondered.'

He hid the ignition keys under the pick-up, spat his tobacco wad into the dust and slapped me on the back. 'Let's go rekindle some old flames. Guard the car, Clinton.'

It was early evening and the boardwalk was busy with slow-moving, easily diverted vacationers, drifting from one fast-food stand to the next via discount stores, factory outlets and craft stalls set out along their route like stations of the cross. Off the streets, up the stairs and on verandas overlooking a darkening sea it was cocktail time, sundown special, happy hour or whatever it took to get the party started early. For me, it never took much.

We took a seat at a tiki bar lit by a fiery sky and availed ourselves of the Sunset Two-For-One.

'What's a Caloosahatchee Crybaby, miss?' asked Brad.

The barmaid bit her lip. 'Vodka, tequila, white rum, gin and sambuca with a dash of Collins mix in it and a shot of one-fifty one on the side. It'll make you cry, baby.'

We drank two each, but they only made us reflective and we didn't find Sherry-Lee.

'We won't,' decided Brad as we hit the street again. 'Not here. It's cheap, but it ain't sleazy enough. But don't worry: the booze will lead us to the cooze. Check it out: pitchers three bucks!' The news cheered him up no end.

When I walked into a bar, people turned to look and kept looking. When Brad walked in, they looked then looked away. It was an effect I aspired to, but tonight my ambition was to stay ahead of my new best friend. It was crucial that he did not stumble across Sherry-Lee, and essential that he remained convinced that I had no idea of her whereabouts. This last requirement was easily met, for I truly did not know where she was, but it made not finding her a dangerous game of chance. I figured I could increase the odds by reducing Brad's mobility, and control the worst possible outcome by knowing his intentions.

'What you going to do if you find her, Brad?'

He was staring through his beer with bloodshot eyes, waiting for the foam to subside. 'Kill her, I reckon,' he mumbled.

I lit a Camel and shook my head. 'What's the point?'

He turned his head slowly, tossing me a tired and murderous look that was out of place in this heaving, seaside good-times bar.

'I told you once. Ain't nothin' changed.'

Loads had changed, but I couldn't tell him what or why. 'Okay,' I nodded, 'kill her. Drink up!' I poured him another beer. 'How you going to accomplish this killing?'

Brad raised a finger to his unshaven lip. 'Hush your mouth, boy – it's supposed to be secret.' He finished the sentence with a belch. 'How am I going to do it? I been thinking about it a lot and I reckon just like that' – he snapped his fingers – 'is the best way for all parties. Most people want to make a performance out of the affair, with an overture and a speech, but I figure the act itself has all the drama you need. What's the point in putting on a show and trying to make an impression on someone who ain't going to exist one millisecond after the finale? It's not as though you're giving them something to think about, is it? I guess all the soliloquising and justification is for the benefit of the party of the first part, and it ain't worth the effort or the risk. You with me?'

I hadn't realised that Brad had put so much thought into the matter. I nodded weakly.

He leaned across the table. 'If I was going to kill you, Marty, you would probably never know. One minute you'd be scrubbing out the ladies' room back there at the trailer park, and the next . . . nothing.'

He mimed an explosion of brain, bone and blood with a chillingly simple movement of his hand away from his face and emphasised it with a discreet sound-effect, then raised his eyebrows. 'You get what I'm saying? If you want revenge, if you want the party of the second part to suffer, then why kill them? Why not keep them alive?'

He sat back and smiled. 'You'd keep them alive, wouldn't you? Keep 'em hog-tied in a shack way up in the woods, half starved and naked, maybe swing by and amputate something every once in a while, wouldn't you? That's the *sensible* thing to do, ain't it? Am I right or am I right?'

He shook his head. 'Just kill 'em, that's my way. I ain't into all that psycho stuff.'

151

'Yeah, but you're still committing an act of vengeance,' I argued. 'You're killing her to get even.'

Brad looked left and right, then leaned over the pitcher, pouring powdered speed into the froth and stirring it with an oil-stained finger. 'That should pep the brewski up a bit,' he grinned, 'and no, I ain't killing no one to get even. I'm killing them because they have committed a capital offence. To whit: murder, theft and betrayal.'

'Theft's not a capital offence.'

'I'll be the judge of that,' he declared. 'Want some of this here crystal pilsner?' He topped up our glasses and lit a cigarette. 'All I'm doing is what our Federal Government should have done a long time ago – getting a return on my tax dollar, so to speak, although it's me paying for the judicial process in gas and bullets and me carrying out the sentence. Makes you wonder what those goddamned judges and politicians do with their time, don't it?'

Brad had clearly given this matter careful consideration, and he wasn't finished yet. 'How many people died in gun-related homicides in the UK last year? Don't know? I'll tell you: ninety-seven. Despicable, ain't it? How many do you reckon died in France?'

'More?' I sighed.

'Forty-four. Japan: ninety-two. Wanna know how many of us Americans died in the same period from the same cause?'

I took a deep breath and doubled the figure I'd thought of. 'Fifteen hundred.'

Brad shook his head with a grin of delight. 'Twenty-eight thousand eight hundred and seventy-four. Nearly thirty thousand people died from gunshot wounds in this great nation last year, and that was a motherfuckin' *improvement* on the year before.' He looked furtively around the crowded bar as though he could make up the shortfall, then swilled the last of his lager. 'C'mon, janitor. I'm deputising you. We got an arrest to make.'

We made it as far as a dive called the Harley Mills. Tourists came here only if they rode bikes and grew their hair long enough to stop their necks getting red. We wove through the staggered ranks of parked motorcycles, up a short flight of wooden steps and into a dark world of smoke, spilled beer and chainsaw blues guitar. Greybeards with bandannas slugged shots at the bar while mustachioed mullets danced with wide-hipped Valium queens and drained cold yellow beer from soft plastic cups. The house band had reduced communication to a variety of whoops and yells, and, in spite of the good time going down, it seemed likely that misunderstandings could easily be reached in a bar that declared itself to be the last resort of what was left of America. Nothing much looked left in here: the Stars and Bars fluttered like bleeding hearts on every denim sleeve while bald eagles soared on hairy arms and barrel chests. If ever I had seen a place where scoring an ounce of weed was a possibility, this was it. The Harley Mills: I committed the name to memory and concentrated on making a good impression. Brad achieved the exact opposite.

I noticed his absence only after the disturbance. The band had been playing a scorching, feedback-heavy version of 'Who Do You Love' when the sweaty, oppressive atmosphere was ionised by the sudden and violent discharge of energy that accompanies a drunken slight in a macho bar. The Telecaster screamed on while tables crashed to the floor, Harley bitches used unladylike language and heavyset men with bald heads and beards interfered in what was essentially a private dispute between Brad and an overweight Angel called Chopper. I wished I could have ignored his plight, finished my beer and gone home, but my best chance of preventing his stumbling into Sherry-Lee's place of work was to stick with him and steer him in the wrong direction. I poured back my Bud, shook my head and went out into the street. Brad had been dragged way beyond the outermost Fat Tail and left lying on his back in the weeds and laughing with a bleeding nose and a split eyebrow. His loss was Sherry-Lee's gain, and I lit him a joint as consolation.

'Still got my chain,' he grinned, wincing as the smoke reached his bruised ribs. 'How do I look?'

'Put it this way,' I replied, stashing my weed back into my sling, 'neither of us is going to pull now.'

We bought a six-pack from a 7-Eleven and drank two on the way back to the parking lot. Clinton paced the bench seat, fogging up the glass with his hoarse barking as Brad stumbled around, trying to remember where he'd hidden the keys.

'Process of elimination,' he slurred when we had gained entry to the pick-up. 'I found the keys by a process of elimination. I'll find my ex-fiancée by a process of elimination. Simple, ain't it? Yes, I love you too, Clinton, baby.'

I nodded. 'Sure is, but that's all for tonight.'

Brad checked his face in the rearview, then stuffed a plug of tobacco into his jaw. 'Ain't nothing wrong here a sticking plaster and a change of clothes won't fix.' He looked me up and down and shook his head. 'Wish I could say the same for you, buddy.'

Cleaned up and bandaged, wearing a T-shirt that declared 'Outlaw Handguns and Only Outlaws Will Have Handguns' and faded jeans, Brad looked surprisingly presentable and depressingly deranged. He rolled through Fort Myers Beach at a steady fifteen miles per hour, stopping for pedestrians and catcalling girls like a regular good-ole boy with a half-witted cousin and a nodding dog out to have some honky-tonk fun. The pistols lay beside his stacked heels, out of sight but easily reached, and when he pulled up alongside a parked police car I felt a surge of adrenalin that cleared my head better than an electric shock.

'Say, Officer, sir,' he called. 'Know any good titty bars round here?'

The cops were sucking soda from twenty-ounce cups, and it seemed that they knew several establishments of that nature in the immediate vicinity. The best, they agreed, was on Route 41 south of Calico Road. Topless only, they warned, but one could buy a beer there. Brad thanked them with a touch to the brim of his cap, wished them a quiet night, and drove away.

I took long, deep drags of the warm evening air, letting myself be driven out of town on the stampeding horns of a dilemma. I could save Sherry-Lee's life by telling Brad the truth about his good buddy Rufus Cooper III, and, by saving her life, I would lose her. I could keep her secret to myself, and deny her to Brad, thus losing her to us both. Alternatively, I could kill Brad, although my chances of success were slightly less than those of Gene arriving back at the trailer with a carload of cheerleaders and a trunkful of weed. I looked across the cab at my tormentor, feeling very small and helpless, an ingénue in a foreign land, Brad was drumming on the steering wheel, using the dog's head as a high hat and singing along to Metallica.

'Off to Never-never Land,' he bellowed. 'I could have been a drummer, you know,' he announced.

'Doesn't surprise me,' I replied.

We spent an hour watching bored dancers with glazed eyes, rubber breasts and wide hips making out with slippery chrome poles at a block-built facility on the Tamiami Trail called the Stud Club. The bar was filled with whooping, shiny-faced students in football shirts and boardshorts and the thudding rock soundtrack precluded any conversation. Shaven-headed security men policed the pit between the bar and the stage, limiting contact with the girls to the purely fiscal, while sweating barmen slid pitchers of froth to thirsty voyeurs. Brad slipped a bouncer a twenty, but all it bought him was a shake of the head.

I poured back a large, watered-down Jack and grabbed Brad, dragging him through the crowd to the entrance lobby. 'See that?' I asked, pointing at a perspex frame displaying red-eyed Polaroids of the cast. 'She ain't here.'

Brad shook his head and pushed a wad of Kodiak into his cheek. 'Got some intel,' he announced. 'Full nudity and no beer. It's called Alligator Strip.'

We swung right before the bridge, following a dirt track into an unlit swamp. Alligator Strip was a sprawling firetrap of nailed plywood and paint on a neon-lit island in a dark sawgrass sea. Rusty gas-guzzlers, shiny pick-ups and beaten-up sub-compacts were scattered through the dusty parking lot like a soiled sample of US society. Brad parked near the road, hid the keys, and led me to the door, where a bouncer who worked hard at looking threatening was refusing entry to a group of college kids. He glanced at Brad and raised the red rope.

'I got to pee,' said Brad. 'Go get a pair of stools at the bar.'

I'd heard a familiar muffled bassline out in the parking lot, and as I pushed through the heavy doors and into the bar, the song hit me hard in the face.

Alice Cooper.

'Poison'.

A naked, oil-slicked girl was twisting herself around a

greased pole on a harshly lit stage. As she spun, her dark hair followed, snapping in perfect time with the beat. She wore earrings like windchimes, a belly-ring and a pair of cowboy boots. Her body was shaved smooth, and as I stood mesmerised at the door, she threw a smile at her unseen audience, turned and took the catwalk backstage, her exit perfectly timed to the end of the song. I stared slack-jawed into her wake.

I'd found Sherry-Lee.

I turned to leave and walked into Brad.

'Titty-bar thataway,' he grunted, pushing me towards the wooden horseshoe that surrounded the stage.

'I know,' I stammered. 'I got to pee, though. Gimme some of that speed.'

Amphetamine sulphate is not praised for its positive effect on the intellect, but I snorted two lines because I wanted to think fast. Sherry-Lee was a stripper, and the revelation was crowding my head. How long before she came on again? How many piercings had I spotted? Had Brad left the firearms in the truck? Was that a birthmark I'd noticed on her pudenda, or a tattoo? I needed to warn her, to tell her to get the hell away from Alligator Strip right now. If that failed, I needed to get Brad away from Alligator Strip.

I licked my finger and stabbed it into Brad's wrap, wishing that the acrid taste was that of cocaine and not this poor man's buzz. I held my breath as the body-checking flash-flood of a speed rush washed through me, steadying myself on the graffiti-smeared stall. I took a deep breath, went through the motions of tearing toilet paper and flushing, rubbed my face, lit a fag and stumbled out of the men's room. I needed to find a route backstage.

Jump-suited early eighties rock was rolling in from the bar as I followed a corridor down to a fire exit. A sign warned that the door was alarmed, but I pushed it open anyway, scaring the smoke from the bunch of college kids who had just been refused entry at the main door. I jerked my good thumb over my shoulder and they got the message. Staying close to the walls and deep in the shadows, I moved around the building, trying every door I found. Sherry-Lee's Mazda was parked at the back, one of fifteen or so belonging, I presumed, to the cast and crew of Alligator Strip. A pool of light spilled on the dirt beneath a cloud of steam from a kitchen window, and it was only when I saw the orange glow of a cigar that I knew I'd been spotted.

'What you looking for, bro?'

'The dancers' dressing room,' I replied. 'It's not what you're thinking: it's urgent. I got to get a message to one of the girls.'

He moved into the light, a huge black man in stained cook's coveralls. 'Why don't you ask at the bar?'

'Can't,' I explained. 'I'm a follower of the Church of Jesus Christ with Signs Following and we believe that man is damned by the sight of naked flesh. It's a pain sometimes.'

He raised his eyebrows. 'I'll bet it is. Give me the message and I'll pass it on.'

I hesitated. 'It might be better if you just show me where the dressing room is . . .'

He cut me short with a long, howling laugh. 'No way, bro. You'll see so much naked booty in there it'll set your Sign Following ass on fire. Give me the message. Who's it for?'

'Sherry-Lee.'

He shook his head.

'Ain't no Sherry-Lee here.'

''Course there is,' I protested. 'I've just seen her.'

The cook started thinking.

I ran ahead and corrected his thoughts. 'I've just seen her car, I mean: the Mazda, over there.'

'That ain't no Sherry-Lee's car. That there's Darlene's car. What you want with her?'

Darlene? She had a special talent for choosing names.

'Just tell her that Martin's out back, and it's, like, mega-urgent.'

The cook looked doubtful. 'How urgent?'

I thrust my swollen hand from the folds of my beer-stained sling and waggled the aubergine digits in his face. '*This* urgent. I got bit by a snake while praising the Lord tonight.'

The cook sucked air and shook his head in disgust. 'Man, you should try my church next Sunday. We all going to heaven too, you know, and all we do is bang tambourines. Wait here.'

Sherry-Lee stomped out in a silver bikini. She was not pleased to see me. 'What you doing here, Martin?'

I shrugged feebly. I was beginning to feel a little unwell. 'Sherry-Lee, I wouldn't have come, honestly, but Brad made me.'

She put her hands on her damnably naked hips and cocked her head. The glitter paste on her chest caught the kitchen light and sparkled. 'Martin, you got to stop bringing Brad into every damn thing. You want to see my naked ass up on stage, you go sit at the bar and pay like everyone else. Be a man about it, Martin, and stop skulking round the dumpsters.'

'He can't see your naked ass up on stage, Darlene,' interrupted the cook. 'It's against his religion.'

Sherry-Lee sighed and tapped her booted foot. 'Brutus P. Desoto, you go flip some burgers, now, y'hear,' she advised, 'before I get real mad.'

'Sherry-Lee, listen, you got it all wrong,' I cried. 'Brad made me come and Brad is sitting out there in the bar, waiting for me to come back from the men's room and you to come back on stage. Go see for yourself! You got to split, right now, a.s.a.p. He's got a Glock and a USP, and he could be packing either. Go see!'

She cocked a hip and studied me in the greasy light, working her jaw as though chewing over my assertion. At last she took a deep breath and spoke. 'Okay. I'll go see, and then what? You think that skunk is going to run me out of my place of work? You think he's going to stop me earning an honest wage?'

I nodded hard. 'I think he's going to shoot you. I've always thought he was going to shoot you. Think about it: he only knows what Rufus Cooper the Third told him. He hasn't heard your side . . .'

'He ain't going to hear it, neither,' she insisted, wagging a finger in my face and sounding like Dolly Parton on speed. 'Now you either git back to the trailer park or git back to the bar and watch me wiggle. I don't want to hear no more of it.' She whirled back into the club, bolting the kitchen door behind her.

I turned and jogged back round to the front, my mind filled with that familiar feeling of guilty impotence.

Three fat men with skinny little beards stood straightening their cuffs in the doorway as three grazed college kids clambered out of the dust at their feet.

'What's in the sling?' asked one as I re-entered the club.

'Snakebite,' I growled.

'Way to go!' he cried, slapping me on the back. 'Have a good evening.'

Brad was coming out as I was going in. 'Where the fuck have you been?'

I opened my mouth to reply but Brad had already forgotten the question.

'Let's go,' he said. 'I've asked: there ain't no Sherry-Lee working here. I got the address of another place written here on the back of my hand. Let's go check it out. I bought you a Coke. Where did you go?'

I didn't answer. He didn't care.

As we made our way back to the highway, Brad sighed 'I should've kept a picture of her.'

I closed my eyes and looked at the image of Sherry-Lee: skinny, cold, oiled and naked but for a pair of earrings, a belly-ring and a pair of cowboy boots, spinning around that pole and burned into the front of my mind. It was a shame that such an intimate encounter had taken place in so public a place, but it would have been churlish to complain. I called the image back for another look, wondering about that birthmark, then lit a cigarette and lay back in my seat. The tension of the past hours had exhausted me, the combination of cheap beer and poor-quality speed leaving me itchy and polluted. The early hours airwaves were surrendered to the slurred requests, drunken whoops and heartbroken dedications of the listening public, their choice of music as predictable as a strip-club parking lot.

'Jesus!' breathed Brad as we pulled up at Monty Venus, a purpose-built adult-entertainment facility with its own cable channel, website and strip of neon. 'These suckers got their own twenty-four-hour porno store! You got a VCR at your place?'

I shook my head. 'Club's closed, too.'

Brad looked at me. 'Got any weed left?'

'A bit.'

'Cool. Got any beer?'

'We got four cans.'

'Outstanding. Wanna learn how to shoot?'

I shrugged. Only a fool would refuse an education.

'This is the magazine,' explained Brad, one eye closed against the joint in the corner of his mouth, 'and this here's the ammunition.' He placed a neat polystyrene box with a red cardboard slip cover on the trunk of the pick-up.

'You put these here forty-cal. babies into the magazine like this, making sure that each round is ahead of the last. See?'

He plucked shiny copperheads from the box, pressing each down into the magazine. A low mist draped softly over the sawgrass, cloaking any witness to my instruction in this dark art.

'Now we place the charged magazine into the butt of the weapon and we press it home.'

A solid click affirmed that the magazine was home.

'You don't do none of this Vin Diesel slamming of the magazine,' warned Brad, sucking hard on the joint and passing it to me. 'It ain't professional. Pass me my beer. You see where that dumb hound dog went to?'

Didn't know, didn't care.

Brad took a long slurp, belched and beckoned me closer. 'This here's the slide, see? It moves backwards and forwards. What we need to do is get a round from the magazine, here' – he tapped the butt – 'to the chamber, here, and to do it we bring the slide firmly back like so, and let it go forward under its own steam.' He smiled as the slide rolled home with an oily click. 'I love that goddamned noise,' he declared. 'It's what a promise sounds like, ain't it?' He cocked an ear at another sound. 'Quick, go crank that radio up.'

'Brown Sugar' filled the twilight and Brad couldn't help dancing as he continued his firearms introductory course.

Above us the stars twinkled in the velvet night like the reflected eyes of a lake full of 'gators and Clinton rustled through the brittle grass like a canine cottonmouth.

'See what else we did when we pulled that slide back? We cocked the hammer here, so what we got now is a weapon that is locked and loaded. All we got to do now is turn this here little switch from "S" to "F" and we're good to go.' He flipped the pistol, grabbing it by the barrel, and offered me the butt. 'Go ahead, Marty: express yourself!'

The Rolling Stones faded away and the rum-soaked DJ dedicated the next track to Brandi over there in Lehigh Acres as the CCR warned of a 'Bad Moon Rising'. I took the USP from Brad and searched his face for a motive.

'She's a beauty, ain't she?' he smiled, and I wondered if he meant Sherry-Lee.

I turned the weapon over in my hand, the engravings on the cold-forged barrel catching the pale starlight. 'What's USP stand for?'

Brad shrugged. 'Unbeatable Stopping Power. Unfaithful Stripper's Punishment. How do you feel about her?'

We were a long way down a one-way track in a fog-bound swamp, and the radio was predicting stormy weather. I concentrated hard on acting dumb.

'She's a beauty,' I enthused. 'I like her a lot.'

Clinton emerged from the weeds, mud-streaked and dripping, looking over his shoulder as he walked into the side of the truck.

'So get your own,' grunted Brad, his eyes deep in the shadow of his cap. 'Mine's spoken for.'

I was holding his weapon, locked and loaded and good to go, and he was standing less than four feet from the high-visibility front sight. A body could lie out here a long time before it was found. Brad took a step backwards, shifting his weight and letting his right hand hang loosely by his side. That brand-new Glock 18 was somewhere under his shirt.

'Have a go,' he urged.

'What should I aim at?' I asked, wasting time. The spit had turned to mud in my mouth and my back was wet with pungent sweat. I wished I was playing backgammon with Gene in the trailer rather than brinkmanship with Brad out here in Alligator Alley.

Brad shrugged. 'Aim at whatever's in your way,' he advised, tilting his head to put a spark on to the roach in the corner of his mouth. 'You don't need to aim – just point with your index finger and pull the trigger with your middle finger. Bullet tends to go where you're pointing. Suck it and see.'

A bell tolled between my ears, and somewhere further away, beyond the thudding of my heart and the tattoo of my pulse, I could hear the wind moaning as tumbleweed rolled through my empty soul. I stood in a night beyond reason, way past the artificial restraints of the mind. The moon had yet to rise and there was no time left for a considered response, for premeditation. I felt myself falling, sucked away from Brad's sombre silhouette, the pistol like a hammer in my sweating hand, dragging me down with its metaphorical weight.

What I did with this tool would define me. *Carpe noctem.*

I raised the USP, feeling something shrivel deep inside as I placed it carefully on the hood of the pick-up. 'Don't like loud noises,' I explained weakly.

Brad shrugged, spat tobacco juice into the dirt and made the pistol safe. 'Well, at least you know what to do if the time ever comes. C'mon, let's go back to your place.'

It wasn't a request, and I was in no position to refuse.

Brad sang all the way back to Bridgeview while I brooded

in hungover silence. The precise snap of a slide coming home was more than the sound of a promise. At close range it was the voice of the Devil himself, offering for one moment the power of God. A firearm took away the need for superior strength, grisly invention and bloody commitment, reduced determination to a whim and concurrent anguish to the duration of a muzzle flash. It promised instant effect with irreversible consequences, the power to put a man into the ground with less effort than it took to scratch an itch or flick a switch. The firearm didn't care how one coped with the aftermath: the Devil liked caprice and cared little for the detail. Some men are capable of gambling all on a crap game. Brad had handed me the dice and waited for me to shoot. Destiny had offered me a shortcut. The opportunity to deliver Sherry-Lee from evil had been in the palm of my good right hand and I'd let it drop.

A whole armful of rattlesnake bites wouldn't balance out that one.

Neither of us noticed the police car as we rolled into Bridgeview. It was parked alongside the reception building, a yellow internal light and the squelch of the circuit keeping its overweight occupant awake. He hit the pick-up with a beam and Brad cursed, his face a plastic mask.

'What the fuck are cops doing out here?'

'Some kid went missing last week,' I explained.

'Go talk to him,' he hissed. 'Be cool, for Christ's sake!'

I stepped into the beam, sucking on a wintergreen Lifesaver that tasted like cough medicine and was unlikely to save anybody. The cop, however, was just counting the days.

'Heading home, son?' he asked.

I nodded earnestly. 'Yes sir.'

'What number?'

'Thirty-seven D,' I replied. 'Here's the key.'

He looked at the big plastic key fob for a moment, then swung his gaze up to me. 'Glad you ain't working for me tomorrow,' he declared after a moment. 'Keep your lights dimmed as you drive through the park.'

Sherry-Lee's Mazda was parked right outside her trailer and her TV was clearly keeping her company. I led Brad up to the door of 37 D with my fists clenched and my shoulders hunched, like a man waiting for the call. There was no reason why he should recognise her car – the last time he'd seen her she had been driving a Camaro – but after the events of the past twelve hours I was ready for each and every disappointment.

Once inside, Brad grabbed the tequila, punched the radio, fell into Gene's chair and started rolling a joint. I slumped on the sofa, barely registering the Grateful Dead, and when I looked up, Brad was asleep.

Gene woke me at zero seven hundred with a call from a hotel in Jacksonville. He read out a list of names and numbers that I tried to copy down as accurately as my double vision would allow, then asked for my report in return. I briefed him with the current sales and purchase data, listing the total expenditure and detailing the cheques that had arrived for items sold. Mindful that I didn't have a car, he asked me to make the twenty-five-mile round-trip to the autoteller to pay in the cheques, to mail brochures to all the new contacts, to keep purchase expenditure down to ten grand, to clean out the aircon filter and tidy up the yard and not to go anywhere near Lake Okeechobee on Sunday. He didn't once ask me about my arm.

'Anything else to report?'

'Er, not much,' I replied, turning my back on the snoring, homicidal, car-stealing, arms-dealing parole-breaker slumped in Gene's favourite chair with a bottle of tequila and a half-rolled joint. 'There've been a few cops sniffing around the trailer park – they've even got a guard on the gate now.'

'Yeah, well, it's about time they rounded up those fucking illegals and shipped their asses back down to Bananaland,' drawled Gene. 'Anything else?'

'It's nothing to do with illegals,' I retorted icily. 'It's to do with that kid, Solomon.'

Gene worked hard on knowing nothing about his neighbours. In his business, it was a failing. 'What kid Solomon?'

'The one who's gone missing,' I explained. 'They think he's been abducted.'

A crackle rode three hundred miles down the copper wire to Jacksonville, turned round, and crackled back.

'Gene?' It was getting hard not to jump to conclusions. 'Gene?'

He coughed. 'Mind the store. Avoid the cops. If they do a door to door, which they will, tell them nothing. You've got nothing to hide, so make sure they know that. One more thing: when did this little bastard go missing?'

'Week last Thursday.'

'Excellent: where were we?'

I blew air, frowning. My memory was shot full of holes this morning. 'Er, coin fair? Heading to a coin fair?' I winced as Brad shifted in his sleep and farted.

Gene was dragging his memory, too, but in a cleaner atmosphere. 'We were in a motel, the Friendship Motel. I paid cash, so it's our word against theirs. Remember, the Friendship.' He hung up, promising to call back in four hours, leaving me cold and confused in the Sunshine State.

'Who was on the phone?' croaked Brad, like he had a right to ask.

'Mate of mine,' I replied. 'That kid who went missing?

The cops are coming out here to do a door-to-door investigation.' I nodded towards the truck. 'That pick-up your property, Brad?'

'Shit, no,' he groaned, rising unsteadily to his feet. 'I was planning on leaving today anyways. Where's the shower?'

'Oh no,' I warned, shaking my head. 'Me first, then you. Make some coffee.'

I shrugged off my sling and let the dirty elastic bandage drop to the floor of the shower stall. The rattlesnake's damage upon my arm was in decline, and the anticipated clairvoyance had failed to occur. It was disappointing that an event as primal as a snakebite should have no supernatural effects, that it should heal and fade in the same way as a bee-sting. I stepped under the shower, delighting in the hot-water rush across my skin, screwing my eyes tight and trying to see any future at all in this American adventure. I opened them again when I heard a knock at the front door, my queasy stomach shrinking as my weary adrenals responded to another alarm.

'It's only the mailman,' yelled Brad. 'I'll get it.'

By the time I'd dried myself, he had opened the package and was admiring an almost uncirculated 1869 ten-dollar gold eagle. Handle gold coins for long enough and you take on the dreams of those who spent them. The ten-dollar eagle was one of my favourites, a symbol of all things American made from half an ounce of frostbitten Klondike gold. Gobrecht had placed the head of Liberty on the obverse, looking disdainfully towards the left through a spangle of thirteen stars. Mott's spread eagle was depicted on the reverse, its wings outstretched as though flaring for landing, the arrows of armed might in its sinister talons, the olive branch held forward in its dexter. The shield on its breast identified it as an American warbird, and, like Liberty, the bird looked to the left, seeming to offer its own brand of peace as the only alternative to a chest full of arrows. If Brad had asked me, I would have explained it all to him, but he saw only the glister of gold.

'This for me?' he grinned, tilting the coin to catch a sunbeam. 'See that pretty birdy twinkle!'

'Put it down,' I said. 'You're not supposed to handle it.'

'I'll flip you for it,' he countered. 'Heads or tails? Liberty or Twinklebirdy?'

He spun the coin, and my good arm struck like a rattlesnake to snatch it from the air.

Brad raised his eyebrows. 'Good catch, Marty. What's it worth?'

'Couple of hundred,' I shrugged, 'maybe a bit more.'

'Maybe a lot more,' suggested Brad, waving an invoice in the air from Gulf Shores Coin and Collectibles. 'Maybe four and a half thousand dollars?' He let the bill flutter to the floor, stood up and adjusted his hat. 'You're not a trusting kind of guy, are you, Martin? And you know what that means, don't you?'

'It's not that . . .' I protested, but he stilled my flapping tongue with a pointed finger.

'Never trust no one who trusts no one 'cos they can't be trusted with nothing – that's what they say, ain't it?' He pushed past me, his hand on the door. 'I gotta go see my parole officer. I'll see you around, pal.'

He was back a moment later. 'Where in hell are my keys?'

The Lee County Sheriff's Department rolled on to the trailer park at a few minutes after nine that Saturday morning. Aviator-wearing deputies carrying clipboards spread out to tap politely on screen doors and ask a few routine questions. Gene had assured me I had nothing to hide, so I planted myself in a lawn chair and soaked up the rays until my time came.

Sherry-Lee was still sleeping when they knocked on her trailer, and after a suspicious amount of curtain twitching she appeared on her top step, her hair wrapped in a towel and her body hidden beneath her outrageous housecoat. The cops smiled and nodded while Sherry-Lee frowned and shook her head, and then they moved on, leaving Sherry-Lee to her fragrant rest. They blew down my street thirty minutes later. I showed them my passport, told them I was on vacation and that I was an insurance assessor by trade. I admitted that I had met the missing kid, that I had spoken to his mother and that I had no idea where he might have gone.

'When did you get bit, Mr Brock?' asked one of the deputies as my interview came to an end.

'Last Sunday,' I replied, 'up at Lake Okeechobee.'

He nudged his partner and pointed at my arm. 'See? Told you that's what it looked like. Was it a diamondback?'

'Er, canebreak, they said.'

'Same thing,' he shrugged. 'So tell me, Mr Brock, if you had to state an opinion, what would you say has happened to young Solomon?'

I rubbed my chin and tried to look wise. 'I'd say he's been eaten by an alligator.'

The cops tried to hide their smiles in their moustaches and failed.

'Thank you for your input, Mr Brock. Enjoy your stay.'

I watched them until they'd gone, then I got on with my work. The morning delivery was already sold to a coin shop in Union City, Georgia. I'd negotiated four thousand seven hundred and fifty plus carriage for the little Twinklebirdy that Brad had liked so much – no small achievement for a complete amateur and one that Gene would be sure to over-look.

His reaction to the news of Solomon's disappearance had disturbed me. It sounded like the nervous behaviour of a guilty man, or one who feared perception as such. No doubt he was counting the seconds until it was cool to call me back, wandering around a small-town coin fair with a mind full of half-baked excuses for his 7 a.m. panic. I looked forward to hearing them, knowing that whatever he said would never restore the political balance of our relationship as it stood at zero six fifty-nine this morning.

I called Fedex to arrange a collection, rolled a joint and wondered if Sherry-Lee would lend me her car to go bank-ing. There was no harm in asking.

I knocked hard, hard enough to wake a night-worker.

She snatched the door open. 'What do you want, Martin?'

'Er, I wondered how you were feeling today,' I mumbled. 'Just rolled a joint – wanna share.'

She stared at me, chewing on her top lip. 'I suppose you've come for a private show, haven't you?'

It was a nice idea, but now probably wasn't a good time. I rubbed my unshaven face and sighed. 'Did you see the pick-up truck parked outside my trailer this morning?'

She looked past me, out across the park and over the swamp, then back at me. 'No, Martin, I did not.'

'The big red one? A Chevy. You didn't see it?'

She raised her eyebrows. 'I'm not repeating myself, Martin.'

'It was Brad!' I protested, but right now I had trouble con-vincing myself. 'He turned up last night, out of the blue, saying he was going to track you down. He took me drink-ing down the beach, then out to some place called the Stud

Club, then to Alligator Strip. He just missed you – you were up there dancing to Alice Cooper while he was in the john. When he came out, you'd gone.'

Sherry-Lee crossed her arms. 'And where was he when I looked out, Martin?'

'He'd already gone,' I wailed, entirely aware of how weak I sounded. 'He asked around for a dancer called Sherry-Lee and got no joy. That's when he left. It's true, I promise you!'

She squinted at me in irritation, scratched her nose, and leaned towards me. 'Okay, Martin, I've heard you out. Now you hear me out. I do what I do because I'm good at it. I've got a good body and it ain't no sin to be proud of a good body. I'm not hurting anyone doing what I do up there, and all they get to do is look. I dance for men and make them happy, and I pay my taxes and I donate to charity and I go to church on a Sunday. Now don't get me wrong: I'd rather be raising babies and baking cookies for the PTA but that ain't happening right now, so I'm going to keep on doing what I'm good at no matter what you, or Brad, or anyone says, and if you've got a problem with that, fine. Just come out and tell me plain to my face and I'll tell you what I think in return. There's no need to go making up stories to try to scare me out of business. Understand?' She didn't wait for my reply. 'One more thing, Martin: stop trying to make things better. You don't know me and you don't know Brad. Just let things be. Please. Goodbye.'

I figured I'd get a cab to the bank.

8

The Sheriff came for Turn Back Jack on Sunday morning. A small crowd turned out to watch him go, but there was no cheering or jeering, just a sombre, unspoken suspicion that the cops had got the wrong man. Gene thought so, too. I'd been prepared to spend the day fumigating the trailer for his scheduled return, but he called from a Denny's on Route 301 to say he wasn't coming home. He figured he'd head straight on down to the Clearwater show to save time.

I told him that Clearwater didn't start until Thursday. He told me to shut up and let him know as soon as Turn Back Jack had been charged. He still sounded worried.

I spent the rest of the day mourning the death of what little reputation I had nurtured with the beautiful, tattooed stripper who lived over the road. By a combination of chance and design, I had promoted myself as her saviour, the healthy alternative with a cute accent and a crazy English sense of humour. By the same means, I had now become a sad, stalking creep who probably needed a good kicking. I submerged myself in self-pity like a man fleeing a swarm of wasps, scared to show my face for the stings of shame and embarrassment that chased me. I was a fool, I realised, seeing myself in Gene's looking-glass as though through a one-way mirror in a police station. If it had been Martin Brock rather than Solomon Bender who had got lost in the swamp, the cops would have been looking for a skinny Englishman with an expression of permanent surprise. They would have been seeking an individual whose grasp of reality was such that he had seriously fancied his chances with the most beautiful woman in southern Florida; a man who not once but twice accepted a lift from one of America's finest examples of an inbred, gun-worshipping redneck; and a fool who had tried to tickle a rattlesnake. I stepped closer to the mirror and looked myself long and hard in the eyes. I was growing older, but no wiser.

It was time I changed my ways.

I rolled a spliff, turned on Gene's favourite radio station and gave my future some thought. Olivia Newton-John hit the nail on the head: I needed to shape up. Sherry-Lee was never going to see me as anything more than another ogling punter until I made some serious changes to my outlook, my attitude and my appearance. I needed to beat Brad at his own game, and, to do so, I would have to become more like him.

Hidden beneath the worn yellow lino on my bedroom floor, in a standard-issue clear plastic wallet, was a Chinese panda. I'd stolen it a few weeks ago from a crowded stand in Dalton, because I'd felt myself to be under-insured. Like a lot of things in China, this panda had been redefined by the revolution. No longer was it a shy mountain bear with a smackhead's face and reproductive problems. It was now one troy ounce of .999 purity Shandong gold with the crafty collectibility of a Beanie Baby. Gene reckoned that the Chinese panda reflected in its brilliance the essential stupidity of his fellow Americans: millions of greenbacks had gone to the Reds as the capitalist collector invested in communist gold, but there had to a good reason. There had to be.

There was.

The Chinese panda was cute and cuddly, and Beijing knew it. New designs were issued annually, with special editions and commemorative sets distributed at coin fairs and promoted by wildfire rumour. Since 1982 every year had been the Year of the Panda and America couldn't get enough of them.

I flipped the coin and studied the fuzzy bear. This was one panda that America could afford to miss.

I grabbed my ID, stuffed all my cash into my handbag and set off walking. A taciturn ex-cop with a stationwagon full of fishing gear picked me up on Route 41 and dropped me in a dusty, low-rise district on the outskirts of Naples. I ducked into the International House of Pancakes, ordered coffee and trawled the Yellow Pages for pawnbrokers. There were dozens listed, but I was looking for the specific type that lacked both scruples and curiosity, and it was hard to tell from the listings. The straight lineage listings seemed most promising, so I scribbled a few on a napkin and set off to find the first.

You're lost in America without a car. Walking the edge of a four-lane highway or wandering along the wide back streets of a commercial district imparts a feeling of utter loneliness and disturbing vulnerability. A pedestrian in America is likely to be labelled a madman, an unsuccessful criminal or an illegal alien, to be ignored, arrested or run out of town. Waiting to cross the highway, I realised that I was probably all three, which cheered me up no end.

So did the discovery that DeSoto had lied when he'd told the Yellow Pages that his eponymous pawnbroker's was open seven days a week. Angry, footsore, overheated and dirty, I stood at a bus stop for an hour and studied the rest of the addresses. At last a bus full of weary, dark-eyed Latinos picked me up and delivered me to the depot in the centre of town. From there, a Cuban taxi-driver took me to Hallandale Pawn, 'Serving Naples Since 1989'. It was a popular spot on a Sunday afternoon, the parking lot crowded with the same selection of cars that had patronised Alligator

Strip. I mingled with the browsers, a blue-collar mixture of immigrants, crackers and clumsy kids.

The store was a museum of unattained aspiration: electric guitars, carbon-fibre tennis racquets and specialist tools told of inspiration, expenditure and lack of application. Just looking at the goods gave you bright ideas for a new and better future: with an angle grinder and a portable mig-welding kit, I could have set myself up a little bodyshop someplace, like Luther, Brad's old boss back in St Louis. With a cherry-red Squier Strat and a fifty-watt amp, I could have got three chords under my belt and started gigging in the bars around Fort Myers Beach. From there, the only way was up.

I was wasting time: I had a better plan.

Two glass-fronted counters stood at the rear of the shop, one crowded with big-assed women and the other with curious men. I pushed my way through and asked for assistance, placing my Chinese panda on the smeared glass.

A big man with curly grey hair and ironed jeans looked down at the coin and up at me. 'You know what this is?' he growled.

'Chinese panda, 1992 issue. Hundred-yuen face value, contains an ounce of pure gold. Spot price is around three sixty-five, but it's worth more because it's collectible.'

'Is it yours?'

'Sure it is.'

'Can you prove it?'

I shrugged.

'Got a state ID?'

'Got a driving licence.'

He sighed as though I wasn't the first creep he'd encountered that day trying to sell stolen goods and placed a clipboard on the counter. 'Fill in this form. Name, address et cetera. Leave the coin here. You get a receipt and we get three working days to check the coin's not been stolen. Come back then, and we'll give you' – he tapped a calculator – 'two twenty-five. Who's next?'

I slid the coin back into my pocket and skulked out of Hallandale Pawn. In the parking lot a skinny youth with a paramilitary haircut and a yoke of gold chains bummed a cigarette from me and offered some advice. 'Go see Flimmerwitz out on Sable Palm Road. He ain't quite so bureaucratic.'

Flimmerwitz was an overweight chain-smoker with poor eyesight and a neatly trimmed beard. His store was a disgrace, stacked floor to sagging ceiling with broken TVs, cracked hi-fis, incomplete toys and other garbage spurned by charity shops. Flimmerwitz discouraged browsing.

'You want to sell or what?' he wheezed, pushing his sweating face into the slipstream of a portable aircon unit.

I placed the coin on his disorderly counter and he fumbled to retrieve it from its slipcase with fat, nicotine-stained fingers.

'It's a Chinese panda,' I explained.

Flimmerwitz stared at me over his thick, designer lenses, his small eyes pale in a fat, white face. 'I know exactly what it is,' he replied through pursed lips. 'It's two hundred dollars to you.'

'They offered me two-fifty at Hallandale,' I protested.

Flimmerwitz blinked in exasperation. 'So why didn't you take it? Were the forms too tricky to fill in?'

I shrugged. 'Don't want cash. I want to trade it for something.'

Flimmerwitz tilted his head. 'Oh, okay, I get it. You want me to guess.' He held a finger to his lips in mock-puzzlement. 'Now let me see . . . You want a fishing rod. No, wait, a pair of roller-blades. I know! You want a CB radio.'

'I want a gun.'

He pushed the coin across the counter. 'That yellow bear won't get you a gun, young man.'

'It must do!' I cried. 'How much is a gun, for Christ's sake?'

Flimmerwitz frowned. 'Does it say "Flimmerwitz's Gun Shop" outside?'

I was tiring of his unending sarcasm. I put the coin in my pocket. 'Must have made a mistake,' I muttered, turning to leave.

He let me get to the door. 'Two seventy-five,' he called.

'Haven't got it,' I replied.

'I'm so surprised to hear that,' he sighed. 'How much have you got?'

'Fifty bucks and the panda.'

'So come back here already.' He placed a small, dented blue cardboard box on the counter. 'Are you a police officer or a representative of any Federal law-enforcement agency?'

I shook my head.

'Say it,' he snapped. 'My attorney can't use a shake of the head.'

I said it, and he lifted the lid from the box.

'Two-fifty and I never saw you.'

A grubby little automatic with cheap plastic grips and a late seventies styling lay like a poor-quality Chinese hand tool in the bottom of a presentation box that would lower the standards of any occasion. A chipped black magazine lay alongside, its oversized butt-plate promising inconvenience and unreliability at best, the electric chair at worst. A car is a car, but even your grandmother can tell the difference between a Lada and a Lamborghini, and this Saturday Night Special didn't even have seat-belts. It was immediately recognisable as a pragmatic, cynically forged hunk of low-melt

steel designed for single use and immediate disposal. It was
exactly what I was looking for.

'What ammo does it take?'

Flimmerwitz showed me his palms. 'How should I know?
Read the manual, why don't you?'

'You sell ammo?'

'Only second-hand and used. Here.' He dropped a handful of empty cases on the counter. 'You want this gun or
not?'

I didn't want it, but I bought it all the same, pushing its
cold and greasy barrel into my waistband like a desperado. I
walked back to the bus station weighed down with guilt
and my Jennings K80 semi-automatic. It pinched my belly
with every step, reminding me of its malicious presence and
threatening to leap from my jeans and into the street. A
USP wouldn't allow itself to be carried in such a manner, but
the Jennings, like a bad friend in need, was right where it
belonged. It knew I despised it, and it knew I needed it, so,
for as long as it was in my company, it would call the tunes.
It grazed on my newly resprouted dope-smoke paranoia,
reminding me that I was now carless, illegal and carrying an
unlicensed junk gun through the streets of Naples, FL. I was
a single stop and one bad judgement away from judicially
sanctioned sudden death and a couple of column inches in
the local news, and as my carcass was consigned to the local
morgue the Jennings, like an unrepentant repeat offender,
would spend a few years in custody before being sent laughing to the crusher.

I kept my shoulders hunched like a fugitive against the
indignant stares of every passing motorist, terrified that the
next car would belong to the Naples PD. The handgun
wanted to go back to my place and get drunk on my liquor,
and, already tired of its chafing I pulled it from my pants and

stuffed it deep into my handbag. I'd started this day feeling stupid, lost and sorry for myself. Now, after having determined to improve my situation through the application of intellect, I felt scared, alienated, vulnerable and stupid, like a paroled sex offender coming home.

The sun studied the back of my neck as it arced towards the Gulf, sucking a nervous sweat through my dirty shirt as I plodded north, holding a hopeless thumb over the highway. By the time I'd reached the north Naples city limits, having crossed an urban desert of drive-in fast-food joints, car dealerships and furniture warehouses, I had a plan.

Sherry-Lee was going to Mexico.

To raise kids.

With me.

Simple.

9

I carried my handgun back into Bridgeview on broken feet at a little after nine. The police guard had been stood down since Turn Back Jack's arrest, and groups of men stood huddled around barbecues and beer cans debating his chances.

I grabbed a cold one as soon as I was home, ignoring the scolding of my snakebitten arm for taking it out unslung. I drained my Bud in one long swallow, then took a roll of duct tape from under the kitchen sink and limped around the back of the trailer. Thirty-seven D was on the last row of the park, and only the gossiping cicadas saw me as I dropped flat and taped the sweat-stained pistol to the underside of the mobile home. It leered at me like an optimistic psychopath, like Max Cady in *Cape Fear*.

'Make yourself at home, you bastard,' I whispered before heading indoors for another beer and a fistful of medication.

I stayed up all night on the off-chance that Sherry-Lee might have seen the light, and fell asleep as the first stripes scratched the eastern sky. Gene woke me at zero seven hundred hours.

'Phase three kicks off at zero nine hundred,' he announced.

I groaned. What had been phase two? 'Where are you?'

'Tampa. They charge the nigger yet?'

'No. I dunno. What's phase three?'

'Here's the story: we are specialists in collectibles, right? We buy and sell rare coins for numismatic collections. We do not buy bullion coins for investment. Krugerrands, maple leaves and eagles are not our stock-in-trade. However, if one

181

of our clients were to ask us for a sheet of Austrian Philharmonics or suchlike, it would be unprofessional to tell them that we could not fulfil their needs, would it not? You with me?'

I nodded. 'Yeah, so far so good.'

'Okay. I got a call this morning from Lady Monroe. She wondered if we could supply a dozen krugerrands. Go to it, Troop.'

'How much can I spend?'

'Make ten buys at not less than thirty-five hundred each. Check the spot prices on bullion coins and move those babies a.s.a.p. If anyone asks, I'm in London until Thursday. Call my cellphone as soon as you get news on that nigger. Anything else?'

Yeah, Gene, lots. I bought a gun yesterday with a coin I nicked from a show. Carrying it home made me feel cheap and sleazy. I'm so in love with the neighbourhood stripper that I've been ready to risk my life and your mysterious scheme to win her heart. I'm drinking like an alcoholic fish and I'm beginning to panic about where the next bag of weed is coming from. I think you might be a child molester and I'm losing whatever respect I had for either of us. I think I need counselling.

'No, nothing else. When are you coming home?'

'None of your goddamned business. Wash the windows if you get time. I'll be on my cell.'

I did as I'd been told and diligently spent just under forty thousand dollars on bullion coins. Our credit was good with a large and growing number of coin dealers from Key West to Kentucky, not one of whom suspected that Whitehall Numismatics was a front for an operation run by a racist conman and his thieving, gun-toting, illegal alien sidekick. I simply washed my mouth out with Listerine, ran through my lines, and dialled out.

'Thank you so much for helping us out with those exquisite Indian heads last week, Mr Wendelman, and thank you for the prompt delivery.'

'Hey, thank you guys for sending the cheque so soon.'

'Not at all, Mr Wendelman: we expect swift payment so we make swift payment. It's only good manners. I'm hoping you can help us out with another request from one of our English clients.'

'Delighted to, Mr Block: fire away!'

'Could you spare us a tube of maple leaves? We're beginning to attract the odd request for bullion, and we don't hold stock because we're really not set up for that kind of business.'

'Well, you should be, buddy. The way the markets are swinging, there's going to be a lot more folks putting their green into gold, both here and over there in England.'

'I agree with you entirely. Mr Renoir said the same thing himself when he called yesterday from London.'

'So you want a tube of ten? Anything else?'

'One more thing, but give me the trade on these first.'

'Call it three twenty-five a piece. I'll send it USPS.'

'That's marvellous. I'll send a cheque by return.'

'You're a gentleman, Mr Block. Now, what was the other thing?'

Turn Back Jack was charged on Tuesday morning with the abduction and murder of Solomon Bender, aged eleven, of the Bridgeview Trailer Park, Lee County. I called Gene and told him the news.

'I knew it was him all along,' he bluffed, as though it were of little consequence. 'I'll be back on Friday night.

Keep that bullion moving through. I need buys from at least sixty per cent of our trustees by the weekend. Did you wash those windows yet?'

On Wednesday I dropped my bandage in the trash, took a krugerrand from Tuscaloosa, Alabama, and traded it for three hundred dollars at Dave's Pawnshop in Fort Myers Beach. I spent twelve dollars and fifty cents on dry-cleaning my suit and another ten on a haircut. I bought a new shirt and a shiny pair of second-hand shoes that pinched a little but promised to make up for the pain in other ways. I sipped a cold beer in the cool shade of Mike's Leisure Lounge, then crossed the street to Things To Make Her Squeal, a pastel-pink jewellery store with an armoured-glass window that attracted arm-locked lovers like flypaper. I told a bleached blonde, six-foot, crew-cutted salesgirl who introduced her-self as Tania that I wanted a gold coin put on a gold chain. She told me to leave the coin and come back Friday, so I took a cab back to the trailer park and spent the afternoon bagging bullion and the early evening washing the windows.

On Thursday I rose early, took a cab to the post office and sent a single Jiffy bag to each of twelve reputable coin bro-kers in Arkansas and Tennessee. Each packet contained about three and a half thousand dollars' worth of brilliant, uncir-culated 99.9 per cent pure gold bullion, insured by the US Postal Service to the value of twenty-five thousand dollars, and guaranteed to be delivered, whatever the weather. Whitehall Numismatics never sold coins to the dealers from whom it bought, and as far as the Dixie recipients of these glittering prizes were concerned, the seller was a private individual looking for the best return on his investment. My burden eased, I returned to Bridgeview, bracing myself for an encounter with Sherry-Lee.

She was sitting on the top step wearing a pink halter top

and cut-off jeans, her arms resting on her bare knees. She was passing the time of day with the guy who ran the office.

I waved a cheery greeting like nothing had happened, and she raised a solemn hand in salute.

'Hello, Martin.'

'Isn't it a beautiful day?' I smiled.

The rodent who ran reception grinned and shook his head. 'Guess you haven't heard, then.'

I looked from his florid face to Sherry-Lee. 'Heard what?'

'The crazy nigger hanged himself!'

How many times was he going to get off on that news today?

Sherry-Lee sighed and dragged herself upright. 'You should have more respect,' she said quietly. 'He was just a poor, confused man who should have been looked after. Good morning to y'all.' She turned and slipped into her shrouded home.

The rodent looked at me and winked. 'She's a fine one to talk about respect, if you know what I'm saying.'

I smiled at the receptionist. 'I would dearly love to stick a handgun in your dirty mouth, if you know what I'm saying. Maybe next time I see you I will, or maybe I'll save up and pay someone else to do it. What do you reckon?'

Then I turned the other cheek and climbed the steps to Sherry-Lee's trailer.

'What do you want?' she sobbed when I knocked on her screen door. 'Can't you see it's a bad time?'

I bit my lip. I wanted to run. 'I've got to see you,' I replied. 'I've got to talk to you.'

A glass fell to the floor and shattered. It takes some effort to break glass on a lino floor. It was indeed a bad time, but I had everything to lose by leaving now.

'I want to see you,' I persisted. 'Not here, not now,

because I know you're upset about Turn Back Jack and all that. I want to see you tomorrow night, because I want to show you something and I need to tell you something. If you don't want to come, then that's cool. It would break my heart, because it could be our last chance, but it's cool. If you do come, I'm only asking for thirty minutes of your time, and then I'm going away for a while. I'll wait for you tomorrow night, in the Sunset Tiki Lounge down on the beach. I'll be there at happy hour, before you start work, and I'll wait all night. I'd really like you to come.'

I turned my ear towards the door, straining to hear acquiescence in her movement across the trailer. Soft footsteps fell towards the screen and suddenly, like a waiting rattler, I felt her radiation.

'Martin,' she whispered through the stained mesh, her voice heavy with swallowed tears, 'it's another bad day in a bad goddamned life. Please just fuck off and leave me alone, will you?'

I hung on to the door for a moment too long, like a cretin waiting for clarification, then I nodded and sloped back to 37 D, glad only that the receptionist hadn't seen me rejected. I'd tried to add an element of finality to my plea in order to persuade her that tomorrow night might really be her last chance to see the light. It was a stupid, weak, sixth-form ploy, and it clearly hadn't worked. Her kiss-off had been nonchalantly brutal, and now, suddenly scared about the future, I shut myself in my trailer to brood.

Outside, the morning sunshine was soaked up by dense, dark storm clouds piled nine miles high as a deep depression settled over the Bridgeview Trailer Park. Solomon Bender was missing, presumed dead, Turn Back Jack had stretched his own overworked neck and Martin Brock's ill-considered future lay in vicious fragments on the floor of Sherry-Lee's trailer.

I resisted the bottle until noon, and then I made up for wasted time. It had been two years since I'd discharged myself from a five-year enlistment in the Bolivian Army, and, released from the routine restraints of Colonel Charlie, my emotions had grown out like a hippy's hair. They swung in my face, annoying me and blurring my judgement. They made me unattractive to nice girls and prevented me from holding down a job. It was time they were chopped back to a more manageable length. This morning I had been focused and businesslike, working from a list and according to a pre-defined schedule. Now, just minutes into the afternoon of the same day, I was sucking on a bottle of Sauza and scraping the carpet for enough weed to build a joint.

Was it in my best interests to commit myself to a future with a woman capable of this scale of spiritual destruction? Sherry-Lee was just another temptation to my addictive personality, a human substance to be cut and abused, a narcotic that would lift me high above the traffic and leave me broken in the street. I stretched out and stabbed the radio preset to Gene's favourite show tunes and oldies station, hoping for relief and reaping only confirmation: '*Que sera, sera,*' sang Doris.

I finished the Sauza, scored six thousand bucks' worth of Twinklebirdies, sold most of them right off and went to bed with a headache.

I woke up on Friday unsure that I'd even been asleep. I recalled lying awake in an acid sweat, staring at the bug-stained ceiling and trying to see a future in the twilight. Sherry-Lee was the first woman I'd looked at since Luisa, so long ago and so far away, but how could I be sure that she wasn't just another bed and breakfast on the road to the bottom of my life? I knew nothing of psychology, but it seemed plausible that a loser in an alien territory would seek first his own, and, failing that, a native foster mother to hold him to her breast. Maybe all I saw in Sherry-Lee was America itself, and in her love the acceptance of the nation.

Clearly the Federal Government thought the same way: if I married her, I would gain the Green Card that legitimised my residency and authorised me to appear on daytime chat shows. I wished I was tough enough to be that cynical, but all I wanted to do was to make her happy. All she had to do was give me the nod and I would have gone wherever she pleased, stacked shelves in Wichita or bagged onion rings in Grand Island, Nebraska, if that was what it took.

Luckily for both of us, I was only two weeks away from payday and I'd never have to lie on a Wal-Mart application form. Luckily for Washington, I was planning on applying for Mexican citizenship anyway. My dreams were perhaps a needy jerk's reaction to the feeling of loneliness and insignificance evoked by America. It was as though the land itself had been cursed by its dispossessed, ceded in the knowledge that the squatters would never own it, no matter how fine the mesh of highways and railroads they laid across it. Even when claims had been staked on every square yard of every arbitrary county in every state in the Union, when the soil had been compromised, federalised and sterilised, any sense of unity would be a state of mind. Live here long enough and the daily struggle to succumb to the cattle-prodding of the taxman and the advertisers would render the anguish obsolete, and any tendency towards solipsism in one's naturalised offspring would be smothered beneath the three-ply asbestos blanket of religion, morality and filtered knowledge, the trinity of education recognised by the Founding Fathers as necessary to good government. The status of illegal immigrant in the United States of America offered a privileged point of view: I was on the outside, looking in, and maybe Sherry-Lee was simply the nearest to the glass.

I lit a cigarette to freshen the rank smell of my plywood bedroom, both aware and appreciative of my mind's attempts to prepare me for the worst. It needn't have bothered, though, for no matter how persuasive and philosophically sound its arguments were for remaining in a state of existentialist disgrace, I knew that I would be gutted if I thought that yesterday, on a day when a wrongly accused, mentally disturbed man had hanged himself, when a cracker clerk had used the word 'nigger', after an eleven-year-old boy had disappeared in the rushes and a fugitive stripper had dashed a glass against the lino, Martin Brock had been rejected by America.

Exhausted by feverish conjecture, I fell asleep in the dawn's early light, waking some time later to find a brown-edged hole as big as a dinner plate consuming my only bedsheet. I leapt from the bed with a yell, rising into a low cloud of choking smoke. Prickly with embarrassment, I ducked back down, grabbed the sheet, and dragged it into the shower stall. Leaving the water running, I threw open the trailer door and returned to my room to find the source of the fire. Reason suggested that the dog-end had burned through the sheet and burrowed into the mattress. Panic butted in, pushing a picture of a sudden explosion to the front of my mind with podgy, shaking hands. Logic sneered, pointing out that horsehair and coils hardly counted as a volatile combination, but I was with the fat, sweaty guy on this one. I grabbed the lumpy mattress, flipped it on its side and dragged it into the front yard, knocking three nights' worth of food and beverage packaging to the floor as I passed.

A postman who looked like he should have been surfing

accosted me. 'Whitehall Numismatics?' He looked first at me, then at the smoke escaping from the trailer like bubbles from a sinking ship.

'That's us,' I replied, covering my nakedness with an imaginary Savile Row suit. 'Where do I sign?'

'Er, here,' nodded the postman absently. 'Dude, is your trailer on fire?'

'That?' I glanced back at the Corporate HQ. 'Nah. Toaster needs turning down, that's all.'

I took the package and tossed it on the table. There was no hole in the mattress, so I returned to my room to find the butt. Maybe the answer was to let off a fire extinguisher in the hope that it found the malicious Marlboro and choked it. It was a decision that might have made things worse, and in a way I was glad that Gene stopped me.

'What the fuck is going on here?' he yelled. 'What's this?' He kicked a pizza box into the yard. 'And these?' He punted a selection of cans after the pizza, raising a stale-ale odour that mixed with the smoke and evoked an image of the morning after at a burned-out nightclub. At least the fire had overwhelmed and erased any traces of marijuana abuse that his finely tuned nose might have detected.

'And *what the fuck are these*?' he screamed, brandishing the package I had just tossed on the table. 'Fucking gold bullion! Left on the table like Mom's fucking apple pie! With the door wide open!' He rubbed his face, the package gripped in a white fist, then pointed at me, a vein throbbing in his temple. 'One hour,' he whispered. 'In one hour I will return. You will either be gone or there will be no trace whatsoever of this fucking holocaust and you will be ready to report. Got it?'

For thirty seconds I considered the first option. I could pick up my handbag, pull on my boots, and go. Sherry-Lee didn't want me, and if I left now I could be in Memphis by sundown, which sounded like a good thing. I had a small amount of cash, a cheap firearm and a fake driving licence, and I could probably find a job as a taxi-driver. I could work hard, lay off the booze, save money, acquire some qualifications, gain a measure of respectability, meet a nice girl, settle down in a small house in the suburbs, have kids, take a mistress, play golf on public courses, pay Mediplan, take my grandkids fishing, fall down and die and be interred in the ground I never owned.

It was easy to dream, but now I had only fifty-nine and a half minutes to regain my seat in Gene's passage to Easy Street. I hastily applied my nose to two finely chopped lines of Brad's crystal meth, lay back and let the speed do the cleaning. Like guns and roses, amphetamine sulphate and housework are a surprisingly pleasurable combination and one that I would recommend to any housewife. They're good for the figure, too, and in fifty-eight minutes the billet was squared away. My only worry was Max Cady, my handgun, still taped under the trailer. Common sense told me it was best left in a state of plausible deniability, but I'd already promised to spend the day with panic. I dashed around the back, snatched it from the cobwebs and stashed it in my handbag.

Gene returned moments later, slamming the car door by way of alarm. He stepped into the trailer with the expression of a man climbing into a cesspit and flicked his narrow eyes around the trailer like a feather duster, searching for evidence of carelessness, corruption or conspiracy. I stood nervously by, my foot tapping like I'd eaten an Acme earthquake pill and chewing my lip, confident that Brad's remarkably fine speed had erased all the evidence.

At last Gene looked straight at me and shook his head. 'You must be some kind of fucking animal,' he decided, 'and if your mother ain't ashamed of you, then you should be ashamed of her.' He poked a Marlboro into his mouth and lit it with a Zippo engraved with the Globe and Anchor of the US Marines. 'Show me the books and make a pot of coffee.'

The sales and purchases were entered on facing pages in a cheap, A5, spiral-bound exercise book. Phone calls and contact reports were logged in another, while all receipts for gas, postage and miscellaneous expenditure were stored in an A4 box file. Gene's inspection of these ledgers showed that I was a diligent animal, if not a clean one, and he searched hard for evidence of cookery. Three cigarettes and half a pot of coffee later he sighed and returned the books to their cardboard box. If he was impressed with his clerk's record-keeping, he kept it to himself.

'How's the slut?' he asked.

I concentrated on polishing the draining board. 'Which one?'

'Her over the road, the waitress.'

Polishing things, I had just realised, was immensely satisfying.

'She's not a waitress,' I countered. 'She's a stripper. And she's crazy about me.'

Gene shook his head in exaggerated disbelief. 'Christ Almighty!' he cried. 'This great nation . . .'

'I'm blowing her out,' I continued, 'tonight. She's a security risk. Did you notice I had my hair cut, by the way?'

If he had, then finding me stark-bollock naked with an undischarged fire extinguisher in a smoke- and garbage-filled trailer with an overflowing shower and a table stacked with unsecured bullion had caused him to forget to comment. Under the circumstances, I let it go.

'I'm seeing her tonight, early, in town. No speeches, no explanations, no nothing, just a short, sharp . . .'

Gene held up a hand. 'Spare me the goddamned close-ups. What news on the kid?'

'Still missing. The suspect topped himself yesterday morning, and the buzz is that the cops got the wrong man.'

Gene put his head in his hands and groaned. 'It would help if the little bastard's corpse showed up somewhere.' He stood up. 'I'm going over to Cape Coral for an aromatherapy. Sort the contacts in my briefcase and send out compliment slips. I'll be back at five.'

'No problem,' I smiled. 'I'll do it just as soon as I've put another coat of Kleer on the lino. Oh, yeah, Gene?'

He paused heavily on the threshold, his face sagging under the weight of unmentionable worries. 'What?'

'Can I borrow the car later?'

That cheered him up no end.

I took a taxi into Fort Myers Beach, called by Mike's Leisure Lounge, the dry cleaner's and the jeweller's, then hailed the same cab for the return journey.

'Jew get everything you need?' asked the driver, a sad-eyed Guatemalan with a porn star's moustache. I caught his drift immediately.

'Not everything. I couldn't find anywhere selling weed.'

'How much jew want?'

I bought half an ounce and took his card. At least I could cry on Maria-Juanita's shoulder after Sherry-Lee stood me up.

Gene was in a different mood when I returned. Although no happier than before, he seemed more relaxed, and somewhat deflated. He ate a cold meatball sandwich while watching the market reports, shaking his head in ongoing disgust at the constant stupidity of everybody else in the world.

'I thought you said you'd washed the windows,' he called.

I pressed the iron carefully along the sleeve of my new shirt. 'I did.'

'Most people wash both sides.'

I sighed. Some people were never satisfied. 'I'll do the outside tomorrow.'

'You're coming to Miami with me tomorrow, early, so don't be late back.'

I gave the collar another pass. 'This won't take long tonight. I was thinking about a spot of backgammon later, if you're up for it.'

He picked up a glossy aviation magazine and flipped the pages as though searching for a free gift. He didn't find one. 'Backgammon would be good,' he nodded at last. 'Take the car tonight but don't get it towed.'

The dirty bandages of low cloud that had spoiled the sun-bather's day had dragged a stack of bruised cumulonimbi up the coast behind them and it was raining by the time I parked up in Fort Myers Beach. I was wearing my black suit, a green shirt with a big collar and horses on the front and pointed thrift-store shoes that were already going back on their promises. If I stood still, I looked good, although I hadn't sought a second opinion: Gene, after all, would have told me I looked like a Dade County pimp. I took a candlelit table overlooking the beach and ordered a beer to quench my thirst. Hard summer rain fell like bullets on the empty beach, kicking up spurts of sand and turning the shoreline to Alka-Seltzer. Further out, unbroken, ill-bred white horses galloped parallel with the shore, whipped on by a feverish southerly blown up from Havana, but beyond the chop, maybe a mile and a half out, the Gulf sparkled in the setting sunlight.

I watched through a veil of rain as the sun dropped from behind the black clouds and sank wearily towards its glistening bath. There was something significant in the circumstance of watching a sunset through a storm, but I was too preoccupied and insufficiently stoned to notice. I'd promised to wait all night, but it meant nothing if she wasn't coming, so I decided to wait until the end of happy hour, go smoke a fat one on the beach, then drive home and get beaten at backgammon by Gene. It was a good plan and it upset nobody.

It was two-for-one time at the Sunset Tiki Lounge so I shouted up a couple of Caloosahatchee Crybabies to celebrate, and toasted every degree of the orange sun's decline. By the time I'd started on the second cocktail, it was half immersed in the Gulf of Mexico, sinking as steadily as my spirits.

It had all gone wrong at the strip club: none of this would have happened if she had been a waitress at Denny's. There were dozens of attractive women in Fort Myers Beach, scattered across the white sand like a daily edition of *Sports Illustrated*'s Swimwear issue. There were thousands of beautiful women in the Sunshine State and hundreds of thousands across the continent. It was unambitious and short-sighted to commit myself to the first pretty girl I'd seen in America, and downright dangerous to involve myself with one to whom snakebite, firearms and bloody revenge were all routine.

To top it all, she was a stripper, and the problems with that were all mine. Exotic dancing was a career like any other, and as Sherry-Lee herself had pointed out, she worked the shifts and she paid the taxes, albeit under an assumed name. She wasn't shagging the punters, just dancing for them, and I had no issues whatsoever with her nudity. It was just that I'd been anticipating enjoying it in private, and there was no pleasure in seeing the woman you loved gyrating naked a few feet from a barful of sugared-up rednecks sipping Jack from hip flasks – not to me, anyway, but maybe I was repressed. Reason, however, was of no consequence in matters of the heart, and the plain truth was that, as far as I knew, as far as I had ever known, I loved her.

None of it mattered now, I recognised, raising my glass as the sun's crown slipped beneath the waves.

'If we run upstairs, we get a second chance,' said Sherry-Lee.

She turned and ran across the bar, taking the steps three at a time to reach the restaurant level above the bar. I followed, arriving at the Gulf-side window just in time to see a second sunset. Sherry-Lee turned to face me, her skin glowing gold in the low light. She was wearing a short yellow dress and black espadrilles, and there was a cute nervousness about her.

'Buy me a drink and tell me what's so important,' she said, glancing around the room. She didn't notice I'd had my hair cut.

I gave it to her straight. 'I know you've heard this before, and you believed in it, but it didn't happen. This time it will. I'm going to Mexico. I'm going to buy a place on the coast, somewhere down Cozumel way, and I want you to come with me.'

Her eyes widened and she opened her mouth but I stilled her tongue with a masterful gesture.

'That's what I'm doing, and this is how I'm going to do it.' I pulled a single gold coin from my pocket and placed it birdy side up on the table. 'This is an eagle. The US Treasury makes them. It contains nearly ninety-two per cent pure gold, weighs in at an ounce and is good anywhere in the world.'

Sherry-Lee brushed the twinkling raptor with her long fingers. 'How much is it worth?'

'As cash? Fifty bucks. This coin could buy us a cheap

dinner. As bullion? About three sixty-five at today's rate. I know what I'm talking about, because this is what I do for a living. I've been over here helping Gene to set up his business, and now my work is nearly done. In two weeks he's going to pay me off, and it's going to be a big cheque.'

'How big?' she whispered.

'Big enough to buy a house and make a life for two in Mexico.'

She was still stroking the coin. 'How come you guys are living on a trailer park, and how come you haven't got a car of your own if you're such high rollers?'

I let my fingers touch hers. 'When I first came here I was supposed to be living at a place out in Cape Coral. Three bedrooms, a veranda, small pool. Then I met Brad, and he brought me to Bridgeview. Then I saw you. I live on a trailer park because I wanted to be near you.'

She wanted to believe me. 'What about your friend? Why does he live with you?'

'Because neither of us saw any point in wasting money on temporary accommodation. That trailer is our home and our office and it makes sense that we share.'

I sat back and let the waiter trade empties for full glasses. I was on my fourth Crybaby; Sherry-Lee was on her second Miller. I lit a cigarette. Sherry-Lee looked long and hard at the coin.

'Word around the park is that you fellas are lovers.'

I choked on my smoke. 'You what?'

'They say you're Bridgeview's first gay couple.' She couldn't help but smile.

'Jesus Christ!' I barked. 'Two blokes share a trailer and suddenly they're ginger?'

'Oh, come on,' grinned Sherry-Lee. 'There's more to it than that!'

'Like what?'

'Like Mr Renoir, for Pete's sake,' she cried. 'Now I don't come across a great many homosexual men in my line of work, honey, but he is just about the gayest thing I've ever seen.'

'Gene? Gay?' I spluttered, as though the thought had never occurred to me. 'He's an ex-Marine, for crying out loud. He served in Vietnam, got medals and everything.'

Sherry-Lee raised a coquettish eyebrow. 'So? Can't you be gay in the Marine Corps?'

'Well, he did mention decorations . . .'

'And what about that robe?'

'What about it?'

'Oh, come on!' she gasped. 'That is so gay!'

She was right, and she'd met him only once. I didn't mention the matronly obsession with cleanliness, the trunk-sized toiletries bag, the impeccable taste for the finer things and that bloody show tunes radio station. She didn't need to know about his love of antiques, his fondness for Paris, his boundless misogyny or his hen-like jealousy. She had already known he was gay, and knowing he hummed opera while in the shower would only compound her belief that I was his rent boy.

Sherry-Lee raised her glass and chinked it with mine. 'I never thought you were gay, honey,' she smiled. 'Bi, maybe, but not gay.'

'I'm not bi, neither,' I blustered, lowering my voice to match my conviction.

'Well . . .'

'Well what?'

'There's that purse you carry around.'

'It's just a bag,' I insisted. 'I explained it already.'

She closed her hand over the coin. 'There's a lot you *haven't* explained.'

'Like what?'

'Like what you guys are really up to in that trailer. I know you're up to no good, riding around in your high-powered suits and living like the rest of us slobs. You're plotting something bad.'

I sidestepped the accusation like a matador. 'How can it be bad if I'm doing it for us?'

She rolled the coin like a butterball. 'Is this for me?'

I shook my head and loosed another button on my shirt. I lifted a chain from around my neck and held it above the table, letting the gold coin mounted upon it glisten like wet skin in the flickering light. 'They say gold should be seen only in sunlight and candlelight,' I said. 'This one's for you: it's a Gibraltar angel, ninety-nine point nine-nine per cent pure gold – as fine and as pure as you will ever get. Take it.'

She blinked hard as I dropped it into her hand, her shock becoming a frown as she studied the coin's surface. 'You're giving me a picture of your miserable Queen?'

I sighed. 'Turn it over.'

She did as she was told and gasped at what she saw. She kept blinking, trying to hide the tears that brimmed in her eyes. Bouguereau's cherubs fired their golden arrows from the reverse of the coin, breaking her will and spilling tears on to the table.

So far, so good.

'It's yours,' I whispered, 'yours to keep whether you accept this offer or not.'

She wiped her eyes with the back of her wrist. 'Martin, they're beautiful . . .' A fit of sobs cut her short. 'I'm sorry. You're so sweet and kind to me. Nobody ever gave me any jewellery before. It's been so long since anyone gave me anything . . .'

It was time for Martin Brock, gilt-tongued seducer, to

work his magic and mine the seam his gold had uncovered. I took her hand and gently closed it around the angel.

'It's been so long since you were given a gift because it's been that long since anyone loved you, Sherry-Lee. Now, look at me: I want to tell you why I want you to come to Mexico with me.'

She blinked again, looked straight at me and nodded. 'Tell me.'

'Because I love you. I adore you. I fell in love with you that God-awful night back in May when I first laid eyes on you. I moved to the trailer park to be near you and I stuck my hand in that box of snakes to prove I would do anything for you.'

'That was the dumbest thing you did,' she sniffed.

'I know,' I acknowledged, 'but love has made me do dumb things. I know you don't believe me when I say that Brad was out there at Alligator Strip last week . . .'

She grabbed my wrist. 'I do believe you,' she whispered. 'I saw him there. He saw me. He got up and left.'

This revelation derailed my train of thought, and all I could do was stare at her for a moment. Then I reminded myself that Brad was history.

'I love you,' I repeated, 'and I've devoted myself to you. I never knew what I wanted to do with my life until I met you, and then you told me.'

Tears were running down her face and her grip on my wrist was firm. 'What did I tell you?' she sobbed.

'You said you wanted to raise babies in Mexico. I knew then that I wanted to raise babies in Mexico with you. I just didn't know how to tell you.'

'Oh, Martin,' she cried.

'Oh, Sherry-Lee,' I replied.

★

I left my shoes on the boardwalk and we wandered along the beach. It had stopped raining, but a bank of low black cloud obscured our actions from the stars and made them cross. Her hand was small and soft in mine, and every hundred yards or so she would stop, turn and kiss me. I was cool with that for as long as it lasted, but I hadn't yet heard her answer. I lit a spliff and we sat on the tideline, watching the reds and the greens rising and falling on an agitated ocean.

'Wish we were on one of those boats, right now, plotting a course for Quintana Roo,' I mused.

Sherry-Lee blew a cloud towards Mexico and nestled her head against my shoulder. 'This is so romantic,' she sniffed, passing me the joint.

I took a long pull, then flicked the roach towards the ocean. She was clearly still trying to make up her mind: maybe she needed a little more persuasion. I turned and placed my hands on her shoulders, pushing her down into the wet, white sand and kissing her softly and feeling through my central nervous system that delightful tingling numbness that comes only with true love and good weed. I pulled away slightly and she hauled me back, her nipples hard through the thin fabric of her yellow dress. Parts of me were developing the same condition, but it was essential that she respected me in the morning. I wanted to have her, right then and there, regardless of the mutual abrasion, but I also wanted her for ever, and the former jeopardised the latter. I backed away, strongly, decisively, and pulled her breathless to her feet. She clasped her fingers around the back of my neck and looked into my eyes.

'That was heading somewhere nice, honey, but a Southern gentleman should really go on the bottom.'

'Not yet,' I said, ignoring protests from all over my body. She turned around. 'Is my back all covered in sand?'

A thick skim of sand coated her from her shoulders to her heels. It glistened in her hair and had soaked her cotton dress.

I patted her down. 'There's a little here and there,' I conceded, paying particular attention to a deposit on her right buttock.

Flickering lights bobbed and weaved at the back of the beach in a punchy breeze that carried thirsty snatches of strangled wah-wah through the night. Captain Jack's Crab Shack was in full Friday effect and I was suddenly curiously hungry.

'Let's go eat,' I said.

'What about my work?' she replied.

'Fuck work.' It was one of my mottoes. 'This is life.'

She grinned, then frowned. 'How do I look?'

I put my hands on her shoulders. She looked like she'd just been shagged in a wet sandpit.

'You look beautiful,' I replied.

The Hawaiian-shirted staff at Captain Jack's Crab Shack smirked as we came through the door.

I assumed my finest English accent. 'Our yacht foundered in a squall just over there. We had to swim ashore. We're perfectly all right, thanks for asking, but we're ravenous. Do you have a table for two?'

'Absolutely,' grinned our waiter, showing us to an intimate table that Gene would have described as front and centre.

'Nice one, buddy,' nodded a fat man in pressed polo shirt as we passed.

Cold beer, frosty glasses and short candle were placed between us and Sherry-Lee admired her angel in its wavering light. I reached across and touched the chubby golden cherubs.

'That's you, and that's me. Armed angels with beer bellies.'

She smiled from the nose down. Above that the tears

were welling again. 'There's not just the two of us in this matter,' she announced.

My heart fell through its cloud. Brad was in the past, and I was interested only in the future. She read my mind.

'It's not Brad. Oh God, Martin. I feel like I've been living in Purgatory these past five years, and then you come along and you're so sweet and kind and caring, and you give me this beautiful Jellibar angel . . .'

'Gibraltar,' I said. 'It's Gibraltar.'

'I know,' she sobbed, weakly attempting to sniff away the tears, 'and it's all too good to be true, like a fairytale, and I'm so scared that it ain't gonna happen and it's going to be me and not you who ruins it, but you've got to know it's not just me . . .' She bit her lip, wiped her eyes with a napkin, lowered her head and looked at me across the table. 'There's another angel in all of this. *My* angel. My daughter.' She swallowed as goosebumps rose along her arms and the house combo kicked into 'Gimme Shelter'.

'You've got a kid?'

She looked at me like it was important. 'I've got a daughter,' she nodded.

'How old?'

'Five in April. You've met her.'

I shrugged and swallowed my beer. The waiter caught my eye and registered my need. 'I've met her?'

'Sure you did, couple of weeks back. You tortured her. She asked about you on Sunday. She asked when Tomás the Talking Martyr was coming back. She's my beautiful girl.'

'What's she doing up there? Why isn't she living with you?'

Sherry-Lee looked at me with pity. 'Ain't you seen that Metallica video? "Nothing Else Matters" or something? The one about the dancer who lives in a trailer with her daughter? I ain't raising my child like that. I haven't been fit to raise her at all these past years.'

You didn't need a snakebite to see why. Sherry-Lee had escaped Federal justice for the murder of Rufus Cooper III, but she'd gone down all the same. She'd sentenced herself to life without parole for a crime that the courts would have called self-defence and which she defined as cold-blooded murder. Sherry-Lee's soul had the whole incident on tape. Playing it back every night, over and over, had made no difference. He hit her once, discharged a firearm in her general direction, and raped her. In return, she had turned his head into a crushed watermelon, denying him the opportunity to be rueful. A dark and vengeful spirit had seized her on that warm Saturday evening in the Ozarks, and she had executed Rufus Cooper III on her own say so. Her actions, she believed, had been extremely wicked. Extreme sin demands extreme religion, and it was kind of fortunate that snake handling ran in the family, although Pastor Zachary and his family were doing little to rehabilitate her up there in Okeechobee. I'd heard it in their voices around the table, seen it in the eyes of the women gathered there, felt it in the way they had welcomed me as her friend. Sherry-Lee was the congregation's own little Jezebel: a whore, a murderer and an unfit mother. She was a living, breathing TV movie, a benchmark for Jerry Springer, and it made them feel good to have her around. Sherry-Lee was the only person they knew who had been touched by the Devil without being bitten, a broken example of hope without faith. She had communed with Satan, supped with the Red One.

She had lain down with Rufus.

I tried to be cool. 'Rufus Cooper the Third is her father, isn't he?'

Sherry-Lee lit a cigarette with short, sharp movements

designed to hide her face from the waiter as he delivered more beer. When he'd gone, she looked up. 'I laughed when I fell pregnant: you got to admire a God with a sense of humour like that, don't you? Damned is the word most folks use, but I carried her and bore her up in Okeechobee. Can you believe she was born on my birthday? Soon as she was born my aunties took her away. I left all the money for her upbringing, for clothes and diapers and all, but they gave it all back. Said they didn't want to corrupt the child with no blood money. I take them cash every Sunday, but I don't think they spend that, neither. Mrs Olson told me once they give it all to charity. You remember Mrs Olson? She's prone to speaking in tongues.'

'How are you going to get Angie back?'

She took a long drag on her cigarette, her eyes like two Glocks, side by side and front on. 'I'll get her,' she declared.

I reached across the beers and took her hand. 'I'll come with you. I love you and everything that comes with you. That includes Angie. Look at me, Sherry-Lee.'

Her lip was wobbling and her eyes were becoming bloodshot from all the tears.

'It's over,' I said. 'You're free. I'm your parole officer and I'm tying you to a thirty-minute lockdown. Understand?'

She shook her head.

'That means you got to report to me every thirty minutes. Naked.'

She sniffed and laughed and my heart soared.

We ate and we drank and we laughed like the condemned, too long and too hard, and then we left. Out on the boardwalk the clouds had parted for the stars and a fat yellow moon hung low in the south-eastern sky. Suddenly she grabbed me and dragged me into an alley between two clapboard buildings.

'We got to go down the beach,' she announced.

'Yeah?' I replied.

'Absolutely,' she confirmed. 'I've got to show you my tattoo.'

How could I refuse?

It was a tiny rattlesnake, coiled low down beneath her smooth bikini line, and it could truly be appreciated only from very close. It was a pleasure to behold, quite safe to touch and, as a Southern gentleman, I feel there is no more to be said about it.

Loved up and stoned, we wandered into a beach bar with damp clothes and dishevelled hair to order a couple of night-caps. Nobody seemed keen to serve us, but only because there was something better on the wall-mounted widescreen. I stood on tiptoe to see over the broad, singlet-clad shoulders before me and cursed out loud.

Bridgeview Trailer Park was on TV.

By the time we got back, the outside-broadcast units of six TV companies were parked up around reception and a porky gang of mustachioed technicians were standing around drinking beer from foam coolers. They shook their heads when Sherry-Lee asked about Solomon, saying that there was no news yet and warning us that the National Guard were going to be searching the whole area over the weekend.

The cameras had brought the residents out of their homes, and a party atmosphere prevailed beneath the sparkling sky. I parked the car some distance from 37 D and walked Sherry-Lee to her steps.

'No lights on in the Bender residence,' I observed.

She turned to see. 'None in Turn Back Jack's, neither. It's so sad. Stay with me tonight.'

What else could I do?

★

I tiptoed home at six-thirty, leaving a kiss on Sherry-Lee's lips and creeping into my trailer like an unfaithful spouse. The table was laid up for a backgammon marathon, the ashtrays clean and a fresh pack of Marlboro for each player. The pieces had been set out, the doubling die on the bar and the leather-bound dice cups locked and loaded. A sealed half-bottle of Jack with a price tag from Clearwater Wine stood beside a shot glass on my side of the table; an empty Coke can on the other. I tried to swallow my guilt: this was the gay equivalent of a dinner in the bin.

I filled the coffee machine as my mind ran from room to room like a frantic mother, desperately seeking an excuse. The house of lies was empty, so I searched the yard, but by the time Gene shuffled past me in leather slippers and silk robe I'd found nothing with which to explain myself that wasn't lamer than a three-legged ass on a tail of broken glass.

Under pressure, I chose to open my defence with a promise. 'Coffee's on,' I called, cheerily.

He nodded as he absently stacked the stones.

'Sorry about last night,' I continued. 'It took longer than I'd planned. You know women . . .'

He didn't, but he shrugged all the same. 'No matter. Can't be helped.'

I eyed his bald patch suspiciously as the percolator spluttered in sympathetic disbelief. 'You seen the telly?'

'Last thing we needed.'

'What are we going to do?'

'Oh, I wouldn't worry, Martin,' he replied in a silky voice. 'I've got it all covered.'

His legs, I noticed, from the tops of his socks to where they disappeared beneath his robe, were hairless. I wondered for a distracted moment if depilation was a nationwide custom or merely a local one. I handed him his coffee. He nodded and took it to the shower, pausing at the door to comment on my garb.

'That suit looks like you drowned in it. You need to press it, and lose that fucking pimp's shirt, will you? It's Saturday, remember? Number twos.'

I sat on the sofa and switched on the TV, counting my chickens as the RCA warmed up. It looked like I'd escaped another bollocking.

The early morning news channels were busy disseminating bite-sized details of a new UN resolution, a train crash in Bavaria, a bomb in Jerusalem and a new-born panda in Durban. Statewide, the headlines included some pretty good aerial footage of a crashed petrol tanker on Florida's turnpike north of Yeehaw Junction, reports of a self-cleansing action by a Miami drug cartel that was all flashing lights, yellow tapes and strobe-lit pools of Latino blood, and shots of a new-born dolphin at Islamorada. A still picture of the Bridgeview reception area was accompanied by a promise that we would be going later to the Lee County trailer park where the search for missing eleven-year-old Solomon Bender was now entering its sixteenth day.

I switched off. We were already there.

A few carloads of over-enthusiastic National Guardsmen had deployed on the approach road to the park as Gene and I left at a few minutes after seven. A ragged sleeve of cloud was swinging in from the south-east and threatening to rain on their parade. Gene couldn't have cared less.

'Fucking weekend warriors,' he sneered as we passed. 'Look at that: some of the fuckers are saluting us. You don't salute goddamned civilians.'

He bought a local newspaper from a machine outside the first Denny's we passed on I-75 and read it in muttering silence at the dark end of a booth while I concentrated on consuming a Grand Slam breakfast with a short stack on the side.

'Kid's dead,' he announced at last. 'Kid was dead six hours after he kissed his momma goodbye. Can't keep 'em alive for long.' He tossed the paper on to the couchette and sipped his coffee. 'So the slut is gone?'

I winced, then nodded. 'Yup.'

He watched me, waiting for some verifying detail as I concentrated on my lean Canadian bacon strips.

He didn't get one.

'Very good,' he announced at last. 'Clean break. No contrail. Very professional.'

'You know when you were in Vietnam?' I asked, going on the offensive through a mouthful of egg. 'Did you ever get hit?'

'Why do you ask?'

I shrugged. 'Just wondered. Thought you might have a Purple Heart.'

He made a cathedral of his fingers and hid his mouth inside. It's hard to lie in body language. 'I don't like to talk about Vietnam,' he replied. 'You finished yet?'

South of Naples, we swung east into the backend of the sunrise and followed Alligator Alley across the sawgrass desert of the Big Cypress National Preserve. I was both pleased and disappointed with what rushed by. I'd always pictured the Everglades as a dark and creepy land, with drowned forests and wide pools of black water where alligators and water moccasins held power like Colombian dynasties, where chained fugitives were pursued by baying hounds. Gene shook his head.

'That's Louisiana you're thinking of. This here's no land at all. It's a river.' He swept his hand from north-east to north-west. 'Fifty miles wide, moving at one hundred feet per day, from Okeechobee in the north all the way to the Caribbean. This here road is a bridge.' He pointed to a distant copse. 'That there's a hammock. All these trees need is a few inches of dry elevation, and they're all crowded on like survivors in a flood. What did the cops ask when they came round?'

National Geographic had turned into *True Crime* with no commercial break. I lit a cigarette and wound down the window. 'Not much. I told them I was a tourist, that I'd seen the kid around once or twice and that was that.'

'They ask if anyone else lived in the trailer?'

'Nope, but maybe the receptionist guy told them who lived where.'

Gene shook his head. 'Roscoe wouldn't have said nothing. I kept him sweet.'

It wouldn't have been helpful to recount my last conversation with the greasy little git, so I merely nodded. 'Cool.' I wondered if Gene needed me to tell him that he hadn't abducted Solomon Bender, because he had been with me, heading west, somewhere between Pensacola and Tallahassee, at the exact time when the kid went possum hunting. He was not a suspect, and there was no reason whatsoever why anyone should consider him to be one.

Unless he had form.

I held the thought for a moment, then let the slipstream suck it from my mind. Gene's past and his future were of neither interest nor concern to me. Payday was ten days away; Mexico two weeks tops. I was less than a month away from living the dream and saw no need to shine a light on Gene's nightmarish past. Live and let live, as Turn Back Jack liked to say.

★

Miami was a place where they spelled cool with a capital 'C' and treated it like a designer label that could be bought and flaunted. I'd seen the same outfits worn with the same slightly bored expressions in other jumped-up seaside towns, and I found them all to be pretentious and insecure. Gene didn't like the place much, either.

'Bunch of fucking idiots living out here,' he growled as we rolled past the Holocaust Memorial. 'I bet this is the kind of place you'd like to live, ain't it?'

'No way,' I protested. 'This place sucks. It's too harsh here, too . . .'

We stopped at a pedestrian crossing and watched as a sixty-year-old bleached blonde with wrinkled brown limbs and a leopardskin bikini was dragged on high heels across our front by a pink Chihuahua.

'. . . It's too much,' I finished lamely, as two tall, slim, tanned bachelor boys with baby-smooth faces and child-sized swimming trunks rode past on a tandem. 'I'd have thought it was more your cup of herbal tea,' I added.

By two-thirty we had turned a sackful of gold into cash and cheques and were in Freddie's Diner munching on gourmet burgers and fries.

'You missing her yet?' taunted Gene, wiping ketchup from his chops.

I shook my head and swallowed. 'Not as much as she's missing me.'

'You bang her?'

''Course I did,' I nodded.

He loaded a cluster of fries with mayonnaise and dropped them down his gullet. 'All they're good for, those trailer park sluts.'

I nodded. Ten days until payday. If I hadn't bitten my tongue clean off by then I could tell him to go fuck himself.

'What now?' I asked.

He placed five hundred-dollar bills on the table. 'Here's an advance on your disbursement.'

'Nice one!' I moved to scoop the cash and he held up a pickle to stop me.

'Hold on: let me have some of those C-notes back. I'll give you smaller.'

I shrugged. Cash was cash. 'Go ahead.'

He retrieved four of the bills, slipped them into his bill-fold, and placed two twenties in their place.

'What are you playing at, Gene?' I cried.

He grinned, fat and cheesy, the cat who'd got the face-cream. 'That's one-forty. Five hundred minus three-sixty is one-forty, and three-sixty was the amount you embezzled from company funds to buy an unregistered coin last week.'

He'd busted me on the angel. Even though I was happy to pay for it, I thought it only polite to protest. Gene told me not to bother and snatched another hundred for board and lodging.

'Unfair!' I cried. 'You've left me with forty bucks!'

He bit the tip from a pickle and watched me as he chewed. 'So? All you need is beer and cigarettes. It's not like you're buying flowers no more, now, is it?'

'That's not the point,' I whined. 'You're just being mean for the sake of it. I—'

He shut me up with a wave of a greasy hand. 'Stop piss-ing and moaning. Next week we reap what we have sown. We've got to be focused, alert and sober for the next ten days because, frankly, the harder we work now, the richer we get. I need to be able to rely on your application, honesty and integrity one hundred and ten per cent from hereon in, and I want you to consider yourself to be in the field from this moment onwards. No more fires, no girlfriends, no snakebites. It's my way or the highway. Deal?'

'When do I get to know what's going on?'

He stuck out his lip and shook his head slowly. 'You don't. You just do as you're told and you get rich.'

'What's my take going to be?'

'How many dealers on the A and B lists?'

He knew the exact number, but I played along. 'Hundred and ten or so.'

'One hundred and thirteen,' he corrected. 'Multiply that by fifteen K Your cut is thirty per cent of that.'

'Five hundred and eight thousand, five hundred dollars,' I told him. I've always been good at maths.

He sat back and smiled like he was proud of me. 'There's your answer.'

It did the trick. I sat in the Toyota spending my ill-gotten fortune on cars, tequila and a sea-view *hacienda* while Gene looked at small aircraft in an ocean-front dealership. He'd never struck me as a flyboy, but I found it hard to care. I reckoned I'd buy my step-daughter a horse and my soul-mate a diamond and myself one of those glass-fronted fridges that allow you to keep a constant eye on the beer stock.

And a modified Cadillac Brougham Deville, the kind of car that made even the bugs smeared across the grille look official.

It would be good to live in a Spanish-speaking country again, and all I had to do was whatever Gene asked, with certain exceptions, for the next ten days. A reckless shiver of anticipation ran up my spine like a rocket, exploding in the back of my mind in a shower of sun-baked visions and half-baked dreams. I counted my chickens for the second time that day: the clutch had grown and the fact that none had yet hatched was a mere detail. As long as I kept my hopes and dreams warm and cosy they'd all be hatched by the end of summer.

We left Miami in the sunshine and followed the Tamiami Trail west, running into a thick, grey rain a few miles past Sweetwater. The forecast predicted a weekend of high humidity, freshening winds and prolonged showers, some heavy, all points south from Hendry County.

'There goes the summer,' drawled Gene, a Marlboro poked in the corner of his narrow mouth.

I didn't care: permanent vacation was just a couple of weeks away. I dozed as we drove through the driving rain, dreaming of a hammock in a land where all the snakes respected me as an equal. I'd never been to Mexico, but I'd sampled and approved a great number of its exports, I spoke its language and I loved a bit of mariachi. It had been the asylum of choice for the discerning fugitive ever since they created a border, and in that respect was the New World equivalent of the Spanish costas that I knew so well and missed so sorely. My arrival in Mexico with Sherry-Lee and Angel would be a return, a homecoming, to a place where I would be familiar yet unknown: Martin Guerre without the war.

In the meantime, like the proverbial fool, I'd made a rod for my back and I needed to decide how best to wield it. I'd set Sherry-Lee on fire and told Gene I'd blown her out, and I couldn't please all of the people all of the time. The spider who lived in the dark and dirty cupboard behind my eyes sighed and started spinning, weaving a reasonably straightforward web of deceit. I would simply tell Gene that I needed to return some trinkets to my ex, using the opportunity to tell Sherry-Lee that Gene had ordered a twenty-four-hour curfew for the next two weeks. A nod and a wink would do the rest, but, as it happened, it was a waste of silk.

The Tamiami Trail, linking Miami to Tampa, must have been a bitch to build. The seventy-mile stretch from the Atlantic west to Naples on the Gulf runs through a level wilderness of stagnant, mosquito-infested swamp, a kind of Club 18–30 for unintroduced viruses to meet and mutate. I shivered as a squall slapped the car like a strip of seaweed: I wanted this country road to take me home. Suddenly Gene swung left at the kind of crossroads Robert Johnson would have passed with his head down and took us down a wet road lined with stunted, dripping trees backed by dark sloughs of feverish black water.

I tipped my seat forward. 'Where we going?'

'Everglades City,' replied Gene.

Five miles of two-lane swamp road took us over a hump-backed bridge and into a one-sided settlement of wooden shacks on wide, open lots. Gene pulled up outside a convenience store.

'Cleaning materials,' he announced, handing me a list. 'Go get 'em, boy.'

I was in fishing country, I noticed, as I waited with my trolley at the check-out. The clerk was only partly succeeding in trashing a mutual acquaintance's reputation over the phone and scanning my shopping at the same time. I browsed through the flyers on the counter, noticing that all the guides were captains, they all knew where the snook and the tarpon lurked and they all lived in the city.

Probably because they couldn't get any service out here in the sticks.

'Bloody weird people round here,' I told Gene as we drove along a road like wet china clay past signs advertising air boat tours, kayak safaris and more and more fishing charters. Everywhere else seemed to be selling bait. Gene cursed as the Toyota crunched into one pothole after another.

'Surely this isn't the main road into the city?' I asked, wincing in sympathy with the shocks.

'What city?' asked Gene irritably.

'Everglades City,' I replied.

He laughed, unamused. '*This* is Everglades City, you dumbass. That was the commercial centre back there. You just passed the city bank. These here are the 'burbs.'

'You're joking,' I snorted, but he wasn't.

We stopped beside an unpainted wooden house balanced atop a dense criss-cross of stout wooden stilts. I could see a river gleaming through them, and a steep flight of steps leading up to a padlocked screen door.

Gene handed me a tiny key on a yellow plastic fob. 'Off you go.'

'Where?'

'In there.'

'What for?'

'Take a look inside, then take a look at the purchases you've just made. Then have a wild guess.'

'Housework?' I spluttered.

'You're gifted, Troop. Go on.'

'Why?'

He inclined his fat head in mock-regret. 'Need to know, Troop, as in you don't. I'll be back in a few hours.' He wound up the window, drove away, stopped and reversed back. 'You forgot your fag handbag.'

I froze in panic as he lifted it from the footwell.

'Jesus Christ, what you got in here?' he asked.

I reached in and snatched it from him before he and my handgun came muzzle to muzzle.

'Lipstick, eye shadow, pair of dice,' I growled. 'Just the usual girl's stuff.'

As he drove away chuckling to himself, I remembered the

bait he'd used to lure me here from my comfortable, hash-rich life in Morocco. Where was the expensive tailoring, I wondered, as I stood soaking in a fetid rain, fumbling with a cheap lock on a flimsy door in a shanty built on false pretences in a swamp at the arse-end of civilisation? And where was the frequent-flyer programme? At least the snook and the tarpon round here got something to bite on before they were reeled in – I'd been caught with pure hot air.

I snorted two lines of speed from my dwindling stash from the top of a rough wooden table and took a look around the property. Clearly a rental with an absentee landlord, it looked like a choice venue for bachelor fishing parties and displayed all the interior-design finesse of mountain refuge. A large living room with a basic kitchen area opened on to a west-facing veranda with a view across a black river and a rainswept mangrove swamp. Holes and rents in the fly-screen windows had been repaired with silver Duct tape and a strip of yellowed polythene had been stapled around the door frame to stop the blood-sucking critters squeezing in through the cracks. Left of the living room were two bedrooms, each with a pair of stained striped mattresses on low iron bedsteads and separated by a bathroom full of rusty fittings from the thirties.

I filled a heavy tin bucket from a groaning tap and set about putting the freshness back. Gene knew as well as I did that I would not be re-enlisting at the end of this tour and he was making damned sure that I earned my keep until demob. There were no documents in the house and no name on the door, but it was obvious that this outpost on the tidal mouth of the Barron River was Gene's hidden asset, and as I swept the floor I counted myself blessed that the house had been more valuable as a rental property than as a corporate headquarters.

Buzzing away on poor man's charlie, I fairly whizzed through the house, treating ants, cockroaches and centipedes with the same chemical disdain, but taking precautions to protect the numerous lizards squatting in the rafters, for they were the foot soldiers, the second line of defence against the whining airborne divisions of black mosquitoes already gathering without the screens.

By six I considered my work done and sat on a wooden chair by the window to watch the flank of a passing storm. I'd smoked twenty cigarettes, scratched my ear bloody and tapped blisters into my feet before Gene came back for me.

He swaggered in with his hands on his hips and played the colour sergeant, running his fingers along ledges and lifting the threadbare rugs in the bedrooms for the signs of an amateur. He found none, and for once he was impressed. 'You're going to make some man a damn fine little wife, one day,' he announced. 'Go get your stuff from the car.'

I was halfway through the door when I realised what he'd said. 'What are you talking about?'

He gave me a look like I was a half-witted dog. 'I said go get your stuff. Leave my kit. I'll get it myself.'

I looked through the gathering dusk to where the Toyota was parked at the foot of the steps. Everything that had been in the trailer was packed inside. 'What's going on?'

Gene strolled across to watch the sun setting through the shredded tails of the storm. 'Relocation. It was always part of the strategy and now it's a tactical move. Last thing we needed was the goddamned media spying on us.' He turned to reassure me. 'Don't worry, Troop, everything's taken care of. The United States Postal Service will forward all deliveries from Thirty-seven D down here, and Ma Bell has transferred our numbers. Our dealers will never know we've moved, and, most of all' – he spun round, his arms out-stretched – 'we've got peace, quiet and privacy'.

At that exact moment a roar that sounded like someone taking a detuned helicopter apart with a chainsaw shattered the stillness. I glanced up through the screen door, cringing in anticipation of a Cessna tearing the roof off the house. The noise grew, its crescendo overlaid with an even louder hillbilly soundtrack, and then, from across the room, I saw a man in a baseball cap and plaid shirt skim across the swamp on a high chair.

'Motherfucking airboats!' hissed Gene, shaking his head. He glared at me as though Everglades City had been my idea. 'We're going to have a problem here.'

I grabbed the binbag containing my personal effects from the car and lugged it sullenly up the steps. Gene had already claimed the room with the view as his own, and I was assigned the remaining bedroom, the one without cur-tains that allowed the morning sun to come streaming in like God's great wake-up call. My whispered mantra was too grim to keep me in a state of serenity, and ten days sud-denly seemed like an eternity. I was inclined to agree with Gene in this respect: we were indeed going to have a prob-lem here. I'd been counting my chickens since five-thirty this morning, checking that the clutch was warm and safe with every idle thought, and now the Queen of Saigon had stamped all over them in his Gucci jungle boots. I lay back on a blood-speckled mattress with the orthopaedic proper-ties of a sack of pig iron and stared at the bug-splattered ceiling.

What the hell was Sherry-Lee going to think?

I covered my face with my hands as her point of view came into focus. History had repeated itself. The trailer was empty and another smooth-talking bastard who had promised her a new life in Mexico had shagged her and fucked off into the night. Once again she had been taken in by lies and seafood, by the glister of gold and the promise of a future. Yet again she had been duped by a man who protested his love and adoration, and there she was, alone in the park. My reputation in Lee County was in grave jeopardy, and I needed to contact the only person whose opinion counted as soon as possible to reassure her that I was, and always would be, for real. The problem was that she wasn't connected. But I reckoned Alligator Strip would be happy to pass a message on to Darlene.

I sloped into the living room, clammy and irritable as the speed began to wear off. The smart way to avoid a downer was to snort a few more lines of whatever dog had bitten you, but my amphetamine mongrel was virtually hairless and I needed all his remaining fur for my forthcoming housework.

Gene was on his knees, connecting his laptop to a phone socket.

'I'm going out,' I announced. 'I fancy a stroll.'

To the nearest phone booth and then the nearest bar.

'Where to?' grunted Gene, a modem cable between his teeth.

'Just along the river bank and back. Check out the birds and stuff.'

'Hang on,' he urged, 'I'll come with you.' As if Gene had ever checked out a bird in his life.

A Treasury Department surveillance team would have heard the bitching and the slapping long before they saw us coming down the riverside lane. For a man who had spent months on deniable black recon ops deep in the Laotian jungle, Gene was a bit of a sissy when it came to bugs. I welcomed them with open veins, certain that I could bear their biting long enough to lose Gene. As soon as he retreated I would hook a left and take a stroll downtown.

'What do you know about fishing?' he asked, waving a lit cigarette around his head.

I slapped an overweight mosquito from my wrist. 'Snook and tarpon are good in these parts.'

'Sure are,' agreed Gene. 'What else do you know?'

I shrugged. 'Not much.'

American men do not like to be perceived as ignorant in piscine matters. Black, white, gay, straight, WASP, kike or wop, none will admit that he doesn't know his bass from his rainbow. Evil, foreign counter-intelligence agencies should take note: all it requires to catch an American agent is the loudly expressed assertion that nobody round here knows a damn thing about bonefish. Against this solid fact it was somewhat unrealistic of Gene to insist that we pretend to be fishermen. He was fat, gay and urban. The only fish I knew anything about was the roach. And Everglades City was not a village for spinning a line. Inconveniently, however, there was no other reason to be here.

'That settles it, then,' nodded Gene grimly.

'Settles what?'

'We dig in. No socialising, no contact with outside parties until D plus three. No bars, no restaurants, no nothing.'

I stopped and slapped him hard on the ear. He yelped and leapt backwards, clapping a puffy hand to the side of his head. 'What the fuck are you doing?' he cried.

'Skeeter,' I replied, stone-faced. 'Big as a rabbit, chomping down on your lobe, man.'

He gave me a long, uncertain stare, rubbing his ear with one hand and scratching his belly with the other. 'Let's go stock up at the store.'

★

The sign on the door of Everglades City's only supermarket stated that the store was open until eight. I rattled the handle and peered into the unlit interior.

'Closed early tonight,' reported a fat kid on a mountain bike, 'on account of everybody going to the Booster Club dance.'

I could see the beer through the grimy glass. I slapped the door. 'Fucking marvellous. Where can we get food?'

The kid shrugged. 'Try the Cat House.'

I glanced at Gene, trying to look like the outdoors type behind the wheel. 'Nah, my mate won't like it. Anywhere else?'

'You guys fishermen?'

I nodded. 'Yeah, why?'

'Try the Rod and Gun Club. All the fishing guys hang out there.'

I shook my head. 'We'll try the Cat House.'

The kid laughed: it was an old joke but it got them every time. 'It ain't a whorehouse,' he giggled. 'It's just a restaurant and a bar.'

'Yeah? Well that's another reason why this place ain't a proper city,' I sniffed.

The Cat House was a nautically themed diner on the road out of town. They served beer at the back and deep-fried everything in the front, except tonight, because everybody had gone to the Booster Club dance. There was a chance that we could order food from the bar, but, warned the elderly broom-pusher, it wouldn't be nothing fancy. I looked around. It would never have been anything fancy.

The bar at the back, on the other hand, was as good as it got. Highly combustible and easily hosed down, its most attractive features included a full-length bar with footrail and matching stools, a jukebox, an Addams Family pinball machine and a pair of fight-inducing pool tables. I looked around, beaming: Everglades City had just gained its charter.

We took a booth as far away from the bar as Gene could place himself – a move that succeeded in making us even more obvious to the three laconic patrons watching Nascar on the big screen. Silent and scruffy in three handy sizes, they looked like the nation depended on them, like the ravens at the Tower. If all three left at once, the White House would fall to a Democrat. It was a heavy burden, and one they bore with the sobriety demanded by such a weighty obligation.

The barmaid was overweight and overdue, and when she eventually came to take our order she made it clear that she too wanted to be at the Booster Club dance. I ordered a pitcher of beer, two glasses and a selection of deep-fried varmints cooked in batter. She poured the pitcher, left it on the bartop, and slouched into the kitchen. I went to collect it, and no sooner had I turned my back on him than Gene pulled. She was tall, tattooed, powerful and fell right into Gene's age bracket, if not his preferred gender. She wore skin-tight jeans, a low-cut gingham blouse and a bleached denim jacket with Old Glory stitched across the back. Her thick red hair was piled high on her head and it was fair to assume she was already a few beers ahead of us.

'This your son, sugar?' she slurred as I shuffled around her backside.

Gene thought for a moment and nodded.

She studied me with the disdain of a lady magistrate. 'Didn't get his daddy's looks, now, did he?' She perched daintily on the table and turned back to Gene. 'Aren't you going to buy me a drink, sugar?'

Gene rubbed his swollen ear and glanced nervously around the bar. He was all alone. 'Sure,' he smiled, firing a glare at me.

I smiled back.

'What can I get you, ma'am?'

She scratched her ear thoughtfully. 'I'll have a rum and Coke, please. Call me Candi. What's your name?'

'I'll get the lady her drink, Dad,' I smirked, leaving him to introduce himself.

'Hey, Derrick,' grunted the barmaid as she poured the Cuba Libre.

The largest of the three patrons, a scar-faced man with a Zapata moustache wearing a vintage creation from the house of Harley, raised an eyebrow. 'What?'

'Go get Candi before Cecil comes in and catches her.'

The aged biker looked round. 'She fishing for tourists again?'

He lifted himself from his stool with creaking bones and limped over to where Gene was being seduced. My dad was squirming as I delivered the cocktail, assuming that Derrick was Candi's man, and that he was on the country road to a redneck kicking. I sat down and sipped my beer, using the foam to hide my grin. Candi did not want to leave.

'Billy-Bob here has bought me a drink and I'm going to sit here and drink it,' she insisted. 'Honestly, Derrick, I'm not giving him head nor nothing.'

Derrick grunted and Candi turned to Gene.

'Derrick here's afraid my man's gonna come in through that door and cause a big old scene, ain't you, Derrick?' She leaned closer, as though sharing a confidence. 'Derrick's kind of new round here. He drives a tow truck for a livin'.'

'Dad, why don't I pour Derrick a drink?' I suggested.

Candi turned to look at me, wobbling slightly. 'He's got nice manners, your boy,' she declared. 'What's his name, Billy-Bob?'

'Judas,' smiled Gene sweetly, through cracking teeth.

'Well, hi there, Judas,' she cried. 'I'm Candi, this here's Derrick and any minute now Cecil's going to come by, but we ain't doing nothing but being friendly.'

'Let's hope your husband sees it the same way,' chuckled Gene. He was very pale.

'Hell, Cecil ain't my husband,' screeched Candi. 'Barron's my husband and he's up in Charlotte at the minute.'

Christ Almighty, I thought, they're all at it.

'Lots of women round here got menfolk in prison,' sniffed Derrick. 'You don't see them fooling around.'

'Correction,' cried Candi. '*You* don't see them fooling around. Rest of us do. And I'm marking time for Barron.' She hooked her top back with a white-painted talon and pushed her cleavage towards Gene.

'See that, Billy-Bob? I got a tattooed tear – one for every year he's away.'

'S'lucky you got such big old titties, then,' said Derrick, ''cos your Barron going to be away a long, long time.'

'Well I'm entitled to a little R 'n' R from my long, painful vigil, don't you think, Billy-Bob?'

Derrick turned a salt-tanned face to Gene and raised an eyebrow. 'Well, what *do* you think, Billy-Bob?'

Gene slurped his beer, looked round and clocked the lower half of a faded blue tattoo on Derrick's broad right arm. He smiled. 'I'd say that to err is human and to forgive is divine, but that neither is Marine Corps policy. What do you say, Derrick?'

The old soak grinned and raised his glass. 'Don't mean nothin'. What outfit were you?'

'First of the Ninth, airborne recon.'

'Goddamnit!' cried Derrick. 'What did you say your name was?'

While Gene was dug in and under fire I slipped away

from the table and headed for the payphone outside the restrooms.

'Information. What city, please?'

'Fort Myers, Florida.'

'Business or residential, please, sir?'

'Business.'

'Name, please?'

'Alligator Strip.'

'One moment, please . . .'

I drummed my fingers on the scratched black tabletop. My message would be cool, confident and weighted with gilded promise. Concise, reassuring and . . .

'I'm sorry, sir, we have no listing for Alligator Strip in the Fort Myers area. Do you have another enquiry?'

Suddenly lost, I panicked. I urged the operator to recheck her database. I spelled out the name. I described the location and the nature of the business. While she was happy to search for the listings of similar establishments in the greater Fort Myers area, she had no information on Alligator Strip. A sudden crash and an excited clamour of raised voices came from the bar. I killed the connection and went back in.

Candi was brushing beer from her blouse and shaking her head while Derrick, restrained by one of his buddies, was receiving a lecture in public relations from the other. Gene was nowhere to be seen. I tiptoed past the scene like a runaway dog, but Derrick spotted me as I neared the door.

'Son,' he called, 'you tell your daddy I ain't done with him yet, y'hear?'

I showed no reaction, no emotion, and scarpered.

It probably wasn't the first time Gene had been caught out. He'd caught a fat lip to complement his cauliflower ear and he sat seething and smoking in the driving seat of the Toyota. I jumped in and we drove the half-mile back to the stilt-shack in silence. Once indoors, I handed him a cold flannel.

'What happened?'

In Gene's world, everything was someone else's fault, and right now he had only me to blame. The self-loathing and shame that are the cruel companions of an unexpected kicking spilled over and burned acid holes in the wooden floor as Gene reworked his memory of the evening to clear himself of any wrongdoing. He had in fact done little that I had seen or heard to warrant a slap, but he kept curiously quiet about his part in Ho Chi Minh's victory. Like he said, he didn't like to talk about Vietnam. I could understand his logic: I didn't like to talk about Vietnam, because I'd never been there either.

When his ire had boiled dry I made him some coffee and laid out the backgammon board. We ate a dry ration of potato chips, my despair somewhat assuaged by the diplomatic suspension of Gene's frankly ludicrous imposition of prohibition on his dissolute staff. Brighter than Bligh, though no less bruised, he realised that suspension of the rum ration would lead to mutiny and issued me his barely adequate homecoming gift of a half-bottle of Jack. He stuck to freshly brewed Mountain Blend, the combination of caffeine and nicotine keeping him aggressively alert and viciously competitive. Every double he rolled was an uppercut to Derrick's jaw, and every time he blitzed my lone stones it was a kick in the nuts for the real Vietnam vet. I quit when the score reached forty-eight to nine, leaving the table and bidding my conqueror goodnight like a black-tied earl in Monte Carlo. My resemblance to outsmarted Old World aristocracy ended there: I was gagging for a spliff. But with the lights on and everybody home it wasn't happening tonight. Nor the next day.

On Monday I awoke with Sherry-Lee's angry despair

lying beside me like a bloody horsehead. As I lay staring at a lizard on a water-stained wall in a stilt-stacked shack in Everglades City, I knew that she would be lying wide-eyed and restless in her narrow, fragrant bed, staring at the cracked ceiling and chuckling at God's capacity for cruel and unusual punishment. My apparent betrayal of her trust wouldn't have stopped her visiting her daughter in Okeechobee yesterday and I wondered if Angie had asked where Tomás the Talking Martyr had gone. I rolled out of bed and checked the Sunshine State. A low, fast-moving front of sweating, over-weight cloud rolled grimly to the west, spilling its guts over the swamp in dense, grey, flying columns. Lower down, squalls kicked a spray from the puddles in the street and a hapless crow dropped his plans to fly straight to Miami as an intemperate easterly pushed him backwards into the trees.

'Summer's gone for sure,' announced Gene cheerily from the coffee machine. He liked announcing the bad things in life, as if their revelation served to reduce others to his low life of miserable cynicism. Gene enjoyed the idea that there was work in the morning, that Christmas was over for another year, that last orders had been called and that the end was nigh.

I grunted and pulled a cracked mug from the cupboard. 'What are we doing today?'

He pointed at me with both index fingers and nodded. 'Good question. Today we start placing orders. We buy krugerrands. We buy pandas. We buy maple leaves, and, above all, we buy eagles. Minimum buy ten pieces; maximum order value twenty thousand bucks. We start with our favourite suppliers – the A list – and we work our way down. Same story to every dealer on the list, same promise of prompt payment on signed receipt. Got it?' He checked his watch.

I nodded distractedly, wondering what was stuck in my hair and realising how much we take the First World for granted. We expect information on demand and long-distance communication at the lightest touch of a button. We know that a twist of the tap will summon hot water, and the movement of a thumb will spark a flame. In one bored minute we can call up more entertainment and education than we could absorb in one year, yet all it takes is an unlisted number to drop us into the heart of darkness. The assumption that I could call up Sherry-Lee's place of work and leave a message any time I felt inclined so to do had supported me like a cheap inflatable. Suddenly I found myself sinking, fighting against a rip that was sucking me away from Fort Myers Beach. I needed to stop drifting and start swimming against the tide. I needed to contact Sherry-Lee.

'Incoming!' yelled Gene.

I jumped, spilling coffee on my clean work surface. 'Jesus Christ, Gene!'

'Jesus Christ? What the fuck has He got to do with anything? The only second coming round here is going to be the USPS hauling out a supplementary delivery of gold to Whitehall Numismatics, understand?'

I sighed. 'How we going to pay for all this?'

He rubbed his grazed chin and grinned. 'We don't.'

In the six months since Gene had established the company, Whitehall Numismatics, in name and in deed, had gained the confidence of a three-page listing of Dixie's coin dealers. We knew what we wanted, and we negotiated hard to achieve workable margins. We were tough and professional, but we were fair, and our oversized cheques arrived when we said they would. We had succeeded in making an impression on our suppliers by giving them the red-carpet treatment. Now we were going to rip it from under their feet. If I had possessed a cigar, I would have given it to Gene.

'It's as good as it ever gets,' he grinned. 'We order, and they get the cheque three days later. Week in, week out, Whitehall Numismatics keeps its word. Buy or sell, we're consistent, and now we're pursuing a new and profitable line in bullion. Here comes Labor Day, and what happens?' He knew I didn't know, so he continued, throwing grand gestures to the room like an evil and slightly underestimated genius. 'Labor Day: you want to quit work on Thursday night – take the Friday off and make a long weekend of it. Couple of days prior you get a call from those nice guys at Whitehall Numismatics: fifteen grand's worth of eagles, cheques in the post on signed receipt. That's cool, because those Whitehall boys are cool. Nice sale, too, just before the holiday, something to celebrate over the weekend, and you ship those birdies a.s.a.p. You know you ain't gonna get a cheque before next Tuesday at the earliest, what with the national holiday and all, and you'll give it 'til Thursday before you call. That gives Whitehall Numismatics a fucking week to dispose of your gold before the alarm bells start ringing, and at the end of the day, what are you gonna do? Call the cops?' He pulled the kind of grin Jack Nicholson had to practise. 'Are you fuck! You're gonna kick yourself hard and put the whole thing down to experience. Bullion dealers, like us, are selling confidence: confidence in the future. They start admitting that they've been had by a team of grifters it ain't going to look so good on their reputation, is it? "Hi, we're Mom and Pop Coin Investments, the one's who got ripped off last Labor Day. We really need your business, 'cos we're dumb fucks who can't hold on to our assets." These sorry assholes are going to meet with each other all over the American South and they ain't gonna share

for one moment that thing that they all have in common –
that they lost fifteen, twenty grand in one day last Labor Day
to you and me. And that, Troop, is why this is the perfect,
white-collar, unstained crime. Get dialling. Get buying.
Dixie's got cotton needs pickin'.'

I had to admire the bastard, even if I was beginning to
loathe him. He'd lit a Marlboro and he was beaming, and if
he'd really been to Vietnam I might have overlooked my dis-
taste and considered myself a member of the A-Team.

Face Man, probably.

10

'Hi, Martin Brock here from Whitehall Numismatics.'

'Good day to you, Sam! It's Gene Renoir calling from Fort Myers – got a fat order for you buddy!'

'Absolutely, Dave, but growth is always encouraging. What krugerrand stocks are you holding?'

'Yeah, I can shift those maples. I'll give you a call later in the week. What do I owe you?'

'That's correct Mr Wildstern: same address by USPS registered. We'll mail a cheque for the full amount on signed receipt, just like always.'

'What's that? I lost you for a minute there, Ted: it's blowing up a gale down here in Fort Myers. Say it again . . . Yeah, okay, call it a round five K on top of the sixteen-eight and chuck 'em in. Mail 'em separately, though . . .'

By Monday lunchtime – a period Gene irritatingly referred to as the 'midday rest break' – the buying department of Whitehall Numismatics had placed orders for just under one hundred and eighty thousand dollars' worth of transferable gold bullion.

Gene worked on while I stood at the window, blowing smoke into the face of a thuggish storm. The summer was over but Christmas had come early – the chocolate coins were on their way. I should have been excited and motivated by the imminent arrival of ill-gotten wealth, by the finale of this gilt-edged American adventure, and instead I was staring north through the rain, feeling angry, frustrated and scared. Most of the anger was wrapped in bright red paper and labelled 'Gene' in scratchy black ink. This little one was for pretending to be a war hero. That one was for abducting me from my home, not once, but twice, and for doing so under false pretences. Another, with ripped wrapping that threatened to reveal its contents, was for his hatred of Sherry-Lee and his seemingly successful attempt to split us up. There was token anger for his muesli and prissiness, a little something for his smugness and a bagatelle for his evasiveness. Everything about Gene was fake and tedious, and when I looked hard at what I felt for him I could see that even my ire was small and cheap and plastic. I'd blown my savings this year on a great big piece of genuine rage for myself and my remarkable ability to fuck everything up without getting killed. I had represented myself to Sherry-Lee as her personal saviour, to Brad as his conscience, to Gene as his fool, and I had failed them all because I didn't recognise the face in the mirror. I did now, though: my ghost looked back at me from the rain-streaked glass, a smoke-wreathed projection on the river and the swamp.

I was Jumpin' Jack Flash and it was a right old gas, an adventurer in the worst sense of the word, seeking to increase my wealth by unscrupulous means. My career path had followed an undulating downhill trail past the indefensible positions of drug dealer, thief, fugitive and uncertified tour guide. Although the post of assistant grifter marked a rare peak on a downwards plot, I now owned a cheap gun, had developed a taste for amphetamine sulphate and was becoming increasingly attracted to pick-up trucks, especially the models with big chrome roll-bars and lighting rigs. If I failed to halt my decline here the next stop was homelessness and addiction. I wasn't really so very far from that part of life's valley occupied by the *basuco*-addicted garbage-pickers of Bogota, rummaging through the rubbish heaps and scraping together their *centavos* for the next hit.

I shivered, pressing my hot head against the cold glass, the dog-end burning my fingers. Payday was coming, but it wouldn't take many poor decisions for me to become parted from my fool's gold. Vagrancy was a real possibility, and I realised with resignation that I'd probably make a pretty good wino. I was skilled at getting drunk, adept at getting high and already had a reputation for mumbling to myself. I lived for the day – or, more specifically, the night – pursuing short-term plans and demanding instant gratification, and the lower I sank, the simpler it became. Sleep, get high, get drunk and die.

I needed Sherry-Lee, and her daughter was a God-given bonus, a ledge upon which I could rest and build a shelter. Without them, I was Midas, and all the gold in the world only made me ill.

The house wobbled precariously on its stilts as a pair of airboats roared down the river, causing the glass to vibrate in salt-rotten frames and small falls of dust to spill from the rafters.

Gene tossed his pen at the window, his curse lost in the blast from two rear-mounted aero-engines. 'What the fuck was that?' he cried, clutching his ears as they skimmed into the murk.

'Florida crackers,' I replied, 'going fishing in the rain, the mad fuckers.'

I lit another cigarette and switched on the TV, hoping for news of the missing kid, but yearning more for footage of the trailer park that would give me a clue how to contact Sherry-Lee. Everybody was talking about the weather, so I switched off, went to my room, and wrote a letter on company notepaper:

Darling S-L,

It looks bad, doesn't it? Looks like I just upped and split, but the truth is that I had as much idea as you that this was going down. I'm not far away, holed up in a leaky shack in a dump called Everglades City, somewhere south of Naples. We're in the process of winding up the business, and my plans for the future remain the same as we discussed. It's hard to concentrate on the details because all I think of all day and all night is you, and Mexico, and I hope with all my heart that you still trust me. I will come through with the goods, and I pray that you'll be packed and ready. Give me a call right now — the number's at the top. If Gene answers, say your name is Lisa from Cornish Coins, and I'll know it's you. What are you waiting for? Call now! I love you.

Martin.

I wrote, 'News From England' on the envelope, sealed it with a kiss and wandered back into the living room, stretching with false nonchalance like someone with something to hide. 'Need any letters posting?' I wondered, vaguely.

Gene looked up suspiciously. 'No.'

'Okay,' I shrugged. 'Just fancied a bit of air.'

'Just fancied a little weed, don't you mean?' he sneered.

I made a half-hearted attempt to defend my integrity. 'I don't smoke weed! How can you say that?'

Gene shook his head. 'Because you do and I can. Now get back to work.'

We knocked off at five, having nearly doubled our take on the day. Gene yawned in a pleased yet apprehensive manner. He looked at his watch. 'Wanna ride with me to the store?'

I hesitated. Going with Gene would give me an opportunity to post my letter, while remaining behind would give me freedom of the phone for as long as he was gone. The chance to buy beer swayed my decision, and I rode with him to the store, slipping the rain-stained letter into the mailbox while he fumbled with his big, gay umbrella. Back at the shack, I stuffed my frozen chilli dinner into the oven and took a beer to the bath while Gene minced around with garlic, onions and zucchini, sipping sparkling elderflower cordial from a Collins glass.

I hadn't bothered reading the cooking instructions on the packaging but my dinner seemed to have benefited from the extra thirty minutes' cooking time. I sat on the sofa and crunched on it while waiting for shots of Bridgeview Trailer Park to come on the local news.

Gene made a big show of uncorking a bottle of Californian Chardonnay and wafted across the kitchen area, enthusing about crème fraîche. 'I could have been one of those TV gourmands, you know,' he called. 'It's amazing that down here, on the southernmost fringe of the United States, in some God-forsaken convenience store that's closer to Havana than it is to the state capital, I can buy fresh veal, imported polenta, the freshest 'erbs.'

And I couldn't get the number of a strip club. The frontier was not what it used to be. 'It's herbs,' I yelled. 'Why do you Septics always say 'erbs? And anyway, you should be drinking Pinot Grigio with that veal. The Chardonnay is way too fragrant.'

'Hark at the connoisseur with his burned TV dinner and his Bud,' grunted Gene.

'It's not burned,' I retorted. 'It's supposed to be this colour. And beer is the correct accompaniment for chilli.'

'*Burned* chilli,' said Gene, determined to have the last word.

I let him have it, my smouldering anger now attracted by television's obsession with the weather. I punched through the six channels that made it this far, one after another, over and over again, and all I saw were men in suits, big-haired women and log-end weathermaps. I switched it off and stomped across to the window.

'You should pay attention to met reports,' said Gene.

I lit a fag and stared out at the rain. 'Don't need a weatherman to see what way the wind blows.' Gene sipped his inappropriate wine. 'Very counterculture.' He joined me at the window.

'We're bang in the middle of the hurricane season,' he declared, pointing at the rushing clouds. 'That's why they're panicking on the TV. Hurricane Andrew flattened this state back in 'ninety-two, and with *El Niño* out there like some delinquent *Chicano* fucking with the weather system, they're worried he's going to father some mean bastards.'

'That's not what they said on TV,' I remarked.

'What the fuck do they know,' sneered Gene. 'You do not want to be here when a hurricane hits, believe me.'

'But we are,' I pointed out. 'Why didn't we stay in the trailer?'

Gene laughed like a smartarse. 'Yeah, right. A trailer will be real safe.'

'But it's up in Fort Myers, not down here in Everglades City.'

'And that's a fifteen-minute trip for a one hundred and sixty-mile-per-hour gust. Hurricanes aren't your weak-ass English thunderstorms, Troop. They're the closest thing God's got to nukes. Here or Naples or Fort Myers don't make no difference.' He sniffed me. 'You been using my Turkish lemon balm bath soak?'

'Course not,' I scoffed, moving away. 'Don't you think we should evacuate?'

He nodded, watching the clouds fly past. 'Absolutely. As soon as the last penny drops, we're gone, over the

Mason–Dixon Line, selling coins for cash at bargain prices.'
He cast a sideways glance in my direction. 'Ever been to
New York?'

'Not yet,' I replied.

Gene grinned. 'You'll like it there. It's full of idiots.'

A bad day turned into a worse night as I learned that my
contract stood until the last of the stolen coins had been sold.
Furthermore, for sound security reasons, not a single twinklebirdy would be offered for sale anywhere south of
Hagerstown, Maryland, the point where 'y'all' became
'youse' and Old Glory stopped flapping. It was twelve hundred miles north of where I wanted to be.

I watched the weather reports with a face like thunder
while Gene chewed on his veal and browsed through the
latest copy of *Recreational Pilot*. A stiff-haired blonde in a
blue wool suit was reprising the news for those who had just
tuned in.

'Weathermen keeping a close eye on the tropical disturbance developing three hundred miles east of Miami
reported this afternoon that an increase in wind speed had
caused the event to be officially upgraded to a tropical
depression. Whether it will deepen to become an official
tropical storm or merely blow itself out is dependent on
high-altitude winds and is, in the words of Jeff C.
Mackleman of the National Oceanic and Atmospheric
Administration, "anybody's guess".' She gave a little shrug
that asked more questions about tax dollars and meteorological research than a board of inquiry and shuffled her papers.

'Well, we've got Pablo Trushell from the Emergency
Management Division outside in the rain right now. Pablo,
they don't yet know if this depression will develop further or
whether it will just fade away. Is it fair to say that the summer
is officially over?'

An immaculately windswept man in an orange weather-proof appeared beneath a dripping umbrella. 'Well, Nancy, Labor Day is only a few days away now so I guess it is officially the end of the summer. It is, of course, incredibly difficult to predict how storms are going to develop, but I would remind you all that this is the hurricane season, we've seen them here before and we'll no doubt see them again—'

It was all conjecture, and hot air caused storms. I switched over to watch a rerun of *The Dukes of Hazzard* and then, exhausted by an only partially accountable anxiety, I crashed into hot and restless sleep.

They were all wrong: Gene, Pablo from the Emergency Management Division, Nancy Rodriguez with her scary blond hair. The summer must have left the iron on, or forgotten its passport, because when I woke up, foul-mouthed and itchy on Tuesday, it was back. The US Postal Service vans came and went in bright sunshine beneath deep blue skies. I watched the crow set off for Miami from the steps, then took another four Jiffy bags in to Gene.

He opened each with ear-to-ear glee, ticking the senders off a two-page list. 'We're getting rich, Troop,' he announced. 'Check it out!'

The treasure pile of my imagination was built from wobbly stacks of gleaming golden coin, heaped to different levels like a yellow bar chart of comparative dishonesty. Reality, as ever, was more prosaic. Krugerrands, maple leaves and eagles came wrapped in space-saving Treasury tubes that stood like a convenience-store display of miniature, tooth-cracking potato chips. Pandas arrived in sheets of transparent plastic that smothered their romance and suffocated their lustre. Packaging reduced the coin to a mere commodity, and it seemed that careful precautions had been taken to protect the gold from human soiling. Maybe it was the other way round; maybe the intention was to save man from auriferous contamination, as if it were understood that this beautiful, enchanting and powerful element could poison the mind in the same way that unshielded radium could pollute the body.

Gene held a sheet of pandas up to the light, chuckling like a fat man trapped in a deli. He was already tainted, irradiated and showing the first symptoms of gold fever. Paranoia, megalomania and self-destruction were sure to follow, but with luck and determination I'd be in Mexico by then.

With Sherry-Lee.

I left him counting his money and started dialling. Waiting for Preston Investment to pick up, I practised positive visualisation, projecting an image of the only stripper I cared for on the back of my eyelids. She was walking in the sunshine, holding a bunch of yellow flowers and wearing no shoes. I didn't notice any clothes, either. She was heading to the reception block to pick up her mail. Roscoe, the bloated swamp rat, had been fired and a kindly faced older gentleman had replaced him. Sherry-Lee smiled as she wafted into reception, and the old man, the twinkle in his eye reflected in his half-moon glasses, shuffled through the mail to see if there was anything for her . . .

'Preston Investments, Preston himself speaking. How may I help you this morning?'

Another day, another truckload of gold dollars. I worked in shorts and nothing else, my bare skin shiny with sweat in the oppressive humidity. When the sun finally called it a day and slipped into the bath we had ordered just short of five hundred thousand dollars' worth of bullion. I heated up something called a Cheesy Lunch for my dinner and washed it down with beer. Gene prepared a seafood linguine with a herb salad and a glass of oaked Chardonnay. I told him that a Sauvignon Blanc would have been more suitable, and he told me to fuck off. He beat me ninety-two–eight at backgammon, then took his aviation magazine to bed. I sat and watched the telephone for a while, willing it to ring and wishing that Gene would slip into a deep, dark sleep and give me the opportunity to dial out.

Neither happened.

His light was still on when I went to bed, and he looked tired and irritable on Wednesday morning. He was waiting for me when I breezed into the living room, rough-faced and red-eyed like a father who had been up all night. 'You seen my spare set of keys?' he growled.

I pushed past him and poured coffee. 'Nope. Which keys?'

'My car keys. The set with the Cessna keyring.'

I shook my head in denial

Gene shook his in disbelief. 'Well, they're gone. They're not where I left them, and I don't lose things. Yesterday they were there, and today they've gone.'

'So?' I shrugged. 'You've got another set, haven't you?'

'That's not the goddamned point,' he muttered, what was left of his temper crashing to the floor as the first airboat of the day howled past. Gene crossed angrily to the window and snatched the drapes closed. 'Fucking hick assholes staring in through this window every time they pass. They don't look in no one else's house, do they?'

I took a deep, slow breath. The day had started badly for Gene: he'd lost his car keys and the neighbours were spying on him. The yellow dust was corrupting his mind, and here came the paranoia.

I kept my head down and dialled out, starting at the top of

the second page of marks. The post arrived at ten, and I rose, stretching, to meet the mailman at the door.

Gene ended his call and overtook me. 'Go make some more calls,' he ordered. 'I'll sign for the packages from now on.'

I looked into his face long enough to register my acknowledgement of his distrust, then nodded nonchalantly. 'Fair enough.'

'I'm not asking for your permission and I do not have to explain myself,' he replied, his voice rising. He would have added more, but the mailman interrupted him. The first of several deliveries that day cheered him up somewhat, but his happiness was shallow and unhealthy. He dragged the black polyester holdall from his room and emptied the wrapped bullion from it, standing the tubes on the tabletop in ordered ranks. Swelling them with the new arrivals, he counted over and over again, scribbling and scratching with a short pencil on his yellow pad. 'Keep those calls short,' he snapped as I hung up on Terry's All Gold in Macon, Georgia. 'All I'm hearing is your tongue flapping. You're not supposed to be shooting the breeze with these people – just get in, place the order, and get out. That way we might just make our target.'

I bit my lip. I had my own reasons for keeping my call time to a minimum: I was expecting a call any minute from Lisa of Cornish Coins, and I was scared she'd give up on me if she found me engaged. It had happened before.

The lunchtime news reported that the tropical depression now spinning like a cracked plate on a wobbly stick somewhere east of Eleuthera had gathered enough momentum to qualify as a tropical storm. This upgrade brought increased benefits and concessions to the busy whirl of thunder and lightning, including entry to all the best golf courses in the state and access to any marina it wished to visit. I watched it on the Doppler, a jerky, two-dimensional, mono-chrome representation that looked like an ultrasound scan of one of *El Niño*'s bastards. I couldn't yet tell if it was a girl or a boy, but the atmosphere was pregnant with foreboding and outside it was still summer.

I made my last call of the day at five-thirty, ordering a sheet of pandas and two tubes of eagles from Union Bullion of Baton Rouge and bringing the total value of our gold orders up to eight hundred and eighty-five thousand dollars, with one day to go. The US Postal Service and an assortment of courier companies had already delivered 650 eagles, 240 maple leaves, 230 krugerrands and 200 black-eyed pandas, a hoard which weighed just under ninety-five pounds and was worth just over four hundred and seventy-five thousand dollars.

Gene sat at the table, mesmerised by his fortune, licking his lips and rubbing together his sweaty palms as he ordered and reordered the eighty-eight US Treasury tubes, the twenty-four rolls from the Royal Canadian Mint and the twenty polythene sheets packed in Beijing.

I cooked myself something called a Wang Dang Doodle and ate it from its disposable packaging, averting my eyes from the unhealthy glow as I watched the news with sauce dripping down my chin. Nancy Rodriguez looked glamorous, successful, fit and rich, but she didn't look like she had much fun. She slipped on a serious expression and gave it to me straight.

'At four-thirty this afternoon the Federal Emergency Management Agency issued a hurricane watch for the south Florida area. Now remember that a hurricane watch means that the area may experience hurricane or tropical-storm conditions within the next thirty-six hours. Emergency Management spokesman John Billman explains what we should be doing to prepare: John?'

'Hurricane's coming,' I reported.

'Told you,' replied Gene.

'There's a lot of stuff we're supposed to be doing,' I observed. 'Where are the radio and the spare batteries kept?'

Gene studied an unwrapped eagle in the same way that I might have studied Miss August. 'No idea,' he drawled.

'We've got to get flashlights, spare food, beer – obviously – and we're not allowed to let the gas tank be less than half full. How much gas have we got?'

Gene sat upright and stared at me, a tight smile on his thin mouth. 'You're scared, aren't you?'

'No,' I countered. 'I just think we should be prepared.'

He yawned and shook his head. 'I've been studying the met, and the chances of this thing making landfall are minimal. If she does, she'll be coming overland from Dade, so there's no risk of a storm surge. This house' – he stood up and stamped his bright white trainer into the floor – 'was built in 1934, way before the Southern Building Conference came up with their precious code. It survived Labor Day in 'thirty-five, Donna in 'sixty, Isabell in 'sixty-four, that pussy Andrew in 'ninety-two and Georges a couple of years back. We'll sit tight, carry on as normal, and when she's blown herself out we'll split. Happy?'

Not really. One minute he was telling me that God was dropping nukes on us, and the next he's saying it's cool to ride it out in a wooden house. I felt like the good-looking one of the three little pigs.

'They reckon the roads will get washed away. What happens if we get trapped here?'

Gene waddled over to the sink and poured water on to his plate. 'We won't get trapped.' He turned and tossed me a wink of intrigue. 'Who said we needed roads, Troop?'

They were showing *Surfin' Mutts 1, 2* and *3* back-to-back

on one of the better-quality channels and I watched the crazy canine antics of the nation's nuttiest sea-dogs for over sixty minutes while Gene prepared a smoked-chicken Caesar. I was down to my last beer, Gene was all out of the wrong wine and neither of us had the heart to face the other over the backgammon board. We sat and watched the weather reports like political prisoners from opposite camps awaiting liberation; or an old married couple waiting for deliverance.

I left him watching *Outrageous Behavior 9: The Cop Files* and fell on to my bed like a gut-shot fugitive. Something Sherry-Lee had said, a splinter of conversation, had risen to the surface like a shell fragment and it needed attention before it went septic. I looked up and out at the same stars that had smiled on us last week on Fort Myers Beach and heard her words again.

She'd seen Brad at Alligator Strip. He'd seen her, then upped and left.

So what?

Maybe it turned out that Brad didn't have the heart to carry out his small-minded crime of passion, and then he didn't have the balls to tell me the contract had been cancelled. Maybe his mean-spirited departure on that faded Saturday morning had served to save his face and his reputation. Either way, it didn't matter.

Except that it did, and I was neither stoned nor drunk enough to work out why.

I studied my sweating palm in the orange light of a lighter's flame. The rattlesnake's kiss had corrupted the flesh into a carbuncle of knotty scar tissue that broke my lifeline and then the line of my heart. I held the flame closer, feeling no heat and no pain. I'd always reckoned on a snakebite leaving two holes, but the Okeechobee canebreak had given me four. That was America for you: always expect more. I looked to heaven for accord, but the stars had gone, their cold light replaced by the opaque glow of a rushing overcast.

On Thursday the van of the storm arrived, taking Everglades City like a riled-up mechanised battalion, rushing through the rainswept lots, knocking on doors and rattling windows, seeking out resistance and advising all well-meaning citizens to remain indoors. The tall palms rolled with the punches, bending in the recommended manner with the resignation of those who'd seen it all before. A vicious gust knocked the paper boy flat and tossed his folded copies of the *Naples News* into the column like shared booty. I watched as the printed pages flew like whitewater rafts above the deserted streets, wondering if there was any news of Solomon Bender. The foul weather didn't stop the US Postal Service, and if our gold was being delivered, it was reasonable to expect that Sherry-Lee had received my letter. I stubbed out my cigarette, finished my coffee and started dialling. Maybe she'd call today.

By two in the afternoon we had called every dealer on the list, and our orders totalled one million, three hundred and thirty-five thousand dollars. Deliveries were valued at just under eight hundred thousand, and even Gene couldn't help but be happy. He rolled a Twinklebirdy through his fingers like a speedfreak with obsessive–compulsive disorder, and when he spoke it was too fast and too loud. He hadn't shaved since Tuesday, and a dark cast lay across his sagging jawline like the shadow of the coming storm.

'Bet you've never seen such wealth,' he grinned, licking the scum from the corner of his mouth. 'Ten years in the conception, two years in the planning, and here we are, with one day to go and a table that's creaking under the

weight of it all.' He held up his eagle in the grey light, turning it over and over in his greasy fingers. 'See how it seems
to *generate* light?' he whispered. 'It's a goddamned shame to
sell all this off, you know.'

I didn't agree. I knew how he felt – I felt the same way
about big blocks of hash or crisp bundles of *muestra*-quality
cocaine – but all I saw on the table was an awkward commodity that was useless until converted into greenbacks.
Maybe I needed to enter into the spirit and catch a little gold
fever for myself. I picked a loose maple leaf from the table,
rubbing the Queen's cheek with my thumb.

'What the fuck are you doing?' barked Gene.

I stopped touching the Queen. 'What?'

He looked like I'd just stepped on his ingrowing toenail.
'Put it the fuck down! There's no need for it.'

'For what?' I cried.

He stood up and narrowed his eyes. 'Put that fucking
coin back on the table!' He stared right through my head, his
bloodshot eyes forbidding defiance.

I stared back, turning the coin in my palm as the wind
gasped and groaned, throwing hot Atlantic rain against the
window like handfuls of gravel. The Saturday Night Special
was still in my handbag, still ready to join any fight, and a
weak nine stones of bullion could be easily taken from this
overweight, out-of-shape, deranged fantasist. Maybe now
was the right time to talk about Vietnam, to get the skinny
on those Laotian ops, to have a frank discussion about treating people right, about respect. I'd been bitten by a
rattlesnake, and that made me lucky. Gene had been bitten
by the gold bug, and that made him sad, and extremely vulnerable. Sometimes I felt that our partnership could end
only badly. A loud hammering at the door checked my
derangement.

'US Mail – registered delivery!' yelled the mailman.

I dropped the maple leaf and walked away to watch the weather. We spoke just once more that foul and stormy day. I asked Gene when we would be leaving, and he replied coldly that we would depart as soon as the last package had been delivered.

I said fine.

He agreed.

What little trust had existed between us was blown away by the storm, and I realised that I couldn't sleep while there was a chance Gene would leave me snoring and head north through the rain with a trunkful of gold. Unfortunately he couldn't sleep either while his second set of car keys remained unaccounted for, and it was inevitable that we should pass the darkest hours of the night over a backgammon board. The TV burned blue in the background, and at eleven-thirty a grim-faced John Billman announced that the hurricane watch had been upgraded to a full-on hurricane warning.

'And that, for those who don't know, means that sustained winds of speeds in excess of seventy-four miles per hour are expected in the area within the next twenty-four hours. Residents on the barrier islands should already have actioned their evacuation plans and all boat owners should have been proactive in securing their vessels. Those of you who, for whatever reason, are not evacuating should have your hurricane kits ready for use and have decided where in the house you intend taking shelter. Those who are wisely choosing to follow official advice and evacuate the area should follow approved evacuation routes only, as shown on this station and on our website. Remember that if you do not have anyplace to go to get away from the hurricane you may use the county shelters, which, in most cases, are located in local high-school buildings. Just about now, Emergency Management officials aided by peace officers will be touring all areas to advise citizens on matters such as emergency evacuation routes and the location of shelters. We should all be tuning our radios in to the appropriate local emergency broadcasting frequencies for updates and advice from the Emergency Management teams in the affected areas. In a moment we'll be checking with the National Weather Center to get an exact update on the position and the status of this storm, but right now a brief message from our sponsors . . .'

I swivelled in my chair to look at Gene.

He rolled a double three and made the most of it. 'Hunraken was the Mayan god of wind and storms,' he announced. 'He was also the god of evil. His master was Gucumatz, son of the moon and the sun, the great feathered snake god.' He looked up from his manoeuvres, laying his small eyes upon me as though the rising winds and falling pressure were all my fault. 'You know what that implies?'

'That the Mayans hadn't the faintest grasp of reality?' I suggested.

'That the Mayans blamed hurricanes on serpents.'

Lightning flashed like paparazzi catching the God with a mystery blonde, and thunder crashed like the artillery Gene had never heard. I looked at my snakebite, feeling dreadfully unprepared for the worst.

The Kittie-Krunch commercial ended happily and John Billman was back, wetter and more worried than before. A link to the National Weather Center showed why. An unadorned brunette with tied-back hair and glasses who could easily have been a porno librarian told us the worst: Hurricane Louisa had just registered surface winds of one hundred and thirty-one miles per hour.

Gene whistled. 'Fucking cat. four,' he whispered.

Louisa was following a north-westerly course, stomping along at twenty-five miles per hour in the footsteps of her brother Georges, squashing bananas in the Lower Antilles, uprooting the dead in Haiti and drowning the tobacco crop in Cuba. Right now her roving eye was on Guinchos Cay, and Deadman's Cay was feeling the full force of her vicious temper.

Gene took this news rather badly, leaping up and rushing to the TV screen. 'Fuck it!' he yelled, running to his room and returning with his attaché case. 'Clear that shit off the table,' he ordered, unfolding a large air chart. He used his fingers as dividers and walked them crab-like from Rum Cay up to Everglades City. 'Shit,' he hissed, looking at his watch. 'That bitch'll be knocking on our door in six hours, and she'll be category five by then.'

'Is that bad?'

He nodded, ignoring the opportunity for sarcasm. 'It's fucking bad, Troop. Back-door we could have handled, but a landfall off the Gulf will fucking drown us. I figured this would happen. We're going to get a fifteen-foot storm surge coming through here like a fucking freight train full of TNT.' He looked at me as though I might have an answer.

I looked back in the same way, recalling that this was exactly what Gene had figured *wouldn't* happen.

He rubbed his chin. 'How much gold have we got?'

'Sixty-six per cent.'

'Sixty-six per cent,' he sighed. He lit a cigarette and sucked on it like they were blowing the 'Last Post'. He crossed to the window and stared out at Louisa's billowing, flash-lit petticoats, then turned and pointed at me. It was an Eisenhower moment.

'We go. We're splitting, getting out of here, right now.'

'What about tomorrow's deliveries?'

'Fuckin' Pony Express don't deliver in hurricanes, and by nine tomorrow morning this place will look like downtown Nagasaki after a wet night. Get your number twos, whatever's got your name on it, and leave the rest.'

I worked my jaw until my ears popped.

Gene noticed. 'Feel that?' he asked. 'That's the pressure going straight to hell. Now git.'

I grabbed my handbag and a change of clothes, stuffed them into a binbag and met Gene at the door. He handed me two soft-leather Mulberry grips and his vanity case, ordered me to load them into the trunk and caught up with me at the bottom of the steps hauling nine stones of gold in that black holdall. Fat rain whisked across the swamp like a besom, thrown before an unhinged wind that was clearly looking for trouble. Flashing blue lights were visible to the north as we first drove east and then doubled back, driving through an airburst of snatched leaves and broken palm fronds. Horizontal squalls rushed through the quivering headlights, and for a moment the wavering beams spilled across a sign that read 'Everglades Airpark, X01, Everglades City, Florida USA'. I looked at Gene, and he concentrated on the road ahead, pulling up beside something that looked disturbingly like a shrouded aircraft. He killed the engine and stepped into the rain, cursing as the wind got the door for him. I followed him, my hand on my head to stop it blowing away.

'You're having a bleedin' laugh, aren't you?' I yelled, but a vigilant gust caught the words and tossed them into the foaming ocean. The sight of the storm-whipped sea pulled me up and I stared like a Midwest moron at the white spikes and barbed-wire curls as they ripped the shoreline one hundred feet away, across something that looked ominously like a runway. 'You're fucking joking,' I called after him as he strode towards a low-lit office.

The wind howled like a widowed wolf as Gene tapped on doors and pressed his nose to the streaked glass. He spun on his heel and walked back towards me, an indignant incredulity on his face, as though it were inexplicable that a building thirty yards from where the storm surge would make landfall should be deserted at eleven-fifty on a Thursday night.

'We'll have to serve ourselves,' he muttered. 'Get the lights on.'

I held up a hand. 'What are we doing here, Gene?'

He stopped beside a wrapped tailplane and put his hands on his hips. 'Get the fucking lights, will you?'

I shook my head. 'You cannot possibly be contemplating taking an aircraft up in *this*. You can't even fly, for fuck's sake!'

He began removing the dust sheet from the tiny plane. 'Who says I can't?'

I did. 'Whose plane is that?'

He sighed in exasperation. 'It's mine, goddamn it. Now will you get the fucking lights or do I have to do it myself?'

Numbness crept like hemlock from my toes to my belly as I walked back to the car. I was no aviator, and I knew little of meteorology, but it seemed reasonable to consider an attempt to launch a pram with wings into a hurricane to be utterly fucking mental. I hit the headlights and told him so.

'Stay here and drown, then,' he replied.

'As opposed to go with you and die in a fireball, you mean?'

He shrugged. 'Whatever, but the gold comes with me.'

A kiloton gust slammed into the airfield and the little plane bounced against its tie-downs.

'Why can't we take the car?' I protested.

He shook his head in tired exasperation. 'Too risky.'

I laughed out loud. 'And taking this toy airplane up in this weather isn't?'

'This', he yelled, snatching the last of the tarpaulin from the fuselage, 'is not a toy aircraft. This is a 1974 Piper Cherokee One-Forty, and it will put us down in Frederick, Maryland, in a little over eight hours. Speaking of hours, I've got over three hundred clocked up on fixed wing, so do not tell me I cannot fucking fly!'

It still looked like a toy plane to me. Not much longer than a van, with low wings and a cabin like a Ford Sierra, it seemed flimsy and unassertive, like a rubber-band plane that went where the wind took it. It was not the type of aircraft I would have booked a seat on in bright, still, summer daylight conditions, and Gene could see my reservations.

'Look,' he shouted, his voice rising and falling through the gusts. 'Every sorry bastard in Collier County is in his car right now, with the kids and the dog, hauling boat, trailer and whatever else they can carry. They're out there on Forty-one and Seventy-five, nose-to-tail, going nowhere fast. Pretty soon the cops will start herding them into high schools, and when this bitch makes landfall, that's it. Road closures, disaster zones, looting, and random checks on vehicles leaving the areas affected. If we get caught up in that chaos, it could be days before we get our asses out of Florida, and days, Troop, is what we don't have. Furthermore, if we get pulled I do not want to have to explain a trunkload of bullion to some zitty little cop cadet. Flying out of here was always the plan, and I'm not going to let some surface-level disturbance stop me. We wait for a gap in the wind, get airborne, and in twenty minutes we're out of the zone and heading north. We drop down at Waycross-Ware Field in Georgia to refuel, and arrive in Frederick at' – he checked his watch – 'say, zero seven-thirty tomorrow morning. Jesus Christ! I don't know why you're pissing and moaning.'

He looked at me as though it were the most sensible plan in the world. Then, as though under the control of his twisted will, the wind dropped to a whisper.

'It's my way or the highway,' he declared. 'Now get these tie-downs, will you?'

It's hard adequately to express the depth of foreboding experienced when manoeuvring an aircraft so light that two men can push it into the outskirts of a hurricane. Rowing a skiff into a storm swell or crossing the snowline in trainers are similar acts, accepted by disasters everywhere as bona fide invitations. We wheeled the skinny Cherokee through the rushing night and filled her wing tanks with fifty gallons of gas from a credit-card-operated pump.

Gene disapproved of the innovation. 'They used to run an honour system after hours,' he lamented.

I empathised: 'honour system' meant 'free' to me, too.

After refuelling Gene spun a slow, cautious one-eighty, scanning the shivering treeline for signs of surveillance or approach. Satisfied, he drove the Toyota on to the shiny runway and we heaved the gold and our personal effects into the rear of the tiny cabin.

'Go park this somewhere innocent,' he said, handing me the keys to the car and forgetting that I'd had only one beer and no drugs.

'Yeah, right,' I countered. 'I was born at night, but not last night, baby. You go park it and I'll wait by the plane. '

He wiped a sheen of sweat from his pate and stared at me, a silver-tainted grin slowly stretching his shiny jowls. A fox, a chicken and a bag of grain. 'My, but you're a distrustful son of a bitch,' he smiled. He pointed at the sky. 'Looky there: stars. I'll be back.'

I stared into heaven and leaned against the wing until I realised that my weight might break it. Off shore a tall fleet of full-masted cumulonimbi formed up in lightning-lit battle formation and made ready to bombard the unprotected shore. Fresh salvoes of warm rain splashed over the Cherokee's fuselage despite the clear skies overhead, and the wind began a new and unsettling ululation. The shallow sea beyond the runway moved like a panicked crowd as the servant of the snake prepared to whip it into submission. I sat on the tarmac beneath the stubby wings and rolled a damp joint, suddenly knowing exactly how those who flew on a divine wind must have felt.

Sometimes weed is not the answer. Every suck on the soggy spliff ripped a layer of denial from the cracked wall of my mortality, and even as the THC rubbed the sharp edges from reason it seemed suicidal to climb aboard this aircraft with Gene at the controls. I flicked the roach into the night as he came jogging from the bushes.

'Don't smoke under the fucking airplane,' he sighed. 'Now get in.'

I climbed into a cabin that smelled of sweat, mould and fear. The worn vinyl seats were made to be wiped clean and the lap-belt was frayed, with a chipped buckle. Gene made the short trip around the Cherokee, rocking the wings, kicking tyres and lifting flaps like a disrespectful pimp. Satisfied, he wiped the rain from his brow, climbed aboard, pushed an antique plastic headset over his ears and grinned.

'More comfortable than British Airways, ain't it?'

I shrugged. 'Are you sure you know what you're doing?'

He let his hands hover over the control column, scanning the instrument panel like a brilliant but forgetful concert pianist. 'Absolutely,' he replied. 'OK, here we go: master switch, on. Fuel quantity, checked. Flaps, down. Blah de blah de blah . . .'

'Hang on,' I called. 'What's this "blah de blah" thing? What kind of safety check is that, man?'

He took a deep breath. 'Will you just shut the fuck up and let the pilot do his thing?' He handed me a white plastic anemometer. 'Stick that out of the window and tell me when the wind drops to twenty-five knots or so.'

I did as I was told, keeping one eye on the spinning egg-cups and another on Gene's pre-flight checks. He did actually seem to know what he was doing, but then he'd impressed crippled paratroopers with his fake war stories.

'Okay,' he repeated, 'throttle, quarter open; master switch, on; fuel pump, ditto; mixture, full rich. Here we go!'

The engine backfired, farting a puff of blue smoke, and the propeller disappeared in a blurred whirr. I fumbled one-handed to clamp the cold grey headset over my ears and heard Gene's crackling voice.

'Wind speed?'

'Forty . . . thirty-five . . . forty. Let's take the car, Gene, can we?'

The plane was rocking on its tricycle undercarriage, slapped around by the wind and weighed down with gold.

'Speed?'

'Forty . . . forty-five . . . Still forty-five. This is lunacy. You're a maniac.'

'Fuck it,' he growled metallically. 'Let's go on the next thirty-five.'

The nose seemed to rise and fall with the pitch of the pro-peller, the tiny wipers inadequate to clear the rain from the cloudy plexiglas windscreen. Waves crashed in white flashes along the right-hand side of the runway and the sheet lightning flashed in the west like a creeping barrage. I shuddered, then remembered something important.

'Where's my parachute?'

Gene's laughter sounded like Muttley through my headset. 'We don't got no parachutes, boy,' he announced, still cackling.

I was flabbergasted. He had no respect for air safety whatsoever. 'That's fucking marvellous, that is,' I declared, shaking my head in disbelief.

'Wind speed?'

'Forty.'

'That'll do,' he decided, sounding for the first and last time like Mel Gibson. He slid the throttles forward, reaching full power in five seconds, then slipped the parking brake and let the Cherokee roll. He chewed his lip as he gave the aircraft full aileron, leaning it into the crosswind as it accelerated along the runway. I braced myself against the instrument panel, pushing myself back into my seat as the waves to my left leapt and receded like the abandoned refugees at Saigon airport. The unlit runway ended a few yards from the mouth of the Barron River, and, as the tarmac ended and the grass began, I felt the nose lift and a gut-dropping lurch as we left the earth behind and skimmed over the raging water. Millimetres of vintage sheet metal separated me from a sobbing drop into oblivion and I lifted my feet from the cabin floor as Gene climbed to the west, the falling distance becoming less relevant with every swing of the altimeter. Distant voices unaware of our flight crowded my headphones, speaking in the tongues of navigators and harbourmasters. Gene flicked a switch and something sophisticated lit up. He flicked another and the cabin light came on.

'See if there's a road atlas under the seat,' he said.

I rummaged and pulled out a 1984 Rand McNally.

'Excellent. Look up Everglades City. I want to follow Forty-one to Naples, then swing north on the Seventy-five.'

I gave him a long, hard look. It seemed that pilots' licences were issued like firearm licences in this absurd country. Any irresponsible idiot could get one.

'Where's your flight plan? Where are your air charts?' I squeaked, like a shrew. 'You cannot fly to Maryland using a road atlas.'

Gene lit a cigarette, moving his mouth – yadder, yadder, yadder – like a long-suffering but culpable husband. Outside, the piled night sky was rent by rips of white lightning that stood on the horizon for longer than their reputation suggested, colossal cortices connecting the earth's body and soul, sending jets through the cloudtops and sprites into heaven. The Cherokee rose and fell like a storm-tossed trawler.

'Some asshole somewhere has seen a white blip come out of X-o-one, and he's watching it on an FAA screen. Pretty soon we're gonna get an ident. request, which, for obvious reasons, I don't want to answer. We head north and lose ourselves in Fort Myers' air traffic, then pop out the other side, switch on the avionics and follow the VOR all the way to Waycross-Ware.' He took his eyes off the road to return the look I'd given him. 'The appropriate response is "Fine, Mr Renoir," seeing as I'm the fucking pilot and you couldn't find your way home on a cloudy day.'

I missed the end of his observation. A thin blue *frisson* had lifted every hair on my body and my fingertips seemed to glow with St Elmo's fire. I opened my mouth to tell Charles Lindbergh, and in the tenth of a second between my observation and my determination the Devil licked the plane with a whiplash crack that killed the cabin lights and set something buzzing on the instrument panel.

Gene stubbed out his cigarette and cursed. 'We've taken a hit!' he yelled. 'Look at the compass!'

I couldn't look at anything with my eyes squeezed shut. 'What's happening?' I cried.

The engine was whining like a psychiatric patient, moaning and sobbing and too weak to carry on.

'Throttle cable must be fried,' announced Gene, shaking his head as he pushed the toggles forwards to no effect. 'Look at the revs, for Christ's sake!'

'Find an airfield!' I cried.

Gene worked the throttle like a beer pump, hauling on the control column to keep the aircraft straight and level. 'Yeah, right,' he replied. 'I'll find a non-existent airfield and you put on your non-existent parachute. Where the fuck are we?' He leaned across and slapped me on the thigh. 'Where the fuck are we? Look for lights, cars, anything. Jesus Christ, I can't see the horizon!'

'I can't see fuck all,' I added. 'Just a great big black bastard of a swamp down there and a fucking hurricane over there.'

'We're slipping to port,' called Gene. 'I can't trust the horizon indicator. Look at the altimeter!' He pointed at an instrument that was winding down like a death-row clock, spinning backwards to the time when it all went wrong. Panic leapt into my arms like a scaredy cat, pursued by a spayed hound of impotent anger. 'I told you we should have taken the car,' I howled. 'Now we're going to crash into a fucking alligator-infested swamp—'

'Shut the fuck up,' screamed Gene, his face wet with sweat in the stroboscopic lightning.

A triple flash lit up the rainswept night for two, maybe three, seconds, and I saw the silver capillaries of streams, the pulsating sawgrass and the stark shadows of hammock trees spread out less than one hundred feet below us. Gene dragged the control column backwards, kicked his pedals and rammed the throttle forwards with no sympathy for the choking carburettors. Suddenly the engine spluttered, then roared back into full voice, revived like an Irishman at the bottom end of a stout.

Gene looked at me and smiled his smuggest little smile. 'Fixed it,' he said.

Then we hit a tree.

11

Imagine yourself on a cheap kitchen chair. You're tied in with a belt around your middle, and you're sitting by the picture window at the back end of the kind of caravan farmers keep for their lowliest cowmen. It's raining, and so dark that all you can see in the dripping plastic is your own face looking back. Suddenly, an eighty-foot cypress tree weighing fifty tons comes out of nowhere and smashes into the caravan, ruining your reflection at ninety-five miles per hour. It would hurt.

If Gene had hit the tree head on, we would both have died. Instead, he clipped it with the starboard wing, tearing it off at its root and pivoting around the solid trunk in a screeching disaster of twisted, buckled and torn metal. The engine squealed like a gunshot swan, the propeller snatching at the air as though it could still drag us out of the swamp, but a hard wooden fist punched through the Cherokee's thin skin as we spun into another tree, knocking the wind from me and dragging us down. I screamed throughout, stopping only when Gene's heavy head cracked the bridge of my nose and sent me off to Never-never Land, less than two seconds after he'd claimed everything was fine. That's the way it all ends for some.

God, my hair grew fast. It was all over my face like Cobain and my fingernails were coming out like Freddie Kruger. It didn't matter, though. Everyone here was ugly. Even the bartender looked like he'd just climbed out of an auto-wreck. He poured me two fingers with his good hand and backed away, wiping the bottle with a square of stained purple silk. Brad came back from the restrooms, one hand on his chin and another on his fly. He shouted up another round and yelled to hear himself think: 'I miss anything?'

I shook my head, my ribs too painful to yell back. He'd grown a beard, I noticed, a sure sign that a man has something to hide. I beckoned him closer and spoke into his ear. 'Put your hands on the bar where I can see them.'

He drained his Bud, necked his shot, and dropped the USP and the Glock on the countertop. Their slides were open, their oiled barrels exposed and their butts empty. Brad showed me his palms. 'I got nothing to hide, buddy. I was always straight with you, always told you exactly what was going down. Now why don't you show me your hand?'

I'd always wanted to, but now, when it mattered the most, I couldn't. My left arm hung uselessly at my side, weighed down by a bag of gold. Brad was waiting, and I appreciated his need for a show of reciprocation, but I simply couldn't drop the bag.

I shrugged and offered him a cigarette.

'They'll kill you,' warned an ashen-faced cowboy as he passed by.

Brad sucked on his Marlboro, shook his head in exasperation and pushed the USP towards me. 'Pick up that hand or pick up the gun,' he ordered, his long, muddy fingers closing around the Glock.

I tried to explain but his attention had wandered. A new song was playing, an old song invested with far more value than it deserved. All around us the bitching and the brawling stopped as everybody sang along.

'*Your cruel device, your blood, like ice . . .*'

'I love this song,' I told Brad. 'Haven't heard it in ages.'

'I hate it,' he grimaced. 'Reminds her of work.'

I couldn't feel my arm any more. 'Reminds who?'

He nodded towards the stage. Not everybody in here was ugly. 'Her,' he grunted.

'*You're poison, you're poison running through my veins . . .*'

My baby came on strutting, wearing nothing but button and a bow. There was a powder burn like a bruise on her right temple.

'That's my ex-fiancée up there,' grinned Brad proudly. 'Ain't she pretty in pink?'

She turned, showing her exit wound to the roaring crowd, a blood-blackened hole the size of a fist edged with smashed bone and fringed by her long, shiny hair.

'You're bleeding, man,' cried Brad. 'Get out of here and clean yourself up. Jesus, no one bleeds in here!'

A thick crimson thread swung from my nose, splashing on the bar and dripping on the floor. I pinched my nose with my good hand and struggled through a disapproving crowd of ghouls to the door. The car park was a scrap yard, the pick-ups and the Camaros stacked on their sides like broken biscuits. I found Brad's ride and climbed in through the broken windshield, strapping myself on to the bench seat with a fur-lined seat-belt. My nose was still dripping, but there was already blood all over his cab, and I'd left my bag behind. It hurt when I laughed, but I could have shown him my hand as I was leaving, and none of it mattered now anyway.

12

I opened my eyes. I was cold and wet. I felt sick, and there was blood all over my T-shirt. I was lying on my side, foetal on the floor, and the rain was falling through a broken skylight. My breath came in short, agonised gasps, and as I struggled to relieve the pressure a shrieking train of uncontained pain ripped through my side, its passage marked by a feeble whimper. I reached out to grab the wet webbing seatbelt dangling beside me, and tugged on it to give my chest a break. My nose was blocked with hard, black plugs of coagulating blood, and when I tried to clear them the bleeding started up again. I snatched a rag from my shoulder – I seemed to be draped in scattered clothes and pine needles– and staunched the flow.

I was both victim and survivor of an air crash, I realised; no doubt about it. I couldn't deny the evidence before me: smashed instrument panel, cracked windshield, a pair of control yokes dancing like morons to whatever tune the wind blew across the control surfaces and a flapping cockpit door. I turned breathlessly to look to where the gravity was coming from and saw a length of dented white wing stretching down and away into the night. To my right, above my head, the rain fell like arrows, their shafts lit by lightning and driven on a wind that rocked the wreck backwards and forwards, round and round, with the tree that had brought us down. I had to laugh: I was strapped in to a wrecked aircraft caught halfway up a tree in a swamp in a hurricane. You had to admire a God with a sense of humour like that.

Furthermore, I was injured, dripping with aviation

fuel . . . and *alone*. I took a deep breath. 'Gene!' I yelled. 'Gene! Where the fuck are you, Gene?'

Swallowed blood, shock, high-octane vapour and the pitching of the wreck in the howling, gusting squalls brought the bile into my throat, and I realised that the vomit would kill me if I passed out.

'Gene! Help!' I screamed, but the wind snatched away the words, ripped them into syllables and scattered them unheard across the swamp. I was slipping back towards the downside cabin door, my bodyweight bearing down on the damaged side of my chest. If I didn't move, I would suffocate, and if I didn't climb out of the wreck before the next big blow, I would be killed in the second plane crash of the night. The will to survive is not an art, a craft or a technique, despite what those who want to sell it say. It is an inclination, an innate gift that can be imitated but not assumed. Anyone can be taught survival skills, just as anyone can be taught karate, but a black belt won't save you from a kicking if you're not a born fighter. I was a born survivor, my aptitude the honourable obverse of the cowardice I wore around my neck like a Gibraltar angel. Gene, I observed parenthetically, was a born fucking bastard.

Wile E. Coyote would have appreciated the irony in unfastening a seat-belt to escape a plane wreck and falling sixty feet through an unlocked door, so I thrust my hand beneath my body to feel for the door handle, rattled it awkwardly, and convinced myself that it was secure. I popped the buckle on the harness, gripped the pilot's abandoned seat-belt and pulled myself into a cramped upright position. The pain was so intense that it was almost worth the suffering for the headrush. I coughed, which hurt, and then I puked up blood, beer and my Wang Dang Doodle, and that hurt a whole lot more. I didn't need a doctor to tell me that I'd

broken my ribs. Every gasping breath exhaled in my endeav-
our to reach the ground was going to impale me like a
bayonet, but that was the least of my worries. I brushed my
ribcage with trembling fingers, braced for wetness and pain,
but felt only the latter. The skin was swollen but unbroken,
although there was no way of knowing if I'd punctured a
lung. I'd know that only when I started drowning in my own
blood. My legs were sore but undamaged, my left elbow
ached as though chipped. I'd bitten my lip in the crash, and
Gene, as a final gesture, had broken my nose with his big, fat,
treacherous head. I was hurt, but I wouldn't die if I could
escape from the mangled corpse of the Cherokee.

I stepped on the side of my seat and stuck my head
through the uppermost door and into the wet white teeth of
the storm. Rain rattled like birdshot against the dented fuselage and the thick limbs of the black tree that held it,
bending beneath the sustained truck-horn blast of a runaway
wind. Thinner branches whipped my face, stabbing my
streaming face with needles, as though blaming me for the
calamity. I squinted back along the aircraft to where it was
jammed in the crook of a trunk, and in a flash I saw the
sheared wing and crushed tail assembly reflecting from white
two storeys below. The creaking wreck scraped bark from its
captive's limbs as the unsupported engine tried to dive to the
forest floor. It was time for me to grab what I could and go.

I ducked back into the cabin and looked into the back.
Both windows were popped from their frames and my few
items of clothing were scattered over the seats. Gene's
Mulberry luggage and the gold were gone. I heaved my
belongings over the side and began to climb out. I had two
knees on the fuselage and my hands on the rear window
frame when I looked in and spotted my handbag. Sobbing
with frustration and taunted by the wind, I backed up, re-

entered the cabin and retrieved it, looping the strap over my shoulder. The Everglades were not the shrine I had in mind for this sacred relic. Taking a careful breath, I again broke through the line of fear that urged me to indulge the pleas of my trembling legs and stay put until help came. Help wouldn't be coming: I'd learned that a long time ago. I hauled myself back on to the fuselage and crawled along its buckled edge, keeping low to avoid being picked off by a sniping wind, placing hands and knees carefully on the wet metal to avoid the vicious shards on the stump of the torn-off wing. The Cherokee seemed bent on taking my drenched scalp to hell, and it wriggled, creaking in the fork of the tree as I picked my way towards a supportive-looking limb. The gun, still wrapped in my handbag, banged along the fuselage, taunting the wreckage like a drunk who didn't know when to quit. Some gusts sighed and others whistled as I reached the safety of an earth-rooted object, and, though I've never really been a hippy, I hugged that tree.

All I had to do now was climb down. I nearly made it, falling just the last fifteen feet to land on my backside on the wet leaf-mould loam. The height of a house above me, swaying in the wind and illuminated by the muzzle-flashes of the lightning barrage, the Cherokee hung like a crucified thief. The air beneath its shattered body reeked of aviation fuel and scattered clothes lay like bodies on the ground, up in the branches or draped across the fallen pieces of debris. I moved away from the cross and leaned in the lee of another trunk.

Maybe Gene was still near by. Maybe his luggage and the gold had simply fallen from the aircraft, and he was lying unconscious and injured in the darkness at my feet. I dragged a crushed cigarette from my jeans and lit it with a trembling hand – there was spirit in the sky but the storm would save me from immolation. The smoke hurt like acid, but it delivered reason to my muddled mind. Gene had split, hauling two leather grips and a black holdall containing nine stones of bullion across whatever lay beyond this wooded island. He'd left me with nothing, not even a binbag in which to pack my sodden belongings, not a dime in cash and not a hope in hell of navigating my way out of the morass that awaited me if I survived this swamp.

Gene had done worse than leave me for dead. He'd left me in limbo.

I sat awkwardly on the sodden ground, chaining a long one from a short one and ignoring the protests of my wounded ribcage. Something sharp was stabbing my thigh from inside my soaking jeans. I reached into my pocket and pulled Gene's spare set of keys jangling into the night, then tossed them into the darkness. I'd taken them when I was sure I couldn't trust him, and how right I had been.

We had taken off from Everglades City sometime after midnight. It was still dark, which meant it could be any time between one and five-thirty in the morning. It would have taken a fat bastard like Gene a good forty-five minutes to escape from the aircraft, gather his wits and his booty and disappear. He was also hauling at least one hundred and fifty pounds of kit, which would slow down even the fittest ex-US Marine, and Gene was neither fit nor an ex-Marine. On the other hand, he could have found a road, hitched a lift and be long gone by now.

Sitting in the bole of a limbo-gumbo wouldn't bring him any closer either way, so I pulled myself weakly to my feet and set about estimating my position. We had headed west after taking off, aiming to follow the Tamiami Trail into Naples, but we'd never overflown the blacktop. It seemed reasonable to assume that the road lay to the north, a great limestone dike across the bed of the swamp. I ran my hand around the slender trunk of a shivering sapling, feeling for moss. Low down, I found it, and I touched up another for confirmation. Now I knew where north lay, and so would Gene. In that direction lay the sodden sawgrass swamp, the wet, black home of the alligator, the water moccasin and the quicksand.

The least that could happen was that my fags would be ruined, so I set about smoking them all before I set off. I pulled the screwed-up pack from my pocket, and something small and light tumbled to the ground. I picked it up and grinned: the last of Brad's crystal meth, wrapped in a voucher for seven-league boots. Rather than risk sharing it with the wind, I popped the whole wrap into my mouth, chewed until I tasted speed, and swallowed. I was now chemically enhanced, running on amphetamines and pure, unadulterated hatred. I would seek out Gene and wreak a terrible vengeance upon him, for he had left me with nothing but despair and a broken nose.

I flicked my last dog-end into the damp undergrowth and followed a worn animal track through the saplings. Knocked flat by a gust, I heaved myself upright and bent over like a soldier under fire, instantly recognising the folly of trying to follow a bearing on this dark and featureless fen. The rain came down like carwash rollers, dense and whirling, slapping at the skin and beating flat the sawgrass. Cruel gusts lifted it again to be beaten down on the backdraft. To try to cross this country on foot on a dry day would have been a challenge. At night, in a hurricane, it was madness, but madness was the *cocktail du jour*.

That and greed.

Gene had left footprints in the mud, a chain of tiny lakes and a deep trench dredged by a dragged bag of stolen gold.

The depth of that ditch belied the expenditure of effort in leaving me behind. He wouldn't be far ahead. I cursed the wind as it slapped me down once more. My left side burned white hot beneath my soaked layers and my nose bled freely into the swamp, infusing a tiny part of Florida with English DNA. Around me and above me the night air was filled with flying debris: palm fronds, twigs, leaves and black teardrops of mud flew through the sky, crackling like a forest fire. The rain hurt now, punching through my clothes like rock salt fired from a shotgun. Knocked back to my knees, I paused before rising, sucking air from an atmosphere of water, my skin contracting as the pelting raised welts across my back.

Gene, too, had been slapped flat: his footprint ponds were punctuated by deeper, wider lakes where his overloaded body had fallen. He was, I observed, making a definite impression on the Everglades.

I found him half an hour later. The speed had kicked in and I was rolling with the punches, moving at a crouch like a stalking Seminole, my hands outstretched to break my fall. Lightning silhouetted Gene three hundred yards ahead, moving backwards, dragging the bullion bag like a stubborn mule urged on by the whipcrack tattoo of rolling thunder. I dropped to my belly, sweating with pain and exertion, my burning lungs clogged, my tongue fouled with muddy spit. Another staggered bolt split the night and Gene raised his fists in fury. His arrogance astounded me: Mayan or Christian, no god sent hurricanes as expressions of delight in humankind. When this howling rebuke roared in from the sea, a justified and violent rage, man hid himself and prayed. Even one as shameless and disgraced as me kept his head down and moved on his knees, afraid to look the storm in the eye. Gene spat in its face, his crimes naked before its bared teeth, because, to him, it was merely a meteorological phenomenon. I watched him, cursing and heaving on the holdall, wishing that my agnosticism was as steady as his in times of trial. As he moved, so I followed, finding his expensive luggage abandoned in the mud at the side of the trail. I took the lighter of the two bags, lessening its load by throwing the less tasteful garments into a slough.

Gene kept moving, sometimes carrying the gold on his back and sometimes dragging it through the mud. He stopped frequently, bent over and breathless or scanning the strobe-lit horizon for hope. A few hours ago, hope had been a phone call from Fort Myers. Now she was a road, a rude and dirty track of yellow mud to lead us out of this black wilderness to a place where Gene's burden had some value.

Without a road, Gene was lost.

And if he was lost, then I was lost, Sherry-Lee was lost and all hope was lost.

Fear and exhaustion conspired to deceive me, their foolishness conjuring cheap hallucinations at the front of my mind. I looked down, and headlights flashed.

Hollow-bowelled with relief, I scanned the horizon, and saw nothing. Moving forward at a crouch, letting Gene do the hard work ahead of me, I paused for breath and heard, between the thunder and the rain, the narrow sounds of a hillbilly radio, then voices, then the barking of a dog. I looked up, and saw more headlights, winking at the edge of my vision, then gone. Whatever trail Gene thought he was following now lay knee-deep in cold, black porridge spiked with sawgrass that slashed like serrated scimitars, lacerating my dripping skin with scores of tiny cuts. My injured side was in spasm, the pain like a vice that gripped me from belly to spine, and as I stumbled into a pool that soaked me to the waist, I considered for the first time that I might not have the strength to escape. The amphetamine-sponsored optimism I had felt so confidently before setting off after Gene had burned away, leaving an agonised despair in its ashes. I fell forwards, tugging at a tuft to drag myself into shallower mud, and lay there, spat on by the rain and kicked by the wind, too hurt, tired and sad to carry on. I wanted to rest, to lay upon the earth and let it absorb me, envelop me and comfort me, but, zombie-like, I rose, my handbag swinging from my neck and a mud-black leather holdall in my hands, an accidental tourist in the Everglades National Park and just back from the dead.

The wind let me stand, pressing gently on my back, and then, like a fan switched off, fading completely. No more rain fell on my blistered back, and as I raised my head, apprehensively, like an abused dog, I saw stars. The night sky lit up like a city after an air raid, the cold stars like the distant, armchair observers of a TV war. Now I could look the hurricane in the eye. I gave it a long, hard glare, defying it to stop me reaching that road, recovering my gold and rescuing Sherry-Lee from Brad. He knew where she worked, and just because he hadn't had the heart to kill her the first time, that didn't mean he wouldn't let his Missouri brooding change his simple mind. I wasn't around to stay his hand and I had a notion that Sherry-Lee, by now a three-time loser, wouldn't necessarily duck when the shooting started. There was no altruism in my ambition: I wanted Sherry-Lee like Gene wanted gold, and I would do whatever it took to drag her out of her swamp.

I scoped a quadrant of the horizon, looking for my partner. His footprints now lay below eighteen inches of water, on a submerged, invisible trail. Tracking was done by sight alone, and as I scanned the darkness with rising anxiety I realised I'd lost him. I pushed forwards, panic driving my soaked and bleeding legs, hearing the thick splashes of my footfalls for the first time in the threatening calm. Silent lightning surrounded me, its afterglow too dim and distant to be useful as I squinted through hordes of marsh-gas ghosts for a sign of the quick.

He was nearer than I thought, collapsed and broken on the black bank of a wide slough, the swag bag half sub-merged, saved only by the narrow shoulder strap lashed like a tourniquet around his white and swollen hand. I stood behind and above him, on the near side of the rain-choked drain, a mere leap from the gold, waiting for the sight of his fallen body to stir an emotion. A single leaf, fresh and green, fluttered from the open sky, turning over and over before landing on his back. Still I waited. Muddied and dishevelled, his arm stretched by the weight of the gold, he had not yet assumed the diminished appearance of a corpse, but I could wait a while longer.

'You left me for dead, you bastard,' I growled, my voice loud and hoarse in the stillness. I leapt the stream, landing with a splatter at his side. I bent down to drag the gold on to firmer ground, and his hand closed around my wrist.

'You *were* dead,' he gasped.

I threw off his weak grip, heaved the holdall from the water and untied the strap from his arm. Those three actions left me empty, and I slumped into the mud, my arm around the bag. Unburdened, Gene rolled on to his back and sucked wind, his mouth gaping, a shiny cut above his eyebrow and his face streaked with mud below a baseball hat that said, 'Florida Pilot'. The word 'Incompetent' was missing from the logo.

'You were dead,' he repeated, his eyes squeezed shut. 'No vitals. No pulse. No nothing.' He winced. It was hurting him to tell me of my demise. 'Figured your neck had snapped.' He opened a blood-red eye and looked at the stars. 'I swear to God, Troop.'

I leaned across, gasping as my splintered ribs rubbed together, and snatched a Marlboro pack from his shirt pocket. The cellophane had saved them, but I lit only one for myself.

'You still left me for dead,' I muttered.

'Because that's what you were,' he groaned.

'Yeah?' I countered. 'Well look at me now. I'm resurrected, and I've come for my gold.' A small but solid brass padlock prevented me from unzipping the holdall.

I turned to Gene and held out my hand. 'Key?'

He shook his head. 'There is no key.'

'Fine,' I nodded, blowing smoke into the stillness. 'I'll take the whole bag, then.'

I climbed unsteadily to my feet, pausing to let the pain subside.

'So where you heading, Troop?' wheezed Gene.

'Mexico,' I replied, bending to lift the bag.

He laughed sadly. 'You'll never make it: look at you!'

'Look at me?' I snorted. 'Look at you, more like. At least I can stand up.'

He shook his head. 'Not after dragging that shit for fifteen minutes, you won't. That's another thing' – pain clouded his eyes, then passed – 'which way you heading with that there big bag of gold?'

I jerked a thumb over my shoulder. 'That way.'

'Interesting,' he mused, rubbing his eye.

I lit another cigarette, tasting blood and speed in my mouth. I spat, a black gob on the black mud in a black night.

Gene saw it. 'You're pretty fucked up there, ain't you, Troop? You haemorrhaging there?'

A whistling zephyr fanned my cigarette. 'Nope,' I replied. 'Bit my tongue, that's all.'

Gene lay back and sighed, his eyes hidden beneath the brim of his inappropriate headgear. 'I'm not going to fuck with you any more, Troop. I'm hurting too much. So I'm going to tell you straight. You do not have a chance of getting out of here tonight, or any night, alone. Me neither. You might make it if you leave the gold behind, but that kind of defeats the object of your visit to this here great nation, don't it? You could hide it here, I suppose, but how in the world would you find it again? On top of all that, this place will be crawling with troopers as soon as the storm subsides, all looking for the passengers and crew of that light aircraft hung up in the trees back there. Which leads me to my proposal. Want to hear it?'

I sat on the bag and blew smoke. 'Go on.'

'We walk out of here together. We split the gold between the two bags and we strike out west, which is that way, by the way' – he pointed to his left – 'to the 92. After that you can do what you like. Padlock combination is eight-zero-eight. Let me know when you've reached a decision.'

I popped the padlock and scooped out a fistful of dollars. Gene watched me, pale-faced, his breathing fast and shallow.

'You could, of course, take what you can carry and strike out alone, but I don't think you'd make it. This ain't your Hyde Park here, and there ain't no straight and narrow paths across the swamp. Take a wrong turn, you'll end up in a quicksand, or up to your neck in the mangroves, or lost in a swamp thicket. Top of that, you got 'gators to think about. Troop, *I* wouldn't even try it alone, and I know this place better than most. It's up to you.'

Gene thought I'd bought his lame story about leaving me for dead in the Cherokee, and now he was working that old magic, stitching silk purses from sows' ears, selling me a treasure map and acting like he wasn't simply trying to save his own miserable hide. He was clearly badly hurt, although he didn't appear to be bleeding, and deeply exhausted from dragging the gold across the swamp. His unfocused eyes and rapid respiration were symptomatic of low blood pressure, which, since he wasn't leaking into the mud, suggested serious internal injury. Left alone, he would soon be making an impression on the Reaper, and his Mont Blanc fountain pen and flashy Miami chequebook would be as much use to him as a sack of gold coins.

Curtains of cloud were falling across the sky as the wind rose in overture to Louisa's second act. Right at the front of my head, where reason and common sense had locked themselves in, it was being suggested that Gene deserved no mercy. It was recognised that he was smarter than me, that he'd confused and misled me like a fox toying with a rabbit. He would solicit my aid and then trick me out of my reward as soon as he was safe. He was even handing me half the gold, or more, if I wanted to carry it, as proof of his good intentions, like a conman giving his wallet to a patsy. My best advice to myself was to keep my mind's eye focused on the truth, to remember that when I was slumped unconscious in a wrecked aircraft, as vulnerable and as needy as Gene was now, he had walked away from me. He deserved no mercy, but it would have been easier to be judicious with a map in my hand. I filled his leather holdall with as many coins as I could lift and stood up.

'Let's go,' I muttered.

Time and distance were measured in aching footsteps as we waded through knee-deep mud into a refreshed wind. I fell every five yards, Gene every three, our ill-gotten gold seeming to conspire with the swamp and the storm to bury us in unmarked, unmourned graves. We had no air to spare for conversation or recrimination, and neither helped the other to his feet after a tumble. Gene was working at the edge of his capabilities, a slightly ironic grimace of determination on his black-streaked face, like a man who knew he'd missed the point. By the time we reached a wide swamp that ran straight and deep down to the sea, the gusts were strong enough to stop us in our ruts. Gene pulled his hat down hard and pointed upstream. Heavy alligators splashed unseen into the water as I approached, but I'd heard so many tonight that I no longer worried. I changed my mind when I reached a narrow wooden bridge spanning the swamp. Something long, fat and dark lay across the boards, its tail dangling above the fast-running water. I backed up, looking around for something to throw.

'What's the problem?' croaked Gene as he caught up.

''Gator on the bridge. Need something to throw at him.' I bent down to drag the mud.

Gene shook his head. 'Swamp,' he panted. 'No rocks . . . no sticks.' He tapped his head, sucking air like an unacclimatised climber. 'Initiative, Troop.'

I approached the alligator, wondering how fast he could move, and if he'd already eaten. 'Get the fuck off the bridge,' I yelled, stamping my foot hard, like Billy Goat Gruff.

The 'gator swung its flat, bronze head slowly and disdainfully, dropped its jaw a couple of inches, and hissed.

I scarpered. 'Go on, git, you fat bastard,' I called back from a greater distance.

This time the alligator didn't bother to reply.

Gene came alongside, shaking his head. 'Not quite the Crocodile Hunter, are you?' he observed, swallowing something bitter.

'Go on, then,' I retorted. 'You get rid of him.'

Gene was shoeless, and in a lot of pain, but I found it hard to care.

'Throw something at him,' he suggested.

'Throw what?' I cried. 'Mud? What's he doing out in a hurricane anyway?'

Gene dipped into his bag and handed me a roll of eagles. 'Throw these. They've got a lower gold content than the others.'

I stared at the tube of coins, then at Gene.

'Well, what the hell else do you suggest?' he asked impatiently.

A roll of eagles weighs ten ounces, and has the potential to hurt if well aimed. I lined up on the 'gator, lobbed it, and missed. A distant splash marked its fall.

'That was a ranging shot,' I explained. 'Give me another.'

'Another what?' he hissed, swaying to keep balance in the buffeting wind. A blast of rain dashed us like handfuls of gravel, washing the muck from my face and rinsing my hands ghostly white. Gene's head remained striped with mud beneath his black cap.

'Another bloody roll,' I replied.

His mouth fell open, about as far as the 'gator's. 'You threw the whole fucking roll?' he barked. One at a time, you fucking moron! That fuck-up you called a ranging shot cost thirty-six hundred dollars! Jesus Christ Almighty! One at a fucking time!'

'Okay, okay, okay,' I yelled back. 'Stop going on about it and give me another roll.'

He refused, so I took one of my own, peeled off an eagle, and skimmed it at the nine-foot monster. The throw sent my ribs into spasm, but it was worth it. The coin caught him below the eye, sending a shiver along his length. He turned and hissed again, but this time I stood my ground. I skimmed another, catching his nostril and eliciting another angry hiss. Throw gold at people and they thank you for it.

Throw gold at 'gators and it pisses them off. That's why *we* have interactive TV and *they* live in swamps. I took a couple of steps closer and zipped another into his head. He showed me a mouthful of daggers and took two lumbering steps through the rain towards me. I let him have another three hundred and sixty bucks, right on the nose, then another, less effectively, on his dinosaur's back. After a total expenditure of seven thousand, seven hundred and twenty dollars, he splashed into the swamp with a final malignant hiss.

Gene shook his head. 'This trip's getting too expensive,' he muttered.

The treeline on the far side of the bridge was coping badly with the hurricane. Royal palms rocked back and forth like nu-metal fans at a Puddle of Mudd gig, head-banging till they broke their necks, while shorter trees caught in the mosh pit were ripped apart, limb by limb, their leaves stripped and scattered across the swamp. It seemed like lunacy to step into a forest of falling trees and flying shrapnel, but the night had been marked by the exercise of poor judgement and it hadn't killed us yet. I lowered my head and went in. Gene caught up with me a moment later, and found me staring wet-eyed at hope.

'There you go,' he slurred. 'State Road Ninety-two. There's a town – I've forgotten the name – and the ocean a couple of miles that way. And Forty-one is six or so the other way. It's up to you now.'

He staggered against a gust and dropped, his fall to the road surface broken by his bag. I fell to my knees beside him, the pain from my ribs a white-noise scream.

'I'm fucked,' I gasped. 'I've got to get some DFs or something.'

Gene smiled like an immolating Buddhist, wiping the mud from his forehead with a trembling hand. 'Head north, to Forty-one,' he advised, his eyes closed as wood whistled all around him. 'I'm going to wait here now. I'm beat.' He wiped the mud from his head again and crawled awkwardly to the roadside, dragging his bag behind him. His movements were jerky and disturbing, as though something dark was tugging on his strings.

I remained kneeling on the tarmac, rocking against the wind, my arms limp at my side.

'You still here?' he called, his voice like an echo. 'Go on, fuck off. You know how to dispose of your share. Just . . . just don't sell nothing east of Texarkana. And everything north of Hagerston is mine. Now git!'

I hesitated. 'Want a fag?'

'Not any more,' he sighed.

'I meant a cigarette, a Marlboro.'

He shook his head very slowly. 'I've given up.'

The sky lit up, and a drop of blood fell heavily from his jaw, disappearing into his soiled shirt. I crawled across to him, sniffing like a hound dog. The baseball hat hid a sticky crown of clotting blood, its wilted pinnacles streaking his face and his neck with an oozing blackness.

'See something you like after all this time?' he wheezed.

'You're bleeding,' I replied. 'Take off the hat and show me.'

'Can't,' he replied, smearing the flow across his eyebrow. 'Take the hat off and you'll take off the top of my head. Kind of excessive for a howdy do, don't you think?'

I stared at the cap in horror, my face a handspan from Gene's. 'What happened?'

'Goddamn Cherokee scalped me,' he grinned. 'Dashed my brilliant mind against a goddamned cypress.' He cupped a palm beneath his swollen ear, then showed me what he'd caught. 'See that? That's brain juice, Troop. I'm leaking like a Mekong junk.'

One eyelid hung heavy across a sunken eye, and the other blinked like it was trying to prove that nothing was wrong. I looked away.

'Hey!' he called. 'The winking's beyond my control, just like the plane crash.'

'Wasn't your fault,' I conceded. 'It was Injun failure.'

The wind whistled.

'Get it?' I persisted. 'Cherokee? Injun failure?'

Even now, he wouldn't afford me the concession of a smile. Instead, he rolled his eyes towards the south. 'Here comes the fucking cavalry,' he announced.

A single headlight approached, its erratic beam like a drunk's train of thought. I limped to the median line and waved until it found me. A battered dirt bike with a farting engine pulled up alongside, the rider's long blond hair plastered to his face. His bare knee was bleeding freely and the skin was scraped from his teenage cheek. His pillion passenger, same hairdo, same age, similar abrasions, was holding his guts, but he managed a nodded greeting.

'We took a spill back there, man,' yelled the rider, clearly stoked. 'Motherfuckin' wind caught Blueberry's board and spun us into the fuckin' bayou, man. I am *all* fucked up!' Somehow, he made it seem like an achievement. 'Figured we could catch some storm swell down there, but it's all fucked up and onshore, and they're talking about a fuckin' twenty-five-foot slosh coming through, so we figured, hey, let's get the fuck out of town. What the fuck happened to you guys?'

If he thought a motorcycle crash was something to crow about, a plane crash would blow him away. Gene headed me off. 'Car got blown off the road down there. We were heading for Forty-one.'

The surfer checked us out, his little bike wheezing in the gale. 'Listen: I got to go and drop Blueberry here up at the highway. I'll come back and get you guys.' He slipped the clutch. 'Hang in there, guys!'

His whey-faced passenger flipped us a thumbs-up, and they whizzed downwind through a whirl of flying foliage.

'Fucking hippies,' grunted Gene, sinking back to the verge. 'Think he'll be back?'

He nodded. 'You don't abandon folks round here.' He raised a wary eye. 'Unless they're dead.'

'What's a slosh?' I asked, sitting down beside him.

'Sea, lake, overland surge from a hurricane,' he explained, his mumbled reply betraying a terminal weariness. 'Used to be called a storm surge. This road used to be called the Ninety-two. Bastards keep changing everything. Wanna play backgammon?' He picked up a stick and slowly, painfully, scratched twenty-four uneven points like alligators' teeth in the road dirt. 'Got your dice in your fag handbag?'

I rummaged past the pistol and dropped the dice on the board.

'Snake eyes,' noted Gene, wiping the blood from his forehead.

A seven-foot palm frond flew overhead like a ragged black albatross.

'What are we using for stones?'

He held up two US Treasury rolls.

'I'll be the eagle. You can be the Queen.'

I pulled two tubes of maple leaves from my bag. 'You sure you don't want to be the Queen?'

He ignored the jibe. 'Best of three. Winner gets first ride with Raspberry. Fair?'

As the lightning lit up the swamp and the wind thundered along the narrow road like a truck driven by a suicidal sociopath, Gene concentrated on his game. With a hand clasped over his dead eye and his blood dripping into the dust, he played like Napoleon, perfecting his strategy in the maelstrom of defeat. The dice were kind to him, as always, but he didn't have the head on him to use their gifts wisely, staring cluelessly at standard moves while I watched him with a sinking heart. For half an hour or so, the hurricane, the swamp, the wound that was killing him, the gold and Sherry-Lee were distant, unimportant concerns. All we saw were the dice, the points and the bloodstained gold stacking up and bearing off. He beat me two–one and raised his hand when I laid out the stones for another round.

'Don't want to play no more,' he shouted.

A hundred-mile-an-hour gust stopped dead, spun one-eighty, and flew back to the coast, snapping the crown from a tree across the road. My ears popped and Gene groaned.

'I'm dying here, Troop,' he called, slurring through numb lips. 'All this talent . . . I can feel it coming. What a waste.' He made a feeble gesture of mock-regret, one side of his face fallen, as though the flesh were already dead.

'Don't be bloody daft,' I scolded him. 'We'll get you to hospital and you'll be sorted in no time.'

It was a weak lie, and neither of us believed it. Nor could I believe that Gene was fading away before me, his skull smashed open and his brain crushed and haemorrhaging down the side of his face. It seemed like only minutes ago that I had been stumbling on his trail through the swamp, wishing him dead. Now, to my horror, my wish was coming true. Hope and Truth took up opposing seats on my shoulder and watched as Gene's balance failed and tipped him into the mud. I leaned forward and lifted him upright, feeling the sticky blood that stained his sleeves. Hope wondered if the two of us weren't being a little overdramatic here, turning this crisis into a death scene when it was more likely that Gene had suffered a minor head injury and was suffering from concussion. Truth pointed out that it wasn't so long ago that Hope was wishing Death on my partner in crime and that if it thought Gene's skull was merely concussed it was as blind as its dim cousin Faith. Truth didn't mince its words: it knew Gene was fucked and urged me to do the right thing before it was too late.

But what was the right thing?

Buggered if I know, shrugged Truth. I'm no expert on etiquette.

'What's that you're saying?' growled Gene.

'Er, nothing,' I shouted. 'Just wondering if there's anything you want to get off your chest before . . .'

'Before what?'

Before you die, you idiot. Before your soul heads off to the crossroads and you're shown which way to go.

'Before Raspberry comes back.'

'You want some sort of confession, is that it? You're looking for a . . .' Gene's lips were still moving, but the howling wind snatched his words and sprayed his face with rain that tasted of the sea.

'I'm not looking for anything,' I yelled. 'I just thought it was traditional, the done thing, you know, at least to offer.'

Gene smiled, short, sharp, sarcastic. 'Thanks for the thought. I'll tell you something in return: don't believe what they tell you about me.'

His gaze slipped from my face and tried to focus on the past. His mind was adrift on a heaving ocean of blood and he was struggling to keep his thoughts on course. 'They'll tell you lies about me. It's all lies. My report says I'm sick, that I'm some kind of goddamned pervert, unfit for command. It's all lies. You ask them if Alexander was unfit for command? If Montgomery was sick? I gave my heart to this country . . . buried my feelings . . . denied myself human contact the better to perform my mission. Then they fuck me the first time I make a mistake. To err is human, to forgive divine . . .' He raised his eyes to mine. 'Neither, however, is Marine Corps policy. Fucking Atlantic City.'

'What happened in Atlantic City?' I asked, and he curled his lip.

'Nothing happened in Atlantic City. Christ, the kid was just trying to save his own ass from the stockade . . . whole thing was so goddamned stupid . . .'

He lowered his voice and let the storm scatter his regrets, distracted now by bitter memories. The wind dropped and he sagged, falling to his side like a man paralysed. As I lifted him back to his knees he was still mumbling curses, but then his eyes locked on to mine, one winking wildly in the dead side of his face.

'Your move, damnit,' he hissed. 'Where's the board?'

'Gone,' I told him. 'Washed away. You won. Two–one.'

He held out one hand. 'So surrender your gold to me.'

'No way,' I cried. 'You get to go first when the bike comes back and that's worth more than gold.'

I turned my back into the wind, flinching under the impact of its blasted debris, concentrating on the vanishing-point of the road until the wavering yellow beam returned.

The surfer was breathless with excitement as he skidded to a halt. 'Awesome, man!' he cried. 'Blueberry got whipped bigtime back there! Branch blew off a tree as we're exactly fuckin' underneath it and gets him – *BOOM* – in the back. Dislocated his shoulder, man, I swear to God. Out-fuckin'-standing! We got to motor, guys. Who's first?'

I pointed at Gene.

He shook his head. 'You go.'

'Quit fucking around,' I shouted. 'Get on and go.'

He held out a shaking hand. 'Sell you my seat for fifty bucks.'

I stared at him. He stared back.

The surfer shook his head. 'Guys, there's like a twenty-five-foot wall of ocean coming down Main Street. Can we make a move here?'

Gene waggled his fingers like Shylock. 'Pay up. You should know by now you don't get nothing for nothing. Haven't you learned anything?'

'Why are you doing this, you fool?'

'Because if I let you go for free it would be an act of altruism, and I'm not happy with the concept.'

'Hey, guys,' called Raspberry. 'Tick fucking tock . . .'

I dipped into my bag and dropped a twinklebirdy into Gene's palm like a lost soul paying the ferryman.

He smiled at the coin, his head bobbing like a rubber-necked sentry, then looked at me with his one good eye. 'It doesn't feel as good as I thought it would.'

'What doesn't?' I swung my leg over the pillion.

'Self-sacrifice,' he replied. 'It's overrated. Don't do it.'

'I'll see you in a minute,' I said.

'Whatever,' he shrugged. 'Just tell me something before you go.'

Raspberry revved the bike.

'Quick, what?' I asked him.

'That fag handbag,' he said, pointing with a stick. 'Why do you carry it around?'

It was a good question. 'None of your fucking business,' I replied.

Raspberry had wasted a lot of valuable study time perfecting his bike-handling skills, and he tore down Hurricane Alley with hair-raising panache, anticipating cross-winds and skirting round broken trees with casual grace. The intersection with the Tamiami Trail at Royal Palm Hammock was aglow with the whirling lights of public safety, and, as we approached, a deputy in an absurd orange sou'wester flagged us down.

'You Blueberry's buddy?' he yelled.

'Yes, sir,' shouted Raspberry.

The deputy looked at me. 'You the guy from the car wreck?'

I nodded.

'Where's the other one?'

'Still there,' I cried. 'We've got to go and get him.'

The Deputy pointed at the surfer. 'Not you,' he bellowed. 'You two get over there and wait with Derrick in the recovery truck.' He ran back to his vehicle, spun it around and skidded on to 92 South, his flashing lights bouncing off the contorted treeline.

'Fucking cops,' sighed Raspberry. 'They love this shit.'

Like he didn't. A redneck tow-truck, lights ablaze, waited in the rain in the lee of the storm-shattered restaurant building. Raspberry wheeled his dirt-bike on to the flatbed while I lugged my bag into the cab, where Blueberry lay slumped beside the fist-throwing biker from Everglades City.

He raised his eyebrows. 'Son of a bitch! Where's your Daddy, son?'

I struggled to make myself comfortable between Blueberry and Raspberry. The sweet smell of reefer filled the cab. 'Who?'

'Your daddy. The captain.'

I pointed down the road. 'Back there. He's not my dad, and you know as well as me that he's not a captain.'

Blueberry passed the joint and I sucked on it like a suffocating man on an oxygen pipe.

Derrick shrugged. 'Well,' he drawled. 'He was a captain

when he sent me to the stockade, the hardass son of a bitch. Ruined my fuckin' military career, did Captain Eugene P. Casseaux, but he never stopped me smoking reefer.' Stoned and genial, he tossed me a conciliatory shrug. 'What the fuck. I did what a man had to do the other night, but I'm over it now. No hard feelings and all. He was a good platoon leader once upon a time. Shipped out to some recon unit and killed a lot of dinks. Got to afford the man some respect now, don't you?'

I bit my lip and nodded. You most certainly did.

'Never figured I'd run into him out here in the fucking boonies, though,' Derrick continued. 'Always had him down as the Miami Beach type. What the hell's he doing out here?'

I handed the spliff down the line as headlights flashed through the downpour. 'I think he might be dying.'

'Fuck,' mused Derrick, taking a hit and stubbing the roach.

'Here comes the cop,' warned Blueberry.

The Deputy rolled alongside, his window wound down and the rain dripping from his hat. 'Storm surge coming!' he yelled. 'I can't get to your buddy, son!'

He looked past us to our driver, his brow brooking no defiance. 'Don't even think about it, Derrick. Bottom Turn Creek bridge is seven, eight foot under already. Poor guy's been washed away. Just follow me out of here.'

Derrick shook his head in sad resignation and floored it, accelerating on to the highway with a swinging door, his CB radio bursting with beeps and excited voices. 'The Corps don't like leaving their dead behind,' he muttered.

Nor did I.

13

I wish I could say that I'd witnessed a twenty-five-foot storm surge inundate the south-west Florida coastline, that I had watched as a pile of wind-driven brine spilled over the land, washing settlements and roads from the map and lives from the national census, but it never came near me. The cop dropped us at a high-school storm shelter in east Naples and told me to stay put until he could spare the time to take a statement.

'Yeah, right!' scoffed Raspberry as he drove away.

We went in and queued on hard orange chairs to be examined by a tired doctor. An obese woman with a volunteer's badge and an air of exasperated self-importance passed us clipboards with photocopied forms to complete.

'So's we can inform your next of kin, if necessary,' she explained through a wad of Juicy Fruit.

I left my form on a shelf and limped in to see the doctor. I showed him my injuries and told him I'd been in a car wreck. He told me I had probably cracked a couple of ribs and might have broken my nose. The nurse told me to take a couple of Tylenol and a sip of water, then sent me to the shelter volunteers in the senior locker room, where I swapped my soaking, torn and mud-blackened clothes for a preppy ensemble of second-hand blue jeans, baseball shirt and tube socks from the donated-garments rail. An old lady with too much lipstick and a twinkle in her eye that said she was having the time of her life handed me a bag marked 'Kiwanis' that contained an economy-class toiletries bag and pushed me towards the showers. Washed and clad in dry clothing, I sipped weak coffee from a Styrofoam cup in the convention-like atmosphere of the crowded school hall, my legs trembling and my mind reeling.

'Sir, are you registered already?' A tanned pensioner in shorts and sandals was in my face. 'You need to register,' he continued, 'so the authorities can—'

I picked up the Mulberry holdall and swallowed my coffee. 'I'm registered,' I nodded. 'Gave it to the lady in the med centre.'

Shock, fatigue, conscience and the law were catching up with me. It was time to move on.

Hurricanes make vagrants of anybody, and on this apocalyptic morning an injured man limping along the highway with a heavy bag no longer seemed such a threat to the American Way. Within half a block I had scored a lift in a shiny SUV driven by the voluble food and beverages manager of a local country club. He asked me where I was headed and I told him Fort Myers Beach. He shook his head.

'Not today, mister. I-Seventy-five and the Tamiami Trail are still closed. Heard it on the radio just now.' He popped a breath freshener and tapped the steering wheel. 'Maybe you could try dog-legging round Immokalee. I'll drop you at Randall and you can try your luck. There's got to be plenty of folks heading round that way.'

He frowned at the rain, and kept asking me if I thought the worst had passed, or if it was still to come, but I couldn't answer. Gene was missing, presumed dead, his ticket to ride sold for fifty bucks. I was shattered, bruised and alive, with nothing to my name but a passport, a cheap firearm, and nearly half a million in gold bullion. Guilt lapped at my feet like a pool of blood, and my depleted soul was soaking it up like dry bread dipped in wine.

'Damn this rain, don't you say?' cried the food and beverages manager. 'You think it's going to stop today?'

I couldn't see it stopping for a long time. He dropped me outside a twenty-four-hour convenience store on the junction of Randall Boulevard and told me to enjoy Labor Day. I bought a pack of smokes and asked the clerk what he knew of Immokalee.

'Kind of like a ghetto up there,' he shrugged. 'It's not really a tourist destination.'

It sounded perfect.

A taciturn maintenance man in a rusting pick-up pulled over and waved me in. His bumper sticker said 'FBI', and, in smaller letters underneath, 'Full Blooded Indian'.

'Where you headed?'

'Immokalee.'

He pushed a plug of Chief into his cheek. 'What the hell for?' he grunted.

An hour later, he woke me with a rough hand and an announcement: 'Immokalee.'

I blinked hard, wiping the dribble from my chin and trying to remember why I was here in this low, grey, washed-out town. Too late to prevent a surge of panic, I saw that the gold and my handbag were still safely between my feet, and, numb with wasted adrenalin, I thanked my driver and stepped from the car into the dirty boulevard.

Rain fell like dry rice across an intersection that split four city blocks. To my left, a huge lot of garbage-splattered wasteland ended at the walls of a distant processing plant with a painted tomato the size of a small asteroid and 'King City Duke' in twenty-foot-high letters beside it. Refrigerated trailer units were parked in neat, tight rows behind a chain-link fence to my right. Ahead of me, a swelling stream of poorly dressed men in cheap yellow waterproofs drained like dirty water towards the centre of town. I wondered for a moment why I had chosen Immokalee in a state with such destinations as Miami and Orlando. I crossed the road and followed the crowd, moving slowly and painfully under the burden of sixty pounds of gold. The pinched, skinny, brown-faced men smiled as they passed, some whispering polite greetings in accented Spanish: '*Buenos dias, Señor.*' They moved quickly, their lunchbags dangling from their wrists, wide straw sombreros or high-crowned baseball hats protecting their dark hair from the cold rain.

'Where you guys heading?' I asked in Spanish.

'The pancake house,' replied a mournful man with a sombre moustache. 'You know the bus?'

I shook my head and struggled to keep up.

'The bus for the work in the fields. The one that stops at the pancake house?'

It sounded plausible. I shifted the bag from hand to hand every couple of steps, but the relief was fleeting and swamped by fresh rushes of pain from my side. Breathless and sweating, I stopped in the lee of a doorway alongside a steaming burrito stand. Single men snatched rolled tortillas in paper towels from the hip-wide counter as they passed while the married men, already fed, hurried past. I was hungry but broke, so I loitered near by, sniffing my breakfast from the air as I caught my breath.

The taco man gave me a suspicious look. 'You here for work, you in the wrong place. Wrong time. Harvest is two, three months away. These guys is planters, skilled workers. This stinking weather, even they don't get no work today.'

I kept my hands on my bag. 'I'm not after work,' I told him. 'I need to find a pawnbroker.'

He raised an eyebrow and took a dollar from a fast-moving planter. 'What you got to sell?'

'A coin,' I replied.

He spooned sauce on to a tortilla and held out his hand. 'Show me.'

'You a pawnbroker?'

He inclined his head. 'No. Too much paperwork. *Comprende, ese?*'

He had a point. I pulled an eagle from my stiff new jeans and dropped it into his hands.

He turned it over and handed it back. 'Give you twenty bucks.'

I laughed, unamused. 'That coin is solid gold,' I told him. 'It's worth nearly four hundred dollars.'

He pointed a dripping spoon at my chest. '*Hombre*, it is worth only as much as you can get for it. Value is relative to need. And, one more thing: don't go flashing gold on the streets of Immokalee. These guys earn fifty dollars a day, if they're lucky, for crawling in the mud planting tomatoes and cucumbers for America. The last seven days there is no work, and there's a lot of hungry babies in a lot of leaky trailers. You understand what I say?'

I gave him a look that conceded the point, then shifted my gaze to his wares. The value of an American eagle on the Brock Exchange was rapidly reaching parity with two burritos and a cup of coffee.

'How many you got?' sniffed the cook.

I watched him from across the threshold, weighing up the risks of crossing it. I could leave right now, find a Yellow Pages, look up a pawnbroker's and wait outside until opening time. With luck, I could turn a roll of maples into cash and be on my way in a cash-purchased car before the lunchtime rush. Alternatively, they could note my seedy appearance, hand me a form and call the police. I took a deep breath and stepped over the line.

'Eleven,' I replied.

He concentrated on his griddle. 'All the same?'

'Yeah.'

'And you want to sell them all?'

'That's right.'

'Okay,' he nodded. 'Let me make a call.'

Jorge Luis owned El Paraiso, a pearl of a bar in the unkempt sty that was downtown Immokalee. He was waiting outside in a black Chevy Blazer with tinted windows, and he never missed a trick.

'*Hombre!*' he observed as I came down the litter-strewn sidewalk, heaving my four-stone load. 'I heard you had eleven coins, not eleven hundred!' He grinned at the Mulberry bag and I shook my head.

'Just books in there. The coins are—'

He raised a hand. 'Not in the street. Come into the bar.'

I expected something sordid and smelling of puke and piss as he unlocked the steel door and ushered me inside. Beauty seemed to have no calling in this uncared-for town, a place where the stateless and the hopeless drank themselves numb with clinical determination. A wipe-clean floor, plastic furniture and neon light would have sufficed for the administration of a soulwash of cheap ethanol, but Jorge either thought his clients deserved better or just liked working in a pleasant environment. The bar ran almost the length of the narrow room, terminating before a pair of blue pool tables. Glazed earthenware tiles formed diamonds across the floor and the bar front was clad in intricately patterned ceramics. The top was solid oak, the fittings polished brass and the stock pure gold.

I ran my hand along the counter approvingly: Jorge Luis was a man of taste. I turned to study him as he locked us

both in, wondering if this was the bit where he pulled a
pistol and robbed me blind. Jorge Luis, however, was way
too cool for that kind of hot-headedness. His clothing created the impression of inoffensive immigrant prosperity, a
big, middle-aged fish with oily hair in a small pond with no
desire to create waves. If I was to be ripped off by this man,
it would happen when he was out at the workers' camp,
handing relief to the poor, with witnesses.

He turned and smiled. 'You like my bar? I build it myself.
You want a drink?'

I glanced at the big clock behind the bar: it was past eight
already. 'Small tequila wouldn't hurt, I suppose,' I mused.

Jorge poured a deep Centenario. 'Tequila man, are you?
Me, *Ron de Cuba*. You been to Cuba?'

'Not yet,' I replied.

'You should go,' he advised. '*Salud!*'

Toast was traditional for breakfast, I supposed. I waited for
another round, but Jorge Luis had better things to do.

'My friend says you have some pretty coins to sell,' he
smiled. 'Show me.'

I pulled a damp Treasury roll from my pocket and laid it
on the bar. 'Ten US eagles, still sealed,' I announced. 'Face
value fifty bucks, market value, say, three-sixty. Ninety-five
per cent pure gold and every one as pretty as this. I got
another roll just like it if you're interested.' I placed a loose
coin alongside the roll. Jorge Luis picked it up, and as the
birdy twinkled in his eye I could see he lacked immunity.
'Twenty-one golden eagles, eh?' he breathed. 'That is a lot of
flocking eagles, no?' He laughed loud at his joke, slapping
me hard on the arm. 'Why you no sell them in Naples or
Fort Myers? They got coin dealers there. You get a good
price.'

I looked him in the eye. 'Because I can't,' I replied.

He shrugged. 'Then you cannot sell these to me for their true value . . .'

'I know,' I replied. 'I need cash. I need it quick. Give me a number.'

He tapped a calculator. 'Can I believe your market value?'

I lit a Marlboro. 'You got a newspaper?'

He passed me yesterday's *Naples News* and I showed him the spot price. 'Three fifty-nine an ounce. That good enough?'

He poked the calculator again. 'Seventeen-fifty. That good enough for you?'

It was an insult, but I didn't have the time to bargain with him. I snatched back the loose coin. 'This one I keep as a souvenir.'

He shrugged. It was still a good deal for one of us.

I licked my lips as he counted out the cash and then he added personal injury to his insulting offer. 'You got a minute to hear a story?'

I shrugged, making little circles with my empty shot glass on the bartop. Jorge Luis caught my drift and poured another *dos dedos*. 'Now you got a minute,' he smiled. 'You see those people out there, shuffling along the street to the market? To you, they are nothing. Economic immigrants, most of them illegal, all of them dirty poor.'

'Dirt poor,' I interjected.

'Absolutely. They come from Mexico, Guatemala, Haiti and from my motherland, Cuba. Now, there's not so many of them, because it ain't harvest time yet, but every day is pretty much the same. They live in trailers, in shacks, in houses on the workers' camp, or here in town, in the flop-houses, sometimes twenty or more in three rooms. Every morning they get up at four-thirty, and they walk to the market, whatever the weather, and they wait for the bus.

Sometimes the bus comes, sometimes it don't, and sometimes they get a seat, and sometimes they don't, but getting a seat is no guarantee of work. They go to the fields, and they wait until the bossmen say it's okay to start, and when he say go, man, you should see these spics go! They run from the buses like Speedy Gonzales, grab their buckets and pick, pick, pick. One bucket, she holds thirty-two pounds of green tomatoes, and the picker, he gets a ticket for every bucket that weighs good. One ounce under, he no get a ticket. Now, once he's working, he can't stop for nothing 'cos anytime the boss can say, "Whoa, hold it," that's it, and once the work's finished, the picker cashes in his tickets.'

He paused to relight his cigar stub, sucked and jabbed the glowing end towards me. 'Forty cents. Each ticket gets him forty cents. He got to pick eighty pounds of tomatoes for a dollar, nearly two goddamned tons to earn his fifty bucks. From that, he's got to pay the rent, buy food for his family, get clothes for the kids, all that shit, and he's got to work seven days a week to put anything by. All the time he gotta keep his head down, keep his mouth shut, not be noticed by nobody. He got no contract, no security, no healthcare, no way of knowing if he's gonna get one hour or twelve hours of picking, or if he's even gonna get a seat on the bus. Man, termites has got more job security than this guy. At the end of the day, if he's got a spare dollar, he comes in here, all dirty from the fields, sneezing from the pesticides, his back all bent from picking those low-down crops, and I look into his eyes and this guy has got more happiness in there than you, my friend.'

He waited for a reaction. I let him wait. He shrugged.

'End of story, my friend. You find the moral. Just remember that sometimes it's easier to do the right thing.'

That puzzled me, but it was still a good call.

He shook my hand at the door. '*Vaya con Dios, desperado!*'

I ate *huevos rancheros* in a fly-blown *cantina* down the street from El Paraiso. The dark-skinned waitress wore plastic flip-flops, a blue nylon dress and the hunted expression of an overworked mother. I checked her fingers as she poured the coffee, but the only rings I could see were those below her eyes. If Jorge Luis could see more happiness in that face than he could see in mine, then I was a seriously miserable-looking bastard. There was nothing wrong with her that a hundred dollars wouldn't fix, as the poet once said, and with the gold at my feet I could repair a lot of faces in this care-worn town.

Charity, however, began at home, and I had yet to find one. I paid with a fifty and left a ten-dollar tip, dragging my bag down the street to the liquor store. I bought two bottles of Sauza and a carton of Marlboro from a neurotic Mexican who seemed used to being robbed, swaying on my feet as I paid.

'You look beat, man,' said the clerk, sounding exactly like Cheech Marin.

'It's all caught up with me,' I confided. 'You know of a second-hand car place round here?'

He directed me down a street of empty storefronts to a fenced-in lot called Scooter's Four Wheel Deals. Scooter's stock was a disgrace, and he caught me shaking my head at a dented Chevy Nova.

'Fine automobile there, son!' he beamed. His spare chins wobbled with enthusiasm as he stretched out a rain-slicked hand to pat the rusting deathtrap. 'Had one myself, once,' he lied.

I was too tired and distracted to endure a salesman's games.

'Cut the crap, Scooter,' I growled. 'Tell me what you've got for a grand.'

His porcine eyes widened a little beneath his hood and he licked his lips. 'Come here,' he said, beckoning me with a fat, pink finger.

I followed him across the crowded lot beneath dripping garlands of tinsel. He extended a hand to let me pass, to let me be the first to see the car of my dreams.

'Behold!' he cried. 'Son, that's a 1978 Cadillac Eldorado Custom Biarritz Power T-Top, new in last week! She's got the original two-tone paint job – Arizona beige over demitass brown, with the light beige and dark saddle interior trim, and the Power T-top is in full working order.'

Suddenly I liked Scooter. I liked Jorge Luis. I liked the burrito guy, and I liked Immokalee. Most of all, I liked the 1978 Cadillac Eldorado Custom Biarritz Power T-Top.

'Last of the big Caddies, she's got a cast-iron, seven-litre V8 block under that hood and she'll give you a full ten miles to the gallon . . .'

'What's a Power T-top, Scoot?' I interrupted.

He grinned, turned the key, and flipped a switch. As the vinyl roof peeled back, attraction became true love.

'How much?' I panted. This was the car that would take us to Mexico.

'It's way beyond your budget,' he shrugged, 'and I can't do finance on this model. Sorry 'bout that.'

'How much?'

He sucked air like a snake, tasting the potential. 'Twenty-two fifty?'

'You take gold?'

He gave me a puzzled, sideways glance. 'Gold?'

Half an hour later I was cash broke, several eagles lighter and heading north-west on 82 to Fort Myers in a car that drank leaded fuel like I drank beer. Gene's ghost rode shot-gun, his presence becoming less ethereal with my deepening fatigue. He wasn't happy about being dead: I could see it in his face. He stared straight ahead, an expression of disappointment on downturned mouth. I turned on the radio and caught the end of 'Jean Genie'. My phantom passenger wasn't amused.

'Turn that shit off,' he drawled, his voice an echo in my throbbing head.

I ignored his command – he wasn't there.

'Top of the hour and the latest news from KXFM. Hurricane Louisa heads out to sea, leaving fourteen dead and hundreds injured.'

Gene's ghost gave me a look.

'Some sources are estimating that the category-four hurricane caused damage to property in excess of two billion dollars. Federal Government has declared Collier County and parts of Lee County an official disaster zone. Despite the storm, word is that tonight's ball game between the Devil Rays and the St Louis Cardinals is on, and despair turns to grief in storm-tossed Lee County as a missing child is found partially eaten by alligators. For these stories and more, tune to KXPN on ninety-eight point four on the FM. Three of the best from Black Sabbath after these messages . . .'

'Fucking hell!' I exclaimed. 'Solomon Bender *was* eaten by 'gators!'

'Told you,' lied Gene's transparent ghost. 'You thought I did it.'

'Never did,' I protested. 'I knew you hadn't done him in, and I couldn't work out why you were acting so guilty. I guessed you must have been on some kind of sex offenders' register, but I couldn't be certain.'

'Now you never will be,' he sighed.

Ahead and above us, a small aeroplane wobbled as it descended through the low cloud cover. I waited for Gene to pour on the scorn, but, perhaps unsurprisingly, he found it hard to criticise a pilot who had made it as far as the final approach. His light beige seat was empty now, but when I checked the rearview he was stretched across the back seat with a Marlboro in his mouth.

'Suppose I was alive and you were dead,' he mused. 'Imagine that, if you have the mental capacity.'

I ignored him, turning up the radio, concentrating on Ozzy's paranoia instead of my own. It didn't help – Gene's voice was in my head.

'Look at yourself,' he goaded me. 'Take a look around. You're driving the car of your all-too-predictable dreams down a rural blacktop, a bag of gold in the trunk and your trailer-trash girlfriend at the end of the road. She's going to fall into your arms and you're both going to take that all-American roadtrip south of the border to waste the rest of your unfulfilled lives on a beach. Jesus Christ! Any moment now the sun's gonna come out as well. Sounds too good to be true, doesn't it?'

It sounded like my just deserts, and, as a lake-sized shadow overtook us, bright sunshine did light up the shiny road.

'It's all in your head,' scoffed Gene. 'Your exotic dancer has eyes for one man only, and it sure as hell ain't you, Troop. Sure, you can turn her head, offer her asylum from her self-persecution, take her away from all this and all that, but you'll never keep her – mark my words. She likes you – she's extremely *fond* of you – but the only man she'll ever love is that redneck maniac from Missouri. Trust me, Troop, I know women.'

He was so full of shit. Even in death he was trying to screw me, and that was what it was all about. Way back in Marrakech

he had made me for an easy lay, one willing half of an old-fash-
ioned master-and-boy relationship. My simple good
neighbourliness had queered his pitch, so to speak, falling as a
lightning seed that ruptured the ground between us.

He was back in the shotgun, one neatly ironed denim-
clad leg propped improbably on the window ledge, like
William Shatner trying to be cool. The sun had gone in
again, but the rain had stopped, so I popped the Power T,
hoping that the slipstream would blow the hallucinations
from my aching head. I lit a cigarette and took a long pull on
the Sauza. A roadside hoarding, once twenty feet high by
forty feet wide, had been snapped in two by the hurricane,
leaving only a pair of robed legs in Birkenstocks and the
words 'ready when He returns'. It was enough, and I got the
message. It reminded me of something Gene had said in a
motel in Saucier, MI.

'We'd have made a tight fucking team, man,' he sighed,
'once you got your attitude adjusted.'

My attitude? What about his?

'Mine?' he cried. 'Now hear this: my attitude was mission
driven from day one. Everything I did was directed towards
the satisfactory achievement of the stated objectives, with the
exception of the occasional aromatherapy massage and the
odd shopping trip. You, on the other hand, pissed and
whined like a goddamned conscript from the minute you
joined. You were a volunteer, Troop . . .'

As far as I recalled, I had been press-ganged after accepting
the old queen's shilling while incapacitated through drink. I
tossed my cigarette butt, the echoes of Gene's militaristic
idiom beginning to give me toothache. I couldn't deny that
he had a right to speak that way after Derrick had vouched
for him back at the crossroads, but it still grated on my shattered nerves.

'Have you thought about last night?' he asked quietly.

'Jumpin' Jack Flash' sprang from the speakers. I turned the volume a couple of notches higher.

'I was finished when you found me, could have died right there on the slough. Don't you wonder why I made the effort to save your life?'

I did, as it happened.

'Yeah, well, I'll let that one keep you up nights,' he smirked.

I'd been under the impression that I was Jumpin' Jack Flash, but it was Gene who'd been washed up and left for dead and Gene who'd been crowned with a spike through his head. None of it had been a gas. I saw his face, striped with blood that shone black in the lightning's blue flash, the baseball cap that was keeping his exposed brain in his broken skull as the fluids spilled from his nose and his ears, and I wondered what he'd done after I'd taken his seat on Raspberry's dirt-bike, leaving him to wait alone in the storm for Death to breeze by.

'Shot craps in the mud to pass the time,' he said.

Dicing with Death on the San Marco road. I wondered how he made out.

'Total washout,' he replied, deadpan. 'Doesn't any of this strike you as weird?'

That I was talking to a dead man?

'Not just that: all of it. The ease with which you got to that shitbag town back there, the way you fenced those coins to the spic barman, this car, the fucking sunshine, everything. It's like you made it all up, dreamed it up on one of your drug-crazed trips . . . You know exactly where I'm heading.'

He was right, and it was towards a question that I didn't want to consider. The radio was playing 'Once in a

Lifetime', and Gene sang along in mocking harmony. 'You know where you might be, don't you?' he grinned.

I ignored him. He wasn't offended.

'Strapped in the cockpit of a one-armed Cherokee, your neck broken in an impact that took place only thirty-three seconds ago.' He raised his eyebrows. 'Spooky, huh? And all this is a mere figment of your guttering imagination, the insane theatrics of a dying brain, random images conjured by your short-circuited synapses from desire and memory, ambition and regret. You watch, Troop: the lower the voltage, the weirder it gets. And when the last spark flares and fades, you'll be glad to be dead, man.'

We'd see.

His piece said, Gene sashayed into a darkened room at the edge of my mind to make an impression on the other ghosts that haunted me. He'd have been dismayed by the company I kept, but he wouldn't have been surprised.

14

The TV trucks and the National Guard had ended their occupation of the road into the trailer park, but Solomon Bender was still the latest news. KXPN reported that the
child's partially devoured body had probably been dislodged from the alligator's underwater larder by the storm surge coming up the Caloosahatchee River. Public opinion was divided on the matter of retribution: some thought the guilty 'gator should be sought out and shot. Others argued that it was just doing its thing, and pointed out that numerous innocent alligators would probably be wrongly executed before the child-killer was found. Nobody mentioned Turn Back Jack.

As I approached Bridgeview, my stomach shrank in apprehension of my reunion with Sherry-Lee. Gene had spooked me with his posthumous insights into her character, and the doubts I'd buried in shallow graves now wandered like zombies through my storm-damaged brain.

I was so close to the end of the page, so near to turning over a new leaf, and so aware that it all depended on Sherry-Lee's heart. My palms were sweaty on the wheel, and an anxious, acid nausea burned my gut as I realised there was more hope, more potential for happiness, in the journey than there would be at the destination. It was a feeling familiar to returning soldiers and parolees: a nervous realisation that happy endings were not guaranteed in the real world. I tried shaking off the doubts, tried to persuade myself that everything would be fine. This time tomorrow Sherry-Lee, Angie and I would be heading west into a golden future, our cares abandoned like roadside garbage. I forced a smile. Everything would be fine.

Unless, of course, she didn't love me.

But even that was cool. Love wasn't a ready-grown pot plant, a perpetual flowering rose that never dropped a petal. Love was a strangling weed grown from seed and once established it would thrive unchecked, covering everything it touched and hiding all sins and transgressions beneath its smothering foliage. Given rich Mexican soil and warm sunshine, Sherry-Lee could take root on me, wrapping her tendrils around my willing limbs, holding me down and bleeding me of my wanderlust. She didn't need to love me *now* — I'd settle for whenever. What mattered was that she loved Brad. And Gene had been a son of a bitch for bringing it up.

I rolled through the gates in my Eldorado, tyres crunching on the roadstone and my mouth as dry as dust. The deserted trailer park looked like a tornado had touched down, scattering toys, plastic lawn chairs and garbage with an explosive flick of its gritty tail. Peeled-back roofs left several trailers open like the mouths of the dead, splintered white verandas lying like broken teeth in the mud. A skinny Puerto Rican, stripped to the waist in the rising heat, stood gaping at a trailer that was dented like a beer can, its plastic windows popped from their frames, the stained nets billowing. He waved limply as I passed. The severed head of a royal palm lay by Sherry-Lee's trailer, its broken crown blocking her door.

I parked the Eldorado on a nearby lot and dragged away the snapped tree. The impact had buckled the door and crushed the steel steps: two feet to the left and it would have smashed in her roof. I stood on tiptoe and peered through the window, shielding my eyes from the reflected sunlight, not knowing what I was looking for. A bottle of nail varnish on the table and a pair of jeans draped on the back of a chair told me that she still lived there and had left in a hurry. She was probably down at the local high-school storm shelter, drinking weak coffee and consoling the heartbroken Mrs Bender.

I glanced across to the Bender residence. Compassionless and disrespectful, Louisa had ripped the roof from the trailer, sucked out the family's clothing and hung it on the fence through which Solomon had crawled to his doom. Bereaved and homeless, the Benders deserved a change of luck.

I walked back to the car, popped the trunk, pulled ten rolls of maple leaves from the swag and wrapped them in a wind-blown carrier-bag. Scoping the park for looters, I heaved it over the dented wall and into Mrs Bender's ruined front room.

Hoping God was watching, I climbed back into the Cadillac, tipped back the seat and made myself comfortable. I was asleep in ten seconds.

It was dark when I woke: 10.10, according to the dashboard clock. Stiff-necked and fuzzy-headed, I rinsed my mouth with tequila and tore the strip from a fresh pack of smokes. It would be four hours and forty cigarettes before she was home, and I had nothing to do but wait. The sky had cleared, so I sat on the hood of the Eldorado, sipping Sauza and watching space rocks burn up in the stratosphere, their aimless drifting culminating in streaks of unremarkable light. I was trying not to think too hard, trying not to worry, but I was weary and my will was a poor shepherd to my itinerant thoughts. I was exhausted by the running, claustrophobic from the hiding and footsore with wandering. I was fed up with the hangovers, the paranoia, the coughing and the shakes that my deeply

unwholesome lifestyle forced upon me; sick of drugs, cigarettes and alcohol.

Maybe that last statement was an exaggeration, but sitting
in the black summer heat beneath the wobbling stars, I felt
my withered soul begging me to find somewhere pleasant to
lie down and be bound. I wanted no more adventures, crav-
ing instead the predictable mundanity of a normal life, even
if the Mexican coast was hardly the 'burbs. Freedom was
overrated. I wanted something that could be lost, but I
couldn't shake the feeling that it had already happened.

Sherry-Lee's wavering headlights pierced my morose
thoughts at a little after two. Something warm and liquid
cracked in my chest as she stepped from the car and walked
slowly, apprehensively, around her trailer, checking for storm
damage. I stayed in the shadows, mindful of her Glock,
watching as she struggled to open her warped front door. I
swallowed spit and wrung my sweating hands as the door
clicked shut and the yellow light splashed on the damp
ground. It was time to go calling.

If she was pleased to see me, she hid it well. She barred
the door with her arm and looked me up and down. 'Well,
well, well,' she announced. 'I do declare.'

'Did you get my letter?' I asked.

'What letter?' she sniffed. She was still wearing the angel,
which was a good sign, I supposed.

'I wrote you a letter explaining what was going on. I left
you my number – I couldn't call you. I tried, but there's no
listing for the Alligator Strip. I couldn't call the office here
because that toe-rag Roscoe hates me and wouldn't pass on
a message if I asked him. I've been pulling my bloody hair
out trying to get through to you, Sherry-Lee.' I ran out of
words, overwhelmed by her fragile beauty.

She gave me a long, judgemental look, taking her time to

arrive at a verdict. At last she sighed, seeming to shrink a little in the porchlight as she lowered her arm. 'You'd better come in. You see they got the power back on?'

I lugged the bag up and over her crushed steps and hauled it through the door.

'What the heck have you got in there?' she drawled, making 'heck' sound like 'hayuck'.

'Get the curtains,' I said.

'The what?'

'The curtains. And lock the door.'

She gaped at me as if I were speaking a foreign language.

'The curtains!' I shouted, employing the foolproof British technique of increasing volume to make yourself understood. I grabbed a handful of flowery print. 'These things!'

'The drapes, you mean?'

'Yeah, the drapes,' I conceded.

'I can't lock the door, though, because it's broke,' she said. 'What the heck is all this about?'

I handed her what was left of the tequila. 'Pour us a toast,' I said.

She shook her head and shuffled to the kitchenette. I unzipped the scuffed bag.

'You know in the movies, after they've robbed a bank or something, when they hole up in a motel and toss all the cash into the air and laugh like maniacs?'

She placed two mismatched shot glasses brimful of liquor on the coffee-table and stared at me.

I lifted the bag high in the air. 'Can't do it with gold.'

I tipped it up and a thudding cascade of rolled gold and plastic sheets crashed to the linoleum floor. Tearing open a roll of eagles, I threw them into the air, wincing as they bounced off the ceiling and clattered into the cheap furniture. Sherry-Lee dropped to her knees beside me and ran her hands through the heaped bullion. I remembered the sparkle in her eyes when she'd touched her first gold coin, and I knew how it got her all hot and feverish.

'Jiminy Cricket!' she whispered. 'How much is there here?'

'Don't know for sure,' I replied, pushing the button on her CD player. 'Want to help me count it?'

It took us all of Dolly Parton and half of Johnny Cash to count 563 eagles, 479 maples and a straight 400 pandas.

Sherry-Lee crouched on her hands and knees like a lean, brown Godzilla at large in a city of gold. 'How much is this worth?' she gasped.

I blew smoke over the towers of coins, kicking the buckled door shut against an insistent gust. 'A little over half a million.'

She sat back, grabbing two handfuls of bullion. 'You can't spend it like this, though, surely?'

'Course not,' I replied. 'I got me a brand-new used Cadillac out there, and I'm going to visit every coin shop from Waco to Brownsville turning yellow into green.'

She smiled, impressed to be in the company of a criminal mastermind. 'So what are you going to do with all the cash?'

I rubbed my palms along my jeans, uncomfortable with the greasy feel of the metal. The unsecured door was flapping in the breeze and annoying me. I pushed it shut and turned to Sherry-Lee. 'I'm going to give it all to you, like I said I would,' I announced. 'But, in return, you've got to give me something.'

She watched me watching her, matching my gaze, blink for blink. 'Give you what?' she asked at last.

This was a significant moment. Our drunken undertakings on the beach had been merely the half-baked, home-made hopes of two deluded losers, making plans for

an imaginary future, enjoying the present through the soft-
focus lens of an envisaged destiny. It had been easy and fun
for Sherry-Lee to pledge herself to my scheme back there at
the Sunset Tiki Lounge, to collude in the bright fantasies of
a shoeless rogue. But right here, right now, with half a million dollars' worth of proof stacked on the lino, commitment
weighed a little heavier. The smiles had dripped from both
our faces, but her eyes never wavered as I took a deep breath.

'Give me a chance with you,' I said, my voice a little
higher than I would have liked.

She swallowed. 'You mean, come to Mexico with you?'

I nodded. 'You, me and Angie, in the Eldorado, first thing
tomorrow morning. I've got it all worked out. We go to
Okeechobee in my car, wait until all the men are milking the
snakes, then grab her from Zachary's ranch and split. What
are they going to do?'

She gasped at the audacity of my plan, and I couldn't help
a little smirk as I pushed the door closed again with my foot.
It bounced off something and sprang back. I kicked it shut,
and it sprang back harder. Puzzled, I turned, and beheld the
scuffed biker boots and frayed jeans of Bradley Erwin Luck,
car thief, convicted drug trafficker, firearms offender and
parole breaker of Crawford County, Missouri.

'I just knew I couldn't trust you, Marty,' he sighed.

A nervous sweat stung my lip as I looked into the oily
accessory screwed into the muzzle of his USP.

'That's a tactical silencer, isn't it?' I observed.

'Good call,' he nodded. 'Knight Arms suppressor locked
into a forty-five-cal. Mark Twenty-three – and that there's a
LAM – laser-aiming module – but Sugarpie there could
have told you that. Now get over there next to her.' He
noticed the gold for the first time since spoiling my troth.
'Where'd all this fucking money come from? You rob the

company safe, Marty?' He reached out and grabbed Sherry-Lee's tasselled handbag from the table, his bloodshot eyes darting left and right like those of a man under the spell of a nightmare. He tipped the bag upside down and shook it. A can of tear gas, a wooden-handled lock knife, lipstick, compact, car keys and tissues fell to the floor. 'Where's your piece, girl?' he growled.

Sherry-Lee curled her lip. 'Find it yourself, creep.'

Brad looked at me, shaking his head. 'Can you believe this? First time she's seen me since selling me out and this is the way she speaks to me.'

'Your attitude is kind of aggressive as well, Brad,' I pointed out.

Keeping the heavy black pistol pointed at us, he rummaged through the coats hanging on the back of the door.

'Yeah, well, I got good reason to be aggressive,' he declared, his self-righteous pout stretching to a grin as he found the Glock in the pocket of Sherry-Lee's housecoat. One-handed, he ejected the magazine and pushed it into his back pocket. 'Twenty-four, huh, Sugarpie? Quality choice.' He worked the slide, checking the chamber.

'You have got a motherfucking nerve, pardon my language, breaking in like this,' hissed Sherry-Lee. 'And I bet you're in violation of your parole, too.'

Brad laughed, a short, foxy bark. 'Violation? Sugarpie, they catch me, they're sending me back to Crossroads for a straight ten with no more parole never. "Contemptuous violation": the judge takes it personal. And that's notwithstanding this here illegal firearm.'

'I won't say anything,' I offered.

'Shut the fuck up, Marty. I never trusted you, and I was damn right all along. You're the worst kind, the type of man who pretends to be someone's friend and fucks them as soon as they've got their back turned. Jesus Christ, you took me for a damn fool, and I knew you were rotten.' He wiped the scum from his lips with the back of his gun hand. 'Chicken, too, and sneaky with it.'

'Sneaky?' I protested.

He fumbled in his jeans pocket and pulled out a folded piece of paper. 'Yeah, sneaky. Recognise this?'

It was a sheet of Whitehall Numismatics notepaper, dated a few days ago. A ripple of relief that I hadn't dissed Brad in writing passed almost unnoticed.

'Pretty words, Marty,' mocked Brad. 'Wish I could write that good. How long you been banging my ex-fiancée?'

'Brad!' cried Sherry-Lee. 'That is not a polite question, and it's none of your business, neither.'

'Yeah,' I added, following her lead, 'and don't be calling the kettle black. Opening other people's mail is just about the sneakiest, rottenest thing a man can do. And it's a federal offence.'

'Wrong,' argued Brad, making his point with a jabbed muzzle. 'Hindering the US Mail is a federal offence. Stealing it after delivery is probably just a misdemeanour. Anyways, it was the desk clerk who stole it. I bought it from him. So, technically, I'm merely receiving.'

'It's still low,' growled Sherry-Lee. 'What else did that greaseball Roscoe give you of mine?'

Brad thumped his head in frustration. 'See?' he snapped. 'This is what I was talking about that night you and me went drinking. You get involved in a dialogue with your victims and the water gets all muddied. I should have done you both right off.' He took five fast, deep breaths. 'Now shut the fuck up, the two of you, and let me think on this a moment.'

Sherry-Lee crossed her arms and sighed, her weary dismay stinging Brad like a slap.

'You can lose the attitude 'cos I still got some stuff I want to say to you, Sugarpie, concerning primarily the matter of sixty-four thousand dollars taken from my daddy's farm,' he warned, still breaking his own rules about wordless executions. 'Marty! You pack all them pretty coins back in the bag while me and my ex-fiancée have us a little domestic.'

I did as I was told, tossing the treasure back into the Mulberry bag while Sherry-Lee and Brad kicked off like an old married couple. It didn't take long to pack half a million dollars' worth of gold. 'Can I smoke?' I asked.

'Knock yourself out,' growled Brad.

'The smokes are in my bag,' I added.

Brad turned and pinned me with a look of incredulous exasperation. 'I don't give a fuck where they are,' he exclaimed, turning to Sherry-Lee. 'What's more, I'm disappointed in you banging a man who carries a goddamned purse.'

'It's a European thing,' she sniffed. 'It's *sophisticated*. You wouldn't understand.'

'Yeah? Well, that ain't all I don't understand, Sugarpie,' retorted Brad.

I leaned between them and grabbed my mud-stained bag. Half a pack of Marlboros lay across my nasty handgun's shiny silver slide like a bad cover for a cheap paperback, and suddenly, as though seen through a tunnel, it was all my senses could process. Somewhere in the darkness beyond the bag, Brad and Sherry-Lee were snarling at each other in red-faced silence, and the fluorescent strip was flickering like a cut-price strobe. I had the drop on Brad, but the advantage was as flimsy as the skin on my teeth. I swallowed hard, and closed my sweaty, trembling fingers around the butt of the heavy Saturday Night Special. Destiny was lost and asking for directions, and I wondered if this was where my other life-line would be broken.

Neither of them saw the pistol leave the bag. Neither noticed as I took two giant leaps across the springy trailer floor. Sherry-Lee gaped as I snatched Brad by the mullet, yanked his unshaven face backwards with my snakebitten hand and jabbed my cheap handgun into the space below his ear where his head met his neck. Blood pressure red-rimmed my vision, and somewhere behind the thumping of my pulse I heard myself shouting as I brought the butt of the weapon down against his temple, splitting the skin and splashing my fingers with his hot blood. A single crack lit up the mobile home like an unseen flashbulb, the suppressed report of the Mark 23 betrayed by an instant crash as a .45 ACP round redefined Sherry-Lee's commemorative shot-glass collection and left through the back wall. Brad's resistance slackened for a moment, and I relaxed my grip on his hair just long enough for his elbow to find my mouth. Blood and phlegm fed my panic as I whacked his skull, primally aware, like a Neanderthal lobbing rocks at an enraged mammoth, that I'd lost the initiative. The USP coughed again, killing the light, and as the lethal beam from the laser slashed through the darkness I threw a roundhouse punch that knocked him limp.

'Go!' I gasped to Sherry-Lee, squinting in the darkness to find the Mark 23 in Brad's twitching hand. It was gone, and as he lashed drunkenly, blindly, backwards, I realised I didn't have the time to find it. I sprang to my feet, dropped my own useless handgun, grabbed the holdall and pushed Sherry-Lee out into the night.

'Car keys?' I cried, my hand hard upon her bare arm. 'Where are your car keys?'

'In there,' she yelled back. 'On the floor somewhere.'

I turned to re-enter the trailer, then changed my mind as a silenced round perforated the door with a whizzing snap.

'Forget the keys! Run!'

I thrust her forwards across the lot, past the wrecked Bender residence to the perimeter fence. Red light rippled along the chain link, its source the laser-aiming module two and a half inches from Brad's trigger finger. As he lurched after us, we found Solomon's gateway to hell and squeezed through, raising clouds of mosquitoes from the damp undergrowth. A narrow white path led through the sawgrass until it ended in a wall of vegetation.

'Go get 'em, Clinton!' roared Brad from our rear.

'This is so dumb,' worried Sherry-Lee, slapping bugs from her skin. 'Why don't you just shoot him?'

'Can't,' I confessed.

'So give me the gun.'

I shook my head. 'Dropped it back at the trailer.'

She shook her own head ... in disbelief.

'Back thisaway, you dumb fuckin' canine,' yelled Brad. 'Even I can see that!'

Sherry-Lee scanned the darkness. 'So what now?'

I stared at the swamp, breathless and spent, my courage and initiative expended in the first seconds of this half-assed escape attempt. She sighed like a Tijuana nun.

'We'll go thisaway,' she decided, pointing to a neck-high swath of rustling grass. 'Go down thataway some, then double back to the fence.'

'Exactly,' I agreed, plunging into the barbed growth, blazing a trail with my swinging sack of gold.

A hollow baying pierced the night, the excited hollering of an ugly hound. Clinton might have been on our trail, but he might equally have been chasing moths. Ankle-deep mud slowed our progress, and the crashing of the brittle sawgrass masked Brad's shouted threats to both pursuer and pursued. We emerged from a dense thicket into a shiny, black plain from which sprouted tufted islands of vegetation. A forest of masts rattled in the distance, and beyond that the lights of the Fort Myers Beach waterfront. Man-made sanctuary was mockingly close, yet haughtily unattainable. I eschewed the hindering cover of the weeds and lumbered, wheezing, through the smooth mud, my shoulders hunched in anticipation of the heart-stopping impact of one of Brad's laser-guided .45 rounds.

'Get up here, fool,' cried Sherry-Lee, hopping from tussock to tussock with unburdened grace.

'Quicker down here,' I gasped, and suddenly it was, in the other sense of the word. I was waist-deep in the mire and, within a second, chest-deep. Foul marsh gas scorched my nostrils as bloated bubbles rose through the emerald-flecked surface. Roscoe would have pissed himself laughing to see me now.

'Don't move!' yelled Sherry-Lee, approaching like a comrade in a minefield. 'Stay *absolutely* still.'

I nodded, and the quicksand tugged me down another inch.

'I got you,' lied Sherry-Lee, searching for something with which to haul me out.

The gold bag was half submerged, only its wide bottom slowing its descent.

Sherry-Lee's expression betrayed the gravity of my predicament as she dropped to her knees and stretched her hand towards me. 'Real gentle now, reach out and take my hand, honey.'

These were the words I'd been waiting to hear all night, but as I jerked my arm towards her, a tiny red dot scurried across the blackness, threaded through the grass, disappeared and then danced across Sherry-Lee's chest. I pulled back my hand.

'Go!' I urged her. 'Scarper. Now!'

The dot ran up her shoulder, slipping off into the night before rolling across her neck.

'Shut up and grab hold.'

'I'm touching the bottom, you dumb bitch!' I yelled. 'You'll never pull me out. Now git before that madman gets a steady bead on you!'

She sat back, a look of innocent wonder on her face as she touched a muddy hand to the spot on her throat where the laser had come to rest.

'It's one of us or both of us,' I hissed. 'What about Angie?'

The dot had stopped moving, and, like a tearful squaw, Sherry-Lee evaporated into the fetid air, leaving only a sad smile. I shrugged, and sank a little deeper, wondering if that little red laser was ruffling the hair on the back of my head. If Brad had any sense at all, he would follow his own commandment and cap me without any preamble. My corpse would sink to the bottom of the swamp and he'd be left with a bag of gold and only one witness to his general witlessness.

I'd always feared that when the end came, I would greet its arrival with craven sentimentality and self-pity. I would choke back tears for the things I had left undone, and let them fall for what I had done. I'd always been aware that Death would come a-whistling by just as I was about to start a worthwhile life, as though he'd been waiting around the corner for me to finish my whisky and stub out my last roach. I'd always dreaded the sadness, the shame and the regret far more than death itself, but, instead, like a man probing a freshly drilled tooth with a Novocaine-addled tongue, I felt nothing but numbness.

I heard his footfalls sploshing to my rear, then a grunt and a thud as he fell into the mud.

'You fuckin' idiot, Clinton,' he shouted. 'Stay out from under my goddamned feet!' The black dog loped past, panting like a locomotive. Brad stopped, shaking his head in fury. 'Get back here, you dumb fucking critter! I swear to God, Marty, that dim dog ran right by you!'

Brad looked like Yosemite Sam, mad beyond the limits of his vocabulary, although he was level-headed enough to appreciate my own sorry situation.

'Got that sinking feeling, Marty?' he panted at last, his red dot spinning a mesmerising parabola in the belching mud. 'Got me good back there,' he acknowledged, showing me a palm shiny with black blood, 'and it's because I appreciate your restraint that I haven't sprayed your Limey brain all over this fucking bayou.'

I nodded in recognition of his mercy, and the mud slapped my chin. 'Cheers, Brad.'

'However,' he continued, 'your present predicament is all of your own making, and I'm damned if I'm gonna help you out of this hole free of charge, especially since you've been banging my ex-fiancée.'

It was banged, singular, not banging, but I let it go. Every breath I drew was pushing my bruised ribs against the crushing counter-pressure of the swamp and hypoxia was making me light-headed. I raised an eyebrow to encourage Brad to continue.

'Now, you can take that there bag of stolen eagles straight to hell, boy, or you can give it up to Mr Luck and have your sorry ass freed from that pit: that's the price of my mercy this evening.' He switched off the LAM and wiped the blood from his eyes. 'What's it to be, Marty? Liberty or twinklebirdy?'

Part of me wanted to sink right there, dragging the coinage down to the bedrock in a spiteful, triumphant gesture of bloody-minded defiance, but it was only a very small part that nobody ever listened to. I raised the soiled leather holdall an inch or two in surrender, the mud level with my quivering lips as the earth tried to swallow me whole. Brad stretched out and hooked the bag, snatching it from my grip and dropping me deeper in the shit.

My last words before sliding under were unmemorable.

The world was cold and dense against my face, pressing against my clenched lips and pinched nostrils. It pushed against my eyelids, forcing its corruption through the cracks in the corners and flooding my ears to allow me to listen to my own fluttering heart. Surely sorrow and regret would stir me now, as I drowned in a sump of slurry, but Death came in the company of fear, disappointment and acute embarrassment. I wondered how long I could hold my breath before my will surrendered to the inevitable choking rush of my instant grave. Peace and quiet and a long, long lie-in were mere moments away, but then stabbing fingers found my scruff and dragged me like a baptised born-again back into the world.

'Scared you, huh?' grinned Brad. 'Scared myself for a minute, too. Couldn't find you down there.'

He pulled me kicking, thrashing and gasping from the mud and dumped me on solid ground like a low-value fish. He rocked back on his knees, the big, customised Mark 23 as black and as evil as the Devil's right hand. 'This is a weird situation,' he declared, panting from the exertion. 'I have fucked with natural justice by pulling you out and I'm kind of concerned about my next course of action here. By all accounts, I should have let you sink back then, but I owe you for the clemency you showed back in the trailer. However,' he dropped from his knees to lie beside me like a cruel lover, 'whatever I decide to do, I'm richer than I was. Get out of the quicksand, Clinton, you dumb fuck.'

'You're not rich,' I coughed. 'You're as broke as me.'

He held a hand to his bleeding ear. 'How d'you figure that, you sorry son of a bitch?'

I arched my back as a shiver ran down my spine, and raised myself to a sitting position. The sawgrass rustled in a cool breeze from the river, turning the mud on my body to crust. It felt like the end of a long day. 'All you got is a bag of gold. You lost Sherry-Lee, just like I did. We're both losers, Brad.'

He lit a cigarette, the flame from a scratched match lighting his bloody face. He didn't offer me one. 'I ain't lost her,' he growled. 'She's still out here, splashing around in the swamp somewheres. I'll get her.'

'And do what?'

He sucked on the butt, rehearsing his lines in his head. 'What I came here to do.'

I laughed, short and dismissive. 'Say it,' I challenged him. 'If you can't say it, you sure can't do it.'

He jerked the handgun towards my face. 'Don't push me, Marty. Just 'cos I treated you lenient just now, don't mean I can't cap you for a different offence. You know what I got to do to that bitch.'

Sherry-Lee was long gone, heading north on the Tamiami Trail by now. Neither Brad nor I would find her if she didn't want to be found; and Brad wouldn't kill her if he did. He'd proved it back there in the Alligator Strip, and every day since then that he'd been keeping her under surveillance. Brad had lost Sherry-Lee over five years before, and there was only one reason on earth why I should have given her back to him. I shivered again, violently, as though gripped by swamp fever. Altruism always left me cold.

'You ain't going to orphan a child now, are you?' I sighed, hearing myself throw it all away. I'd seen the light back at the trailer, shining in her eyes as she had met me on the step, and it had told me I didn't have a whole lot to lose with her. Gene had been right, after all.

Brad frowned and flicked his dog-end. 'What the fuck are you talking about?'

'Sherry-Lee's got a kid.' I glanced up through my eyebrows. 'Didn't know that, did you?'

He studied me for a moment. 'Bullshit.'

'She'll be five on Sherry-Lee's birthday. Called Angie. Now give me your cigarettes and I'll tell you some more.'

Brad did as he was told. I lit up and spilled the beans.

'You know that Rufus Cooper III set you both up, don't you? You know he showed Sherry-Lee a picture of you with some Mexican bird and told her you were screwing her?' I studied my sodden sneakers, talking low and slow like a man in confession. 'You weren't doing the dirty on Sherry-Lee, were you, Brad? Who was she, this Guadalupe?'

He shook his head slowly, distractedly, like a man preoccupied with watching the pieces fall into place. 'Guadalupe was the *jefe's* granddaughter. If I'd nailed her, I'd have been dead before I hitched up my pants. Even Rufus knew that.'

I spat mud and sucked hard on my cigarette. 'Rufus told Sherry-Lee you'd turned state's evidence to avoid copping a ten to twenty, and that you'd incriminated him. Told her to go ask you herself if she didn't believe him, and I bet he told you to refuse to see her if she came.'

He nodded, hard and fast, like a schoolboy. 'Damn right he did. Told me not to trust her. Said she'd been wired up and that I shouldn't see her.'

I lay back and blew smoke at the stars. 'You know what

else he told her? He said you'd been screwing around for years, and that *he'd* always loved her. Completely fucked her up. And there's more.'

He stared at me like the second-dumbest dog in Florida.

I threw it back, straight in the eye. 'At a rest area, somewhere between Carson County and St Louis, Rufus pulled a gun on her and raped her. *That's* why she shot him. You managing to keep up with all this?'

Brad blinked several times. 'She tell you this?'

I nodded. 'Guess what happened after the rape?'

He raised a hand. 'Hold up there a moment. Are you trying to tell me Rufus got biblical with Sherry-Lee?' He looked as though I'd told him that Jesus was Jewish.

'Stay focused, Brad,' I sighed, 'it gets better. Sherry-Lee found herself to be pregnant soon after, but you and me know something, don't we, Brad? We know that kid isn't Rufus Cooper III's, don't we?'

I'd known it the moment I'd seen her, and my lovesick heart had ignored the evidence as I ruffled that blond hair and looked into those crazy blue eyes she'd inherited from her lunatic father. Angie wore Brad's genes like a designer label: I just hoped she'd got her brains from her mother.

'The fucking *quebrachon* never ...' Brad's mind caught up with his mouth and he slapped a muddy hand across his lips to stem the flow.

'What's a *quebrachon*?' I asked.

He looked at me, his eyes white in his blood-blackened face. He was thinking hard and fast, but he possessed limited resources.

'Nothing,' he replied eventually. 'It's just spicano slang. Don't mean nothing.'

I watched as he grunted and twitched and mumbled and shook his head as the issue percolated through his overburdened brain. After a few moments he scratched his head with the silencer, his finger still on the trigger.

'Why you telling me all this?'

I took a deep breath and let my heart do the talking. 'Because I've forgotten what it's like to do the right thing. Because I'm sick of being wrong all the time: in the wrong place at the wrong time with the wrong people for all the wrong reasons. You three weird bastards belong together, and I have no right or reason to keep you apart. I love Sherry-Lee, and I saw her as my guide out of the swamp I'm lost in, but I can't follow her. She's yours, Brad, and you're hers, and that blue-eyed kid belongs to you both. How could I come between you? You all share the same birthday, for fuck's sake.'

Brad sniffed. 'I appreciate your candour, Marty. Now give me back my smokes.'

I checked the pack. There were three left. 'No way. And give me back my gold. Way I see it, you get the girl, I get the gold, and everyone's happy.'

'Hey!' he protested. 'Give a man a cigarette, for Christ's sake!'

'Fuck off,' I scoffed. 'Give me the gold.'

Brad shot me a look he'd been giving weaker kids ever since he was six years old. 'I ain't giving you the gold back, buddy. It's my gold now, and you can keep your stinking butts. I could buy a whole goddamned warehouse of smokes with this here money.'

I shifted uncomfortably in the mud. It looked like I'd turned an opportunity into a crisis.

Then Brad remembered he had a firearm and things got worse. 'Give me those fucking cigarettes now,' he insisted, pointing the Mark 23 at my heart.

'Jesus Christ, Brad!' I whined.

'Shuddup,' he warned, 'I'm trying to think.'

It didn't take long. I watched Clinton lick the mud from his balls until a self-affirmative grunt suggested that Brad had reached a verdict.

'Now listen up, Marty,' he announced, rising to his feet. 'I'm going to pronounce my judgement on this here case. You listening?'

I stared at him and sighed. He took it for a yes.

'On the matter of you being a false friend, a deceiver and a betrayer of a man's trust, I find you guilty as charged on all three counts—'

'Objection!' I called.

'Overruled,' barked Brad, jabbing the Mark 23 at me like a lethal gavel. 'There's also the matter of adultery to be addressed. It's a goddamned commandment, Marty, for Christ's sake.'

'Come off it,' I sneered. 'You weren't married or even engaged, so how can it be adultery?'

'Well, it's coveting your neighbour's ass, then, and it's still a commandment,' insisted Brad, 'and the sentence should in all honesty be death, either by shooting in the head or tipping you back in that there sinkhole. Personally, I favour the former since the latter is both cruel and unusual, but I'm the first to admit there's been some extenuating circumstances here.' He tilted his head to one side. 'You want to move over here a ways, Marty, by this here sawgrass? It's just that you're sinking again.'

I was being tried by Judge Luck in the Caloosahatchee County Courthouse. *Of course* I was sinking again. I moved to more solid ground. 'Pray continue, Your Honour.'

He ignored the sarcasm, or maybe he just missed it.

'In the matter of the extenuating circumstances, I maintain my position that mercy is due to you in respect of the restraint you exercised back there at the trailer when you were entirely justified to use lethal force. You could have shot me, and instead you just battered my head. I respect that, and I thank you for it. Furthermore, you came forward of your own free will and offered me important information in regard of my personal life, to whit informing me of the existence of my own little daughter, which I still cannot fucking believe to be true.'

'Language, Your Honour,' I warned.

'Fuck you,' he spat back. 'Anyways, the verdict is this: the death sentence is suspended and on top of that I'm going to reward you for coming forward. How do you feel 'bout that, Marty?'

'Fucking delighted,' I grunted. 'What's the reward?'

Brad unzipped the holdall and pulled out a sheet of pandas.

'How much are these worth?'

I gave them a glance of appraisal. 'Fifteen bucks apiece.'

Brad frowned. 'See? You just can't help being dishonest and deceitful, can you? You're incorrigible is what you are.' He rummaged through the bullion, his tongue poking out of the side of his mouth. 'Let me find something here I recognise ... Here we go: one of them there twin-klebirdies.' Starlight turned the Eagle silver as he held it in the air. 'Now I know for a fact that this here coin is worth seventy-five hundred dollars 'cos I saw one exactly similar in your trailer last month. In fact, this one's probably worth more than that 'cos it's newer. Now, I ain't gonna give you just one of these birdies. Bud, I'm gonna give you two. That's at least fifteen thousand dollars. What do you say to that?'

Together, the coins were actually worth seven *hundred* dollars: not even enough to fly me back to Marrakech. But

Brad was never going to believe that. Tired of the whole affair, I waved a mud-stained hand at his offer. 'Keep your stinking gold.'

Brad lit up hungrily, inhaled and blew smoke at the stars. 'Take it,' he insisted. 'You earned it.'

'Bollocks,' I replied. 'You stole it from me fair and square. Keep it.'

'I did not steal it,' he retorted. 'I took it in payment for saving your life. How soon you forget.' He tossed the coins at my feet.

'I got the gold. I got the girl. You deserve a reward for your contribution to my good fortune.'

'I don't want your bloody reward. You've taken half a million dollars for saving my life and now you want to give me two bits for saving yours? Get the fuck out of here. Way I see it, you should give me back at least half.'

Brad sighed and dragged his fingers through his hair.

'Are you dumb or something, Marty, 'cos that crow don't caw. We ain't friends, thanks to your past behaviour. We ain't business partners. And you've already proved that there's no honour among thieves. We're rivals, you and me, plain and simple. I'm trying to keep it nice and all, but at the end of the day, when all's said and done, I earned this here gold. That pair of twinklebirdies ain't charity: it's a businesslike payment for services rendered. So put them in your pocket and shut the fuck up before the verdict gets overturned and I cap you.'

I reached wearily for the coins, and as I grasped them Sherry-Lee stepped from the foliage like a VC sapper, streaked in mud and bleeding from the spiteful slashes of the sawgrass. My Saturday Night Special, big and crude in her small hands, found enough light in the darkness to gleam like a mugger's grin.

'Drop it, Brad,' she growled.

'Baby!' cried Brad.

'Don't you dare "baby" me!' She pulled back the hammer with the timing of a TV-movie heroine. 'Toss that firearm over here, you son of a bitch!'

'Darlin',' smiled Brad, lobbing the Mark 23 into the mud without a thought for his three-hundred-dollar silencer.

Sherry-Lee bobbed down and picked it up. She was doing great. She must have doubled back to the trailer, found the gun where I'd dropped it on the lino, and run all the way back out here to stop Brad from killing me. The madman was right: she *was* a darling. And my bruised heart beat only for her.

'Bradley Luck, you're a despicable man,' she said.

'Hey, honey,' pleaded Brad. 'We got so much catchin' up to do.'

'We ain't got no catchin' up to do whatsoever,' countered Sherry-Lee. 'Martin, honey, pass me that bag there, would you?'

'What bag?' I asked.

'She means this bag, dummy,' said Brad, kicking the holdall.

'But that's my bag,' I protested.

'*My* bag, you mean, don't you?' retorted Brad.

Sherry-Lee discharged one round into the mud with a muffled crack that grabbed everyone's attention. '*My* bag, I think you'll find, gentlemen,' she smiled. 'Now pass it on over here before I kill someone.'

I looked at Brad. 'Go on then: pass her the bag.'

He gave me his death-row glare. 'She asked you.'

'Right!' yelled Sherry-Lee, flipping on the LAM with a painted nail. 'Where's that dog?'

We watched as the laser probed the darkness before

coming to rest on Clinton's wet nose. He sat hypnotised by the dot, like Bambi with the butterfly, his tongue lolling from the corner of his frothing jaw and his tail slowly wagging in dim delight.

'One ... two ...'

Brad scooped up the bag and dropped it at her feet. 'That's a heavy bag, honey,' he said. 'Why don't you let me carry it for you?'

Sherry-Lee swung the red dot from Clinton's gormless face to Brad's overworked brow. 'That's real sweet of you, Brad. Now let's all head on back to the trailer, real slow.'

I knew she was going to say that.

'And don't neither of you think of trying nothing neither.'

And that. She was ripping us off, and while I was reluctantly admiring her survivalist pluck, Brad was trying to work an angle. It said something depressing about us all.

'What do you say, Marty?' called Brad as he led us in single file through the sawgrass. 'Was that eleven rounds or was it the full dozen?'

'Shut up, Brad,' warned Sherry-Lee.

'See, if it's twelve shots fired from that there precision firearm, that'll make it emptier than my hound dog's head ...'

'And if it's eleven?' asked Sherry-Lee.

'Well then, darlin', I do not doubt your ability to place the twelfth in the back of my handsome head,' admitted Brad. 'However, by my counting, I make it twelve already. What do you say, Marty?'

I made it seven, which gave her another five to play with.

'You forgot something, lover,' announced Sherry-Lee with far too much latent affection for my liking. 'I got Martin's little junk gun here as well, and while it most definitely lacks the power and sophisticated engineering of your big old USP, I'm quite sure it will do a fine job of mashing up your dumb skull. So quit talking quit talking and keep walking.'

And that's what it had been about all along, I realised as we ducked through the chain-link fence and crept back into the civilised world of the trailer park: the limited but adequate ability of Martin's little junk gun to fuck big Bradley Luck in the head. It hurt like soap and powdered glass, and the best I could hope for now was a share in the gold, so I gave it my best shot. 'What you going to do now, Sherry-Lee?' I asked as we walked past the Bender residence.

'I'm gonna leave you two here, 'cos you're both as bad as each other, and I'm gonna take this gold, get my daughter and disappear like the Cheshire Cat. Does that sound fair, considering what the two of you have put me through?'

'What about what Rufus Cooper III put you through?' I countered.

I had a plan. Like an unwanted kid, it was weak, ill-conceived and unlikely to succeed, but it was all I had. Sherry-Lee, bless her soul, would never be mine, and deep down I'd known that all along. Furthermore, my willingness to let her return to Brad proved perhaps that I'd never really wanted her. Maybe I'd been infatuated with the idea of settling down with a ready-made family, but when the opportunity had arisen to make it happen I'd panicked and given it away. Sherry-Lee Lewis and Bradley Erwin Luck were made for each other, and I didn't belong here.

'What about Rufus Cooper III?' hissed Sherry-Lee.

If I could only persuade Sherry-Lee that the red-headed charmer had tricked her, that Brad had never cheated on her and that she, him and Angie belonged together in a de-luxe trailer park where you could raise kids, hogs and hound dogs, brew moonshine and discharge firearms in peace, then she might see that there were some things that stolen money just couldn't buy. If she could see that I was giving the three of them something that was not available in the shops, then perhaps she would understand what Brad had failed to comprehend, and perhaps she would do the right thing.

Which at this moment was to give me back my gold.

I nodded towards her trailer. 'Let's go inside.'

The morning star was bright in the eastern sky by the time I'd unravelled the five and a half years of misunderstanding that lay between their tangled hearts. As I spoke, Brad still held the bag of gold, Sherry-Lee clutched two firearms, and I clung to the faint hope that there was some profit in this exercise. By the time the first rays of Saturday morning had kindled the frayed edges of the broken clouds, my throat was raw and sore from explanation, so I left the trailer and went into the Florida dawn to gargle with tequila. Part of me still expected Sherry-Lee to shoot Brad and throw herself into my arms, but it was the same part that wasted time chasing rainbows. I shook my head and returned inside to claim my pot of gold.

'Come right in Marty,' cried Brad. 'I want you to see this.'

He placed his right foot on the edge of the table and hitched his right trouser leg to the top of his boot. Flakes of dry, black swamp dirt fell to the floor as he pulled a stubby blue revolver from his boot and slapped it on the tabletop. Sherry-Lee opened her mouth but he held up a hand.

'Hold that thought, honey.' He raised his shirt to reveal another handgun stuffed in his waistband, then pulled a stiletto from his left boot. He pointed it at the revolver. 'Smith and Wesson Thirty-eight snub. Design classic. Next to it is a Taurus Millennium. Cheap ghettoblaster. Like Lana

Turner standing next to J-Lo, and they both been in my pants.' He dropped the knife and it stuck into the tabletop like a dart. 'Made that one myself. Gonna call it Angie.'

He was clearly trying to woo her, but Sherry-Lee looked on impassively until he tugged at his T-shirt and dragged up the chain from around his neck, just as I had once done in Fort Myers Beach. 'Kept this for you.' He unclipped the chain and slid a cheap ring on to her shaking finger.

Personally, I thought the Gibraltar angel had been a far classier gift, but there was no accounting for trailer-park taste.

Brad held on to her hand, staring deep into her tearful eyes. 'Wanna go to Mexico, Sugarpie?'

Everybody wanted to take this woman to Mexico, and all of a sudden I felt old and unwanted, like the last, sour goose-berry on the bush. It was time to reclaim my stake and split. I adopted a casual approach to its recovery, hooking my thumbs in my back pocket and tapping the Mulberry holdall with my toe. 'Reckon you kids'll need a little travelling cash,' I drawled. 'Let me see if I can help you out some.' I bent down and grabbed the bag.

'What the fuck you doing, Marty?' asked Brad.

I carried on dragging the bag, avoiding his startled glare. 'Gonna give you guys some of my gold, just to get you started. What's wrong with that?'

Brad stamped on the holdall. 'I'll tell you what's wrong, Marty,' he said. 'It's not your gold to give. It's my and Sherry-Lee's gold.'

I tugged harder, losing my cool. 'It's my bloody gold, Brad. I stole it, fair and square, not you.'

'Er, hello!' cried Sherry-Lee in a valley-girl voice. 'I think you'll find, Martin, that Brad stole it from you, fair and square and all, then I stole it from him ...'

'I did not steal it,' protested Brad. 'I earned it. Fair and square.'

'Whatever,' continued Sherry-Lee, 'and seeing as he and I are engaged and all, that makes it our gold. Am I right, Brad?'

Brad folded his arms across his chest. 'What's yours is mine, honey, and vice versa.'

These two were beginning to sicken me. I looked at Sherry-Lee, hoping that all the shock, the despondency and the pain caused by her betrayal was dripping from my face. 'How could you?' I spluttered. 'After all we've been through?'

She put a hand on her hip and cocked her head. 'We ain't been through much, Martin. Church, drinks, dinner: it was hardly a relationship.'

I opened my mouth and closed it again. Then I opened it again, but there was nothing to say, so I closed it again. 'What about the angel I gave you?' I managed at last.

'What about it?' countered Sherry-Lee. 'You want it back?'

I shuffled my feet despondently. This was all going horribly wrong. 'No,' I mumbled.

'Well, that's mighty kind of you, Martin,' beamed Sherry-Lee with no apparent sarcasm. She stepped forward and took my hand. 'Listen, Martin: it would never have been any good between us. I'd have been poison running through your veins – you must know that, or else you'd have never done what you did to bring me and Brad back together. And when you showed up here last night, what did you tell me?'

I began to reply but she beat me to it.

'You said you were giving all this gold to me, like you promised, so's I could take Angie south of the border. Am I right? And ain't that what you've done? And on top of giving me all this, you've given me my fiancé back and given all three of us a new life. Ain't that right, Brad? Ain't that a truly wonderful thing?'

Brad was examining my junk gun. 'Yup,' he nodded, without looking up. The connection between my clemency and my lack of ammo had passed him by.

'And if we have ourselves a little boy, I reckon we'll use your name in there somewhere when we baptise him,' enthused Sherry-Lee.

'Or maybe a hound dog or something,' suggested Brad.

Sherry-Lee looked deep into my eyes, searching for understanding. 'You've done a good thing here, Martin,' she insisted. 'Don't go and make it bad.'

'We gotta go, Sugarpie,' said Brad.

'You're right, lover,' agreed Sherry-Lee, dropping my hand. 'I'll go get my stuff.'

She stepped into her bedroom, leaving me with nothing to do but stare at Brad. He stared back from the high ground.

'Best man won is all, Marty,' he shrugged. 'No hard feelings.'

'Fuck off,' I growled.

'Hey,' he grinned, 'you'll be Ok. You still got them coins I gave you?'

'Yeah, for what they're worth.'

He fished a new roll of maples from the bag and tossed it across the room. They hit me square in the balls.

'Put them away,' he warned. 'Sherry-Lee will go crazy if she finds out I'm blowing the housekeeping.'

I stuffed the roll in my back pocket and something in my doleful expression took the triumphant smile from Brad's face.

'Listen up, Marty,' he said. 'I can't give you no more of this here gold than I've given you, but I want you to have something else to remember me by.'

'As if you've not given me enough already,' I grunted.

He shook his head. 'I mean it, man.' He fumbled with his necklace. 'I want you to have this,' he declared. 'Ten point nine mil., switchblade curb ...'

I stepped backwards and away. 'No, no, no. I couldn't possibly.'

He frowned in confusion. 'Why not?'

''Cos it's too classy.'

He couldn't disagree. 'Take the dog, then.'

'No way.'

'Then you got to have the chain. It ain't no consummation prize nor nothin'. It's a gesture of gratitude; something to remember us all by. Don't insult me now.'

'Keep it, please,' I insisted.

Brad squared up to me. 'Take it, goddamn it!' He leaned forward and draped the dreadful gold rope around my neck. 'Looking good, Holmes.'

It felt like the albatross of bad taste. I looked up and Sherry-Lee was ready to go.

'Nice chain,' she smiled, with no irony.

'I made him take it,' said Brad. 'It was the chain or the dog. You ready, baby?'

She nodded, biting her lip. 'Wanna go start up the truck, honey, while I say goodbye to Martin?'

Brad shook my hand in an unfamiliar jailhouse fashion, slapped me on the shoulder and dropped into the new day. 'Tell me something before I go, bro,' he insisted, pointing at my handbag.

'It belonged to Luisa,' I told him, guessing the next question. 'She was another hurricane who wrecked everything before blowing herself out.'

Brad frowned like something significant had just flown way over his head, nodded and left.

Sherry-Lee waited until she heard him shouting at Clinton before stepping forward and taking both my hands in hers.

'I'm really pissed off, you know,' I muttered.

'Don't be,' she smiled. 'You'll be Ok.'

'I thought I could at least trust you to be fair.'

She dropped my hands and brought her fingers to her temples, as though I were giving her a headache. 'Look here, Martin: there's half a million in that bag, but me and Brad ain't never going to get the true value. I'm reckoning on three hundred grand, and that's hardly enough to settle down on, 'specially since we don't have the option to come home. Now, I ain't never lived in no foreign country before, but it's my opinion that you need a comfortable sum behind you to make it work.'

'I had thirty-five bucks when I arrived here,' I said.

'Yeah, well, look at the way you've ended up,' she replied. 'You're hurt, homeless and you've just been robbed by trailer trash.'

A long blast on an airhorn declared Brad's impatience. Sherry-Lee stood on tiptoe and whispered in my ear. 'You'll be Ok, Martin. You can trust me on that.'

I pulled away. 'I don't think I can trust you on anything.' I pulled a seashell from my pocket and handed it to her. Way back when the future was bright, I'd promised to save it for her. 'Keep this in remembrance of me,' I said.

She looked down at the shell, her eyes widening in tearful recognition. 'I've left you something pretty to remember me by, too,' she whispered. 'And now I got to go. I'll never forget you, Martin.'

She rose on her tiptoes again to kiss my cheeks and my lips, softly and gently, then she was gone. The door slammed, the engine revved, the gravel roared, the trapdoor opened and I fell far enough for the golden rope around my neck to break my heart. It was over now: executed at dawn. And as Gene had forecast, it didn't feel as good as I thought it would.

Sherry-Lee had left behind her radio, and rather than listen to the throbbing in my head, I switched it on. Emmylou Harris and Gram Parsons were singing 'Love Hurts', as if I needed telling, but I sat and listened hard, the hairs erect on my arms as I waited for the tears to fall.

They didn't come – they never did – and as the song faded I wandered into her bedroom to lie on her narrow bed and dream up a new plan.

She'd left a cheap vinyl bowling bag on the nylon counterpane. The contents were wrapped in a Wal-Mart carrier-bag. I tipped it on to the faded pink bedspread, smelling the dried-blood odour of old money as dozens of bundles of banknotes bounced on the mattress like reasons to be cheerful. I didn't need to count it: this was the answer to the 64,000-dollar question concerning the whereabouts of the money Sherry-Lee had taken from Brad's daddy's farm. Her conscience had never let her spend it, and it must have been here all the time, hidden in the closet like a severed head to remind her of her crime. Now it was mine, and under the circumstances I thought it the prettiest thing to remember her by. Best of all, she'd done it behind Brad's back, and I derived almost as big a thrill from that as I did from the loot itself. I wished only that I'd been sweeter when she had left, but then again, what was the point? Life was too short to waste making friends.

I scooped the cash back into the bowling bag, tossed it into my Eldorado, got on the Tamiami Trail and started looking for an international airport.

It was time to start forgetting Miss Sherry-Lee Lewis.

15

By nine o'clock that blue and sunny morning I was parked outside a mall in West Palm Beach. By nine-thirty, I was a changed man. My filthy, worn-out charity clothes were festering in the bottom of a Lake Worth Garbage Services dumpster and stiff new denim was rubbing my swamp-marinated flesh raw. A girl called Sugar in a mall-side travel agency had told me that flights to Cuba from the States were pretty much impossible for ordinary folks, and she didn't for the life of her understand why. She figured it was probably something to do with the immigration problem, and told me that my best plan was to fly from Miami to Kingston, and to double back to Havana from there. I bought a one-way ticket to Jamaica and told her I'd take things as they came. You never knew how long a stopover in Kingston was going to last.

At eleven-thirty I was waiting for the lights to change at an intersection on the south side of Boynton Beach. A barefoot Latino immigrant loped towards me with a squeegee and a plastic bucket, and I waved him away. Then I changed my mind. '*Hombre,*' I called. '*Dica mi: que es un quebrachon?*'

He gave me a look of the deepest suspicion. I waved a ten to cover it. He puffed up his chest, rubbed his beard, and approached the car, looking around, as though he were walking into an ambush. A *quebrachon*, he explained, was the sort of man I could find in spades an hour or so south in Miami Beach. A *quebrachon* was a man who preferred *riata* to *chocho*, a fellow who liked to *tomar el culo* rather than to *hacer una cubana*. A *quebrachon* was a *soprapollos* of the worst kind, if I knew what he meant, and one most unlikely to participate in heterosexual relations, whether consensual or not.

Brad's partner in crime, it seemed, had been as gay as mine, and that raised a number of awkward objections to Sherry-Lee's carefully crafted tale of rape and murder. It just went to prove that there were three sides to every story.

I thanked the Mexican for the information, offering him a nearly new 10.9-mil. switchblade curb, fourteen K, twenty-four-inch, one-fifty-gram necklace for his trouble.

He gave it the once over and shook his head. 'Too flashy, man.'

'What about the car?'

He scratched his head. 'What about it?'

'You like it?'

'Sure I like it, *ese*.'

'You want it?'

'Don't fuck with me.'

I wasn't fucking with him. The Eldorado was a beautiful car, mine for a day, but it belonged to another time. If the Cadillac couldn't go to Mexico, then the next best thing was to give it to a Mexican.

'Get in,' I said. 'I'll drive it to the airport, then it's yours. You're no one in this country without a car.'

He tossed his bucket into the back of the Eldorado and hopped the door. 'You're not some kind of *quebrachon* yourself, are you?'

I shook my head. 'Nope. I like strippers and waitresses.'

'Then what are you? A *pocoloco*, an angel, or what?'

I rolled up the on-ramp to I-95 South.

'Just a generous kind of bloke, *hermano*.'

AC/DC were on the radio and it was turning out to be a fine day. I hoped God was watching.